PLAYER *of* MINE

HANNAH COWAN

Portions of this book are works of fiction. Any references to historical events, real people, or real places are used fictitiously. Other names, characters, places and events are products of the author's imagination, and any resemblances to actual events or places or persons, living or dead, is entirely coincidental.

Edited and proofed by: Sandra at One Love Editing @oneloveediting

Cover design by: Booksandmoods @booksnmoods

First Edition

ISBN: 978-1-7779955-9-1

Reading Order

Even though all of my books can be read on their own, they all exist in the same world—regardless of series—so for reader clarity, I have included a recommended reading order to give you the ultimate experience possible.
This is also a timeline accurate list.

RECOMMENDED READING ORDER

Lucky Hit (Oakley and Ava) Swift Hat Trick trilogy #1

Between Periods (5 POV Novella) Swift Hat-Trick trilogy #1.5

Blissful Hook (Tyler and Gracie) Swift Hat Trick trilogy #2

Craving The Player (Braden and Sierra) Amateurs In Love series #1

Taming The Player (Braden and Sierra) Amateurs In Love series #2

Vital Blindside (Adam and Scarlett) Swift Hat Trick trilogy #3

CRAVING the PLAYER

HANNAH COWAN

Dedicated to all of my ex-boyfriends. Thank you for making me feel unworthy and subpar. Because of you, I pushed myself to find what makes me happy, and have found my self-worth again.

Suck it, assholes.

1

Braden

SHARP NAILS TEAR THEIR WAY DOWN MY BACK, RIPPING THROUGH the sensitive skin and drawing blood. The blonde beneath me moans in my ear, begging me to pick up the pace.

We've been going at this for what feels like hours now. She's come more times than I can count, quite the opposite of myself. I've been unwantedly edging myself.

"Just like that!"

My frustration is obvious as I pull out of her in one swift movement and lean back on my legs, dick starting to sag.

"What are you doing?" she whines, lips jutting out in a juicy pout.

"Sorry. I just remembered that I have to go pick up my grandpa's friend's dog from the vet." My tone is dry and careless. I move off of the silk red sheets left in a disarray on her bed and toss the unused condom into the nearby trash can.

"You could say my name, you know." Her breathless voice only frustrates me more. In all honesty, I don't remember her name.

I try to block her out and focus on finding my clothes. I can just about plant a thank you kiss on the lamp in the corner of her room when I spot my button-up hanging from it. "And you expect me to believe that you have to pick up this dog in the middle of the night?"

She doesn't spare me an unconvincing frown as she wraps the blanket around her otherwise naked body—a wise decision on her part. It was her hot body that enticed me enough to come here in the first place, and as much fun as it is to stare at her smooth, olive skin, I already have a terrible case of blue balls. The thought makes me reach down and anxiously rub at my limp cock with a deep, aggravated sigh.

"Sorry, what?" I slide my arms through my shirt. My back burns when the material rubs across the new cuts in my skin.

"What is your deal?" she snaps.

I run a hand through my messy hair and pull my phone from the pocket of my jeans. As soon as I switch it on, I'm met with several texts asking about my whereabouts and disappearance.

"You're unbelievable!" she scoffs, pulling the blanket tighter around her. In a flurry, she rushes into the ensuite bathroom, slamming the door behind her.

Well, that makes things easier.

I pull my keys out of my pocket and the cold metal bites into my palm. The nauseating smell of her fruity perfume wafts throughout the house, making me rush to the front door even faster. I slide my sneakers on and fight back the urge to kick myself in the ass for letting my dick get me in trouble again.

I'm out the door and in the driver's seat of my car before my stomach has a chance to start swirling with disappointment.

"IF YOU KEEP DROPPING your arms like that, I'll gladly bruise up that pretty face, Clay."

Clayton takes another risky swing at my chest and I roll my eyes at his poorly placed move. "C'mon, buddy. You gotta do better than that." I grab and twist his arm behind his back. I turn the six-foot ginger around and shove his face into the boxing bag in front of us.

Poor guy didn't stand a chance in hell with that sloppy throw.

"Your mouth twitches before every swing. That needs to stop. Anyone who studies you even in the slightest will know your tells. You'll never win like that. *Ever*." I move back a step and lift my arms into position before nodding for him to try again.

His eyes narrow as he bounces on his feet, observing me. Trying to learn *my* tells. As if I would put them on display for him. Less than a second later, his top lip lifts just the slightest bit, causing mine to lift in a grin.

In an instant I'm tucking myself under his right hook and swinging my left arm. I make contact with his abdomen, and the air is pushed from his lungs in a raspy wheeze. He clutches his stomach and curls over.

"Fuck you," he coughs.

"Damn, I guess I should have put my gloves on. My bad." I shrug.

"Remind me again why I can't have another trainer?" He asks me the question like he doesn't already know the answer while pushing himself upright again. After a few seconds, his grimace slowly evens back out into a scowl.

"Because nobody else wants your whiny ass," I snicker, walking toward my gym bag and pulling out my gloves. The gold stripes wrapping around the slick black material never fail to make my chest swell with pride. I worked day and night to afford these babies, and damn are they *ever* worth it.

"We both know that you just don't want to get rid of me."

"Yeah." I snort. "That's it."

Sliding my hands in my gloves, I clench my fingers and tighten the Velcro strap. Patting both gloves together, I raise my brow and nod for him to try again.

The balls of my feet tap against the concrete floor as I bounce, keeping my eyes locked on my best friend. He's finally got his arms in the correct position, at least, but the tension in his shoulders worries me.

"Drop your shoulders!" I bark. "You're going to hurt yourself."

"I'm trying," he snaps but drops his shoulder slightly, most likely to humour me more than anything.

Without a second thought I send my fist toward him, but stop mid-throw when he drops his arms just enough to expose his face to me.

I warned him. Pushing my arm forward again, I hear a loud *smack*.

"What the fuck!" he shouts with eyes full of fire as he grabs his now bleeding nose. I bite back my laugh.

"It's not broken. Relax." I grin to myself and give my head a quick shake. "I told you that if you dropped your arms again, I would mess with your pretty face."

I turn away from him and reach into my gym bag, pulling out two towels. After I toss him the darker coloured one for his gushing nose, I keep the lighter one for myself. The sweat covering my bare torso is wiped away quickly before I discard the towel.

"What if you would have broken it?" he groans.

"Then you wouldn't have dropped your arms next time. Take the pain as a learning experience."

"You were coming for my stomach!"

"It looked like I was aiming for your stomach. You would have no idea if that were a trick or not. That's why you don't drop your arms," I say with unwavering confidence. I've trained to be a boxer nearly my entire life, learned almost everything there is to know about the sport. He needs to gain a bit of confidence in me. If my ego weren't the size of Texas I would have been offended. "Anyways, pizza for dinner?"

"Sure," he replies, voice nasally from the pressure he's applying to his nose. His ability to go with the flow is one of the reasons we get along so well.

"Come on, if you get blood on the floor Dad will kill me." I lead the way to the showers.

"Maybe I'll leave a trail then."

I scowl.

Working for your dad has its benefits, but dealing with his rage when you break one of his rules is not one of them. No bloodshed is the most crucial rule in this gym. It has been since before I can remember. We Lowry men don't follow many rules, but the ones we do, we live by. As if by breaking a single one would throw the entire universe off kilter.

"If you want to go that far, I might as well get a couple more hits in. Soak the floor in your misery," I half-heartedly threaten.

He just scoffs, shaking his head. "I'd like to see you try."

"Yeah? Want to bet on how long you'd last in the ring with me?" I tilt my head and straighten my back so all six-foot-three of me tower over him.

Clay gulps but keeps his lips pressed together. "Whatever. Arrogant bastard."

I laugh. "Always full of compliments, Clay. So, stuffed or regular crust?"

"GRAB ME A BEER, WOULD YOU?" I shout as I drop back on the couch. My words are muffled as a slice of pepperoni stuffed-crust pizza is clenched between my teeth.

"Do I look like your damn mother?" Clayton calls back.

I shove my hand between the couch cushions and grab hold of the TV remote. My greasy fingers fiddle with the remote before finding the power button and the familiar sound of my favourite, hot-as-hell sports announcer fills the room.

"Pretty please can you bring me a beer?" I try again, snickering to myself when I hear the fridge door slam shut.

"Here."

I catch the cold can midair when he throws it toward me like a softball. I turn to face him and crack it open nice and slow. I take a long swig and rest my head back against the couch. "Thanks."

"Don't mention it," he grumbles and sits down beside me, holding out a paper plate. He wears a look that dares me not to use it, so I take it with a huff and set it down on my lap.

My attention drops to my phone when it vibrates, shaking the glass coffee table it's lying on. Reaching for it, I notice several names spread across the screen.

I lean back and unlock the phone, grinning. A picture of a naked body fills the screen, and my eyes narrow. The girl's athletic, toned figure lies outstretched on what looks to be a bed, with a sheer, white, silky robe sagging off of her narrow shoulders. Her knees are bent, legs are spread wide open, the soft pink skin of her bare pussy glistening between them.

"What are you smirking at?" Clay asks. When I don't answer, he leans over my shoulder to look for himself. "Holy shit. Who is that?"

Locking my phone, I roll my eyes. "Fuck off and go find your own."

"I have my own." He sounds less than mildly confident in that statement.

"Then what are you waiting for?" I raise a brow, testing him before he flips me off and pushes off the couch. "Maybe if you got laid, you wouldn't be so damn uptight. You're acting like a twenty-seven-year-old virgin."

"Not everyone wants to be a 'fuck it and chuck it' kind of guy until the day they die. We're not all that young anymore, dude."

Registering his words, I nearly blow chunks all over the living room. "I stopped ageing when I turned twenty-four, remember?"

"Right." He snorts.

The reminder of how old we are was unnecessary. It's not like I don't know how close I am to reaching my thirties. With Clay getting his shit together with most things, I'm reminded nearly every damn day of the week. The thought of becoming someone that needs to start meeting society's standards makes a knot form in my stomach the size of Texas and my blood run ice cold.

I feel proud of Clay for realizing what he wants in life goes farther than a good fuck and a cold beer afterward. But his path will never be mine. The whole idea of going to a job I hate five days a week before coming home to a wife and three identical kids waiting on the porch of a two-story suburban home makes me want to kneel and pray to be shipped off to another planet.

Nah, I'm happy with staying twenty-six forever. Society can kiss my pearly white ass for demanding a change

I've just wrapped a towel around my waist when Clayton pushes open the bathroom door, eyes droopy and dull as he shoves past me, stopping in front of the sink.

He follows the same routine as every night: wets his toothbrush with cold water, smears a thick line of spearmint toothpaste onto the rough bristles before shoving it into his mouth and brushing his teeth for precisely two minutes. I'm no shrink, but I would confidently diagnose Clay with a case of obsessive-compulsive disorder any day of the week.

We've been living together for two years now, and I'm still trying to come to grasps with his overly cleanly, organized ways.

After exactly two minutes of scrubbing every square inch of his mouth, Clay spits into the sink and wipes a fresh towel across his lips. He doesn't tear his concentration from the small container of dental floss pinched between his fingers as he mumbles, "I forgot to tell you that there's some sort of concert tomorrow night at SP, and you need to be there."

I raise my brow. "There's a concert? At Sinners? Since when do they do that shit there?"

"Don't know. Ethan got tickets or something from one of the bouncers last week. There's one for both of us."

"Could be fun." I shrug and rub at the sting in my eyes, exhaustion stepping on me with its dirty shoe. I don't give the invitation much thought. Ethan is an eighteen-year-old boy stuck in the body of a twenty-six-year-old man. This isn't the first time that we've been *told* to go out with him, and it won't be the last. I just nod my head and follow along. Night-clubs aren't my venue of choice anymore, but beer is beer regardless of where you drink it.

Clayton gives me a nod but doesn't look away from the mirror.

"I'm going to bed. Don't forget that I need you ready to go to the gym at eight," I remind him before leaving the bathroom. I don't get anything more than a brief grunt in response, and I chuckle.

Our two-bedroom apartment—if you could call a full bedroom and a small den without a window two bedrooms—is so damn tiny that it only takes me a whole two seconds to walk down the hallway and reach my room.

I was lucky enough to earn my right to the actual bedroom by sucking back two more shots of tequila than Clay at a pub on Halloween the night before we moved into this place. I'm damn grateful for my stomach of steel, too, since there's no door or a lick of privacy leading to the den Clayton calls the Boom Room. But boom, it does not.

Where I might seem picky about the women I bed, Clayton damn near refuses anyone that doesn't meet his iron-set criteria to the absolute T. It's safe to say the Boom Room is filled with more tepid echo than anything else.

I don't bother turning on the light as I quickly swap out the towel for a pair of briefs that I find in a rare, clean basket of laundry and crawl into bed. When I get under the covers, I close my eyes and pray to God himself that I'll pass the fuck out soon.

2

Sierra

"I'M EXHAUSTED," I GROAN IN DEFEAT.

The three brown bags in my hands—each one filled with enough clothes and uncomfortable shoes to make my bank account and self-confidence beg for mercy—threaten to drop to the floor of the packed shopping mall. I can't say that I would complain if the ruby red high heels my sister forced me to buy ended up lost in the crowd of babbling shoppers, though.

"Tell me about it. At least you get to go home and relax now. I have a daughter just waiting to rip my head off for hiding her tablet before I left." My older sister, Clare, huffs while pulling open the heavy frosted glass door with the name *Courier Strip Mall* scrawled across the pane and leads us into the packed parking lot.

The autumn sun beams down on my exposed, pale shoulders. "At least Liz is cute." I offer her a quick sympathetic smile.

Raising a hand above my eyes, I squint to try and find her car.

"Of course, she is. She takes after me." She fishes out her

keys and hits the lock button twice. When the beeping rings out, we spot the shiny silver car.

Once we reach it, we shove our bags in the trunk. I slide into the front seat and cringe when my bare legs stick to the hot leather seats.

"I want a picture of you tomorrow morning before you go to work, Sierra. I'm so damn proud of you." Clare plops down in the driver's seat with a grin so wide I'm surprised that I don't see the corners of her mouth splitting open. "You got hired by one of the top marketing firms in the country! This is amazing."

My cheeks get warm as I wave her off. "It's a start."

"A start? Sierra, you spent a year working your ass off trying to market freaking dog food at your old job, just to end up even farther back than when you started. By the way, that dog food that in my honest to god opinion, shouldn't even be allowed to be labeled and sold as dog food in the first place. Their name speaks for itself. I mean, come on! *Poochie Goo Dog Food*? No way the ingredients are even legal. I say the job switch is happening at just the right time. I couldn't imagine what other companies Julia would have had you work with had you stayed." She finishes her speech with a long exhale and pulls out of the parking lot.

I fidget in my seat, shaking my legs and twiddling my thumbs to the point Clare reaches over to place a steady hand on them to get me to stop.

I've worked so hard to get this chance. To find a company that actually wants to show off my skills, not just shove a failure of a project in my lap that nobody else wanted so that I can fall to the back of the herd—alone and unnoticed.

Julia Stroll is a successful woman. I had hyped myself up to the point of near explosion the first day I met her, naïve with the idea that she would want to take me under her wing. You know, show me the ropes. Be my *mentor*. Or better yet, a *friend*. I hadn't had many of those after I graduated college. I spent far too many weekends with my nose buried in a textbook or watching Ted Talks to build any friendships that I would want to carry with me in the real world. But from the moment she laid eyes on me—those stone cold, vacant brown eyes—I knew that my perfect idea, my perfect *plan,* had already found its way into the shred pile.

Now here I am, three years and a briefcase full of less than admirable dog food and lice shampoo marketing experience later, about to be the new girl again.

"I'm a bit nervous, honestly," I admit.

"You'll be great. You've worked your ass off for this job. If Liz ever gets lice, I would use Itch Be Gone shampoo without a doubt." She bites the inside of her cheek to avoid laughing.

"Wow, you always know how to say the right thing. How did I get so lucky?"

"I wonder that myself." She smiles with satisfaction and flicks on her signal light before turning into my neighbourhood.

The continuous rows of green spruce trees bring a sense of familiarity to the air that I can almost smell and feel brush my skin. As we pass the beautifully bricked, colonial style houses lining the street, I can't help but feel an inch of jealousy climb up my spine.

After growing up sharing the only extra room in our childhood home with Clare, I've always dreamed about owning one that was a little larger than necessary. Not anything that would feel empty and cold on the days where my future children were at school and my imaginary husband was at work. But somewhere that we would never fully grow out of. A home big enough to host holiday dinners and my weekly book club meetings with all the neighbourhood mothers where we would get drunk off red wine and reminisce on the old days.

I had hoped that I would end up scoring large with one as soon as I finished school, but reality hit like a bitch when I realized I was aiming a bit high. Okay, way high.

Being fresh out of four years of college left me with nothing but a heaping pile of student debt, and a drinking problem that didn't seem too much like a problem at the time. The negative balance in my bank account kept my housing options pretty small once it was time to move out of dorms. I was lucky enough to find a decent-sized apartment within a few weeks of graduating, but my low budget pushed my living quarters way farther away than I had wanted from my old job, and even further from my new one.

The car comes to a slow stop outside of my small two-story apartment as Clare turns down the radio. "I'm serious about the picture, Sierra. I need to see how beautiful you look tomorrow."

I unbuckle my seatbelt. "I will. I promise." There's no way I would live it down if I forget to take the damn picture. Clare would guilt me for it long after I died. Hell, her parting words while leaning over my casket would be, *"How could you forget the picture, Sierra? I would have had that picture to look back on today."*

I climb out of the car and with a final goodbye, shut the door and wave.

She rolls down the window. "Love you!"

"Love you too." I blow her a kiss and grab my bags before walking to my building.

As I'm placing the last plate into the dishrack, the intercom on my wall wails out a screeching cry. Wiping my wet hands on my cookie monster pajama shorts, I blow a stray piece of hair out of my face and head for the speaker by the front door.

"Open up. I got ice cream!" Sophie's voice pierces my ears. I shake my head and buzz her in.

When it comes to my best friend, I know that ice cream is code for some sort of drama involving her, or something that's about to involve her when she sticks her head in the middle of it.

A minute later, there's a string of knocks on the door.

"What kind of ice cream do you have? And remember, there's only one right answer!" I shout through the door.

"Cookie dough. Now let me in before someone snatches me and leaves you without a best friend. The crime rates lately have skyrocketed."

I unlock the door and step back just before all five-foot-nothing of her plows her way inside, heading straight for the kitchen. The grocery bag she brought is planted on the countertop as she pulls open the cupboard above the sink and turns around with two huge ceramic bowls in her hands.

"Three or four scoops?" she asks, her face hard with concentration as she digs through my utensil drawer for an ice cream scoop. Her perfectly waxed and tattooed eyebrows draw together as she focuses.

"Just two."

Her head turns to me so quickly that my eyes bulge. She cuts a hand through the air. "Three it is."

I move toward the counter and lean a hip against it. "So, are you going to tell me what's wrong or should I start guessing?"

"Nothing," she groans, shoving the scoop in the open tub of ice cream with a surprisingly terrifying amount of force.

"Right." I move around her to grab two spoons. "Then do you wanna tell me what the poor ice cream did to you before you got here?"

"You know Ethan Langton, right?" she asks with a weighted sigh, spinning on the heel of her still booted feet to face me.

"The guy that used to host all of the frat parties in college?"

The guy was a total tool. The only thing he had going for him was his washboard abs. But even then, the appeal faded fast as soon as he opened that sexist mouth of his. Guys who think that a woman belongs in the kitchen in the 21st century have no right being so good looking.

"Unfortunately," she grumbles while grabbing her nearly overflowing bowl of ice cream and stomping across the apartment to my thrifted navy couch.

The four-seater, velvet couch is for better words, extremely out of style and butt ugly. But when you're twenty-six with absolutely nothing to your name but an outdated shirtless firefighter calendar and a pair of scuffed Louboutin's that you got as a present from your ex but are too stubborn to retire, you take what you can get.

"What about him has you so pissed off? We haven't even seen him in years." I grab my bowl and join her. It isn't until after I sink into the couch cushion that I notice the regretful look on her face. I swallow heavily as the realization dawns on me. "Oh. *Oh*. So, you slept together then? I mean, it isn't the end of the world. Right?"

"Isn't the end of the world? I slept with a man child."

Her head falls back and she grumbles a few sentences under her breath in Spanish. I hide my amused grin behind my hand. Sophie only rambles in Spanish when she's flustered, angry, or both. But both is *never* good. And from the flush on her cheeks and the way her back teeth are grinding together, I can only assume that she's definitely both.

Scooping a hefty amount of ice cream onto my spoon, I shove it in my mouth and sit quietly. Sophie has never been shy about her sex life, but Ethan Langton? That *does* surprise me. Overcompensating dickbags aren't usually her go-to, regardless of how deep the itch might be.

"When?" I ask after a few silent seconds.

"Two nights ago. It was a rare moment of weakness. There was a pool, and you've seen Ethan without his shirt."

"I have." I laugh quietly. "He's hot for sure."

"And boy, is he ever packing a rocket."

Crinkling my nose, I brush off her comment. "If it was so good, then why are you upset? Was he too quick on the trigger or something?"

"No! God no," she rushes, dropping her spoon in the melting glob of ice cream. "He wants to, like, go out. *On a date*."

My brows jump up and questions fill my mouth like I'm playing a game of chubby bunny. But I sit in silence, waiting for her to elaborate. Only she doesn't say anything else. She puts the bowl of melted ice cream beside her and folds her hands together in her lap instead, looking anxiously around the apartment. With a nervous knot rooting in my belly, I try to fill the silence.

"So, are you just not into him then? I mean, a free dinner is a free dinner. Even if it is with a guy like Ethan, and *especially* if the sex was good."

"Maybe if it were dinner I would go. But he invited me to watch some band play at SP tomorrow night and you know how much I hate it there."

He invited her to a club? As a date? Yikes. What's that saying? Disappointed but not surprised?

"I didn't even know they let bands play there." I stretch my legs out in front of me and set my bowl beside Sophie's.

"That's beside the point, Sierra!" She slides a quick hand down her hair and squeezes her eyes shut. "I want to go, but I don't want to go alone. Who knows what would happen to me if I went into the bathroom without a partner."

"I think you're being a little paranoid, babe."

I, for one, haven't been to a club in years. But the memories I do have of the drunken nights spent with my arm laced through Sophie's, and a piece of paper over our drinks still burn in the back of my mind. Her parent's might have let her watch a few too many episodes of Dateline when she was an early teen. We did stay safe though, so I really shouldn't complain. Sophie was always one hell of a safety buddy.

"Why don't you come with me?" Her back straightens as she turns to me with wide eyes. I gulp. "Please?"

"I'm not third-wheeling for you at Sinners. Plus, I'll be way too tired after work."

Grabbing my bowl, I practically run to the kitchen, cursing under my breath when she chases after me, a long blonde ponytail slapping against her back.

"Please do this for me. I'll literally get down on my knees if I have to."

I drop my bowl in the sink and let out a sharp exhale. She won't stop until I agree. I know that for a fact. "You owe me for this. I'm serious."

Flailing arms slide around me, the smell of cotton candy overwhelming. "Yes, I do. You're the freaking best."

"I know. Now let go of me before I get a sugar rush from that damn perfume of yours."

3

Braden

HAVING MADE IT TWENTY-SIX TRIPS AROUND THE SUN HAS ITS benefits, regardless of how shit it might make me feel.

There are countless things that I've learned and collected in my head like a chipmunk storing nuts for the winter. And every once in a while, I make use of all of that information.

I've learned that if you want to be taken seriously in this competitive—sometimes unforgiving world—you have to carry yourself with an unwavering sense of confidence. Without confidence, how do you expect anyone to take you seriously? Without a sense of high-strung determination and power, attempting to skip a long line to get into a club you don't even want to be at would be nearly impossible. But with it . . . that's a whole different story.

"Big Dave, have you been working out?" My voice carries strong across the packed, brightly lit sidewalk as we walk toward the front doors of Sinners Paradise.

The at *least* three-hundred-pound protector of the neon gates turns away from the bloodshot-eyed teen in front of him, his lips lifting in a twitching grin. Clayton chuckles beside me when I raise my hand in a quick wave.

"I have, actually. You can tell?" Dave asks once we push our way in front of two women.

One of them has a waist long, platinum ponytail that reaches the top of her ass and if I had to bet, wouldn't even reach my shoulders with six-inch heels on. The other, a taller, dark-haired beauty grabs my attention by the balls and clasps a tiny fist around my throat, stealing my air. Her eyes are hard, narrowed on the dimple in my chin, and for some fucking reason, that has my blood burning with frustration, I wish that she would shift her gaze to mine.

With a shake of my head, I turn back around and force myself to refocus on the burly, unattractive security guard. "Of course. Those guns could end world wars, buddy."

There's an unnecessary flex of his arms when he puffs out his chest. I chew the inside of my cheek to keep from smiling.

"I'm still waiting for those boxing lessons." Dave says, moving the black rope aside that was keeping us from entering.

"Anytime. You know where to find me." I pat his round arms and nod to Clay for him to follow me inside.

"Are you seriously going to let them in before us?" I hear a snarky voice snap, the strength in the tone taking me by surprise.

Turning around, I lock eyes with a pair of narrowed ones —the colour of molten silver right before it's poured into a mold, glistening in the brass pot. They belong to the brunette I noticed when we first arrived.

She stands with a nearly overwhelming sense of confidence and poise, like she doesn't fear anybody or anything. Like we should all fear *her*. And maybe, if I was any less of an egotistical prick, I would have been terrified to piss her off even further, but that's not me.

Instead, I decide to lift a brow in a silent taunt before crossing my arms and snapping, "That a problem?"

Her narrowed eyes roll as she places her hands on one of her full hips. They're nice hips. Ones that I could grab and squeeze and knead in my palms until the skin was red and sore.

"Considering we've been out here waiting for over twenty minutes to get inside, yes. It is a problem."

"Sorry to break it to you, fighter, but that's not my problem," I say.

She laughs humourlessly, shaking her head. "How typical."

I cock my head. "What's that supposed to mean?"

"Leave it, Sierra," her blonde friend sighs.

Sierra, hey? I can already imagine that rolling off my tongue later while I'm fucking that attitude right out of her.

"Have fun inside, Sierra. I would say let's do this again, but I would rather light myself on fire."

Sierra doesn't get a chance to reply before Clay and I are heading inside. I can faintly hear her snap at Dave before we're sucked into the loud music thumping in the club.

I laugh under my breath at the memory of her snarky comments. That one doesn't lack fire, that's for sure.

"YOU MADE IT!" Ethan slurs, stumbling over to our spot at the bar. As graceful as a baby deer, that one.

"I see you started without us." I stretch my neck so I can eye up the crowds grinding and drinking until they stumble, bumping into each other with grins that show they couldn't care less.

Most of these people won't even remember who they met or what songs they dirty danced to when they wake up. But that's what's fun about being young and careless, right? The lack of repercussions for our actions and mistakes. So why does the idea of tipping back shot after shot until I can't manage to walk three steps ahead of me without falling on my face not give me the same buzz as before?

Fuck, I really am getting old.

Ethan grins, naïve to life outside of places like these. "Do you have a drink already?" He's moving toward the bar before Clay and I have a chance to answer. "Two pornstars!" he shouts at the bartender.

"I forgot how annoying he is when he's sloshed!" Clay shouts, bumping my shoulder.

"Just when he's sloshed?" I snort. Clayton laughs.

"Here you go!" Ethan slides the red and blue-filled shot glass toward us with a sense of urgency. Some of the liquid sloshes over the top of the glass and sticks to the bar top.

"Thanks." I throw back the shot and fight back my gag when the horrendously sweet mixture slides down my throat, making my stomach whimper. Ethan is already making his way through the crowd when I push the empty glass back where he used to be.

"I'm going outside for a minute," Clay says, I nod, and he disappears in the crowd.

I settle my forearms on the bar and look around, quickly realizing that there's no way they're fitting a band in here.

Peering over a few heads, I search for anything that the band could even use as a stage but come up empty-handed. Unless they plan to shove a drum set in the middle of the dance floor, I think they're out of luck. Pushing myself away from the bar, I feel a small hand attempt to wrap around my bicep and squeeze.

My jeans pull tighter when I look down and catch an eyeful of a set of creamy tits spilling from a tube top. I place my hand back down on the bar and toss her a star-studded smile. The girl gives me a wicked smile in return. She pushes herself closer to me, sending the blood rushing straight to my groin when her tongue slowly slides along her bottom lip, her hooded eyes locked on mine the entire time.

"Hey, gorgeous," I say, hovering my hand over the bare skin of her lower back.

"Hey, Braden. Do you remember me?" she asks, a slight glimmer of hope lighting up her eyes. I frown.

"No." I sigh, long and hard. As much as I would love to have those tits smother my face all night, I'm not about to lie to get her in bed. That seems to be more Ethan's style than mine.

She stands silent for a moment as she processes my blunt answer. If she were smart, she would turn around and run straight for the hills. Remembering names isn't really my specialty, among other things.

"Fuck you," she spits, dropping her hand from my arm and stalking off.

I run the pad of my thumb over my bottom lip. *You almost did, sweetheart.*

With a dampened mood, I head for the little lit-up bathroom sign across the dance floor. I keep my back rigid as I move around the sweaty bodies, desperately avoiding the couple close to filming a damn porno beside me before I'm stumbling into the back of someone, an uncomfortable groan spilling between us as an elbow hits my spine.

I turn around to yell at whoever shoved me, only to see the back of a short guy as he pushes through the crowd, away from me.

What a damn pussy.

With a scowl, I start for the bathroom again, only to have something firm pushed into my crotch, moving in slow circles against me. Surprised, I drop my eyes to see a round ass grinding against me, matching the deep pulse of the song pounding around us without a care in the world.

Throwing all caution to the wind, I yank the girl closer to me, pressing my front to her back and letting my fingers dig into her flared hips. The smooth material of her black, strappy dress sticks to her body like a second skin, leaving nothing, yet far too much to my imagination as I let my eyes trail over the smooth, freckled skin of her shoulders.

I drop my head and brush the top of her ear with my nose. "You're bold, rubbing against me like we've known each other for years."

"Maybe we have," she replies breathlessly.

Reaching back, she scratches her nails up my arms before gripping onto my bicep and squeezing, pulling me tighter against her until there's no doubt in my mind that she can feel every pulsing inch of me pressed against her.

I move my hands to her exposed shoulders and trace the thin strap resting on her collarbone. She leans back against me and rests her head against my chest, swaying side to side with the music.

Her hair is soft, so fucking soft as I push it off her shoulder and bare her neck. A rich mix of cinnamon and orange penetrates my senses, making my mouth water with the need to drag my tongue over her pulse point and taste every inch of her. A thought that should seem ridiculous, considering I don't even know her name.

"I would have remembered a body like yours," I mumble and spin her around to face me. My breath catches in my throat when the same silver eyes from outside fall on me, this time half hidden by her droopy lids and thick eyelashes. I swallow my groan. "Or maybe I didn't."

Her eyes don't waver from surprise—not like mine. Instead, she presses her hands against my chest, fingers spread wide. I can't help but wonder if she recognizes me. If she does, I would assume from the attitude she had outside that she wouldn't be letting herself touch me or vice versa.

But she is. And I would be lying if I said I wasn't hoping that she remembers exactly who I am.

As she keeps her palms flush to my stiff abdominal muscles, I raise my brows, intrigued and unbearably captivated by the stunning siren in front of me.

Her gaze falls when her touch begins moving up my chest, and heat engulfs my groin as she watches her own movements. She scratches at my t-shirt with white-tipped nails, exploring my chest, moving her hands over my pecs and to my collarbone before eventually wrapping her hands around the back of my neck, fingers looping aggressively in my hair. Her eyes lift to meet mine again. She oozes confidence, and I can feel my underwear stick to the moisture collecting on the tip of my dick.

"I want to know how you got in so easy," she mumbles when I drop a hand to her ass. "Better yet, why didn't you take us in with you?"

I blink, surprised. "Your instant hatred toward me outside wasn't an obvious enough reason?"

She laughs. "Okay. Fair enough."

We continue to dance, but there's only one thing that I can think about. Sierra remembers who I am, and I've subconsciously made it my plan to give her a night that will ensure she never forgets it.

"What if I made it up to you?" I ask.

"How?"

I bend down and lean toward her. My words brush the top of her ear. "Let me take you home instead."

She shivers. "I thought I hated you."

"Hate sex is the best sex."

Sierra pulls back just enough for our eyes to catch. "Take me home then."

That's all I needed to hear. In a flurry, I grab her hand and pull her through the dance floor and out the front doors.

The chilly air nips at our skin, and I use it as an excuse to pull her tight to my side. I push us away from the bystanders still waiting in line to get in, and toward a yellow cab waiting along the curb. Throwing open the door, I let her climb in first before I slide in and pull her onto my lap, pelvis to pelvis.

"42 Clanmore Street," I shoot at the driver before grabbing the back of her neck and pulling her to me, pressing our lips together in a kiss I'm sure I'll still be feeling in the morning.

4

Braden

All I taste is cherry Coke when my lips meet hers. The addicting flavour has me snaking my tongue between her already parted lips and exploring her mouth.

Her need is as apparent as mine as her hands move over every inch of my chest, like she's trying to memorize the feeling of my skin under her touch the same way that I am with her. Her fingers slide under my shirt, meeting the bare skin with her nails as she drags them along every indent resting there.

My hand fists in her hair, wrapping the long brown strands around my knuckles as I pull her impossibly closer to me. I swallow the gentle moan that slips from her lips when I reach between us and lift her dress, letting my fingers trail up her inner thigh. I keep my touch soft, teasing.

I rest my head against the seat and groan when I reach the hem of her panties, the only boundary left between me and the skin I will undoubtedly find swollen and wet.

My knuckle finds her slit, and I know it would be easy to fuck her right here, in the back of this cab, with how wet I find her. "Fuck, you're dripping."

She doesn't answer, only inches back to move her lips to my neck, sucking, licking, kissing, *worshipping*. I desperately shove away her panties to the side and drag a finger up her sex. She sucks in a breath and her thighs clench around me momentarily before relaxing completely, leaving herself open for my touch. "Yes. *Yes.*"

My eyes dare to roll back, the intense feeling I get from hearing her sounds of approval shoots through my veins like a reeling junkie who's just got his fix. I know instantly that I want more of those noises.

I spread her open with two fingers and she hisses from the sudden exposure before I'm sinking a long finger inside of her. *Holy fuck* she's tight, stretching around the intrusion. I press my palm to her swollen flesh and my finger slides deeper with a new sense of urgency.

Sierra lifts herself from my lap until just my first knuckle remains inside of her, and I take the chance to line up a second finger before she comes back down, taking them both this time. My palm slides against her pussy, wetter than before when she begins to rock against it, grinding her clit on my skin. Her face falls in my neck, opened mouthed, and warms the exposed skin with her laboured breaths.

"Is that good? Is this what you want?" I use my free hand to shove down the strap of her dress and free her left breast, grateful when I notice the lack of bra.

Not wanting the cab driver to catch a glimpse of what's mine for the night, I lean toward her chest and suck her pretty pink nipple into my mouth. Her gasp is barely audible, like her body doesn't want anyone to hear it but me. My cock aches, hard as stone as it presses painfully against the zipper of my jeans. I want inside of her. *Now.*

It's like she's running on the same frequency because the next thing I know, her palm is pressing down against me, eliciting a grunt of satisfaction from deep in my throat.

The cab comes to a sudden stop, jerking us forward as my knuckle rubs against her clit, drawing out a soft cry from her before she jumps from my lap.

"Thank you for the ride!" she squeaks, eyes glazed over, avoiding looking at the driver as she shoves the door open and flies out of the cab.

With pussy-soaked fingers and a hard cock, I manage to pull out a wad of cash before setting it on the passenger seat and sliding out of the cab, not speaking a word to the silent driver.

Slamming the door shut, I turn around and pick up her waiting figure, sliding my hands under her ass and grinning into her hair when her long, toned legs wrap around my waist. Her grip is tight as she presses herself against me, not wasting any time before starting to play with the button of my jeans.

Her impatient touch has me nearly running up the sidewalk and tripping over myself when she slips a hand inside my boxers, grabbing onto my arousal eagerly.

She pulls back slightly when we reach the door but her small hand stays wrapped tightly around my dick. I look down at where she has me in a tight fist, pumping the thick shaft like she loves doing it.

"My cock looks good in your hand, baby."

I would take a picture if I didn't think it would creep her out. It looks like a fucking wet dream.

"It feels even better." Her thumb collects a bead of precum and swirls it over the head. *Jesus Christ.*

I reach into my jeans and grab my keys before opening the apartment door. After slamming it shut behind us, I spin around and slam her back against the wall, cursing into the empty apartment when her grip on me tightens.

"Keep doing that and I'll fuck you right up against this wall," I threaten, dragging my parted lips down her neck and biting the delicate skin hard enough to ensure there will be a mark tomorrow.

"Is that a threat or a promise?" she asks.

No, I want you in my bed. Now.

I move us inside my bedroom, leaving the lights off as I throw her down on the bed. With her knees bent, she lets her legs fall open in front of me, and I lick my lips, desperate to taste her.

I rip off my shirt and throw it across the room before stalking toward her like a predator to prey, only stopping when my thighs hit the mattress. She takes me by surprise when she sits and starts to pull up her dress, keeping her eyes trained on me as it inches up her skin.

My lungs burn, and I realize I've been holding my breath, watching her strip for me.

My jaw slacks, blood burning as I take her in. I knew she was hot, but I didn't realize she was rocking such a dangerous body. A dipped waist met with full hips, thighs that I want to suffocate me, and an ass that any man would kill to feel in his palms. She's fucking gorgeous. And it's more than just her body. It's her narrow cheekbones, plump cheeks, and full lips. Her sharp jaw and round eyes. Fuck, I scored large tonight, that's for sure.

I grab her ankles and pull her to the edge of the bed, watching as her perfect, handful-size tits bounce with the movement. I slide my arms under her thighs and pull her even closer, until I can smell the sweet arousal and see the outline of her pussy through wet panties. With firm hands, I push her thighs apart. My mouth waters.

She pulls off her panties and exposes herself to me.

My cock throbs with need. I'm a starving man, out of control when I see her bare, swollen pussy without the restrictions of her silk underwear. With a groan, I dive between her thighs and run my tongue flat along her wet slit.

Her hips buck up at the sudden contact, but I grip her legs and hold her in place, keeping her still.

"More," she pleads, voice shaking. Hearing her without the spine-straightening confidence that I've quickly learned to expect only intensifies my need to satisfy her.

I want her to unravel in my bare hands. I want her to remember who made her come harder than she ever has long after she walks out my front door tomorrow morning.

"More? You want my tongue inside this tight cunt?"

I let my eyes move from the glistening pink flesh in front of me and work my way up her stomach, paying extra attention to the scar underneath her belly button where a piercing used to be and the large paw print tattoo underneath of her right breast. I chew on my bottom lip to suppress a groan when she palms the same tit, covering both her hardened nipple and tattoo.

My gaze falls to her face quickly, unable to stay focused on anything but her parted lips and eyes so heated I can almost feel them lighting a match to my insides, burning me alive from the inside out.

Dragging one hand to press flat against her hips, I use my other to spread her apart, and begin lapping at her arousal, moaning in the back of my throat at her soft sounds of approval that fall in the dark.

I plunge a finger inside of her before adding another right away with the knowledge of just how ready she is for me. They slip in easily and her eyes shut, chin lifting in the air and hips pushing up from the bed before I'm shoving them back down.

"Play with those nipples for me, Sierra. Need you to come."

My words are nothing short of a demand and she responds without a fight, twisting and pinching both of her tightened peaks between her fingers with a sigh of relief. I have no idea where the sudden need to be vocal is coming from, but I'll take it. Now isn't the time to question this shit.

I pick up my pace, slipping in a third finger and curling them, hitting the spot that has her gasping.

"Don't stop. *God*, I'm almost there."

I wrap my lips around her clit and suck hard enough that it releases with a pop before I punish her with a nip to her swollen flesh. She tries to kick out her legs, fingers gripping the sheets. My next words come out tight and harsh.

"It's Braden. Not God. Say it and I won't stop right now. Don't make me stop, baby. You're taking these fingers so good."

She has me hanging on by a fucking thread. I need to be inside of her, but I also have to know that I made this tight pussy come all over my fingers, soaking my hand while she screams my name.

Sierra tightens around me with each shuttered exhale, and when I suck on her clit for a second time, she stills before every muscle in her body tightens. She reaches her high with her chest rising and lip held between her teeth. I take everything she has to give me with a cocky grin on my lips before slipping my wet fingers into my mouth, staring into her pupil-blown gaze with my own as I suck them off.

I love the way her cheeks flush, as if me sucking her juices from my fingers is more intimate than me just eating her pussy like a starving man.

I crawl over her with the taste of her still on my tongue and reach into the side table, pulling out a condom and covering my cock with it before settling it between her legs. She's warm and wet against me as I rock against her center, feeling myself slip between her folds and my tip brushing her clit on every upstroke.

There's a beautiful flush on her cheeks, and her lashes flutter disbelief before I kiss her. She responds eagerly with a just as bruising kiss before nipping at my bottom lip and slipping her tongue in my mouth, commanding and leading me, using me for her own pleasure. It's so fucking sexy I begin to worry if I'll become a one pump chump once inside her. *I need to calm down.*

Fingers work their way into the hairs at the base of my scalp and yank hard enough to pull our lips apart and expose my neck to her wet, open-mouthed kisses. I need to reel her in. I need to take back the power before I lose it completely.

"You're going to be so tight, aren't you? You could barely take my one finger earlier. I'm going to stretch you out so good," I mumble.

Moving away from her lips, I shove my head in her neck. I begin to feast on the immediately addicting taste of her skin. Peaches and fucking sunshine. I've never compared a taste to goddamn sunshine before, but I would happily do it again because that's the only way to describe it. Warm, clear, *free.* She tastes like fucking sunshine. My hot breath fans out on her skin, bringing goosebumps to the surface.

"I need you inside of me *now.* Stop playing with me," she growls.

I laugh at her attempt at a glare but don't dare disagree. "Put my cock inside you then, *fighter*. Take what you need."

And she does. *Fuck,* she does. My jaw slacks when she guides me inside and then stops, sending me a look that says, *I'm not doing all the work, asshole.* With a brief shake of my head, I thrust the rest of the way inside and bite my tongue hard enough I taste blood when I feel her tighten around me like a damn vice.

"*Fuck yes.* Take every last inch."

Her nails scratch at my back. "Please, just fuck me."

More than satisfied with her plea, I pull out, thrusting back in again when I feel her become more adjusted to my size, building momentum every time my balls slap her ass, filling her to the hilt. I lean back on my knees and pull her toward me, entering her again with a guttural sound that I hardly recognize as coming from my own mouth.

Gripping her ankles, I push her legs up into the air and continue barreling into her, the sound of slapping skin echoing around us, intensifying the electricity zapping in the air every time our bodies meet. I can feel my high building—biting at my spine and forcing my thighs to clench tight. My stomach tightens, and I fumble with her clit, pressing down on it with the pad of my thumb and rotating, determined to get Sierra off before I fill this condom.

"Oh, my god!" she cries, eyes squeezed tightly. "Harder. I'm gonna come."

"That's a good girl. You take this cock so fucking good. Come for me, Sierra."

"*Yes*!" she screams, her pussy clamping down on me, holding me in place just as I feel my orgasm barrel into me.

My head falls back, and I thrust into her again before stopping, muscles quaking and my release filling the condom.

Sierra stays silent, both of us catching desperate breaths. I pull away and discard the used condom before coming back and seeing her lying on her stomach, arm tucked under my pillow, dead asleep.

I swallow down my laughter and mumble under my breath, "Goodnight, then, fighter."

5

Sierra

I'M PULLED OUT OF DREAMLAND ONLY TO HAVE BRIGHT SUNLIGHT burn through my eyes, piercing into my skull. As if the tequila headache wasn't enough, the nausea swirling in my belly definitely is.

A thick ink-covered arm weighs down my chest as I try to focus on the *now,* not the before when I was gulping back alcohol like water after a marathon, and shaking my ass on anyone within arm's reach.

Letting out a shaky sigh of regret, I trail my eyes up the arm and try desperately to ignore the pulse between my legs that thumps like a raced heartbeat when my heavy eyes fall on the deep purple bruises covering Braden's throat. Dammitt, Sierra. Hickeys? Are we *sixteen*?

The memories of last night come flooding in, making it pound hard enough that I begin rubbing my temples in search of relief.

Getting drunk was not a part of my plan last night. But neither was coming home with a guy who reeks of broken hearts and probably has a nauseating number of nudes in his camera roll. I want to hate myself for being weak enough to throw myself at by far the hottest guy I think I've ever seen, but I'm far too prideful to look past the fact that I actually got him to sleep with me in the first place to follow through with the self-hatred.

I squeeze my eyes shut and try to come up with a plan.

There's no way that I'm staying here to deal with his no-doubt typical morning-after speech, so I guess that only leaves me with one viable option: disappear before he has a chance to rip my self-confidence to shreds.

The last thing I need to deal with is Braden's cocky, pussy wetting arrogance.

What happened last night, I know that that's not me. I'm not the type of woman who drops her panties for the hottest guy that comes up to her at a club. I'm normally too chicken-shit to do anything like that. But last night, I was that woman.

I was the one that other women whisper about while watching her make a total fool out of herself by falling all over a guy who won't remember her in the morning. And as much as I would love to blame it on the heart-crunching pain I felt watching my ex-boyfriend push the girl he cheated on me with up against the back door of said club, I know that it goes far beyond that.

Braden jostles beside me, pushing the blankets down subconsciously and exposing the hauntingly mesmerizing eight-pack to my sleepy eyes. I can almost feel his gentle touch running along my body before I mentally curse myself out. No. Just *no*.

Eying the room, I spot my dress lying across his dresser, my panties somehow looped around the bedroom door handle, and both shoes lying on opposite sides of the small room. He doesn't lack finesse, that's for sure. Or maybe that was all me. At this point, I can't be sure. I seemed to have become a different person last night. One with no inhibition or fears. Just a pair of wet panties and a one-track mind focused solely on the giant god of a man rubbing against me and dancing along to a thumping beat without tripping over myself.

I want to shove my palm against my forehead at the memory of the arrogant dick parading around outside of the club like he owned the damn place before eyeing me up like a cat to a canary. My anger grows into a full-blown punching attack in my gut when I remember how riled up it made me to have that same man pressing his dick against my ass on the dance floor, and how quickly I had fallen under his lust trap.

Jesus, Sierra. I wasted no time in practically dry-humping him on the way outside and letting him do all sorts of things to me in a cab. A *cab*! Heat crawls up my neck.

I use my free hand to peel Braden's fingers from my skin and inhale sharply when his arm topples toward the mattress. He doesn't stir any further, just mumbles something incoherent under his breath before burying his head further into his black pillowcase.

I slip from underneath the covers and sigh as the heat that was once suffocating my body is replaced with a light, cold breeze flowing in from the slightly cracked window across the room. I collect my clothes and get dressed quickly, not attempting to hide my shame as I fist the straps of my shoes and open the door. Softly shutting the creaky wood behind me, I wait for the small click and drop my hand.

"Made it," I whisper, relieved.

The sound of a throat clearing has me jumping out of my skin.

"Ah, you must be the owner of the voice I had the pleasure of hearing all night long," a rough voice chides from behind me. There's not even a hint of annoyance in the statement, only utter amusement. I grow confused.

I spin around and gasp, a sweaty palm moving to rest against my throat. My shoes fall to the floor before bouncing a few feet away from me and stopping with a *clunk*. The smug look covering the man's impressively well-carved features is not enough to hide his shit attitude as he eyes me curiously. His low-riding boxer shorts remain the only piece of clothing covering his tan skin as he crosses his arms and lifts a thick, confident brow.

Flustered, I quickly collect my shoes and stand up, pulling my dirty dress down as far as I can stretch it, not wanting to flash him. "Uh, yeah. I was just leaving." My words are rushed and almost . . . squeaky? I nearly sprint to the front door.

"You're not going to tell me your name at least? I think you owe me that after you kept me from receiving my proper beauty sleep. Now look at me, my looks are faded," he teases with an exaggerated pout. A large hand runs down his obvious six-pack. He's not as muscular as Braden, but I would have been attracted to him regardless. He's a handsome guy.

"Are you brothers or something?" I ask, not sure why I'm interested. Would it matter if they were?

"Hell no. Not in the ethical sense, at least. I'm Clayton, your bed buddy's better-looking best friend."

"Clayton and Braden, clever." I snort. Half squatting, half bending, I put on my shoes.

"Definitely." His mouth quirks. "So, your name?"

"Why does it matter? You'll never see me again."

"Just curious." He shrugs, openly checking me out. I want to reach down and cover my breasts, knowing how open they are for viewing in this dress, but he looks away before I have the chance.

"My name's Sierra. Now can I leave?"

"Sierra, right. I heard that a few times last night."

I narrow my eyes and place my hand on the doorknob,

squeezing. "You knew? Then why bother asking in the first place?"

"Double checking." He chuckles, a dimpled smile beaming back at me.

"Great," I groan. "Well, if there isn't anything else, I'll be leaving."

"See ya, sweetheart." He waves me off with a mock salute before I'm walking out the door.

I'm not sure I'm a big fan of this Clayton guy. But then again, I'm sure that I'm not a fan of Braden either.

"IT WAS MORTIFYING, Soph. You should have seen the arrogant look on his face when he saw me." I continue ranting to my best friend, wrapping my hair around my finger as I lean back in one of her patio chairs later that day.

"He sounds kind of hot." She takes a big sip of her lemonade, nearly finishing it off in one go.

"Sophie," I reprimand her.

"What? He was, wasn't he? You have to help me out here. Last night was one big cyclone of blurred figures for me."

"Well yeah," I scoff, incredulous. "Not as hot as Braden, though. Not by a long shot." An array of dirty thoughts—or more so memories—infiltrate my scattered brain before I quickly shake them away.

"Right, the guy you ran off on after he rattled your insides like no other guy has before." She shakes her head like a disappointed parent.

Brushing off her last few words, I bite my cheek. "You would have acted the same way. He's too hot, you know? Like the hot you can only read about."

Right," she drawls. "Silly me to think you would have

stayed for at least one more orgasm before ditching."

Thoughts of what would have happened if I hadn't run out before Braden woke up have been festering all day. Would we have avoided the painful good morning and moved straight to slipping back under the sheets? Or would he have looked at me with regret and revulsion, questioning why I was still in his bed? I'm not sure the chance of *maybe* having his tongue between my thighs again would have been worth the risk of embarrassment.

"How did it go after I left you and Ethan alone, anyway? You haven't said anything." I change the subject with a newly formed twist in my belly and adjust my sunglasses to distract myself before I can dwell on it for too long.

"Before or after we came here?" she asks coyly.

"You came here?" I ask, startled. "And?"

"I don't kiss and tell." She fights back a grin and her neck flushes.

I send her a pointed look. One that says, *you're really going to pull that shit?* "Hypocrisy at its finest."

"You love me anyway."

"I do. And if you love me, you'll let me out of this damn sun before I turn into a lobster. You know how bad I burn."

My lips tug as I slide my sunglasses up into my hair and stand. I walk around her parent's oversized rectangular pool and pull open the glass patio door. Sophie's sandals slide across the patio tiles as she steps up behind me. A searing pain flames from my shoulder when she flicks my burning back, giggling maniacally before pushing past me.

"Sophie!" I shriek and chase after her, face tense with irritation. Her laughter reverberates through the house and weakens my resolve.

Damn her for falling into the vacant spot of best friend all those years ago. She's exhausting, but I don't think that I could imagine her any other way.

6

Braden

I PEEL MY EYES OPEN, MY LIPS TIPPING IN A LAZY SMILE WITH THE memories of last night. I stretch my arm across the cold sheets, scowling when I don't make contact with the warm body I was expecting. I search the room but come up short of anything but the searing feeling of disappointment.

And here I thought I was going to start my day with breakfast.

My eyes move around the room in search of the clothes that were ripped from Sierra's body last night. She could just be in the bathroom or something. Right? The gnawing in my stomach becomes more intense when I don't see her clothes. I groan, the sound a mixture of pure sexual frustration and . . . rejection? I push myself out of bed and pull on a pair of sweatpants from the dirty laundry bin.

I yank open my bedroom door and breathe in the rich smell of coffee before spotting Clayton draped over the couch. Dressed in only a pair of black boxer briefs, he covers his bare stomach with a bowl of Lucky Charms, milk splattered on his pecs.

"Sierra's not here," he sings while watching last night's Vancouver Warrior's hockey game on our shared flatscreen.

I don't watch a lot of hockey anymore. It unsettles me now more than anything. I guess giving up on one passion to pursue another does that to a person. I chose boxing over hockey and tried to never look back. Some days, I stumble and find myself reminiscing, though. Those are days that I like to forget, sunk deep inside of a woman who won't care if I remember her name in the morning. A woman who doesn't know the old me. The one that I've become accustomed to forgetting.

"What did you do to her?" I move toward him, feeling my skin start to beat with warmth. My harsh tone grasps his attention. He turns to look at me, more curious than afraid.

"Me? Nothing. You, on the other hand." He shakes his head disapprovingly. "She couldn't seem to get out of here fast enough. Are you having problems in the sack? It's okay if you are. I won't judge you."

The devilish grin tugging at his lips makes me think otherwise. "Fuck off." I glare at him, throwing up my middle finger. "Did she say why she was leaving?"

"Nope. But she did look quite upset." I lose his attention as soon as the Warrior's buzzer sounds, the signal that the opposing team scored a goal. "Stop sleeping, defence! What the fuck!"

Yeah. What the fuck? She was upset? After that mind-blowing sex? Yeah right. I might be an egotistical asshole, but I *know* when I satisfy a woman. And last night, she was more than satisfied.

"Her loss," I mutter. I'm not sure if I'm trying to convince myself or Clayton at this point.

I head toward the bathroom, passing my room on the way. I fight back the urge to take a can of Febreeze to the whole fucking thing when the smell of her still lingers in the air, clinging on to every possible surface.

I mutter a curse. Just the memory of her sprawled out, exposed and eager for me, on *my* bed is enough to make my dick harden. I don't know if I should feel surprised or pissed that she left without saying goodbye. Maybe I should be relieved. Everything I remember from our conversation outside the club doesn't lead me to believe that she's my type at all. High-strung, smart-mouthed women are more Clayton's style. Alcohol was probably the only reason why I found her tolerable last night.

The bathroom window provides more than enough light as I push open the damaged door, cringing when the top hinge threatens to give out. I manage to close it without losing it and pull open one of the vanity drawers, digging for my toothbrush. When my gaze flickers to my reflection in the mirror, I spot a quick flash of red clinging to my back.

"Holy hell," I mutter, turning in the mirror. I squint and peek at the five long scratches racking down the entirety of my upper back, three of them deep enough to leave scabs on my shoulder blades. *Kitties got claws, that's for sure.*

With a shake of my head, I turn on the shower, more than ready to cleanse myself of last night's sins.

WITH A CLEAR HEAD, I step out of the shower, wrap a fluffy white towel around my waist, and leave the steam-filled bathroom.

"Bad time, Son?"

My head snaps to my dad, his brown eyes beaming under the cheap fluorescent lights hung above the kitchen table. He sits with perfect posture, shoulders held high and chin pointed to the sky. With shoulder-length brown hair tied back in a loose bun, and a clean-shaven face, he looks way younger than forty-eight. I think it's gone to his head. He's far too confident for his own good. Even more so than me.

"I didn't know you were coming," I reply, too busy moving inside my room and ripping through one of my dresser drawers to look at the annoyed scowl I know he must be wearing.

"I tried calling a few times, but *clearly*," he clears his throat, "you were busy. I was in the area, anyway. Figured I'd just stop by to invite you to dinner in person."

"Come on, Dad. You came here so that I was forced to give you an answer as opposed to ignoring your calls and messages." I straighten my spine, standing stiff, shoulders straight and lifted like I'm preparing myself for a hit from behind.

"I told you not to call her that. She's not a fucking child." He lets out a long sigh, one that lets me know just how pissed off I've made him and how hard he's trying to reign in his anger. "I've let you avoid her long enough."

"Give me a break, Dad."

He waits until I join him in the kitchen before replying. "We're getting married. You can't stop that just because you don't like her."

I rip open the fridge and pull out a bottle of water with a dark laugh. "You're right. I don't like her. And I think you're making a mistake."

His huff is music to my ears. I drink the entire bottle and toss it into the trash.

"She's too young for you. I probably could have fucked her a time or two." I face him and shrug. The blonde swimwear model that can now label herself as his fiancée, is *my* age. What twenty-six-year-old woman wants to marry an old divorced guy with two kids the same age as her unless she has some hidden agenda? Some secret that she doesn't plan on spilling until she has whatever she wants? *Gets* whatever she wants.

See, my mother's new husband is exactly how I pictured—a wrinkly old investment banker/restaurant owner who tries embarrassingly hard to have a substantial part in my life, knowing that we will never be close, but still cares enough to try. That marriage is normal. This one, on the other hand, is *so* not.

How does he expect me to respect this woman? She has no more life experience than I do. Does she even want a family? What is her own family like? Do they support this marriage?

"Braden," he scolds before his jaw clamps shut, back teeth grinding.

I throw my hands up in surrender, leaning back against the counter. "I'll come to dinner, but I make no promises that I'll be able to behave myself."

"Thank you." He nods once, but his eyes remain narrowed and dark, moving around the room so he can avoid looking at me.

He didn't get the answer he wanted, but he's smart enough to take what he can get right now. I won't budge on my feelings so easily.

"It will be my absolute pleasure, Pops." I force a smile and push myself away from the counter. After he sucks in a long breath, he stands up and starts walking to the front door.

He only makes it a few feet away before he stops and turns to face me, looking me in the eyes this time. "Don't forget that I can still kick your ass if you fuck this up for me. You don't understand, and you don't have to. I'm a grown man. But I would appreciate your support. Whatever you think you can give me, I'll take it."

I feel immediately guilty at his confession. I'm a stubborn asshole, but I'm not a complete sack of shit. My relationship with my father is something that I appreciate more than anything. I would never forgive myself if I was the reason we lost that bond. So, I stomach my feelings and give him an inch, knowing Brooks Lowry isn't the guy to take a mile.

"I'll try. But that's all I'll promise."

His eyes lighten the slightest bit, no longer as dark and gloomy. Things have been tense between us recently, but I'll gladly be the one to clear the fog and let the sunshine back through.

"My house tomorrow night at six. Don't be late."

"Yes, sir." I salute him with two fingers, making him laugh as he leaves.

It's a loud laugh from deep in his belly. The kind that sounds like pure happiness. A laugh that I'm going to lock away and keep for later, knowing damn well I'm going to need to remember the sound of it tomorrow.

7

Sierra

I HATE DRESSES. THEY'RE ONLY GOOD FOR TWO THINGS. DRAWING unwanted male attention to your body, and making you worry that you're going to flash your goods every time that you have to pick something up from the bottom shelf. The chafe currently living between my thighs would be enough to make me throw my stapler across my office in a fit of pained anger if my boss didn't happen to be standing in front of me. He's watching me oddly as I awkwardly shift my ass around on my leather office chair to avoid stripping off the top layer of skin.

"Are you alright?" Cole Travis, the head of marketing at my new job asks, the corner of his lips twitching.

"Yeah, of course." I clear my throat and attempt to sit up straight. The sharp-featured male lets a star-studded smile bless my eyes as he nods, seemingly happy with my reply. He toys with one of his gold cufflinks, drawing my eyes to the crisp, perfectly tailored navy-blue suit he's wearing. A blush pink tie is knotted perfectly at the base of his throat, sticking out against the white dress shirt beneath it. He looks wealthy. Wealthy enough to intimidate me.

"Have you chosen a project yet? I know I gave you quite a few options."

"Almost. I'm stuck between two right now." I smile back, clicking my pen repeatedly before I realize that I'm fidgeting and drop it on my desk, placing my palms on my thighs instead. Somewhere safe.

"I want to ask which two, but I think I'll wait and keep your decision a complete surprise." His eyes move around my surprisingly spacious office when he adds, "I'm excited to see what you accomplish here, Sierra. I don't believe you've ever been pushed to your full potential."

I take his words with a grain of salt, knowing better than most how quickly things can take a turn for the worst. Especially in a company like this. One where disappointment and one wrong move can ruin your career.

"Thank you for the opportunity, sir. So am I." Heat rushes up the back of my neck, and I drop my gaze to my open laptop, a bright, somewhat cliché quote beaming back at me.

A goal without a plan is just a wish.

"I'll check in with you in a few days. If you have any questions—anything at all, don't hesitate to ask." His kind tone is comforting as he gives me one final nod before slipping out the door. A dangerous amount of pride fills my chest as I finally let my grin breakthrough.

"Actually." Cole's voice startles me, causing me to jump slightly. I spot him peeking back through the doorway. "How about you take the afternoon off? It's a beautiful day."

"Are you sure?" I slip my bottom lip between my teeth. Is this some sort of test?

His unique turquoise-coloured eyes hold a playful glimmer as he shakes his head lightly. "I'm sure."

"Thank you, sir."

"Cole works," he replies, winking, before leaving my office—for real this time. Leaning back in my chair, I snatch my phone from my desk drawer and call my sister. She answers on the third ring.

"Sierra? Aren't you working?"

"That's why I'm calling! Now shut up and listen!"

"Okay, okay. Down girl."

"What do you say to margaritas and dancing tonight?" I can't hide my sudden excitement. Happiness warms my blood, and I buzz in my seat. It's been months since Clare and I have gone on a night out together.

"You had me at margarita," she replies excitedly.

"Perfect. Meet me at my house at seven."

Braden

My single-story family home sits on the other side of a newly patched road. It glares at me, mocking my level of nervousness as I continue stalling my arrival.

It's not like I'm not happy that the old man is finally happy again. It's the overwhelming and honestly, disturbing fact that he's marrying someone *I* could be marrying that freaks me out. Out of every other single woman in the world, he had to go and choose someone twenty years his junior. Figures.

I spot my brother's brooding figure in the living room window, his head shaking at something being said to him. It's still so weird using that term. *Brother*.

"Crap," I mutter when Tyler's head turns to the street, blowing my cover when our dad follows his gaze, eyeing me up. Throwing open my door with a louder than needed groan, I head to the house.

"Jerking off out there or something?" Tyler asks the second I walk inside and kick off my shoes.

"Fuck off."

"No can do, buddy. Lana made us a fancy dinner that we definitely don't want to miss." His annoyed expression matches mine to a T, not like I'm the least bit surprised. Tyler and I are similar enough that if you hadn't ever witnessed his grumpy "I hate the world" attitude and borderline anger issues, you would assume that we were twins. Of course, I'm the better-looking brother, but that's a discussion for another day.

"Did she? I can't wait."

"Drop the sarcasm, dip shits. She can hear you," Dad snaps, his voice menacingly low. Dropping down on the cushion beside Tyler, I lift my brows and clasp my hands behind my head.

"Where's your wife? How come she gets a pass on dinner?" My question is directed at Tyler, but I look to my dad as he leans against the large arch separating the kitchen from the living room, wearing an innocent expression. One that says, *Gracie is my favourite, that's why.*

"She's teaching a dance camp," Tyler says, smiling ever so slightly.

He's proud of his wife, no doubt. She opened her own dance studio last year, using it to help little kids whose parents can't afford regular dance lessons. She doesn't charge them anything. Not for their uniforms, shoes, or competitions. It's really something out of a fairytale for those excited new ballerinas. Something that Gracie's able to do because of the millions racking up in my brother's bank account from years spent playing professional hockey for the Vancouver Warriors. They're both so incredibly selfless that it makes me want to be better. *Do* better. Unfortunately for me, it's not that easy.

"I hope everyone's hungry!"

Oh, joy to the fucking world. Here she comes.

Three sets of eyes fall on Lana as she comes rushing into the living room, an apron wrapped around what looks to be a very tight red dress matched with a pair of terrifyingly tall heels—always dressing to impress, this one.

"Starving," Dad replies sweetly, slipping an arm around her waist. He looks hopelessly in love with her. It should make me happier to see him like this.

"Brooks!" She giggles when Dad's hand disappears behind her, grabbing her ass. Holding back my vomit, I turn to see Tyler doing the same. His hand moves to shield his eyes.

"Dad." I clear my throat. I can feel my eyes rolling when he ignores me and starts placing sloppy kisses on Lana's exposed shoulder. "Dad, the food's going to be cold," I say again, louder this time.

"Right!" Lana's the one to pull away first, finally taking notice of the people around her. "The kids must be starving, baby."

Her comment has my nostrils flaring. I'm *not* a kid.

"Right, right. Sorry." Dad chuckles nervously before waving us toward the kitchen.

"Thanks. For a minute there I thought I was going to empty the contents of my stomach on the floor," Tyler mumbles under his breath when we reluctantly start to follow Dad toward the kitchen.

"Next time it's on you."

There is no number of mental speeches I can recite in order to feel prepared for this dinner. No matter what I say, or how many fake smiles I wear, I'll never accept Lana as his wife. I don't know how, and I'm not sure I'll ever even want to.

"Deal," Tyler agrees.

"What the fuck?" I say under my breath when we reach the kitchen. "It smells like a teenage girl's bedroom in here."

At least ten vanilla-scented candles stretch across the length of the new, sleek black table placed in the centre of my dad's outdated, crowded kitchen. The dark wood looks like it can seat at least eight people, which is confusing in itself, considering that there are only five of us on a good day.

What limited walking space there used to be in this yellow-lit room has shrunk by more than half. Tyler and I are forced to walk shoulder to shoulder just to get to two empty chairs on the left side. We choose the ones farthest from the Stacey's mom wannabe so we don't have to listen to the love birds whisper dirty things to each other when we inevitably fall into tense moments of awkward silence.

Dad sits across from us with Lana on his right. He wears a broad smile while rubbing his stomach in big circles. "This looks delicious."

I can sense the double meaning in his words before I see his gaze moving up and down his fiancée's body with a nod of approval. It's something I would say if I were in his shoes. It takes a solid two minutes before he actually looks at the overly extravagant meal laid out across the yellow, tulip covered table runner.

"I made all your favourites!" Lana smiles wide, proud of herself.

Oh, I bet you did.

Cocking my brow, I trail my eyes over every dish, getting more confused by the second. Kale salad, salmon with tofu. Is that *quinoa*?

"When did you start eating rabbit food, Dad?"

His tight-lipped scowl doesn't pack the same punch it did when I was younger. I easily brush it off and speak again.

"If I had known that she was stuffing you full of green

shit, I would have brought pizza." My lips lift slightly when I hear Tyler snicker before attempting to cover it with a cough.

"Braden," Dad snaps, steam nearly shooting from his ears.

I can't seem to shut myself up, though. Something about seeing someone make him eat like he isn't already as healthy as a fucking horse makes my insides churn. My dad has been a boxer for his entire life. He's probably healthier than I am. He doesn't need to be on a damn diet. Lana clearly doesn't understand how much we need to eat to keep up with the sport so that we don't wither away to nothing. Dad's probably just too nice to say anything.

"Yes, Father?" I sing, watching as he tightens his grip on the edge of the table, fingertips turning white.

"It's okay, Brooks," Mommy Dearest sighs. She places her hand on top of his in hopes of relaxing him. The rock on her ring finger that emptied out the entirety of my dad's savings account sparkles under the hanging light. If I have to sit here any longer, I might just end up eating my own fucking tongue for dinner. She looks at me. "I'm just trying to keep his cholesterol down."

"His *cholesterol*?" I nearly choke on my spit. My head spins in my dad's direction now, my eyes flaring with unspoken anger. "Do you have high cholesterol?"

He blinks a few times, mouth unmoving. His shoulders vibrate, most likely from shaking a long leg beneath the table. I lift my brows and clear my throat, growing impatient. "Do you, Dad?"

"No. But it's always good to take precau—"

I stop him mid-sentence. "Well then. I'm glad that that's settled. But as much as I would love to eat *whatever* is in front of us, I actually think that I left my fridge open." I click my tongue, planting a disappointed smile on my face. It's clear nobody buys the excuse, but I honestly could care less.

"Clayton would kill me if I let his yogurt spoil. You know how he is, right, Dad? Just crazy about that yogurt."

"Don't you dare leave me here alone," Tyler threatens in a low voice, turning to watch me stand up from my chair.

"Sorry, Ty." I mean it. "I didn't sign up for this."

"Neither did I!" he replies, voice raising an octave.

"Braden Christopher Lowry," Dad growls, standing up, his chair sliding across the tile before smacking against the wall with a decent amount of force. "Sit back down. *Now.*"

"Don't use your *'dad voice'* on me." I laugh, brushing away his red-faced anger like it's nothing. "It doesn't work anymore."

It's not hard to imagine the lengthy list of colourful words he's thinking about yelling at me from across the table as I roughly push my chair in and lift my glass of water, finishing it in a single gulp. He chooses to keep them all to himself, for Lana, I suppose.

"It was lovely to see you, Lana. Maybe pizza next time, though?"

Her glossy lips open like she's going to say something before she nods her head instead, not muttering a single word.

"Awesome. I'll leave you guys to it then." I shoot my dad a dimpled grin before walking away from them, not stopping until I feel the cool breeze on my skin.

I've once again found myself stuck in the shittiest bar in town, a dewy long-neck bottle cool against my warm palm.

I don't wander my way over to Jim's for the expensive beer or the rude bikers smoking their joints in the back-corner booths—but for the silence. It's an odd place to go in search of silence, but that's exactly what I find here every single time.

Jim's is far from a busy place, which means I can come here to think without anyone breathing down my neck and asking me if I'm okay. If I need to *talk*. I'm positive that I don't have half as much shit going on in my life as most of these other fuckers trying to drown their feelings with overpriced whiskey, but we all have one remarkably simple personality trait in common.

We're all selfish, unapologetic pricks in need of someplace to relax. Everyone here has a story, one that they don't ever plan on sharing with anyone.

Maybe they lost everything in a divorce because they were too prideful to apologize after every fight with their ex. Maybe they're losing at some sort of internal battle that could have easily been won by a few trips to a therapist. Or, just maybe, they could be struggling with the realization that their life means nothing past boxing matches and pussy, yet not have the want or fire under their ass to do anything more. Wait, that one's just me.

Nobody cares what your story is once you cross the threshold and breathe in the old wood smell that paints the air of Jim's. You're just another faceless figure here. Just how I like it.

"Want another?" A familiar voice asks. I simply nod and meet Jade's vacant stare with my own.

Jade is one of the only two bartenders in this dump. She's a single mom recovering from years of cocaine addiction while working every night at a place full of *other* addicts. Ones who are either in the middle of recovering, pretending to be recovering from something, or boldly refusing to recover. I feel for her, I really do.

"How's your baby girl?" I slide my empty bottle of beer across the counter before grabbing the new one, raising it to my lips and taking a long swig. Jade slings a small white towel over her shoulder before cracking open her own beer and copying my movements.

"Excited to be starting preschool next month," she replies with a small, rare smile that I only see when she's talking about her daughter, Samantha.

I return the smile before taking another sip. "And her dad?"

The skinny prick used to show up here every night, blown out of his mind and just itching for a fight. Most of the guys, myself included, used to love giving him a reason to throw his fists around so Jade didn't have to be on the receiving end once she got home. Finally, after a hard long year of seeing her show up to work covered in more colours than a colour wheel, she kicked him to the curb.

"Hasn't shown up since. You don't have to keep worrying, Braden," she teases, but I can see the appreciation pass through her green eyes.

I shrug. "As long as you and Smartie are safe."

Her smile is genuine—warm even, as she sighs and pulls the towel off of her shoulder, opting to wipe the counter. Our conversation ends when I see her turn her attention to the shadow walking up to the bar, stopping a few feet away from me.

"Could I get two Margaritas?"

"Sure," Jade replies, the amusement in her tone puts a smirk on my lips. I don't miss the barely there noise of disbelief she makes while moving down the bar to mix the drinks.

Turning to look at the oblivious woman beside me, the one who ordered a girly mixed drink in a bar full of old men and doped-up bikers, I shake my head.

"I think you stumbled into the wrong place, Barbie."

With her fancy designer bag, platinum blonde hair, and

glossy pink lips, the girl looks like she was meant to be at Sinner's, not this hole-in-the-wall dumpster fire.

"My name's not Barbie, asshat," she shoots back with an angry scoff. There's a look in her eyes that I can't exactly pinpoint. A look that says, *I think I know you, but I can't be too sure.* It confuses yet intrigues me.

I push my now empty beer bottle away from me before resting my elbows on the bar and leaning forward, testing her. "And my name's not asshat, but you already knew that."

"Right," she hums in agreement. "It's Braden." She avoids any further eye contact, staring forward at the wall of glass bottles so that I have trouble catching the slight twitch in the corner of her mouth.

"Do I know you?" I ask tightly. When I was younger, I would have taken her knowledge of me as a compliment. But now, with a famous half-brother and a newfound love for privacy, I'm not that guy anymore.

"Not really."

My face tightens as I zone in on her proud expression. What the fuck does that mean?

"Here you go. I'm sorry that it took so long. We don't usually carry the mix up front," Jade mutters, joining us again, this time with two green plushie-filled glasses.

"That's okay. Thank you." The blonde shoots her a look of appreciation, wrapping her small hands around the two glasses, and glaring at me before walking away with a strong sway of her hips.

"Margarita's, huh," Jade mumbles to herself, shaking her head in disbelief. She rounds the bar and walks to an empty table, starting to wipe it down.

I keep my eyes locked on the back of the blonde, watching her maneuver around the empty tables before stopping in front of an occupied one. She sets the first drink down in front of a brunette facing the opposite direction before placing the other down in front of an empty seat.

The blonde is wearing a wicked grin when she sits, now facing my direction. She says something to her friend seconds before the brunette whips around, her wild eyes searching the bar before stopping on mine.

I feel my jaw unhinge when our eyes meet. *Sierra?*

8

Sierra

"Have you been here before?" I ask, dragging my eyes across the wooden sign that dangles awkwardly from above the door of this supposed Jim's bar.

"A time or two." Sophie replies casually, like it's not out of the ordinary for her to stumble upon places like this. I suppose it isn't. Sophie's always been the fearless leader between the two of us, not afraid of anything or anyone.

My best friend has a natural type of confidence, the kind that doesn't waver regardless of the situation. I'm the opposite. I wear a false sense of bravery like my favourite oversized sweatshirt: *constantly*. It's become second nature to me. I must be a glutton for punishment because there's really no time to be shy in my world. Let alone my type of work.

Sophie and I stand out in this neighbourhood. We look out of place with our expensive heels and glossy blown out hair. And when a man stumbles out of the bar dressed in a pair of oil-splattered coveralls, his hand finding the wall for balance, it only serves as a reminder of that. The putrid smell of vomit blows off of him in the wind and in our direction.

I spin to face the street, my stomach swirling. I slide my

hand into the right pocket of my wool coat and wrap my fingers around a pen, clicking down on the end over and over again as if on instinct.

When my stomach settles, I spin back around. Sophie is trapped inside her own bubble of excitement as she completely bypasses the drunk now collapsed by the door, and takes a step forward, yanking open the door.

I stay rooted in place and listen to the creaky hinges with a judgmental brow raised to the sky. When I make no immediate move to follow her inside, my best friend wraps a dainty hand around my forearm and pulls me in with an unbelievably firm grip.

The musky smell hits me like a brick wall when we cross the threshold, making my nose crinkle. I attempt to find an empty table through the thick layer of cigarette smoke in the air. "When I told you that Clare ditched me, I was expecting you to take me somewhere a little less . . . dirty," I grumble while squeezing my body through a small gap between two occupied tables.

I sound judgmental, and I know that I'm being exactly that. But I don't do well in new places unless I'm five tequila shots deep.

"Well, suck it up, buttercup. I'm tired of the same old, same old. Live a little, Sierra."

It's not hard to see where she's coming from and wish that I could swallow my own worries in order to make her happy. But it isn't as easy for me to "live a little" as it is for her.

"Okay. But why here of all places? Those guys are literally smoking joints back there."

She stops us in front of a bar-height, two-person table, and tosses her purse down on the top beside the words *suck a dick* that have been etched into the wood. Following my stare, she looks at the group of intimidating bikers before giggling like a schoolgirl.

"When's the last time that you smoked pot? It's been a couple of years at least." She's grinning now, sitting on her chair as I do the same with mine.

"Back in freshman year." I fold my arms and lean back.

God, we were wild in college. *I* was wild. Back when everything was as simple as waking up for an afternoon class and then stumbling back home wasted out of your mind the following morning. Weekdays blurred into weekends when I was living on cloud-nine, naive to the world and drunk ¾ of the time. But life is a nasty vengeful bitch just waiting for her chance to push you off a cliff and watch you drown in a world of responsibilities and credit card debt once you hold that diploma in your hand.

"Those were the days," she sighs.

"Being a grown-up *could* be worse. My new boss seems super nice. Especially considering he walked in on me having an internal freak out and didn't say anything about it. Even told me to call him Cole." Pushing a stray piece of hair out of my eyes, I watch her eyes double in size.

"Is that his first name?"

"Well yeah."

"Yikes."

"Yikes? Why yikes?" I rush.

"He wants to bang you, babe," she replies, her tone too casual for my liking. This is not the time to be *casual*.

"This is *so* not a joke, Soph. Maybe he's just the laid back, down to earth type. It's pretty common for employers to tell their employees to call them by their first name, right?"

"Maybe," she starts carefully. "But you're too hot for it just to be a casual thing. I would watch out, S. He might go cray-cray on you."

"Noted," I mumble, dropping my gaze to the cracks running along the wooden table. It looks like somebody attempted to fill them with a brown crayon.

"Want a drink? I do. Be right back!" Sophie is out of her seat and rushing past me before I can reply. As I watch her natural curls bounce with each step she takes, I find myself tugging at my straight strands, too thin to stay in a curl for longer than five minutes tops.

When we were teenagers, Sophie would spend an hour every other morning curling my hair for school. She was and still is, the only one that could get it to cooperate.

A few minutes later, a massive round glass is set down in front of me, the familiar slush of a margarita bringing out my smile.

"Thank you." I wrap my lips around the thin straw and close my eyes, nearly moaning when the sweet flavour hits my tongue. I peek open my right eye when I hear Sophie throw herself in her seat. There's a wicked smile tugging at her lips, and I shake my head before she has a chance to speak.

"What?" I ask, growing more confused by the second when I notice her eyes ping-ponging behind me.

"So, you remember that guy from the other night, right? The one with the hot roommate and the huge di—"

"Yeah, I remember him, Sophie," I interrupt. She knows that I haven't forgotten about him. How could I? I spent far too long in the bath last night because of him and the memory of his tongue between my legs.

"Well, he's sort of sitting at the bar right now."

"What?" My stomach drops to the floor, heat rushing up my neck. I nearly choke on air when I spin around in my seat and meet a pair of bold amber brown eyes waiting for me. I'm embarrassingly breathless when he grins, a set of adorable dimples resting on both of his cheeks.

Braden slowly raises a glass bottle to his parted lips and takes a longer than needed drink before setting it back down gently. He starts to trail his eyes down my figure, catching on the deep V in the tight maroon dress. My heart thrashes in my chest.

The intensity in his stare heats my skin. I know what he's doing, staring at me like he wants nothing more than to bend me over this table and have his way with me, and fuck do I wish that I don't crave the same thing.

A twitch in his right eyebrow pulls me back to reality, or close enough to it. Blinking, I watch him pull out his wallet and place a stack of cash down on the bar. He stands up and heads in the direction of the restroom, not sparing me another glance.

With my pulse in my ears, I spin back around. There's an ache between my legs that I have a feeling won't be disappearing anytime soon.

"You're going to follow him, aren't you?" Sophie asks coyly, nodding to the hallway.

"Should I?" *No, I shouldn't.* Right?

Sophie rolls her eyes dramatically before waving toward the restrooms. "Yes, you idiot. Go!"

I can't find the words to reply as my head subconsciously moves up and down. "I'll meet you at home? Or maybe not?"

My margarita remains barely touched as I collect my purse from the back of my chair and beeline it to the bathrooms, not bothering to give Sophie anything more than a quick wave goodbye.

I have no idea what I'm doing, going to meet a guy in the bathrooms for a quick fuck, but all I know is that if I don't, I can't help but feel like I'll regret it forever.

My pulse quickens with each step I take.

By the time I turn down the hallway, I come to an abrupt

stop. I ache to feel the cool metal of the pen in my jacket pocket as my anxiety flashes like a caution sign with the words *turn around* written above it in thick neon letters.

I can always turn around, I remind myself. I don't *have* to do this. But I *want* to. So damn bad it makes my knees shake.

The mere thought of Braden thinking that he's won something here—that I'm just like every other female he's lusted over, the ones that run after him, panties around her ankles, thighs slick from her excitement—makes me want to kneel over and vomit. The last thing a guy like Braden needs is another sexual win. But would it be a win? Or would it be something more along the lines of an agreement? A win for both sides. I get another mind-numbing orgasm and he gets to add another tic to his win column.

I shake my head profusely, annoyed with myself for even entertaining this idea. But it's too late to turn around now. *It's time to be a big girl, Sierra.* Take what you want and stop questioning yourself. Relax.

With that mental pep talk, I start for the bathroom again. The hallway rounds, and I take as many deep breaths as I can before I make the final stretch. I turn the corner and freeze.

"Took you long enough."

Braden's pink lips are tilted in a grin, his back against the wall, arms crossed and biceps stretching the tight sleeves of his t-shirt.

"I wasn't sure if I was going to come." *A lie.*

"You wanna know something?" He doesn't wait for me to respond before pushing away from the wall and taking two large steps toward me. "It hurt my feelings when you ditched me the other morning. I had big, *big* plans for you."

I can't help but drop my gaze to the noticeable bulge pressing against the zipper of his jeans, remembering exactly how it felt to have his cock throbbing inside of me.

Gulping, I reply, "I just figured that I would beat you to it."

"You figured wrong." He closes the distance between us, making my lips part in surprise. His breath is hot on my neck, causing the hairs on my arms to rise. "I guess you'll just have to make it up to me now."

I gasp when my back hits the wall, his body moving to shield mine as he places his palms on either side of me, boxing me in. He leans forward, his nose rubbing against mine, the smell of him surrounding me. The mixture of leather, spice, and pure masculine energy makes my mouth water, craving to have it as a permanent stain on my skin.

"Somebody could walk down here any minute," I whisper, my eyes falling to his mouth, watching his tongue swipe across his plump bottom limp.

I know that nobody would see me, not with this man covering my tiny body with his giant one, moulding them together into one. And honestly, I'm not sure if I even care if anybody could. Not anymore. My words are a cop-out. A lame one at that.

"Don't go shy on me now, baby. We both know you're anything but."

The words spark something dormant from deep inside my chest, something that flares into a ball of fire, pushing me to make my next move.

I waste no time in grabbing the back of his neck and pulling him to me, pressing my lips to his. My eyes roll back at the feeling that lights up my veins, pulsing through my body at his rough touch.

His hands are everywhere, yet nowhere close to where I crave them to be. He nips at my bottom lip, forcing my mouth to open for him before his tongue is trailing along mine, moving in ways that make my core ache with need. God, the things he can do with that tongue—

"Hold on tight," he murmurs before grabbing my thighs and lifting me. I wrap them tightly around his waist.

The breathy groan that escapes his lips when I press myself against the bulge in his tight jeans is enough to send me straight to hell.

I reach between us and grab him through the scratchy material, sliding my palm along the hard outline of his cock and squeezing.

"That's it, fighter. It's nice to see you again," he rumbles, his long lashes fluttering.

"Is it?" My nails scratch at the skin above his underwear, making him shiver before I'm popping open the button of his jeans.

Suddenly, he's moving us while looking over my shoulder to guide us toward what I hope is the bathroom. His lips close over the sensitive skin of my neck, sucking, biting, tasting, leaving a trail of marks behind. My back hits a solid surface for the second time in the past few minutes as he shoves open the door and flips the lock.

The dirty tile countertop is covered in God knows what, making me cringe when Braden stops in front of it. I gawk up at him as he debates whether or not to drop me on top of it.

With a scowl, I say, "I'm not placing my bare ass on that."

I release his cock and wiggle against him until he loosens his grip enough for me to set my feet on the ground. He watches me place my palm firmly on his chest, his eyebrows raised and something carnal in his eyes.

"We'll have to find another way," I mumble, staring at the bulge in his jeans with an eagerness that surprises me. My clit throbs, tired of waiting.

He inspects my body with dark primal eyes, and it makes me feel more confident than I think I ever have. The way he's staring at me, almost like he's taking mental pictures of what every inch of me looks like in this moment—my skin flushed and body eager—and keeping the images for later, is both intimidating and sexy at the same time.

His heated gaze gives me the push I need to raise my fingers to the thin straps of my dress and gently slide them down my shoulders, letting it pool at my feet.

I know the decision to skip a bra tonight was the right one when Braden's eyes widen, his surprise evident in his stuttered breathing. It doesn't last long, though. I knew it wouldn't.

He narrows his eyes and stalks toward me with purpose. It only takes him two steps to reach me, and when he does, his eyes are so dark with built up sexual tension that I want to jump him right there.

"No bra? Why am I not surprised?" he asks. His huge hands push against my bare chest, squeezing the two breasts with a grateful sigh that shoots like liquid fire up my spine.

Spreading his fingers, he slides them across my nipples while looking up to watch my lips part with a slight whimper. He gives a sharp tug to my left nipple before shaping my body with his calloused palms. My back arches, a deep-rooted want so apparent in my actions as I push against him eagerly, *desperately*.

He slides his fingers under the band of my lace underwear before dropping to his knees in front of me. Warm, wet lips press against my chest, covering every inch of available skin in sloppy, open-mouthed kisses. When his mouth closes around my nipple, sucking and licking the hard bud, I reach behind me and fumble with sweaty palms to grab onto the countertop, desperate to keep myself steady.

"Fuck, you're so responsive."

Braden's voice vibrates against my skin before crawling inside my chest, burying itself deep. He starts sliding his mouth down my stomach, getting closer to the pulse between my thighs.

"I'm always like this. You're not anything special," I rasp.

His fingers continue to dance along the top of my underwear, teasing me to the point a growl of pure frustration builds in my throat. I refuse to give him that level of satisfaction. If I had more strength in my arms, I would reach down and force him to stop teasing me.

"Oh yeah? I'd like to know the names of every other man that's made you this wet this fast before."

Fucking prick.

"That could take all night. There's just been so man—"

I gasp when he finally moves a finger to the centre of my panties. He smirks when he feels the wetness waiting there for him, soaking through the thin material and covering his finger. My breathing shallows out when he peels away the only thing keeping him away from where I ache, desperate for release.

I'm surprised to feel a heavy knot form in my belly when he rids me of my panties. I don't know why I've become so damn nervous watching him narrow his gaze on me the way he is—like a man starved of food for too long—after everything that we've already done together, but I am.

The sudden urge to reach down and shove him away is overwhelming, but the need to have him spread my legs and dive in face first is even stronger.

My jaw drops, a sigh falling in the air when he answers my silent prayers and swipes his tongue along my slit. He places a hand on my stomach, steadying me as my grip on the counter loosens, muscles and bones quaking.

Squeezing my eyes shut, I feel him push my legs further apart and swirl his finger in my arousal before sliding it deep. His deep chuckle is wrongfully sexy, running over my skin like warm honey and leaving a trail of goosebumps behind before his mouth is back between my legs.

The toe-curling pleasure his mouth brings has me curling

my fingers in his hair, pulling him closer to me. His eyes meet mine when he slips a second and third finger in and flicks at my swollen clit.

My head falls back when the tightness in my belly starts to grow. He closes his lips around my clit when he senses how close I am, sucking and biting while keeping his fingers snug inside me, moving them in ungodly ways. His eyes stay connected to mine the entire time I fall apart, watching with laser focus as I sob in satisfaction.

"Good girl," he groans against me, twisting his fingers a final time before I'm whimpering a strangled version of his name and clenching my thighs tightly around his head.

The idea that I could strangle him right here and now is an interesting one, but I let my legs go limp. I'm too selfish to skip out on another orgasm.

He pulls his fingers out and stands up, quickly stripping out of his jeans and boxers. I feel my mouth water as I watch his thick cock slap against the rippled muscles of his abdomen. How he even fits that monster in those tight boxers is beyond me.

"Face the mirror and bend over," he commands with a growl that sends a throb to my already soaking pussy.

I force myself to nod and do as he says, sliding my hair over my shoulder when I hear the tearing of a condom wrapper.

Looking forward, I place my palms on the edge of the counter and watch him eagerly through the lipstick-covered mirror. I catch sight of my reflection and shudder.

I'm the perfect picture of helplessly aroused and dangerously eager.

He slides the condom on swiftly, expertly. There's a smirk on his lips when his attention falls on me again, taking notice of the fact that I've actually followed his instructions. I see his heavy approval in his eyes, and revel in the fact I've pleased him before I look forward and clear my throat, shaking the image from my mind. *No. Not happening.*

I'm relieved when he grabs my hips with steady, commanding hands and tears me from my thoughts. He uses his left hand to slide up my back before pushing me down so the cold counter presses against my heavy breasts. The sudden action takes me by surprises, and I gasp, more turned on than I expected by the feeling of my hard nipples rubbing against the cold surface. Suddenly the state of cleanliness in the bathroom carries no weight.

Braden gives me no warning before I feel the tip of his cock push into me, easing its way inside, slow and steady as I clench tightly, trying to accommodate all of him. His size makes me sigh, waves upon waves of pleasure tinged with the pain of being stretched so wide swirling together into a feeling of euphoria. It's a feeling that I could see myself getting used to, regardless of the fact that I know I shouldn't be thinking like that. Especially right now.

I sneak a look at him over my shoulder and find myself consumed with the look on his face, unable to look away. His lip is between his teeth, head hanging back, neck limp. The scar etched through the middle of his right eyebrow is emphasized when both brows pull together in a way that has me pulsing around him. The sight of unmistakable pleasure spreading across his face has my grip on the counter tightening.

He slides the rest of the way in and groans, "I forgot how tight you are."

My breath comes out of me in a rush when he pulls all the way out before slamming back into me. His thrusts become rough, unforgiving, and I cry out, begging him for more. I need him to keep going, to keep fucking me until I beg him to stop, unable to take anymore.

He curses under his breath and grabs my hips, squeezing them to the point of bruising.

"Don't stop," I whimper. "Don't fucking stop."

Braden shakes his head once. "Just keep taking it like that . . . *fuck yes*."

His movements don't falter as he reaches forward and grabs hold of my hair, wrapping it once around his knuckles and yanking me back toward him. His front presses against my back, warm skin slick with sweat connecting with every thrust of his hips.

Our eyes meet in the mirror, the sight so erotic my knees threaten to buckle. I can feel his hot breath on my shoulder, neck, then ear as he mumbles, "I need you to keep quiet for me now, Sierra."

Nodding quickly, I reach back and squeeze his forearm, letting my nails dig into his skin. My tongue slides between my teeth as I hold back a loud cry. I feel my legs give out from under me when my orgasm sends my body into a fit of trembles. White-hot pleasure shoots up my spine, sizzling my nerves, fraying them. I cry out when he reaches around me and plays with my clit, rubbing it until my high falls, leaving me breathless and jelly-like.

Braden lets go of my hair and I fall forward on my hands. He grabs my waist, holding me up, not stopping his unforgiving thrusts as he does so.

"I'm almost there," he grunts, eyes squeezed shut.

My strength starts to come back a few seconds later, and I manage to stand on my own, throwing myself back to meet every single one of his thrusts. Fingernails dig into my skin at the same time he throws his head back, releasing a deep guttural groan while filling the condom.

I can't seem to look away from him, too entrapped by the complete satisfaction and relief etched in his tightened features. His sharp jaw is rigid, teeth grinding so hard I'm surprised I can't hear the sound.

His movements slow to a stop as he places his hands down beside mine and rests his forehead against the middle of my back.

Braden's words are slurred whispers. "So, are you going to run away from me again? Or have I convinced you that it's no use?"

9

Braden

I'M PLEASANTLY SURPRISED WHEN I WAKE UP TO HOT BREATH fanning across my chest.

An explosive tingling sensation shoots up my right arm when I attempt to pull the numb limb from under Sierra's body before giving up with a quiet groan. For such a small person, she creates way too much damn heat.

As if hearing the silent insult, Sierra mumbles incoherent words in her sleep, her voice light and delicate—the complete opposite of the brash one tht I've become so accustomed to. She nuzzles her face into my neck, and my chest rumbles with a silent laugh.

I let myself relax again and soak up the sight of the naked body curled around mine. Circular bruises peek out from under her messy hair, decorating the smooth skin of her neck with hues of purple. The possessive marks bring the memories of last night back full throttle, and my cock thickens.

After leaving the bar and hailing another cab—no emotionally scarred drivers this time—we stumbled inside my apartment where I bent her over the back of the couch and thrusted into her. It wasn't long until we were christening every surface we could find, and then stumbling into the bedroom where she rode me until we both passed out.

Each memory from the night before creates a heavier need to wake her up with a morning fuck, regardless of the ache in my muscles and her ridiculous rule.

No morning sex.

I have no idea how, or *why* I agreed to such a stupid rule, but now that I think about it, it was definitely the booze. It's always the fucking booze.

I look up at the ceiling and use my free hand to push my shaggy hair out of my eyes, the strands damp with sweat. Dropping my eyes, I watch Sierra's dainty hand stretch across my abdomen, her manicured nails scratching at the toned muscles. It feels good, relaxing even. She pulls herself closer to me with a sigh.

The movement causes the thin black sheet to move down her torso, exposing her bare chest and hardening nipples. The bared skin taunts me, silently beckoning me forward. I swallow the growing lump in my throat.

I've never been a big fan of waking up beside someone, especially not somebody that only my penis is overly acquainted with, but if waking up to a body as gorgeous as this one is what I've been missing out on, then fuck have I been an idiot.

Sure, there are some women who seem to get the wrong impression after coming home with me, waking up tucked into my side, freshly fucked and hungry. They assume that maybe I'll wake up and realize they're my soulmate, my *person,* as Clay would call it. But the mirage usually fades quickly. It's a hit to the pride being told that he's just not that into you.

"You're the worst pillow ever. You fidget too much." Sierra pushes herself off of me before letting her head fall onto her unused pillow with an exaggerated huff. Tangled but glossy caramel-brown hair spreads out around her, smelling strongly of mangos and a bit of her floral perfume.

"Maybe that's because I'm not a pillow." I chuckle lowly.

She grabs a handful of the blanket and tucks it under her chin. "Whatever."

"Someone's a grouch in the morning."

I force myself out of bed and stretch my arms above my head, knowing damn well my dick is rock hard, nearly pulsing with how worked up I've found myself this morning. Sierra attempts to keep her eyes to herself but fails miserably.

Her gaze is narrowed, eyes hot as she trails them down the tight ridges of my stomach before focusing on the thick length right in front of her. I watch her lips part, still swollen from last night, and crave the feel of them around me again.

I want my hands in her hair as I fuck her mouth until she gags, forcing her to take as much of me as she can, spit dribbling from the corners of her mouth. My palm twitches, desperate to wrap around my shaft and give it a pump or two, suddenly claimed by the thought of her.

"Are you going to move or stand there all day?" she asks smugly, her legs now crossed in front of her.

I blink twice and realize I've been staring at her mouth for a creepy amount of time. "It's too early for your snark, Sierra."

I clear my throat and pull on a pair of boxers. "There should be something for you to wear in the bin by the bed unless you want to put your dress back on."

Without giving her a second look, I leave her to get dressed. When I get to the living room, I spot two sock-covered feet dangling from the couch and grin, feeling my blood cool to a normal temperature. I move quietly around the sofa and give each foot a hard yank. I burst into a fit of laughter when Clayton jumps into the air, terrified and about two seconds away from snapping.

Hating jump-scares: another one of Clayton's many quirks.

"Morning," I snicker, falling back in a fluffy maroon armchair across from him. Clay folds his arms and turns the volume up on the TV. He tries to tune me out, but I only speak louder. "Sleep well last night?"

"You're a prick," he replies.

"Oh, I'm sorry. Did we keep you up or something?"

He stands up from the couch and grabs his empty coffee cup from the coffee table. He stomps off to the kitchen and disposes of it in the sink.

Sierra comes walking out of my bedroom a few seconds later, coughing uncomfortably. Her eyes hold a hint of suspicion and curiosity as they flick between Clay and me.

I notice Clayton's jaw slacken when he sucks in a breath, eyes feasting on the image of her. She's decided on wearing one of my old hockey shirts and a pair of rolled up sweatpants. The white shirt is ripped and stained from years of wear and tear. It swallows her whole. It's definitely not what I would have expected her to grab, but I won't complain. She looks fucking hot in it.

"It should be a sin to look that good in the morning," Clay says in approval, taking the words right from my mouth.

She swallows nervously, and drops her eyes to the floor, clearly uncomfortable with the sudden attention from the both of us. Something hot and stiff flicks my spine when she starts biting her thumb nail, an anxious habit I've noticed Lana doing a few times when we first met.

I pin Clayton with a sharp look, regardless of the fact that he isn't, nor doesn't want to pay me any attention.

"Uh, thanks." Her cheeks are flushed as she stares at her toes.

I'm not sure if she's offended by his comment or just not used to receiving them. Either way, I'm immediately not a fan of the way she's shut down, her insides nearly completely bare and in clear view. The confidence and sass that I've begun to associate with this woman is gone, leaving only a nervous girl behind.

I'm about to walk toward her when her walls come back up. With a fake smile and a roll of her eyes, she says to me, "I forgot my phone in your room."

Before I have a chance to tell her to drop the act, she's inside my bedroom, shutting the door softly behind her.

Turning to Clay, I hiss, "Way to go, asshole."

"Me?" he reels. "I was just being honest. You're the one who left a naked model in your bed alone. You were probably the one that offended her. At this rate, it won't be long before she comes crawling to me looking for a real man."

"Trust me. You couldn't handle a woman like Sierra." I sink into the armchair.

The last time Clay tried to score with a girl at Sierra's level was about two years ago, and he was beaten to a pulp by said girl's boyfriend not even twenty minutes afterward. He claims that the blowjob he got in the bathroom was worth it, though, regardless of the fact it was the beginning of a serious life change.

He hasn't pined over anyone since then. I assume he's just not interested in fighting over anyone anymore. It would be ridiculous of me to bug him for that.

It's not only guys that like to play games. We just get the brunt of the blame for it.

"I'm starting to think that neither of you can handle me."

I turn to my bedroom door and see Sierra. She's back to her confident self, standing in front of us with a hand on her hip and an easy-going smile. She looks just as sexy as she did last night, with the addition of some wild sex-hair that I'm not surprised to find still resting on her shoulders. It's going to take a lot more than a hairbrush to get those knots out.

"You wanna find out?" Clay asks, now in the kitchen. His tone is far too hopeful in my opinion.

Sierra tilts her head in mock consideration. "No, I don't think so."

My laugh tears through the room. Sierra seems less than impressed by the both of us as she sighs in what I assume is disbelief, and heads for the front door. My sides start to ache when I reach up and wipe a hand down my face, clearing the laugh-induced tears from my skin.

"Buddy, I think it's time you retire your game. It's rustier than the bathroom shower head," I say.

Clayton's head snaps in my direction, and he shoots me a less-than-subtle warning look. Feigning innocence, I purse my lips and blow him a kiss.

"If you two are done, I want to talk to Braden," Sierra says, staring at Clayton, watching as he nods along with her every word. "Alone," she adds when he continues to smile at her.

"Right." He nods before rushing off to his room. Sierra lets out a thankful sigh once he's gone, turning to look at me.

"Alone at last," I say.

Waving me off with a lazy swish of her hand, she mumbles, "I left my number on your bed."

Surprise floods through me. I'm not sure what I was expecting this morning, but I definitely did not expect it to be this easy. I would have bet my winnings from my next boxing match that I would have had to sneak my number in her phone and call myself to get her number.

"Duly noted, babe."

"Don't call me babe," she snaps. "And please keep this to yourself. Your friend creeps me out."

Blowing out a light laugh, I nod. "So. No strings. Just sex then, yeah?"

She blinks once before saying, "Yeah, just sex."

10

Sierra

"Just sex?" Sophie sputters, spitting lettuce from her salad across my desk. It lands on a picture frame of me, Clare and Liz from our trip to the zoo last month.

Liz sits on my shoulders, wearing a wide smile with two missing teeth and a pair of light-washed, blue jean overalls with bronze buttons. Clare stands beside us, struggling to hold three melting ice cream cones in her hands. It was scorching hot that day. I think I'm still finding skin to peel from the nasty sunburn I got.

It's been a week since I last saw both Braden and Sophie. Work has held me by the tits, keeping me busy to the point of near exhaustion. I don't have much energy left by the time I get home at night to do more than microwave a frozen meal and crawl into bed. My phone remains chalked full of unread texts and unanswered calls. It's a wonder I've even managed to shower and throw on makeup every day.

Sophie wipes her mouth with a napkin that was previously folded on her lap. "Just sex with a guy like that? No way in hell. I'm calling it now, S. It won't work."

"You only think that because you don't even know the

guy. He's a total douche-bag." I stab my plastic fork into my salad container and bring a bunch of leafy greens to my lips.

I never knew how much I would love being able to eat my lunch in an actual office instead of outside or jammed inside a small lunchroom until now. And from Sophie's laid-back posture, I can tell that she approves as well.

"A sexy douche-bag," she mumbles, still staring at me with an unconvinced glimmer in her blue eyes.

"Doesn't matter. I'm not looking for anything more than sex. You know that."

Still not believing me, Sophie scoops up the rest of her salad before shoving it in her mouth and tossing the empty container into the trash can by the door.

"Whafefer," she mumbles with her mouth still full. After swallowing her food, she continues, "All I'm saying is that you might want to be careful if you're so against catching feelings. A guy like Braden won't hesitate to dump you out on the street like it's garbage day once you're no longer all shiny and new."

"I know." I nod. "You don't have to worry about me."

"Uh, yes, I do. You're my best friend, Sierra. I worry about you more than anyone."

Slapping a hand above my left breast, I let out an exaggerated sigh, my eyelashes fluttering. "I love you too."

"Anyways," she sings. "I saw Maeve the other day."

I freeze instantly, blood draining from my face. The mood between us shifts, and I hate myself for allowing just the sound of her name to have such a negative impact on me.

"Oh? Did you two talk?" *Please say no.*

"She saw me before I could turn around." Sophie visibly cringes from the look on my face. I'm not surprised, I don't even need to look in the mirror to know that I must look like a kid who just had their lollipop snatched from their mouth.

"Great."

I push away from my desk and begin busying myself with the lunch wrappers covering the top of it. The slight tremble in my hands only fuels my temper as I drop the empty salad container into the trash can and shove it down harder than necessary. Once, twice, three times. I let my repressed anger break free each time I shove the container further and further into the garbage bin. I close my eyes, letting out a shallow breath before righting myself and turning around.

"She seems a little off," she says slowly, guilt dripping from every word. Her forehead is wrinkled and she avoids my stare. I feel instantly selfish for reacting the way I did, seeing how upset it's made her, but I can't find it in myself to apologize. Neither of us have done anything wrong. Maeve is the one to blame for all of this.

Catching one of my oldest friends having sex with my boyfriend of four years will never not sting. And six months later, I'm still not over it. I'm not sure if I should be by now, but I'm definitely not. I still miss them both so much that I hate them even more for it. They don't deserve to be missed. They deserve to live a very miserable life together. They should be missing *me*.

"I don't care." The lie burns my throat. "She seemed fine when Logan was shoving her up against the wall of Sinners the other night. Actually, she seemed pretty fucking great."

Okay yeah, I'm bitter. I have a right to be.

"What?" Sophie gasps. "She definitely didn't mention that."

"And you're surprised, why? She lied to us for months, Soph." I lean back against the wall with my arms crossed, trying desperately to ignore the pain beginning to grow between my eyes.

"I know. I just thought that she could have changed, you know? If she had gone back to how she used to be, maybe we could have been a group again."

I place my hand on her slouched shoulder. "I hoped for the same thing. But she broke my heart, Sophie. I trusted her with my life and she used that against me for who even knows how long."

She nods before leaning her head back against my stomach. The memories of that night never seem to fade or lose their colour. They stay clear and vibrant, like a freshly painted canvas.

I got home from work and heard him calling out *her* name from *our* bedroom. I remember the spiked up, messy head of blonde hair peeking out from beneath our heavy white comforter. Her short black dress was strung carelessly across the back of my office chair. The sound my wine glass made as it fell from my hands, shattering against the hardwood floor. I can feel the burn in my throat from when my choked sob flew across the room, the two bodies jumping anxiously from the bed.

"Sierra?" Sophie calls, watching me curiously. I force a smile and fall back in the now, shoving the memories to the back of my mind.

Moving my gaze to the sunflower shaped clock hung from the wall behind my desk, I say, "Lunch goes by too fast." I laugh awkwardly. "I'll call you later?" Or, in other words, can you please leave?

"Right." She coughs, standing up from her chair. "Have a good rest of your day, babe. Talk later."

I round my desk and place my palms down on the smooth wood, nodding firmly. An array of emotions flicker across Sophie's face before she settles on a forced smile. She raises her hand in a small wave and pulls open my door, walking through it silently.

As soon as she's gone, I close the door and a choked sob is ripped from my throat. I move a shaky hand to my chest bone and struggle to suck in a shuttered breath. Balling my hands into fists, I clench my jaw, angered by my lack of strength. *Keep it together, Sierra.*

They never deserved you. They mean nothing to you anymore. You can do better. You *will* do better.

I repeat the mantra over and over again until I've made myself believe it. Even for just right now.

As I slide a thick stack of clasped papers into my briefcase, a knock on the door startles me. My eyes—tired and somewhat blurry from the sting of my drying contacts—fall on Cole's broad shoulders as he leans in the doorway, the epitome of confidence and bold male energy. I think it's easy to admit that he intimidates me nearly as much as Braden does.

A heat festers in my chest at the thought of Braden. Nearly six-and-a-half feet of towering *man* and sexual prowess wrapped in a mess of arrogant words, fearlessness, and a whole ton of experience. I'm not sure how anyone could help not being intimidated by all of that. I wouldn't doubt that even someone like Cole would find Braden's presence unnerving.

"Heading out?" Cole asks with an easy smile that makes my nerves somewhat settle.

"Yes, sir. I have a box of toaster waffles calling my name." I laugh lightly, sliding the straps of my purse up my arms until they rest on my shoulder.

"As great as those sound, I actually came to invite you to join me and a few other co-workers at the Italian restaurant down the street. Best fettuccine in the city, hands down." His million-dollar smile does little to calm the growing uncertainty that fills my stomach at the thought of having such a casual meeting with my bosses.

With my luck, I'll crumble under the pressure and end up stuttering a ridiculous attempt at a joke that will end up labelling me as the awkward girl for the rest of my career here. Not the worst label, but not exactly the one I'm aiming for.

"Thank you for the offer, bu—"

"We don't bite, I promise. It'll be fun," he tries again, this time placing his palms together in front of him. The gesture looks like a silent plea, and my resolve weakens.

I'm not sure whether it would look worse for me to decline, or risk making a nervous fool of myself. Not wanting to upset the people who hold my entire career in their hands, I agree.

"Okay. When should I be there?"

He grins. "We can head over now, actually. Everyone is already on their way. I offered to ask you myself. It's only a five-minute walk."

Oh. "Okay." I inwardly cringe at my simple reply before squeezing the strap of my purse with a tight grip and waiting for Cole to lead the way out of my office.

When we both step into the empty hallway, I close my office door and turn back to see him waiting for me. The troublesome nagging in my head becomes quite a nuisance as I feel my palms begin to sweat. Sending him a reassuring look I don't believe myself, I follow him to the elevator.

"So, Sierra. How do you like it here? Any complaints?" he asks when we reach the shiny silver doors. I reach forward to push the down button before stepping back and casually wiping my palms on my skirt.

"It's been great. Everyone's super nice."

"Glad to hear it. Sometimes the pressure gets to be too much for some of our new hires. I think they expect it to be an easy job."

I nod along with his words. I can see where that idea

would come from. Back when I first told my parents I was planning to spend four years getting a marketing degree, they were a little underwhelmed. Although, I think it stems from them wanting me to follow in their footsteps and want to "save the world" or so my father would say.

My parents both spent decades of their lives on humanitarian missions in third-world countries. A job that I'm positive they love more than Clare and me. It's also a job that has been the root of several family disputes over the years. It's easy for them to look down on us for not wanting to do better for the world, putting ourselves and our own careers first. Because of that, we don't spend a lot of time together. We never have. The only difference now is that Clare and I are grown up, meaning there's nothing to force us into seeing our parents like there was when we all lived in the same house.

Nobody puts the effort in, and our family remains distant. I'm sure that's how it will always be. I can't see that changing for anything.

My parents fear what they don't understand. And they don't want to learn any different.

The elevator doors slide open with a quiet ding and we walk inside. I feel tense, rattled from my thoughts. I'm frustrated with myself for letting my parents get to me, but will myself to let it go when Cole settles beside me, the elevator doors closing.

"I'm really thankful for this opportunity. I don't plan on wasting it," I say, confident in every word I speak.

He meets my gaze. "That's what I like to hear. We're lucky to have such a hard worker on our team."

My lips tug up. I stare at my closed-toe black heels and try to relax. It would seem that all of my hard work is finally going to pay off.

Let's hope that I don't fuck it up.

11

Sierra

I wish that the pit in my stomach had shrivelled up and died the minute we walked inside of our destination—the fancy Italian restaurant a few blocks away from the office—Paninaro's, I think it's called. However, I still feel like I could hurl over at any given moment.

The pungent smell of parmesan cheese and breadsticks burning my nostrils doesn't overly help the situation, either. The salad I had for lunch churns and churns, forming a tsunami of lettuce and tomatoes in my belly.

I jump, startled when a warm palm touches my lower back. The contact is unwanted and unnecessary. I freeze, struggling to keep my hands from shaking and clamming up.

"In the corner booth," Cole mumbles, his voice husky and much closer than it used to be. I can feel his breath on the shell of my ear.

My blood runs cold as I struggle to swallow past the boulder in my throat. Forcing my lips to tilt up in a sorry excuse of a smile, I give a brief nod.

Looking ahead, I focus on two tall, well-figured receptionists—the ones I've become accustomed to finding giggling together in the break room every morning, holding tall plastic cups full of some sort of frothy liquid. Tonight, they'll sit in a sleek black booth directly in front of me.

Across from them sits the CEO of Brenton Marketing, Clark Brenton. He wears an easy-going smile, his sharp features completely relaxed. It's easy to tell, even from a distance, that he's extremely confident and self-assured. And I'm sure having two stunning women sitting just a few feet away, completely enamoured by his chiselled jawline and unique aqua-coloured eyes helps with that as well. The two women look about ready to do anything this guy asks of them with a pleasant smile and an excited "yes, sir."

"Hey, Clark." Cole greets his boss like you would an old friend when we reach the large booth, his loud voice—firm yet somehow lazy—grabbing the table's attention. "Ladies." He grins at them both. I'm sure his white teeth sparkle beneath the warm lighting.

The two women turn to stare at us—or me, rather—eyebrows raised with silent judgment. I lift my hand and wave when I feel my anxiety near its peak. They're expecting me to introduce myself, but I can't seem to speak, still too focused on the heat radiating from the hand glued to my back.

Two sets of perfectly lined eyes stare at me with a sort of vacancy that urges me to drop my hand back down. My cheeks flush a deep red, feeling a rush of rejection shoot through me.

"Hi," I squeak.

Frustration as I've never known nips at my spine. My career is the one place, the one *thing* that doesn't make me nervous or anxious. I'm damn good at what I do. I can stand in front of an auditorium full of executives and spectating companies and not blink an eye—because I *love* my job. But I'm acting like an idiot right now in front of two of my bosses all because I'm a little flustered by a simple hand on my back?

"Hi." I hear the woman on the inside mutter, partially under her breath. "It's Sienna, right?"

Ouch. That one burns more than I would have expected.

"Sierra," I correct her.

"Sure." She nods absentmindedly and turns back to her orange drink.

I know that I shouldn't take offence to her apparent lack of interest in me, but I've never been good at dealing with women outside of my field.

"It's Tiffany and Lauren, right?" I ask, forcing my shoulders back in an attempt to try and keep my composure. I bet they're planning ways to get me fired as I stand here. My mere presence is probably a stain on their entire week.

The girl sitting on the outside of the booth—Tiffany, I think—huffs dramatically and rolls her round mahogany-coloured eyes. "Yeah, that's us. Are you going to sit down now? We were waiting for you two to finally get here to order. I'm starving."

The need to shove my face in a brown bag and hyperventilate is starting to make me dizzy.

"Sorry," I mumble quietly and slide into the empty seat beside Tiffany, grateful for the space from Cole. She doesn't bother giving me any more room on the bench.

Pulling down the edge of my navy skirt, I try to ignore the snickers beside me when Cole slides into the booth across from us. He's not hanging half-off the edge of his seat like I am, though.

"I'm sorry for making you guys wait. I left my wallet at the office and didn't notice until we were almost here. I made us turn back to get it," Cole says, and I meet his gaze, blinking, uncertain as to why he just covered for me.

He didn't forget his wallet. Honestly, I didn't even know

we were late in the first place. I usually stay at the office later than everybody else in order to get ahead of my workload for the next day. Still, I wasn't even planning on coming to this stupid dinner. How was I supposed to know that Cole was going to drag me here?

"Oh, it's okay!" Lauren pipes up without hesitation.

"I ordered you a beer, man. Hope that's okay," Clark says, pushing a full glass of frothy brown liquid in front of Cole. Cole responds with a grateful smile before wrapping his fingers around the dew-covered glass. Clark turns to me now. "We didn't know what you would want, Sierra. But the waitress should be back soon."

Great, thanks.

"Alright." I nod and look away from the table to the wall across the restaurant where the bold washroom sign rests. It's not a unique getaway by any means, but it's a getaway nonetheless. I slip off the bench without a second thought.

"Where are you going?" Cole asks, concern washing out his features as he stares at the hands I have clenched tightly around my purse.

"Washroom. I'll have water if the waitress gets here before I'm back."

I don't give him a chance to reply before I'm taking off toward the bathroom, hoping like hell that it's unoccupied. I don't particularly want, nor need, an audience when I hit my mental wall.

I allow myself the luxury of sucking in a shallow breath, hoping it will somewhat calm me when I successfully maneuver around the crowded tables, only bumping into the backs of a small handful of chairs on my way.

Pulling open the women's room door, I beeline it for an empty stall. I push myself through an open one at the end of the line and shut the door behind me, twisting the lock with shaky fingers. Turning around, I let my back hit the metal and squeeze my eyes closed. My palms press against my eyes until I see static.

I don't know what I was expecting, showing up to a dinner I knew I wasn't really invited to, but this certainly wasn't it. It's clear nobody but Cole wants me here, and honestly, I'm still confused as to why he invited me in the first place. I have no relation to these people, there is no work relationship or friendship outside of the office. There isn't even one *inside* the office.

Tiffany works for Clark, I think, but I have no idea who Lauren works for. The only times I've ever seen her are when she's gossiping with Tiffany in the break room. Unless I'm missing something painfully obvious, I find it odd that those two would have been asked to come tonight as well.

I stay rooted in my place for a few much-needed minutes before the fog in my brain manages to subside enough for me to form a clear thought again.

Fixing my posture, I unlock and open the stall. My heels clink against the floor as I walk to the long, marble counter, stopping in front of one of the four sinks. I turn on the tap and collect some cold water in my hands before splashing my warm cheeks.

With the pink fading from my face, I spare a glance at the stalls and find them all unoccupied, which leaves me in the safe confines of this judgment-free zone for a few seconds longer. The cold-water clings to my cheeks as I stare back at my flushed complexion.

The uneven splotches of light brown freckles cover my pale skin, spreading over my small nose, across my cheeks, and down to my small chin. My silver eyes watch my every move, the obvious judgment in them only sparking my growing annoyance with myself.

I could have been in my fluffy pink robe, sprawled out on the couch watching reality show reruns right now. But no, here I am, hiding in the freaking bathroom because I'm too socially awkward to sit through a single dinner with a few colleagues. *Typical* Sierra.

With a final groan, I push my dark hair out of my face with slightly-damp hands and reach for a paper towel to wipe myself down. After throwing it away and preparing myself with one final pep talk, I move to the door and whip it open.

I nearly trip over my own two feet when a familiar masculine voice settles along my skin, worming its way into my chest. Stopping dead in my tracks only a few steps from the door, I slowly spin around.

"I knew it was you who rushed past me out there. I could never forget that ass."

12

Braden

"So, fill me in. Considering that you've been too preoccupied to make time for your old withering mother these past few weeks, I can only assume you've been busy to the absolute tits."

My mother wears a deep-set scowl that makes me laugh. It's the same scowl I've been on the receiving end of far too many times. Ever since I turned old enough to speak or walk, really.

"You're not old nor withering, Mom. Stop being dramatic." I twirl a glob of spaghetti around my fork before shoving it in my mouth. After a hefty swallow, I moan, "Damn, Antonio. Give my compliments to the chef. This is fucking delicious, as always."

My step-dad sends me a warm, appreciative smile and dips his head. Paninaro's has been in Antonio's family for generations, opened up by his great, great grandfather a few years after he migrated to Canada from a small town in Italy. I don't know much more than that. The relationship that I have with my step-dad is slim, only built out of necessity and the respect he's earned from treating my mom so well.

"You're welcome to come here anytime, Braden," Antonio says. *"Quello che è mio è tuo." What's mine is yours.* I know he means it, and for a flicker of time I feel guilty for not building a closer father-son relationship with the guy. He tries really hard. That has to count for something.

I serve the table a tight-lipped smile. *"Grazie."*

Antonio would never say it, but he appreciates the fact that I've tried to learn his language. I can see it in the way his green-speckled eyes shine as they stare at me after every Italian word I speak. Sometimes I'm rather ass at it, but I try nonetheless.

"How's your father and his child bride?" Mom asks the question so casually, her wine glasses tipped back as she takes a small sip, eyebrow lifted. The red liquid sloshes the sides of the glass when she sets it back down on the table cloth. I try to string together a response, but fail.

"Jesus Christ, woman," Antonio whispers, shaking his head and reaching over to place his hand on hers. "You can not call her a child bride. It is rude."

"Is that not what she is, Tony? She is our son's age. It's inappropriate!"

I stare at her, lips slightly parted, unsure of what to say.

My parents got divorced when I was young. The entire thing was messy and rough for everyone, but it was nothing compared to the arguments they've encountered since Dad's been with Lana. Mom doesn't do well with change, and if my shock and confusion was anything like what my mother felt, then I would say her reaction was and is completely warranted.

It's not that we both don't want him to be happy. My father was my fucking role model growing up—my super hero, even. He deserves happiness more than anyone I know. But is this the way to get it? Are we keeping him from being happy? Is he just going through a phase? His version of a mid-life crisis? Fuck. I don't want to think about it anymore.

"You should talk to him about it, Mom. He's still waiting to hear back from you about your wedding RSVP," I say between mouthfuls.

Mom opens her mouth to speak, and from the passion in her stare, I can tell words are being thrown my way. But I'm no longer paying attention. I'm focused elsewhere now, on a figure wrapped in a deep navy skirt and loose blouse, moving with near-lightning speed toward the bathrooms, wound up like a coiled spring.

She seems completely unaware of her surroundings, mind set only on fleeing whatever has her spine straight as a steel rod and hands fisted. I tune out my step-dad's concerned tone as he says my name a few times, trying to grab my attention again, asking if I'm okay. It's not until Sierra disappears behind my mother's back—completely out of my view—that I retrace her steps.

My brows collide, pulling tightly together. I know I'm glaring mildly at the two women residing at the table Sierra scurried from. By the look of relief they both share, they couldn't be happier to see Sierra bee-lining it to the washroom. However, I feel my eyes narrow into a more cold, intimidating glare when I notice the rest of the group.

Sitting across from the women are two businessmen types —the kind of men who spend more money on custom tailored suits and name brand watches than they do on what kind of luxury car they drive. The first one, let's call him *Bert*, sits on the inside of the booth, watching the breasts of the blonde across from him rise and fall with each breath she takes. There's something carnal in the way he eyes her. Something that makes my gut twist. He's clearly a boss or somebody who holds some sort of power over her. I can tell by the way she's watching him: cautious and nervous but trying to play it off with a coy, flirtatious smile.

I've seen Jade wear that same look every time Jim Sullivan walks into his bar. It pisses me off seeing it now, just as much as it does then.

I relax the fingers that I don't remember fisting, and move my stare to the second guy at the table—*Ernie*.

He wears confidence nearly as well as I do. Relaxed shoulders, one arm extended, forearm resting on the table so he can show off his expensive watch. The light from the ceiling lamp above the table reflects off of the tiny diamonds embedded around the face of the watch, making each one in what appears to be a thousand, dance around the room. His jaw is covered in a brown scruff—like he hasn't bothered shaving for a few days.

I decide without a sliver of doubt that I don't like him.

"Excuse me," I mutter, pushing away from the table, ignoring my mom's questions as I follow Sierra. I bump the shoulder of one of the waiters as he rounds the corner and nod apologetically at him before coming to a stop beside the ladies' room door. I fight back the urge to whip open the door and stomp inside to see her with an ineligible grumble. I'm not her boyfriend. She's more than capable of dealing with her own shit.

I'm about to leave in an effort to save my pride when I smell Sierra's perfume. The smell of fresh-cut flowers and vanilla brings out my smile. I turn to her when she steps through the door and covers her shock-ridden, parted lips with her hand.

The tight material of her knee-length skirt emphasizes every single one of her delicious curves—the ones I hope are still covered in the bruises the shape of my fingertips—as she leans back on her right foot with a sense of forced confidence.

She might think that she's pulling off her little "I'm too

confident to be shaken by anything" act that fooled her table, but it won't work on me. I may not know her all that well yet, but I've begun to pay attention to the little mannerisms she tries to hide.

I find myself speaking before I can stop myself. "I knew it was you who rushed past me out there. I could never forget that ass."

"Braden," she sighs, exasperated. "Why am I not surprised to see you here? Trapping women in public bathrooms seems to be your thing."

"They are when it comes to you." My mouth curves up.

It's purely coincidence, really. I wouldn't have guessed that I would run into her at my family's restaurant of all places. Barely anyone I know ever comes here. I like it that way.

"Did you need something? I have to go back out there." Her voice wobbles slightly as she speaks and looks past my shoulder at the table barely visible around the corner.

I follow her gaze and bite back a laugh when I see Ernie cough and reach down to the front of his slacks to adjust his dick, palming it slightly. He's watching the girl beside the blonde suck from a paper straw, clearly hoping she'll suck something else after dinner.

"I think they're fine without you." I laugh, turning back to her, letting my shoulder brush her neck. I feel her shiver. "Who are those people anyway? Don't tell me you work for a sex ring and that's your pimp. I'm way too broke to start paying you."

I want to knee myself in the balls as soon as I've finished speaking. Yeah, that was definitely the wrong thing to say. Her scoff is immediate, cheeks flushing red as she slaps my chest—*hard*. "Do I look like a prostitute to you, asshole?"

Accepting the invitation to openly check her out, I don't hesitate. I slip my eyes up and down her body. She's tall—

taller than most women I go for, but I couldn't imagine Sierra being any shorter. I like that the top of her head meets my chin when I whisper dirty things in her ear and that I don't have to bend down so far to kiss her.

Her legs are long and fit perfectly on my shoulders while her heels dig into my back while I'm eating her out. Why the hell would I want to change that?

The more that I look at her, the more I find myself liking what I see. That thought alone is enough to break the intensity of my stare and force me to take a cautious step back, away from her.

Unable to keep my foot out of my mouth, I tell her, "No, you don't. But you do fuck like one."

Her eyes flare, steam practically shooting from her ears and I know that I'm about to get my ass handed to me on a silver platter.

"Fuck you, Braden. You're unbelievable." She doesn't spare me a second look before she's attempting to move around me.

Sidestepping, I stretch my arm out in front of her. She stops in her tracks, staring at me with an icy glare. "Get out of my way before I rip your balls off and shove each one down your throat. Don't think that I won't leave you here while you choke on them either. I wouldn't even think twice about it."

Her threat has the opposite effect of what she was hoping for. I'm hard as a fucking rock, utterly turned on by her aggression. "I'm confused, Sierra. I thought you liked my balls. Especially when they're hitting your chin while my cock is half-way down your throat."

She glowers at my arm just long enough for the skin to break out in goosebumps before moving her stare to my face. I find myself locked in the middle of a staring match. But I won't be the one to back down first. My pride doesn't like the idea of losing when it comes to *anything,* let alone something so minuscule.

"Half-way down my throat?" she scoffs, never breaking eye contact. "You give yourself *way* too much credit."

"There's the Sierra I met outside Sinners. You're sexy when you're pissed."

She raises a defiant eyebrow and with her chin tipped, leans in just enough that her breath brushes my lips. "Just when I'm pissed?"

I swallow the remaining distance between us and relish in the heat her body exudes pushed up against mine. My eyebrow twitches with a silent dare. I wait for her to make the first move. Not because I have an issue with being the one to shove her back against the wall, but because I would fucking love for her to be the one in control, demanding and taking what she wants from me.

"No," I reply, my voice becoming raspy and strained from the unreleased tension building between us. "You're one of the sexiest women I've ever seen. No matter what you say or do."

I drag my palm down the wall and slowly move it to the side of her arm. Goosebumps rise on the smooth skin beneath my fingertips. She swallows, bobbing her head slightly before she's grabbing the back of my neck and pulling me toward her.

Her lips are on mine instantly. It's an urgent, dirty, needy kiss that has me groaning into her mouth with a feeling of relief and utter desire to have more of her. She swallows the sound, our tongues now tangled and my blood pumping in my ears to an off-tempo beat.

Her palms move to my chest, lying flat and firm before she's pushing me, my back slamming against the wall. I smile against her lips when she slides her fingers under the fabric of my shirt and drags them up my skin, touching as much of me as she can, as if she forgot the feel of my body. The air between us crackles, charged with pure sexual frustration. I want to take her right here, right now. But I'm aware of where we are and who we came here with. It's not the time or place, regardless of how badly my cock wants to fuck her until she can't stand straight.

Deciding that I might as well take as much as I can while she's here, I release her mouth and thread my fingers in her hair, moving it away from her face. A string of muttered words fall between us at the sheer sight of her right now.

Lust-drunk and frazzled, her eyes are half-lidded, pupils blown. I clench my fingers in her hair and take her mouth, rough and hungry. There's nothing gentle about the way I kiss her, like I'm trying to somehow own her lips and the way they return the favour just as feverously. I kiss her like nobody else is here. Like we're alone in the bathroom or inside of my apartment and she does the same.

There's an unnatural amount of chemistry between us, and I plan on taking full advantage of it before it sizzles out and disappears.

Without breaking the kiss, I spin us around and box her in, letting myself completely consume her space like she has mine. She gasps, head falling back against the wall when I move my thigh between her legs and untangle my hands from her hair, planting them on her hips.

I use my grip to pull her toward me, my thigh becoming engulfed by the heat between her legs. She's soaked, I can feel her beneath my jeans.

"It's taking everything in me not to fuck you right here, Sierra. I want you riding my fingers, coating my hand in your cum before you take every last inch of my cock inside you until you come again. I don't want you to be able to walk without feeling the ache between your legs that I created. Let me take you home."

It's a need disguised as a plea, one that I hope she buys into before I spend the rest of my day jerking off under cold water to the image of her and everything that I plan on doing with and to her.

She has me in knots, impossible to untangle.

I feel the frustration and disappointment build to a near point of explosion when her eyes widen, suddenly alert, no longer fogged over. A deep flush washes out her light freckles when she shoves me away and frantically readjusts the bottom of her dress where it had ridden up. She doesn't look at me once while collecting herself with a silent urgency, and it pisses me the fuck off.

"Shit. Shit, shit, *shit*." She presses two fingers to her swollen lips, looking as embarrassed as a teenage boy caught by his mom watching porn for the first time. "No. No way. We're in a hallway. Oh my God." Hands clasp on the top of her head and she begins to pace.

I push my hair back and lick my lips, the taste of her mouth still on them. "Relax. Nobody saw anything." *Who cares if they did?*

"You don't know that. Anyone could have walked by." She frantically tries to flatten her hair. "Cole—my boss could have seen! You need to stay away from me. I don't think straight when you get close to me. I'm not myself around you."

I try not to take her words as compliments, but I'll admit I don't quite see the problem with what she's saying.

"Boss, huh? He probably would have liked to see it. The guy looks like he only knows how to be on the bottom. I'm sure he could have taken some notes."

"This isn't a joke, Braden. Just forget about it. I have to go."

I don't make any effort to stop her when she brushes past me. She wouldn't have stayed regardless, and I'm not about to make a fool of myself by attempting to convince her. "Try to keep it in your pants for the rest of the night, yeah?" My tease falls flat.

"Don't call me. This was a mistake," she mutters before walking away and joining her table again. My jaw ticks with anger at her sudden departure, but I ignore her parting words.

I will be calling her. Preferably sooner rather than later. She can count on that.

13

Sierra

Fuck Braden and his ability to yank me around by a set of puppet strings.

Every single ounce of my self-control is yanked from my grasp the minute he opens his mouth, leaving me with nothing more than crushed dignity and wet panties. It's embarrassing—downright scarring for my self-esteem.

He's dangerous. An all too tempting distraction that I can't afford right now. Or *ever*. The air between us becomes so charged with sexual want and attraction that I can't manage to keep any sort of boundary up. When I try, he just kicks it over, smiling that arrogant grin the entire time.

When I was with Logan, there was always an attraction there. But it never sizzled in the air, danced on my skin, or expanded in my chest until I couldn't damn well breathe. We were together for what feels like forever, having met when I was only eighteen and he was twenty-one. It was a few years before we moved from being friends to being in a romantic relationship, but it was a sudden change. I always assumed that we had a strong sexual connection, a shared lust for one another, but now, I'm positive that we never did. What we had was comfort and trust—a shared responsibility to take care of each other's sexual needs and wants. How utterly disappointing.

I can feel Braden's heated gaze on my back as I walk back to my table. My bottom lip slips between my teeth as I sway my hips more dramatically, knowing full well he was already rock hard when I left him standing there. He deserves to be teased. After all, he did accuse me of being a prostitute.

Lauren is the first one to notice me when I reach the table.

"Oh, Cole. Sienna came back," she cheers sarcastically, toying with the lipstick-coated straw between her long fingernails.

Cole's eyes meet mine when he spins around. "We were just about to send a search party after you." He laughs. "Everything okay?"

"Yeah, just a long line." *A very, very long one.*

I cock a brow at the two girls when they don't move to make room for me and mumble under their breath instead. The snickers they both make in response to my growing anger only snap my last strand of patience.

"Okay. What the hell is you—"

"Baby? What are you doing here?"

I whip around to stare at Braden as he walks up beside me and confidently slips his arm around my waist, pulling me flush up against his side. He's so tall that I have to tilt my head to meet his stare as he settles beside me, palming my hip with splayed fingers. His lips stretch in a boyish grin that draws me close. My arm hooks around his torso, squeezing him with a silent thank you.

When someone clears their throat, I blink twice before following the noise. Cole stares at the large hand splayed across my hip but he doesn't seem to buy into the touch. I lean into Braden.

"Is this the boss that you were telling me about? It's so great to meet you, Colt," Braden speaks up again.

"It's Cole," Cole corrects him when he finally tears his eyes from my body and dares to take his chances eyeing up Braden. "And who are you? I don't think Sierra has ever mentioned you."

The arrogance in his tone rubs my skin like a fresh sheet of sandpaper.

"I'm the boyfriend."

"You're *her* boyfriend? For real?" I hear Tiffany mock, the humour in her tone punching at my bruised ego, leaving behind a dull ache.

"Yeah? What about it?" Braden asks in a low, threatening voice, not missing the obvious insult.

I want nothing more than to jump over the restricting mental ropes holding me back from tearing this bitch a new asshole. But these are my coworkers. I can't do anything that could ultimately hurt my career. I've worked too hard to throw it all away over a few rude comments.

The taste of blood rings in my mouth before I notice that I've been biting down on my tongue. I need to get out of here. With a shaking hand, I tug on Braden's belt loop. His breath fans across the top of my head as I peek up at him and meet his concerned stare with a pleading one. *Please take the hint.*

The top of my head is cold again as Braden looks away, clearing his throat. "You guys wouldn't mind if I took Sierra home, would you? My mom's actually expecting us for dinner."

I send a forced smile to the group and fiddle with the strap of my purse. Catching the glare Tiffany's shooting at me from across the table, I let my teeth latch back onto my tongue.

"Yeah, no problem," Cole clears his throat. "See you

tomorrow." The last words are spat through a clenched jaw as he watches Braden plant a kiss on my head.

"Yeah. See you all tomorrow."

I feel Braden's hand slide into mine, our fingers interlocking as he looks down at me curiously, a softness in his eyes that I haven't seen before. It looks a lot like pity, but it feels the opposite.

"So nice to meet you, Colt. Have a good one."

Pushing out a breath, I tug on Braden's arm and start leading us through the restaurant, focused on the exit. Neither of us speak a word until we get outside. The sun peeks through the clouds, shining in my eyes and fresh air fills my lungs.

The hand once held in Braden's slaps against my thigh as he drops it and steps back. His brows are scrunched between his eyes as he avoids eye contact, opting to stare down at the concrete instead. The silence continues to grow, acting like a barrier between us that I'm extremely grateful for.

Wanting nothing more than to get away from here and end this little charade, I say, "Thank you. You didn't have to do that."

He straightens his back and looks at me again. The softness I saw back in the restaurant is long gone, replaced only by a familiar, vacant stare. "No worries. You looked uncomfortable."

"That obvious?" I laugh lightly, unable to keep it to myself.

"As I said, don't worry about it. You shouldn't let people talk to you like that." His eyes dart around the parking lot. He looks like he wants to be *anywhere* but here. With me. "My mom's actually still inside, so . . ."

"Right." I nod. "I need to go anyway. My car's still at work."

"Yeah. I heard it's going to rain. Might want to hurry." He shoves his hands in his pockets, shoulders tight.

I nod again. "I guess I'll see you around, then?"

"Yeah. I'll see you around." He turns and walks back inside seconds before I feel the first raindrop splatter across my forehead.

I think that sounded an awful lot like goodbye.

14

Braden

RAIN PELTS DOWN FROM THE DARK SKY, SOAKING INTO THE material of my t-shirt, making it cling to my skin. The temperature seems to drop with the press of a button. I shiver, soaked through and through.

"Seriously? What next? Being struck by lightning? Stepping into an ankle-deep puddle and losing my shoe?" Sierra shouts from behind me, the anger in her words so prevalent that I begin to feel guilty for leaving her standing there alone and upset.

I'm annoyed with the way I'm acting, but I need to walk away. I need to leave her behind me and brush off the feeling of protectiveness that's now burrowing itself in my chest. It's a new, uncomfortable feeling that I know right away I don't like, nor have any reason to be contemplating in the first place.

Then I think about her boss and the way he watched her when she got back to their table—like she was a forbidden fruit he couldn't wait to take a nice juicy bite out of. Yet he didn't stand up for her—

not once—when she was being belittled right in front of him.

It pissed me the fuck off, and I knew that I had to do something. Sierra puts on a hefty image of perfection and bravery in front of others, but she's not made out of impenetrable armour. Nobody is.

Regardless of what I know I *should* do, I stand here in the rain anyway, watching her shake like a fucking leaf in the middle of a busy parking lot and wondering how I'm supposed to put distance between us when she's standing so defeated, soaked from head to toe and stranded without a damn car.

I'm not exactly the good guy, but I'm not the bad guy either.

Sighing, I spin around on my heels and choke back a laugh. With drenched brown locks sticking to her pink cheeks, her head thrown back and eyelids fluttered shut, Sierra looks beautiful—peaceful even. I don't bother fighting back my grin as I push my sopping hair away from my face and watch her, the view uninterrupted.

She drops her head now, staring at her open-toed shoes. Her head shakes, fists clenching and unclenching at her sides. The tension in her shoulders keeps her body rigid as she kicks at a cement barricade and groans in pain.

She looks like she wants to light the world on fire and watch it burn to ash. It's a sight that has me on the balls of my feet, anxious to be by her side so we can do it together.

"You want a ride?" The offer slips out before I can stop myself.

Five minutes ago, I was ready to leave her out here alone and delete her number before I ended up walking off the edge of a cliff, falling face-first into an abyss of the unknown. Now I'm offering her a ride home?

Sierra's pretty pink lips part when she spins around, relief washing over her, tense shoulders dropping. If she were offended by my offer, she doesn't show it. "Uh, yeah. Sure. If you don't mind."

I reach into my pocket and dangle my car keys in the air with a brief nod to let her know that it's not a big deal. "It's the red one."

I head for my car but stop after a couple of steps, suddenly frozen in place, watching as her eyes begin to shine and her bottom lip trembles ever so slightly.

An ache grows in my chest as I keep myself from going to comfort her. I've never found myself in this position before—being somebody that might be able to bring comfort to someone else. It terrifies me.

Despite that, I call her name.

She doesn't respond, just wraps her arms around herself and shivers. I close the distance between us and wrap my arm around her, tucking her into my chest with a heavy sigh. "You're going to get sick."

Sierra exhales a shuddered breath while leaning into me, but keeps her arms by her sides. I try not to think too much of it and focus on the way her breathing begins to steady instead, each puff of hot air creating a burning sensation on my frozen chest.

Her touch is electric, sparking under the water running off our bodies. The tingle it leaves on my skin makes it hard to focus—hard to remember where and who we are. It's addicting. It enthrals me and makes my brain fuzzy.

When I think she's a bit more relaxed, I try again to lead us to my car, desperate to both get out of the rain before we come down with hypothermia.

"Wait. Not yet." She pulls away until we're a few inches apart and presses her hands to my pecs, fingers splayed out.

She wears a look of embarrassment that has my jaw tightening, a growl of frustration vibrating in my chest. It was the same embarrassment I saw when she reached her table inside, and having her look at me the same way has my hands clenching until my palms burn.

"I'm sorry if I embarrassed you back there. I should have been able to handle them myself," she whispers, her voice thick with emotion, sounding utterly defeated. Her thumbs rub my wet shirt over and over before she grips it in a fist.

Furrowing my eyebrows, I shake my head. "You shouldn't have had to handle them in the first place. And I meant what I said before. It wasn't a big deal."

"It was a big deal to me."

It was?

She nods, letting her eyes drop to my mouth. Her reaction tells me I said my words out loud.

I don't have time to kick myself in the ass about it before she's pressing her lips gently against mine. I blink a few times before kissing her back, tasting her tears and fighting back the urge to go inside and throw my fist around. I busy myself touching her instead, using her body to calm and steady me. I grab her face in my hands and try to warm her skin by rubbing my thumbs across her sharp cheekbones.

We need to get to the car. I know that I need to get us warm, but when I move my hands to her hips and pull her flush against me, I don't think my legs would move even if I tried.

A set of furious shivers rack through my body, but I'm not sure if it's from the cold anymore.

The rain continues pounding down around us and our clothes are soaked, yet neither of us care. The only thing I care about right now is how good her chest feels pressed up against mine and how badly she makes me want to be inside of her. Whether it be in a public bathroom, my bed, or outside in the pouring rain, I can't get enough of her. I could spend all day with my mouth against hers.

Her lips part as she pulls away, yet manages to stay close enough to brush her nose against mine. "Can you bring me home now?"

I don't need to be asked twice.

SIERRA FLICKS her bedroom light on before slowly turning to me—wearing a coy, almost shy smile—and pushing off her wet skirt. She lets the fabric fall to the ground with a thump, so wet it must weigh a few pounds. Her eyes shine with a playfulness that has my lips twitching.

My mouth waters at the sight of her naked body. My cock hardens in my jeans, feeling nearly painful with how tight they've become. Her blouse is so wet it's see-through, and her breasts spill from the top of her cream-coloured laced bra behind it.

I swallow the space between us and pull off her blouse before reaching behind her, unclasping and throwing her bra away. Without preamble, I grab her hips and pull her to stand in front of me as I sit on the edge of her bed. Leaning forward, I catch her nipple in my mouth, sucking and biting at the rosy bud.

"Yes," she sighs in approval.

Her eyes widen with both shock and a hot flash of need when I reach up and collar her throat, squeezing lightly.

"Eyes on me." It's an order, not a request, and it doesn't take long for her to understand, nodding once. "Good girl."

I want to watch her writhe from the feel of my tongue lashing at her nipples as they ache with need and her skin burns from the rough brush of my stubbled jaw. Every primal instinct is begging me to take us both to the floor and slide inside of her.

I'm desperate to feel her hot pussy gripping my shaft like its very own lifeline, but I won't. I want to take my time with her. She needs to remember exactly what it feels like to have me buried balls deep inside of her in case she ever thinks of letting anybody else between these smooth thighs.

Sierra bucks her hips and her fingers find purchase in my hair, tugging on it hard enough that my scalp aches. I drag my open mouth to her other breast before repeating my actions on that nipple, tasting, sucking and biting down on it, soaking in each whimper that slips from her lips.

I release her throat and my hands begin to shape her body, stopping briefly on her ass as I begin to knead it in my palms. My touch drags to her front, teasing the inside of her thighs.

She whispers my name and I groan, pulling away from her chest to decorate her smooth skin with anxious, greedy, open-mouthed kisses. My tongue dances just above the band of her underwear, still holding her glazed stare before I rip the thong down her thighs and yank her forward until she straddles my left thigh.

She gasps, surprised by the move but recovers quickly when I grip her hips and drag her toward me, making her clit rub against my leg. Her hands find my shoulders as she steadies herself before dragging her bare pussy toward my knee and back again, beginning to ride my leg, using me to get herself off.

I keep my hands steady but relaxed on her waist, letting her be in complete control. My cock presses against my zipper, hard to the point of utter discomfort, but I don't make any moves to get myself off. Watching Sierra fall apart on my leg is too fucking sexy to interrupt.

"That's right, baby," I praise, watching her teeth sink into her bottom lip, wishing that was me. "Make that pussy come. Soak my leg before I fuck you."

Her chin tilts, and I can't find it in me to force her to keep her eyes open when they flutter shut again, her movements becoming ragged, less controlled.

The pressure on my shoulders increases when she uses me for balance, too focused on getting herself to the edge to stay upright. She's getting close when I bury my face in her neck, nipping at the skin below her ear, slashing it with my tongue.

The peaks of her chest brush against me when she arches her back and whimpers, "Please. I need you to touch me."

"Where?" I pinch her nipple between my fingertips. She cries out. "Is that enough? Or do you want both?" I pinch both and give them a hard twist.

She doesn't reply, only increases her movements until her breath hitches and her spine straightens, forcing her to lean away from me.

"Fuck, Braden. Yes, *yes*. I'm coming." The words come out gargled, in broken pieces. Her hands slip from my shoulders, and I move to catch her before she falls to the floor.

When her body goes slack against mine, I grin wickedly. Moving my hand between her thighs, I drag a finger along her drenched slit and groan. With her cum coating my fingers, I slip them in my mouth and suck them clean while she watches with heavy, lidded eyes.

"*Fuck*, you taste good."

There's an insatiable fire in her eyes as she watches me, digesting my words. Knowing she's so turned on by the simple act, even after coming so hard just minutes earlier, has my shaft twitching in my pants, pleading to spring free of its tight confinement.

I pull my fingers from my mouth and wind them in the hairs at the base of her neck, tilting her head and kissing her, letting her taste herself on my lips. Flicking my tongue at her mouth, she parts her lips for me, letting our tongues glide alongside one another, tasting and sipping and memorizing. Without breaking away, I grab her by the waist and stand, hoisting her up. She tightens her legs around me as I spin around and lay her on the centre of the bed, crawling on top of her.

I pin her in place with my hips, grinding my cock against her hot pussy and growling, "I need you so bad, Sierra. I fucking ache to be inside of you."

She bites down on her bottom lip, and her eyes flutter shut. Before I can do it myself, she spreads her legs and pulls me closer, whimpering when my zipper brushes her swollen clit.

I back off the bed long enough to shove off my jeans and briefs. My cock is hard and heavy between my legs as I move above her, nearly losing it from just the heat radiating between her legs when I press against her. I slip a finger between her wet, pink flesh, and rub a knuckle across her sensitive nerves before rolling it between my fingers. Sierra arches her back, pressing hard against me.

My heart thumps hard and fast against my chest. I wouldn't be surprised if she could feel it. I haven't been this turned on in my entire life. The need to touch and hear her makes my blood pound in my ears to a near-deafening point. I desperately want it to stop. For things to go back to the way they used to be. When sex was a simple means to an end.

It couldn't feel farther from that now.

When we're together I fuck for *her*, not me. I want to fuck her to the point my name will be the only one that ever leaves her lips again. Not because she'll miss me, but because she won't be able to think about another cock stretching her hot cunt the way mine has.

Every time she's kissed, I want her to think about how right my dick feels in her mouth and down her throat.

When another man brushes a hair out of her face, I want her to remember the burn of me wrapping it around my fist and yanking her close while devouring her throat like a starved animal.

The thoughts won't leave my head. Won't give me any reprieve. They just keep knocking around in my skull, torturing me until I give them what they want.

But I won't give them what they want. I know I won't. Sierra is not mine. I seem to have forgotten that she is just a fuck buddy and can be replaced without a second thought.

As if needing to prove a point to myself, I grip my shaft and thrust completely inside of her, keeping my eyes locked on her tits as they jolt from the sudden movement. She gasps, hands searching my body for something to grab and steady herself with. I pull out almost completely before plunging back in.

Again, and again.

She feels hot, tight, and like something I could become addicted to if I let myself fall down that hole. My thrusts are savage, unrelenting. There's nothing personal about the way I fuck her. Like she's nothing more than a willing body. The nostalgia of it washes over me and has my molars grinding.

"Braden!" she cries when my thumb slides across her clit. She fists my hair in an attempt to grab my attention but I refuse to give it to her.

Don't look at her. Fuck her like a stranger.

She claws at me harder, more impatiently with every slap of skin. So, I grab her thigh to move it around my hip and slide even further inside that tight vice, hitting the spot that has her seeing stars in hopes that the increase of pleasure will distract her.

It doesn't. Fuck me, it only makes *my* resolve flounder.

Her pussy quivers around me, and I know she's about to come. The pressure at the base of my spine says I won't be far behind her.

Throwing her other leg over my hip, I fuck her harder. My

balls slap her ass and sweat beads between my brows and on my chest.

"I need you to come for me, Sierra. I need you to coat this cock in your cum," I groan through clenched teeth, fighting to keep from taking her mouth and stealing her moans as they barrel into me.

"Look at me," she growls, reaching toward me and scratching at my chest. "I'm not just some faceless fuck."

I almost freeze when she calls me out, completely aware of exactly what I've been doing. I ignore her.

Grinding my teeth some more, I sweep up some of her wetness and rub circles around her swollen clit. It's a jackass thing to do—using her own body against her—but I don't let myself feel guilty for it when she tightens up like a spring and her walls clamp down around me, pulsing as I come right along with her.

"Fuck. Yes." My thrusts become messy, and my vision becomes black around the edges as she milks every last drop of cum from me. A smug smile threatens to pull at my mouth before I swallow hard and blink twice, settling back down on earth.

Neither of us say anything as I pull out and get off the bed. My thighs burn, and my muscles stay tense, pissing me the fuck off.

With a tick in my jaw, I pull my damp clothes back on, keeping my back to her. It isn't until I pull out my phone to check the time that she speaks up.

"You're a real piece of work. You know that, right?"

Her words strike a nerve, and my hands form fists at my sides. I have to focus on keeping my composure and not turning around to look at her. I'm not sure what I would find if I did.

She doesn't sound hurt or offended. Just angry and frustrated. But I won't risk it, even when continuing to ignore her has my stomach churning.

I know that she *is* right. I know that she didn't deserve to be fucked like that—like she didn't matter. Yet I did it anyway. She can hate me all she wants, but I know it was the right thing to do, regardless of how cruel it was.

"Oh, and you're lucky I'm on birth control, dickbag," she adds, each word laced with venom. I feel the colour drain from my face, and my shoulders instantly sag with guilt.

I've never once had sex without a condom. I'm sure there are quite a few in my wallet right now, too. I just didn't fucking think about it in the moment. I'm such a total prick.

I clear my throat and grip my phone so tight I fear it'll snap in half. "Good. That's good."

She scoffs before I hear her get off the bed and the ensuite door slam shut, the lock clicking soon after.

Taking her storming off as exactly what it is—a dismissal—I run a hand through my hair and yank until my scalp burns. The shower starts, and I shove my phone in my pocket before leaving her house with a giant ball of regret in my stomach.

15

Sierra

RUNNING SWEATY PALMS DOWN MY LEATHER SKIRT, I TRY TO convince myself that saying yes to this family dinner isn't going to come back to bite me in the ass. I'm nearly one-hundred percent positive that it will, but I refuse to leave my apartment wired with nerves and nausea.

It's just my parents. How bad could it really be? I nearly snort when I realize just how stupid that question is.

They've been taking some time off work to travel this past year—as if parading from country to country for work the past twenty doesn't count as travelling—and are only *now,* six months later, taking a break to visit their two daughters and granddaughter.

It's so disgustingly typical of them to think that visiting us is some sort of gift that we should worship at their feet for. Like we should be grateful and not so damn stubborn with our feelings of neglect.

I can still hear my mother's clipped tone in my ear from when she called and *told* me that we were having dinner together the night they got back into town. If I had just paid closer attention to the caller-id when she called that morning, at the asscrack of dawn, I could have avoided the entire thing and blamed it on work or something. But since I was too exhausted and worn-out from the complete pity fuck I received the night before, I picked up the phone and was greeted with the raspy, snippy voice that belongs solely to my mother before I had the chance to warn myself.

"We already made the reservation for Sunday night, Sierra. Don't argue with me, it's the least you can do for us. I'm too old to argue. You know this," she said, as if fifty-five is the new ninety.

I simply responded by asking where the reservation was, and immediately had to fight the need to hiss like an offended cat when she responded with, "The restaurant connected to our hotel. The fancy one. Remember? They have the best fish."

I've always hated fish, but I told her I would be there and hung up before I couldn't bite my tongue any longer.

My parents always stay at the same hotel when they visit. Considering they sold our childhood home the minute Clare got pregnant and moved out, there really isn't another option.

I'll never forgive them for leaving me no choice but to move in with my sister while they went and traveled the world, responsibility free.

A hotel is their only option in Vancouver. And for some reason that I really don't care enough about to know, the hotel restaurant is the only place that they will eat. It probably has something to do with the sticks that have somehow climbed further and further up their asses with every trip they take for work, and how it's made them too good to eat anywhere with less than a five star rating, but who knows. Definitely not me. I haven't known anything about them for quite some time now.

The door buzzer makes me jump, yanking me from my

thoughts as I take one last look in the mirror, nod in approval, and grab my purse.

Fidgeting with the high-collar of my button-up peach blouse, I undo the top button and pull the shirt away from my hot neck as I head out. I fan the material and sigh when a cool breeze sticks to the sweat there. If Clare's already down there waiting, I must have been stuck in my own thoughts for far longer than I thought.

With that in mind, I say a quick prayer under my breath and head downstairs with my wool coat under my arm and a grim smile on my face.

"MOMMA," Liz sings from the backseat. She's snuggled into her booster seat with her favourite stuffed giraffe in her fists, not bothered by the lack of light in the car. It's only seven o'clock, but it's already fairly dark outside thanks to the change in seasons.

"Yeah, baby?" There's a slight waver in Clare's voice, most likely from nerves, but I don't mention it. She's already on edge enough as it is.

Our parents have only seen Elizabeth, their *granddaughter*, a total of three times since she was born. She just turned seven this past July.

Their lack of involvement hurts Clare, but they just don't see it. They don't care. I feel awful for my sister, having watched her raise a daughter all on her own after being divorced when she was twenty-three, so young and alone. I know that I was there for her and Liz, but it's not the same. She needed her mom, and she wasn't there for her. It wasn't fair to anyone.

"I don't wanna see Nana and PopPop." There's a finality

to her otherwise gentle voice that makes me wince. *Tell me about it, kid.* "Why do we have to? Do they 'member me?"

Clare sits silently for a moment, tongue pressed to her cheek. I can only imagine the things she wants to say but knows that she can't. Kids are like sponges. They absorb literally *everything*. Not like we both wouldn't love for Liz to let a few of our thoughts slip during dinner. Just not tonight. A scene is the last thing any of us want.

"Because they're family. And we always make time for family, Bug."

I turn to Clare and smile even though she doesn't take her eyes off of the road. I wait for another question to come, but Liz seems satisfied with that answer for the moment.

After another ten minutes in silence, with only the radio playing in the background, we arrive outside of the hotel restaurant.

There's a chill that slides over me when we head for the doors, one that makes my skin prickle and my stomach clench with fear. I swallow and shove my hands inside the deep pockets of my coat, fiddling with whatever I can find.

The automatic doors slide open when Liz skips a few steps ahead of us, arms flapping in the air. She looks the epitome of carefree and naïve.

It makes me jealous.

When we're young, we're always so eager to grow up. All we think being a grown-up means is no longer having a bedtime and being able to eat junk food whenever we want. It's not until we actually do grow up that we realize just how badly we miss our youth, and how we took it for granted.

We would do anything to go back to the days of no responsibilities and worriless nights. But we can't, because like our youth, they're long fucking gone and there's a slim to none chance that they will ever come back.

We pass by a busy stainless-steel bar cluttered with a few

suit-wearing intimidating men perched on leather stools, and the glowing shelves lined with generous arrays of expensive alcohol behind it before we stop in front of a hostess table. The energy in the restaurant is familiar from the various times we've dined here, yet I still can't seem to get a reading on what makes it buzz with a sense of comfort the way it does. Maybe it's the bright, yet somehow not blinding lights that dangle from the high ceilings, or the classical music that plays at just the right volume. Who knows.

Slim fingers grasp my exposed wrist when we stop and wait for the hostess to show us to our parents. My eyes slide to the left and find Clare's waiting gaze. The panic in her wide stare makes my mouth dry like I just sucked on a cotton ball.

"Don't freak out," she says mighty slowly, watching me like I've suddenly become a ticking time bomb that she's terrified of setting off. "ButitlookslikethеybroughtLogan."

I double-blink. "Say again?"

"It looks like they brought Logan, S. I would recognize that sleazy smirk any day. You told them what happened right? That you're not together anymore? *Shit*. Of course, you did. It's been months."

I stop listening after she says his name, the sound of blood thumping in my ears too loud to focus on anything else. My stomach burns as what feels like acid rips holes through my insides.

I swallow past the bile in my throat and follow Clare's stare to the table off to the side of the restaurant, half-hidden behind a massive fish tank filled to the max with exotic fish.

"Did you know he was coming?" I think I mumble, fully aware that my tongue feels incredibly numb. It's not until I wipe the back of my hand across my forehead, testing it for sweat, that I realize that both my hands are shaking. *Pull it together, Sierra.*

My breath catches in my throat when we're noticed and a masculine hand lifts in the air, two fingers creating a "come here" motion when we continue to stand in place.

I can feel Liz's confusion and worry when she uses a small palm to grip my lower thigh, squeezing to try and get my attention. With a fleeting smile, I manage to calm her slightly, her hand not moving, but squeezing much lighter.

The two long fingers continue to wave us over, but my feet refuse to move, glued to the fucking floor like the bottoms of my heels have melted and stuck to it.

I close my eyes and imagine a *Bugs Bunny* worthy X marked below Logan's seat. When I don't hear an anvil fall from the sky and crush the cheating sack of shit into smithereens, I open them again, disappointed. I shake the thoughts away and with a quick inhale, square my shoulders and steel my features.

I tell myself that I can look at him. That my knees won't give out on me and leave me a blubbering pile of embarrassment on the floor.

There's nothing that he can do now that will hurt you anymore than what he already has. I repeat that sentence over and over again until I'm at least half positive that I won't lose my fucking head. He's nothing more than an ugly reminder of why men suck, and why I'm perfectly content with being single until the day I die. He's the past, regardless of how apparent it is that he wishes he still had a place in my present.

Logan Newcrest is like a stray cat—you leave out a bowl of tuna for it one too many times and it keeps coming back for more, no matter how often you kick the scraggly thing away.

Only in my case, I've given my stray cat one too many chances at redemption and now he won't piss off until he gets another.

Feeling a bit more secure in myself, I meet his stare with one full of ice. His lips tip in an amused, nauseating smile.

"Let's get this over with, guys," I say, turning over my hand and grabbing Clare's.

Clare gives my hand a reassuring squeeze that says everything she doesn't. I appreciate that she doesn't say anything. Doesn't ask me if I'm sure, or if I'm positive. There's a quiet voice in my head that tells me I might not have been able to do it if she had.

I'm the one to lead us to our table, needing to take control wherever I possibly can. When we round the fish tank and take in the full view of our table, I don't let myself show even a sliver of the anger I feel pouring from every pore in my body.

My mother, all five feet of her, jumps up from her chair at the far end of the table and claps like the restaurant isn't full and that it's just us at home. Her antics used to embarrass me when I was younger, but not anymore. You get used to it.

"Elizabeth! You look so gorgeous, sweetheart," Dina Caster says in awe of her granddaughter.

She swiftly ignores Clare and me and stares down at the tiny girl that moves to hide behind Clare's leg, eyeing the older woman—who might as well be a stranger to her—like she doesn't know why she's talking to her.

"You remember us, don't you, Lizzy girl?"

My father, Leonard, grins that wide, carefree grin that used to wrap around me like a warm hug when I was Liz's age. It doesn't have the same effect on my niece, however. She moves further behind my sister and grips her thighs like she'll sink through the floor if she doesn't have something steady to hold onto.

"Mom. Dad." Clare dips her head at the two of them before turning to crouch in front of Liz, gripping her shoulders lightly. "Say hi to Nana and PopPop, baby."

My mother clicks her tongue rudely and walks to Clare's side when Liz doesn't immediately do as she's told, attempting to brush her aside to get to her terrified granddaughter. "Don't be rude, Elizabeth. Say hello to your grandpa and me."

"Mother," I hiss, wishing for a second that shoving an old lady, let alone your own mother, wasn't frowned upon. "She probably doesn't remember you. Did you really think that she would? It's been what? Three years?"

"Hello, Sierra," she sighs, eyelids sweeping shut for a moment as if my mere existence exhausts her. She doesn't even bother looking at me when she turns to the elephant at the table. "Are you not going to say hello to Logan? It was so thoughtful of him to agree to come tonight. He is such a busy man nowadays with his company taking off! You must be so proud of him."

Hearing my own mother speak of my ex-boyfriend's accomplishments with a sense of pride that I've never heard from her in regard to my own, only makes my skin burn hotter.

I stare at her without blinking, keeping my features lazy, bored. "Why is he here, Mom? You know full well we're no longer together. I remember telling you why, as well."

It's Logan that speaks next after clearing his throat way louder than necessary. "I'm right here, S. Speak to me. You know I only bite if you want me to."

I spare him a fleeting glance and clamp down on my tongue. If his arrogant, tasteless words weren't bad enough, his choice of outfit accessories is.

The navy and pale pink striped tie that I got him last Christmas is knotted snugly at the base of his throat and lays flat over a crisp, white button-up shirt, while a gold Rolex—the one I saved for for a solid year and gifted him on his birthday—is fitted below the custom cuff-links on his left wrist.

I snort, unable to hold it in. "You couldn't be an even bigger prick if you tried, Logan."

My mother scoffs at my comment while my father lightly shushes her.

"Let's just sit down, shall we?" he suggests desperately.

A set of tired, mahogany brown eyes flicker between Logan and me, yet Leonard Caster says nothing in my defence. Like always, he's too terrified of his wife to ever dare speak out against her.

It's still a wonder to me how he can stay married to my mom—happily, at that—when they're such opposites. Whereas my mother doesn't mind making her presence known in a crowded room, Dad would rather slip under an invisibility cloak to avoid even a single set of curious eyes.

I can almost feel his embarrassment from the scene that this wife has caused, but knowing he probably didn't agree with her inviting my ex-boyfriend, yet still went along with it is enough to keep my sympathy for him at bay.

He will always be the same timid-mouthed man I've known my whole life.

Swallowing hard, I stiffly dip my chin and take the empty seat beside my niece when I notice that everybody else has already sat down. I sigh in relief when I see Clare sitting beside Logan, shooting me a wink when she catches me looking. And when I spare Logan a quick flick of my eyes, I smile at his scowl of disapproval.

Clare and Sierra: 1

Cheating Bastard: 0

16

Braden

"YOU DIDN'T WANT TO CHANGE FIRST? I LOOK LIKE A FUCKING slob beside you." I don't bother looking at my brother when I speak. I'm too busy watching the ice cubes melt in my glass of whiskey.

The Vancouver Warriors just won their home opener—barely, but who cares—and Tyler, being the winning goal-scorer of the game, called to invite me out with the small group of players that wanted to celebrate the win in the public eye. I instinctively wanted to say no, not because I don't love drinking fancy fucking booze in the company of my brother, but because being around so many professional hockey players makes my insides burn.

I miss the damn sport, and knowing that I could have been playing alongside my own brother, not necessarily on the same team, but in general, yet chose a completely different career path, fills me with the smallest nip of regret.

I keep reminding myself that I did it for Dad and that there was no guarantee I would have been drafted into the pros anyway, but not knowing at all, that shit *sucks*. It eats at me some days, but boxing is in my blood. It's a passion of mine that I could never give up.

I'm so damn proud of Tyler for not allowing his own inner demons to stop him from accomplishing what he's always wanted, and for becoming a staple name in hockey.

That doesn't mean I'm not a bit jealous, though. Every time I turn on a game and see my brother and his brother-in-law, Oakley Hutton, and one of my college hockey teammates and good friend, lighting up the rink together with so much skill, power, and confidence, I can't help but imagine myself right there beside them. Just like the good old days.

"We both know that if I went home after the game, Gracie wouldn't have let me back out," Tyler says with a snort. His smile spreads around his clear glass as he takes a sip of his drink. The humour in his dark eyes makes my chest rumble with a laugh.

"Right." I tap the side of my glass with my finger and hum. "How has she been lately? The nausea still kicking her ass?"

My brother's wife is three months pregnant now and has been dealing with some gnarly morning sickness the entire time. If I remember correctly, I think she had to get prescription pills from her doctor when it got so bad that she couldn't even get out of bed most days. It was hard for her not to be able to work, but every time she even attempted it, it wasn't long before she was calling Tyler from the bathroom, begging him to come take her home.

Tyler shoves his empty glass toward the bartender. "Yeah. It's getting better but it's killing *me*, man. She looks so fucking miserable all the time and there's nothing that I can do to help."

I want to give him a reassuring hug, but settle on squeezing his shoulder knowing full well he's not the biggest fan of receiving comfort from anyone other than his wife. "How much longer until it eases? Or will it not go away?"

"Doctor says it should go away in a few weeks. Hopefully, it'll just be a first-trimester thing."

I nod. "Well for all of our sakes, I hope so too. I don't know how much more of your bitching I can take before my ears begin to bleed, Ty."

"Fuck off," he grumbles, even though the corner of his mouth twitches, begging to lift into a grin. "What's up with you? I haven't seen you since you bailed at dinner."

"Not much."

It's only a half-lie. I haven't done much of anything since I left Sierra's house last week. I haven't texted her, and she hasn't texted me. Things have gone back to normal. That is if my new normal has become not being able to get even the slightest hard-on unless I'm flicking through memories of what Sierra's pussy tastes like.

I haven't been able to get it up for anyone, at fucking *all*, the past few days. I even spent my Saturday night in a dark hallway at Sinners with my pants down at my ankles and a hot mouth wrapped around my soft cock, unable to get hard. The busty brunette was offended, not like I could blame her, and left me bracing myself against the wall with my dick hanging between my legs like a limp noodle. I didn't even give myself time to be embarrassed that my cock had become so utterly useless before I left, got in my car, and began slamming my hands on my steering wheel until the anger passed.

"What's the scowl for them? Someone key your car or something?"

"Nobody fucking keyed my car. Nothing's up."

Tyler turns his bar stool until he faces me, right arm planted on the bar top, knees spread wide in his expensive, custom black dress pants and the top two buttons of his white dress shirt unbuttoned. His black hair—buzzed on the sides, longer in the middle—is messy as hell, like he hasn't touched it since he took his hockey helmet off after the game. Knowing him, he probably hasn't. He has a brow kicked up as he watches me, eyes doubtful, making it clear that he doesn't believe a damn word I've said.

"I saw Clayton the other day when I stopped by the gym," he says while signalling the bartender to refill his glass. My stomach drops.

That little shithead.

Tyler's drink is refilled quickly, and he takes a sip before facing me again. "He mentioned a girl. Sierra, I think her name was? Said you were seeing her or something like that. I told him he had to be lying because there's no way my brother had a steady girl and didn't tell me."

I lift my shoulder in a lazy shrug, trying to play it off like the topic of Sierra doesn't affect me. Tyler would never let me live it down if I told him just how much it did actually affect me.

"We were fucking around for a while. It's done now." There's the smallest hint of a smile on his face that has me tonguing my cheek. "I'm serious. I haven't seen her in a week."

"And how has that been?"

The grip on my drink tightens. I swallow hard. "Fine. What are you? A shrink now?"

"Fine?" he echoes, head tilted while he belts out a rough laugh. "You sure about that? You don't sound real sure."

Pushing away from the bar, not wanting to deal with getting the third degree any longer than I have to, I get up, drink still in my hand. Tipping my glass, I gulp down the last few sips before slapping it down on the bar and shoving my hands in the pockets of my jeans. "Going to the bathroom," I mutter and stalk off until his bursting laughter fades into nothing.

I'm rounding an excessively gigantic fish tank when I stop, my chest beginning to constrict. My nostrils flare and my back molars grind together as I take in the scene playing out a few feet in front of me.

Sierra.

Sierra.

Sierra.

The need to kick something dangles on the edge of feeling almost numbing when my cock grows hard, pressing against the zipper of my jeans. There she sits, all perfect posture and self-aware. Straight-faced and confident. Pale peach lips, sharp cheekbones, strong jaw.

She doesn't smile, pout, or frown. Her full lips remain in a straight line, completely still, like she's promised herself a giant margarita if she doesn't so much as budge them with a strong exhale.

The peach blouse she wears is the same shade as her lips, making them pop that much more. It frustrates me that I can't figure out exactly what she's thinking behind those blank silver eyes and long, thick black lashes.

She's put up a wall, it's easy to tell. One that she doesn't plan on letting anybody at her table have the chance at sneaking past. I can't help but stare as she briefly narrows her sights on the slightly hunched man sitting across from her. The same one that I can see clear as fucking day dragging his foot up her leg from beneath the tablecloth before it disappears from view.

He's fucking ballsy.

I've never wanted to rip a limb from someone's body more than I do right now. I stand rigid, glaring daggers at the back of the guy as he slips his hand beneath the table and bends forward.

I blow out a hot gush of air when Sierra flinches and turns toward the young girl sitting beside her.

So she flinches when he tries to touch her, yet invites him for dinner with the other people at the table that I assume are her family? Confusion clouds my judgment, making it harder to stay calm.

My lips curl inward at the thought that she's been out, able to fuck around with other people, while I now have a hard-on for the first time since being inside of *her*. It's infuriating. Absolutely maddening. A spiked pit grows in my stomach that feels a hell of a lot like jealousy.

Every muscle, bone, and fibre in my body wants me to stalk over there and toss the prick from his seat until he's not even in the same building as Sierra. From the fitted suit jacket and shiny black dress shoes that look like they've never been worn before tonight, I know he's here to impress. And that's the last damn thing I want to let him do, for reasons that I will deny over and over and over again until they burn to ash.

I don't want him to see the way her eyes burn with something primal and unapologetic before she tosses out a sassy comment, or how her bottom lip pulls slightly to the right side when she's nervous.

They're completely selfish thoughts. Ones I have no right thinking about. Maybe that's what pisses me off the most.

17

Sierra

Voices around me mesh into a symphony of utter misery.

My heels click-clack on the sidewalk as I move toward Clare's vehicle like my ass is on fire. A deep, dominant voice rambles on and on about something with my father, growing louder and louder by the second. I know Logan is trying to catch up with me, but I only move faster.

My hackles are still raised. I'm beyond frustrated with the way Logan touched me during dinner like he had a right to do so. What started off as simple, yet unwelcome brushes of his foot along my calf soon became firm squeezes of my knee under the table regardless of how far I had tried to pull myself away from his wandering hands.

I've never been one to love the attention that comes with causing a scene in public. Add a very impressionable child to the mix, and I knew that there was no way that I could get away with backhanding the son of a bitch without risking teaching my niece that that is an appropriate way to act.

I can't even remember the last time I was so livid my hands shook and my chest constricted like a python had coiled itself around my ribs, planning on making me its dinner.

Logan was supposed to stay rotting in a cemetery filled with all of the other figures of my past that had hurt me in some way over the years. I've been working so damn hard at moving on with my life, to not see reminders of him in every bottle of rum in my cupboard or picture of London on the wall of my home office.

But of course, it was my own mother that had to pour gasoline all over everything that I've accomplished before sending it all up in flames. I'm not sure why I'm even remotely surprised.

My most prominent childhood memory of her is from Christmas morning when I was ten. Clare had promised me that she would no doubt be winning the Best Sister In History award with the Christmas gift she bought me.

Turns out, Clare had saved up all of her babysitting money from the past two summers so that she could buy me the dollhouse that I had been begging our parents for for the past three Christmases. My big sister hadn't even managed to wrap it in Christmas paper yet before my mother had forced her to return it, claiming that she and Dad had already bought me one while accusing Clare of trying to act like my mother when I already had one that loved me just enough.

I wasn't even surprised when I woke up Christmas morning to find a small, rectangular-shaped wrapped box waiting for me under the tree instead.

"You are never too young to start journaling, Sierra," Mom said with a familiar scowl after I had unwrapped a leather-skinned journal and everyone watched my face fall flatter than a pancake.

It was never mentioned again, not because Mom felt like she did anything wrong, but because her pride couldn't take another beating from her eldest daughter.

Nothing stopped Clare from continuing to buy me gift after gift each year, though. She just learned how to hide them. And once I started making money to buy her gifts, we started celebrating Christmas together. *Alone*. Just the two of us.

Even looking back on it today, I know that I wouldn't wish to change a single thing about it. Our mother would never own up to it, but she is responsible for the tight, unbreakable bond that her daughters share.

My fingers barely touch the door handle on the SUV before Logan shouts, "Sierra! Wait up!"

I suck in a breath through my nose before letting it out my mouth. Ignoring my better judgment, I turn my head to find him waiting a few steps behind me. My parents aren't behind him, most likely already in their car, leaving without a goodbye. I can hear Clare on the other side of the vehicle, buckling in Liz.

Logan's hands—the ones I remember being so smooth, not an imperfection in sight, the kind that belong to a man who hasn't known a lick of manual labour in his life—lay wiggling at his sides, like he isn't sure what to do with them.

I can't figure out if it's regret that has his mouth drooping or frustration from the night not going exactly how he wanted it to. Either way, not my problem.

"I want to go home, Logan. You shouldn't have come tonight. You know that, right?"

His foot lifts off the pavement before planting itself back down again. "I missed you. I don't regret coming."

I nearly laugh. "I'm not sure you know what regret feels like."

"Can you stop throwing cheap shots? You've already shut me out. Don't you think I've suffered enough?"

My jaw unhinges. Anger as I've never known sizzles under my skin, frying every nerve ending in my body that would have otherwise helped me continue to the bigger person and get inside the car.

"You've. Suffered. *Enough*?" Each word comes out in a sharp burst, my hands opening and closing at my sides when they begin to shake.

Logan throws his hands into the air, exasperated. He's annoyed. With *me*!

"How's Maeve, by the way? Does she know that you've spent your night with me and my family? Not sure she'd like that very much." This time I meant to throw a cheap shot.

He shrugs it off anyway, replying like he never even heard me. "I don't know what you want me to say, Sierra. You already kicked me out and blocked my number when I said I was sorry! You know it didn't mean anything. It was an accident."

"An accident? I didn't know it was possible for a penis to fall inside of a vagina *accidentally* but look at that. You learn something every day!"

Logan groans with a roll of his eyes. "Here we go again. I'm not sure why I keep trying. You're always so damn dramatic."

You're always so dramatic.

Dramatic.

I'm dramatic.

The weight of his words doesn't fail to fall on my wounded pride, making it burn like lemon juice squirted into an open wound. I feel squashed down by the unrealistic expectations of everyone around me to the point of pure exhaustion. I feel tired. Tired of having to continue to prove myself time and time again. Of feeling like nothing I do is ever good enough for anybody else. Of never living up to the expectations of my parents.

Any strength to continue this fight floats away, leaving me deflated. My shoulders sag forward and my eyelids begin to droop. Thankfully, my sister, wherever she is, decides that this conversation is over when I don't say another word.

"Get the hell out of here, Logan," she says, voice way too calm and controlled. Slim fingers slip around my wrist and lead me into the car, the door already open. I don't remember her opening it.

Clare gingerly helps me slip onto the seat while I serve her a look that says "I can do it myself." She simply shrugs me off and pulls the seatbelt enough that I can grab it easily and click it into place.

Clearing my throat, I slap on a barely there smile and nod once. She sighs but takes a step back, closing my door and getting in the driver's seat.

No words are said as she starts the engine and pulls out of the lot, merging onto the street. The radio plays quietly, just loud enough to help fill the void of a conversation that I don't want to have.

My head falls against the window, and my eyes have only begun to flutter shut when my phone vibrates in my purse. I debate whether or not to pull it out and look, worried that it might be Logan deciding that the conversation was in fact, not over. But I decide to reach into my purse and pull it out regardless, not wanting to start hiding from my past now.

My stomach lurches when I see the text lighting up the screen.

Braden: Come over. I need to see you.

Tapping my finger on the screen, I chew on my bottom lip, wanting to immediately say no, but stopping myself before I do.

Go over to Braden's house? To what? Get another pity fuck?

There's no hidden reason as to why he wants me to go see

him. There would only be one reason for going over . . . and I know that it would help get my mind off of everything that's been dredged up tonight, pity fuck or not.

Ah. Fuck it.

Me: On my way.

No turning back now. "Change of plans, Clare. I'm not going home."

BRADEN FLOPS down on the bed beside me with a satisfied sigh, wearing a wicked grin that has me questioning my sanity. Our eyes meet, his somehow glowing in the darkness of his bedroom.

The overhanging feeling of confusion that blanketed my shoulders when I arrived earlier—watching Braden eye met up with a less guarded, more attentive expression compared to the last time we were together—has been lifted, replaced with one of satisfaction.

There are questions I want to ask, and things I want to say. But they can wait for a time when my heart isn't racing and the delicious throb between my legs has disappeared.

"Shit, Sierra. I think you've ruined me for anyone else."

He's nearly beaming, his expression so calm and collected, so at peace, while I struggle to hide the surprise from mine. Sometimes it's impossible to understand this man.

He seems to sort through and understand his emotions like it's the easiest concept in the world.

I flip on my side and prop myself up on my elbow, eyeing the dimple in Braden's left cheek. "How do you do that?"

He turns his head. "Do what?"

"Act so calm. You don't try to keep how you feel to yourself. I don't know how to do that."

There's a small part of me that questions whether or not entertaining small talk in bed with this attractive, rough-around-the-edges man will only get me in trouble down the road, but the bigger part of me says to go with it. So, I do.

He seems to gnaw on my confession, two bushy, chestnut-brown eyebrows knitting together in thought. The scar that runs through his left brow has to be pretty old as it's nothing more than a thin white line now. Before I know it, I'm tracing the scarred flesh with my finger, feeling the smooth skin surrounded by rough short hairs and wondering how he got it.

Did he get in a fight when he was younger? Or was he a rowdy little boy who smacked his head on anything and everything? If he was, I hope he's at least apologized to his mom.

My finger stills its movements when he, whether consciously or subconsciously, leans into my touch, pressing his cheek into my palm and hums a deep, raspy sound of satisfaction that I store away for later.

After a few quiet seconds, he speaks. "There are certain things that I do keep to myself. Tons of things, actually."

My elbow gives out, and I rest my shoulder on the bed, stretching out my legs with a yawn. The long hairs on his calf rub the top of my foot as I move it back and forth along the cold sheet. "Could have fooled me."

He winces subtly before fumbling over two otherwise simple words.

"I'm sorry." His warm palm grips the meaty part of my thigh, a few inches above my knee, and hooks it over his hip. "For what happened last time. If I'm being honest, I didn't think you would answer my text earlier, let alone actually come."

I blow out a breath. "Yeah, you were a complete asshole. I almost told you to go to hell. Maybe I should have."

"You should have. I deserve it."

He does. Just because I couldn't help wanting to scratch an itch that only Braden seems to be able to soothe recently doesn't necessarily mean that all is forgiven and forgotten. How he treated me the last time we were together felt like I was receiving punishment for a crime I didn't commit.

It was completely unfair. I wasn't sure whether to be offended, hurt, or confused as I stood in the shower, under the scalding water, praying that when I got out and walked back into my room, Braden was long gone, never to be seen again.

A muscle ticks in his cheek, under the skin of my fingertips. I trace the sharp lines of his jaw, from the tip of his earlobe to the bottom of his chin.

The air is thick as I draw it into my lungs and say, "I'm guessing your explanation for the other night falls in the category of things that you keep to yourself, huh?"

He turns his face into my palm and kisses it once, twice, and a third time before letting out a shaky exhale. His chocolate eyes are warm yet guarded as he watches me with obvious curiosity, like he's trying desperately to dissect my thoughts.

"Do you want an explanation from me, Sierra?"

"If I said yes, would you give me one?" I counter.

"Yeah, I think I would."

Oh. Surprise has my mouth running before I can stop it. "That's okay, I'm over it now."

I offer Braden a weak smile before rolling onto my back, my head colliding with a thick pillow. A pillow that smells more like him than he does. It sticks to my skin and swirls in my belly. *God*. Really?

I hop out of bed and rush out of the room, desperate for some space to get myself together.

It's once I'm nearly out of the room he tells me, "You're invading my life, Sierra. I was just trying to keep you out. But clearly, it didn't work."

THE STREET outside my apartment is dark and empty, void of human life. The time by the car radio shows that it's just past midnight, so I'm not surprised.

My hands are clasped and tucked between my thighs so that I don't fidget with them. The silence in the small car is deafening. It feels wrong. I feel out of place.

It wasn't the right move to stay the night with Braden, not when his admission shook me so thoroughly. I needed space to clear my head, then more than ever.

So, not even ten minutes after I stumbled back into Braden's bedroom, I asked—or begged, I guess—for him to drive me home.

He didn't argue when I asked, didn't beg me to stay the night, and I was grateful for his understanding, even though my request could have been seen as alarming. It wasn't until he led me out of his apartment building, a strong hand resting on my lower back, that I realized he might know me a bit better than I had originally thought. And that didn't scare me as much as I expected it to.

The fact I'm *not* more scared is what scares me the most. *How ironic.*

"Thanks for the ride," I murmur.

His fingers tighten slightly around the steering wheel and he nods, still looking out the windshield. I'm sure that either one of us would be able to hear a pin drop in the backseat right about now.

After a strong swallow, I offer him a tight smile and unclasp my hands so that I can pull open the car door. But the minute they lay flat on my thighs, he's collecting them in his large, strong ones, squeezing like he doesn't exactly know what to do with them now.

His thumbs rub along the top of my hands, and my eyes flutter shut for a second. When I open them again, I find Braden watching me with a look that I recognize instantly. *Vulnerability*.

"I need to walk you inside, okay?" he asks firmly. I open my mouth to agree but he cuts me off before I start. "Don't bother arguing with me either. I just want to make sure you get inside safely."

I shake my head and laugh lightly, feeling the sound bubbling in my chest and ears. "Okay. Walk me inside."

He looks taken aback by my easy acceptance but brushes it off with a grin. After a final squeeze of my hands, he lets them both go and we step outside.

Braden meets me on the sidewalk and like earlier, places a firm hand on the small of my back, guiding me to the building.

When we reach the doors, he reaches in front of me to pull it open, holding it with a strong arm until I've walked inside. I have to use my fist to stifle my laugh when I catch him ducking his head to make it through the doorway.

Sometimes, I forget that he's taller than any guy that I've ever been with. All thick thighs and corded calves. He makes my five-nine height look embarrassing.

Once I've unlocked the second door and we've walked up the stairs to my second-floor apartment, I feel all the happiness from only a second prior fizzle out of me, annoyance taking its place.

18

Braden

I SEE HIM BEFORE SIERRA DOES.

The guy stands a few doors down from her apartment, clearly not sure which one is hers as his eyes flicker from one to the next. He seems relaxed, though. Relaxed but curious, like the building is familiar but he's forgotten what it looked like.

"Who the fuck are you?" I spit.

I don't recognize him at first or second glance, and that annoys me.

"Who are you?"

I wrap my arm around Sierra and slide her behind me, not appreciating the way he looks at her. We're already in front of her apartment, seeing as hers is the one directly beside the staircase. It helps settle me knowing that he's not already too close to her space yet.

Cocking my brow when he takes another two steps toward me, I meet him halfway and place my hands on his narrow shoulders. I squeeze hard before shoving him back.

"Tell me who you are before I drag your sorry ass outside."

"What are you doing here, Logan?" Sierra asks, sounding exasperated with this *Logan* guy. I find comfort in that. She's behind me again, running her hand up my spine.

The little prick takes the short distraction as an invitation to sneak past us, ducking under my arm when I try to catch the back of his dress shirt and sliding into Sierra's apartment. Sierra must have unlocked the door while I was busy trying to get his name.

Grunting under my breath, I follow Sierra into the apartment, slamming the door shut behind us. Logan is standing by the kitchen island, shaking like a leaf with what I would assume to be an ungraspable amount of adrenaline.

It's probably burning his blood, making it thump in his ears. His chest is probably tight, the thought of seeing Sierra give another guy even a spare glance making his vision tint with red, darkening around the edges until all he can focus on is him.

I know that's how he feels because it's how I feel. The only difference between us is that I'm not the one watching her touch another man, attempting to comfort him.

Sierra leans up on her toes, both hands gripping onto my right bicep like it's the only thing keeping her grounded, and presses her lips to the top of my shoulder in a short, sweet kiss. That's his final straw. His control snaps, and he's suddenly in my face.

With a loose jaw and wild eyes, Logan swings his fist in the air, the hit sloppily aimed at my face. I catch his fist mid-swing, wrapping my hand fully around it and squeezing. I don't stop squeezing when he tries to pull his arm back toward him, or when he hisses through his teeth at the pain. I stop when she asks me to, sounding only half like the Sierra that I've come to know.

"Let him go. He's not worth it," she says under her breath,

staring up at me with a silent plea in her steel-grey eyes. "I just want him to leave."

I drop his hand, and he pulls it to his chest immediately, staring down at it like he can't believe it's not broken. It would have been easy to shatter his hand in mine, and I hope he knows that I didn't do just that because I chose not to.

I peer down at Sierra, and the vision rattles me. She clings to my side like an adorable, Sierra-sized koala bear, and I feel a piece of me crack wide open at the sight, baring that small, yet significant part of myself to her whether she realizes it or not.

There's no mistaking the feelings that have begun flapping away in my chest. Yet I can't find it in myself to run and hide from them. I realize now that I actually want them. I want *her*. Not just for one night, but for every night. I don't want to drive her home after having her in my bed, making it smell like her. I want to fall asleep beside her warm, naked body and make her breakfast in the morning. I'm not a cook, but I can try.

I want to learn her every quirk and flaw. I want to hear about every important moment in her life, good or bad, I don't care. I just want to *know* her. She deserves someone who will put the effort in. And I'll be damned if I let another guy seize the opportunity before I can.

It's Logan's voice that pulls me out of my head.

"You sneaky little bitch. It was you that told Maeve where I was tonight, wasn't it? Were you messing around with this guy when we were together, Sierra? Is that why you won't give me another chance?" He's rambling, eyes flinging around the room, pupils blown and cheeks flushed.

Sierra tenses around my arm and moves impossibly closer to me.

The pieces of the unfinished puzzle slowly start to come together as I recognize the fancy buffed dress shoes and ironed suit jacket from the hotel restaurant earlier. Logan is the guy that was grabbing on Sierra like she was his to touch. The thought of that alone is enough to have every muscle in my body coiled tight, ready to throw him to the ground and teach him the proper way to throw a punch.

"You're nothing but a stupid whore," he spits at her, focusing on the way she clutches to me. "You're not worth the trouble."

"I'm going to give you one chance to calm down and leave before I break your skull." My tone is dark, the threat obvious. "Nobody talks to Sierra like that. Do you understand me, or should I show you what I'll do to the next person who raises their voice or calls her a whore?"

Logan slides his venomous stare to me, his brows bunched together in thought. This guy really has no idea who I am or what I do for a living because if he did, he would know that I don't like repeating myself when it comes to scum like him. It's much easier to hit someone instead. They don't second guess you then.

"I don't take kindly to people who find it so easy to talk to women like that. And I especially don't like it when that woman's mine."

Sierra tenses briefly before relaxing again. I almost steal a look at her but chicken out when I realize I might not be prepared for how I'll feel if my slip of tongue impacted our relationship negatively. It's better not to know.

"Oh yeah? And what are you going to do about it if I don't, pretty boy? Stay out of it. This is between her,"—he moves a hand between him and Sierra— "and me."

I wrap an arm around Sierra's waist on instinct and pull her tight to my side, palming her hip in an attempt to calm myself down before I do something I don't want her to see.

"Go home, Logan. I didn't tell Maeve anything. But

regardless, she's your problem now, not mine. You made sure of that."

Logan's Adam's apple bobs. "I know that you talked to her, Sierra. You never could keep your mouth shut when it came to other people's business."

She flinches against me as he continues to scare her. I bite my tongue when alarm bells start blasting in my ears. Holy mother of *fuck*. This guy is fucking dead.

I'm already in front of him, punching him square in the nose before he can blink. The solid crack in the air has my ego swelling as he stumbles backward, shooting his hand up to cradle his shattered nose as blood begins dripping onto the floor.

I unclench my fist and wince at the pain shooting through my knuckles but shrug it off as I move in on him again. He flinches when I grab him by the collar of his shirt and start dragging him behind me all the way to the front door.

I pull it open and shove him through the doorway, fighting off a satisfied grin when he trips over his own feet and falls to the floor, unable to catch his balance.

"If I see you here again, you'll be taken out on a goddamn stretcher. Now fuck off." I slam the door in his face and turn around just in time to catch Sierra as she jumps into my arms.

Sierra

Braden catches me without difficulty, capturing me in strong arms as I wrap my legs around his waist and thank him by placing my lips firmly on his.

I thank him in a way that feels so much deeper than with

common, expected words. He carries me toward my bedroom, shifting us so my butt is perched on his left arm.

With his now free hand, he grips my nape, tilting my head and deepening the kiss. A sudden wave of appreciation has my skin buzzing and belly flooded with a few sets of flapping wings.

I've never been a girl who cheered for violence but watching Braden slam his fist into my cheating ex-boyfriend's face—*shit*. From the bulging of the veins living in his forearm to the flex of his bicep when he swung, I was a goner. I've wanted to pounce on him from the second he called me his woman.

Usually, I would have bristled at the dominant claim, but it had my legs feeling like jelly instead. He might not have meant it, and may never say it again, but I've placed that shit in my memory. I won't forget it.

With a sly swivel of my hips, I feel his arousal press against me and whimper, all past thoughts suddenly overpowered by the liquid heat pooling between my thighs. My palms lay flat on his shoulders before curling into them, pulling at his shirt to bring us even closer together. Our chests brush, a jolt between my legs making me gasp at the sensation that comes from my nipples rubbing against his solid pecs.

"Cold?" He pulls back and grins broadly, his dimples making a beautiful appearance. Brown eyes slide from my face to my chest then back again.

I feel his happiness in the very centre of my chest as I shake my head. "No. I'm perfect."

The silence wrapping around us would usually make my skin itchy, but the only thing I feel right now is a sense of peace. A sense of *belonging*. I want to grip the feeling in my fists and shove it deep inside, storing it for a time when I know I'll inevitably need it.

I'm placed gently on my back in the middle of my bed, and can't help but gawk at the man in front of me. I wonder how I got here, with this powerhouse of pure masculine energy and power towering over me, looking at me like I'm something more than a workaholic with a crooked relationship history and family drama.

I frown as skepticism creeps into my head, and the peace slips away.

It's Braden's whispered words that blanket those pesky thoughts. They're just four simple words. Words that shouldn't have my breath catching in my throat, but do so easily.

"You're so fucking beautiful."

Cautious eyes trace my face. It's like he's scared that his confession will make me run from him and he's looking for something to prove him wrong. But I don't run. I don't think I could regardless of how hard I tried.

The tension leaks from my muscles and I relax. Then comes a moment in time when his expression is completely open, his walls temporarily pulled back. There's a trust there that says more than words ever could.

With a deep groan, he's hovering above me, knees between mine and hands gripping the headboard. I arch up into him and take his mouth, distracting myself from the feeling of heaviness that's fallen over us.

My bottom lip is pulled between his teeth as he nips on it before soothing the sting with a stroke of his tongue. The heat flaring in his brown eyes makes my thighs clench and tighten around his hips, the want to have him touch me is becoming a torturous need.

Again, he does what I want without me having to ask. It's a sort of recognition that has a lump forming at the base of my throat. He's begun to know my body just like I have his.

I swallow back a whimper when he begins undressing me,

taking his time to trail his fingertips over every inch of my body. An involuntary shudder works its way up my spine.

"Stay with me, my little fighter. We're nowhere near done yet."

The raw need burning in his eyes sets my insides on fire. An incessant throb builds between my legs, and I lift my hips, desperately seeking friction. With a steadying breath, I grab the back of his neck and pull him toward me. I barely catch the battle being fought behind his heated stare before he's burying his face in the crook of my neck with a sigh that shoots straight to my clit.

Wet lips part against my hot skin as Braden begins marking it with strong sucks and peppered kisses until he nips at the area beside my collarbone.

"Braden," I whisper.

I could spend hours with his mouth on my body, worshipping me in the way only Braden can.

With a shaky exhale I drop my forehead to his shoulder and hold him against my bare chest. The threat of losing his touch is too consuming right now. I hate that I feel this way. That if he were to push himself away and leave me, right now, it would hurt—*badly*. It wouldn't be like last time. I wouldn't be able to pretend that it doesn't bother me. He would leave his name etched on my skin. I'm just not sure how deep it would be yet.

My eyes nearly roll back into my head when his fingers finally slide over my upper thighs before slipping between them. He pants against my neck while parting my lower lips and dragging one finger through my wetness, right up to swirl it around my throbbing clit. My breathing becomes heavy as I close my eyes.

My bottom lip slips between my teeth when he groans, "Always so wet for me, baby."

I spread my thighs wide to give him the encouragement to

slide a finger inside of me. He does, before quickly adding another, alternating between a slow and fast pace while curling them inward, pressing down on the spot that has me snapping my eyes open with a sob.

"That's right. Let me hear you. Tell me how good I make you feel."

My neck is suddenly cold and it takes me a second to realize that Braden's staring down at me now, no longer pressed tightly against me. His lips are swollen and red as they sit slightly parted. When his tongue swipes out to wet them, I know that I clench around his fingers, my thoughts overrun by memories of having that tongue slide along my pussy until my thighs are shaking.

"Answer me, baby. Tell me how good I make you feel and I'll feast on that sweet, wet pussy until you beg me to stop," he demands with a sharp twist of his fingers.

"Good. *So good.* Please, Braden. I need it."

I'm long past feeling embarrassed by how badly my body needs him or how quickly I fall apart around him. There's no point. I can't stop it, nor do I want to deny myself the feelings he invokes with a single touch or drop of his voice.

Being with Braden like this is the only time when I'm not worrying about a deadline or working myself up over simple everyday tasks. I'm just Sierra. A very horny Sierra who would do just about anything for a mind-numbing orgasm at the hands of a giant, Hulk-like man who knows what my body needs before I do.

Braden's moving down the bed with a groan of approval. I squeak in surprise when two large hands grab under my ass and pull me down the bed so that I'm sprawled out like a starfish. Gripping the skin beneath my knees, he throws my legs over his shoulders and buries his face between them, swiping his tongue from my entrance to my clit, swirling it in a clockwise motion while keeping his eyes locked on mine.

His stare is soft—unbelievably so as he repeats the motion over and over, watching me writhe beneath him, a string of profanities falling from my lips.

I reach for him, finding it hard to suck air into my lungs. My head is swimming, my thoughts clouding. I say his name like a plea, voice thick with need. Words fail me as I gasp and whimper, but he knows what I want. What I *need*.

I'm close, *so* close. I can feel it trying to consume and blind me. My fingers thread themselves in his hair and pull hard as my back arches, hips threatening to shoot off of the mattress. But he reaches up and uses a flat, firm hand to keep me down while also taking hold of my hand and lacing our fingers together with a squeeze.

"That's it, baby," he coaxes, drawing out my orgasm like magic with a jab of his tongue inside of me. "Let me taste you."

I sob unintelligible words as white-hot pleasure shoots through my veins. My muscles tense, thighs shaking and squeezing around Braden's head as he keeps fucking me with his tongue, letting me ride out my high on his mouth.

The intensity of my orgasm has drained my energy, leaving me exhausted. I crack a smile and watch Braden use the back of his hand to dry his mouth before crawling over my body and collapsing on top of me.

"Get off me," I wheeze. "You're too heavy."

He presses a kiss to my cheek, chuckling when I start hitting his back. A roll of my body has me feeling the hardness beneath his jeans and I'm slapped with a pang of guilt. As I'm about to reach down and touch him, he nips my jaw, pulling my attention to his boyish grin.

He pins me with a look. "Don't. I'm good."

I want to argue but nod instead, a feeling of warmth flooding my stomach. "Well then, I'm serious, you behemoth. Roll over."

With a hard pinch to the side, he finally rolls over and lays on his back, head tilted to the side so he can still look at me. Heat climbs up my neck and stains my cheeks when he continues to stare, completely straight-faced.

"What?" I ask.

"You're gorgeous when you come."

I burst out laughing. "Shut up and go to bed. I'm tired."

The humour dancing in his eyes has me smiling long after I'm under the covers and he's flicked off the lights and crawled in beside me. His body rubs against mine as he wraps his big arms around me and pulls me close.

"Thank you," I whisper after a while, running my fingers up and down his abdomen. The hard, warm muscles flex under my touch.

"For what?" I can hear the smile in his voice.

What am I thanking him for? The orgasm? The company? The sense of calm? I let out a long, tired breath before whispering, "Everything."

He presses a kiss in my hair and hums. "Anytime, baby."

I don't even bother telling him not to call me that before I let him hold me as I fall asleep.

19

Sierra

"AUNTIE!"

My niece rips open the front door and rushes toward me, hugging my thighs with a tight squeeze. Her bursting energy has me smiling softly when I reach down and plant an exaggerated kiss on her head.

"Hey, kiddo. Have you been behaving?"

"Of course!" She flashes me a toothy grin, her left hand planted on a jutted hip.

Wearing a pair of dark blue jeans with iron-on patches across the knees and a shirt with a beagle eating a donut triple its size, she couldn't possibly be any cuter.

"That's what I like to hear. Now, where's your momma?"

I reach up to smooth the hairs that have been blown out of place by the wind outside. When my fingers get caught in a giant knot, I know it's already too late to salvage it. Leaving my hair down after my shower seemed like a good idea at the time, however, that may just have been because Braden didn't exactly leave me much time to get ready after sneaking in the shower and eating me for breakfast.

Liz turns toward the back of the house and points to the patio door. "The backyard. We're raking leaves!"

"Let's go then. We're wasting daylight," I tease.

The young, spitting image of my sister bolts toward the door. I pull it open for her and watch, amused, as she sprints off to one of the three piles of orange, brown, and yellow leaves. Clare stands with a rake in her hand, adding to the already giant third pile.

I whistle to grab my sister's attention and wave when she lifts her head, smiling so wide her white teeth shine in the sun. She throws the rake in the pile of leaves without hesitation, pats her hands on her coverall-clad thighs, and sidesteps the battery-operated, hot-pink children's car resting on the grass before walking over to me.

"What are you doing here? Not like I mind the surprise visit." She pulls me into a tight hug.

"I was in the neighbourhood. Figured I might as well visit my beautiful sister while I'm here."

"That's what I like to hear. Come inside. I have iced tea in the fridge. Liz, come inside when you're done playing in the leaves!"

A hand clamps around my wrist as Clare pulls me inside, a slight bounce in her step. Her beaming attitude isn't exactly a rare sight, but it still has me curious. She's usually happy, but not *this* happy.

I sit down on one of the bar stools lining the small kitchen island as she grabs the pitcher from the fridge and pours me a large glass. Placing the dew-covered glass in front of me, she flops down beside me.

"You're starting to freak me out," I say, raising my brow. "What's up with you? You look like you just got lai—" *Oh.* "You got laid, didn't you?"

"That obvious?" Her blue eyes sparkle.

"Oh yeah. Who's the lucky guy?"

"His name is Joel. He works at a mechanics shop only a few blocks away. Isn't that amazing? We've been on a few dates."

"A few? And I'm just hearing about him now? You break my heart, Clare."

"Oh, shut up." She swats my arm. "I didn't want to say anything unless I felt like it could really be something. He wants to meet Liz."

I try to keep my feelings from showing on my face, but my surprise is evident when I ask, "He does? So, it's actually serious then."

She nods once, suddenly stiffer than a board. "I think so. I don't want to rush into it, though. Not when Liz is involved. Plus, I have no idea how Max will react to another man in his daughter's life. It's always been just him."

Hearing the name of her ex-husband is like nails on a chalkboard.

"He doesn't really have a say in your love life, Clare. Not completely, anyway. It's kind of inevitable that you would both find other people. I'm sure he's had his fair share of women over the past three years."

Ever since my sister separated from Liz's dad a few years ago, I don't think Clare has even thought about dating anybody else. I guess in her own way, she was holding out hope that they would end up working out their issues and find their way back to each other. That's just not how life works, though. Not in my experience, at least.

Max and Clare were always the couple that I looked at and fawned over, hoping that that would be my future one day. They met in high school and dated all the way through college before getting married the year after graduation.

When they got married, everyone thought they would be together until they died. But the reality of life got in the way.

It twisted and pulled apart their ideal future until it cost them their memorable love story.

"I know," she breathes, swallowing thickly.

"I say go for it. If you're ready, that is. Don't rush into anything."

"I don't really have time to take things slow, Sierra. I don't really have men lining up on my doorstep. Nobody seems to want to date a thirty-year-old divorced single mom."

"Apparently Joel does." I throw her a wink and place a reassuring hand on her shoulder. "Have faith. What's meant to happen will happen. I promise."

"I guess." She smiles slightly.

"Where did you two meet? Actually, when did you meet? How long have you been keeping this a secret from me?"

It doesn't matter to me where or when she met this guy. I just want her to be happy. She deserves happiness more than anybody that I know. I owe her everything.

"Relax, Nancy Drew." Resting her chin on her palm, she smiles at me. "Remember when I popped that tire back in June? On the way back from the beach? We didn't have the spare so we had to call a tow truck."

I nod. "That was what, three months ago?"

She smiles sheepishly. "Yeah."

"You kept him a secret from me for three months? Oh, man. You *so* owe me, Clare Bear."

She lifts one shoulder in a shrug but I can see the humour flicker in her blue-green eyes.

"Yes. But we didn't start dating right away. He is the lead mechanic at the shop where the tow truck dropped my SUV off, but he wasn't the one that fixed my tire. I didn't meet him until the next time I brought it in. Liz had stuck a barbie doll somewhere under my hood when I was refilling the windshield fluid and I didn't notice until it had melted all over the inside and I couldn't get it off."

My attempts at stifling my laugh fail and I lose it, laughing hard enough that tears swell in my eyes. "I can just imagine you right now. 'Hi, sorry, but my daughter melted a barbie all over my engine. Please help me.'"

A tightness grows in my stomach as I brace myself on the counter, my shoulders shaking. I peek through closed eyes and see Clare staring at me with a look that says "shut up or else" but don't stop laughing until she punches me in the shoulder.

"Stop it." She's blushing.

"I'm guessing he was sweet to you then? Didn't laugh in your face?" I swipe away the tears that have fallen.

"No, he didn't. He was very professional."

I smirk. "Professional? Is that how he wound up between your sheets?"

She glares at me. "No. He wrote his number down on the invoice and glared at the other mechanic when he started teasing me about not using the inside of a car as a barbie dream house or something stupid like that. I don't remember."

There's a sense of pride and happiness that grows in my chest while watching how dreamy she looks talking about Joel. It's enough to have me accepting him already, regardless of not meeting him yet. Any guy that makes my sister smile like that is good in my books.

"Anyway," she says. "Don't think that I haven't noticed the glow to your skin either. You look different. *Happier*."

Do I? I brush off the comment. "I feel the same."

Her stare burns into my face and I take large gulps of my drink to try and pretend that I don't feel it.

"Don't even, Sierra. Have you forgotten that I'm your big sister? That title comes with younger sister reading skills."

"Is that so?" I scoff. Her intense stare doesn't waver as it wears me down way too fast. "Fine! Put that damn look away. I've only been sleeping with someone. It's not serious like you and Joel."

I risk looking at her again just to see her roll her eyes. "Yeah, okay. Try again."

"I'm serious! We're just having fun. Trust me, he isn't a relationship kind of guy." My fingers dance on my leg as I bounce it.

"He's gotta be hot then, right? What's his name?"

I'm flushed when I answer, struggling to keep my voice from wobbling when just the thought of his name has me wanting to rub my thighs together.

"Braden. And yeah. He's really fucking hot," I burst, raising a hand to my cheek to feel the burning skin.

She taps a contemplating finger on her chin and hums. I feel my brows lift with curiosity. "What? You don't like that name or something?"

"Braden," she says slowly, pronouncing each letter like she's never spoken them before. "Braden." This time she rolls the r.

"Jesus Christ, Clare. You're weirding me out."

She swipes a hand in the air. "I was just trying to see how well it rolled off the tongue."

I shake my head at her ridiculousness. "Well? Don't leave me hanging. Does it fit the bill?"

She tosses me a wink. "It's not bad. I'm sure he makes up for having such a usual name in other ways. Tell me, is he tall? You're far too tall to be with a short guy."

"Clare!" I chastise regardless of the smile that stretches across my face. "Don't hate on short guys. The majority of them know their way around a woman's body better than most of the tall guys I've ever met. But yes, Braden is pretty much a giant. Even compared to me. I reach his chin."

She looks surprised. "Really? Well then. I certainly can not wait to meet this guy."

"Keep dreaming, Clare Bear. I don't see that happening any time soon—if ever." I can see that she wants to push me on it but knows better than to try.

I'm grateful when she easily changes the subject to ask if I'm free to come with her to Liz's fall talent show. After agreeing, we make our way back outside to join my niece in her leafy paradise.

Clare and I exchange smiles, both of us starting to laugh before we grab Liz and toss her into the only pile that she hasn't yet destroyed. Her squeal of excitement is like a shot of serotonin. And just like that, I'm home.

20

Braden

"No."

My tone leaves no room for judgement, it's too cold and void of emotion. Betrayal like I've never known rears its ugly head.

Dad's brows move to his hairline as he stares at me, mouth gaping as if he's surprised for some ungodly reason. He was either completely naïve to my feelings, or just doesn't know me as well as he used to.

Whichever it is, I don't care. It's the same either way.

He wants to leave.

"What do you mean, no?" he echoes, and I catch the movement of his fingers curling around his bottle of non-alcoholic beer.

I clear my throat. "Sorry. *Fuck* no."

"Watch it, son," he growls.

Dark eyes burn into the side of my face with a look of rage I've seen only a few times over the course of my life. I continue to look straight ahead, refusing to meet his stare. "I meant, why not? What's keeping you here? The gym? Forget about it. We'll buy a new one in Toronto. Hell, if you come with us, I'll buy you three."

There's no holding in my humourless chuckle. "Really? In case you've forgotten, you drained every last fucking penny you had for the rock on your fiancée's finger. And what about Tyler? You know, your other son? Don't you think maybe he's something that I don't want to leave behind? I'm actually surprised you're so okay with it."

"Tyler spends half the year on the road, Braden. Location doesn't matter to him. Gracie does. And it wouldn't be fair to take her from her family, especially while they're building a family together. Anyway, I already spoke to him today. He turned me down."

I feel the judgement in his words like a sucker punch to the gut. The disappointment that my father feels with how I live my life makes me want to throw my fist through a cement block. The way I refuse to commit to one woman pisses him off—disappoints him. I know it stems from his own past mistakes and regrets, so it's not surprising he projects on me, wanting me to be better than he was.

For a second, I debate throwing Sierra in his face to spite him but stop myself when I remember that while I may want her to be mine to some degree, it's not like that between us. Our relationship, or whatever you would call it, is messy, filled with a never-ending list of questions I don't have the answers to yet.

Every time that I feel myself give in to her pull, I yank back before I give it a chance. The thought of her with another guy makes me want to go postal. I get possessive and lose myself in her presence and the way she makes me feel like I could rule the whole fucking world. But all it takes is one reminder of how broken I am in the world of relationships and commitment to shut down again.

Seeing Sierra makes me happy. I care about her and don't

want her with anyone else, I won't deny that or how selfish it makes me. But I won't let myself give more than that. I don't know how. I'm happy with how things are now. Anything else would be far too complicated.

I would only be digging myself into an even deeper grave in Dad's eyes if I admitted that to him right now.

"So, because I'm not married and expecting a kid, I have nothing to lose by uprooting my life to fit into *your* plans? *Your* future? You can't just expect me to come with you because you're too scared to do this on your own."

I meet his eyes when he slams a fist down on the top of his new kitchen table. His bottle shakes, and the small porcelain jars of cream and sugar clatter. I hold his stare, pressing my tongue to my cheek.

His mouth is held in a firm line that's only broken when he opens it to speak, his refusal to my claims at the ready. But I cut him off with a raised hand in front of me that has a rumbled, angry curse falling between us.

"If you're not scared, then sign over the gym to me and go. It's going to be mine someday anyway. You know I'll take care of it. If there's nothing here for you to come back to, then you really can start over with Lana."

He visibly flinches. Adam's apple bobbing with silent emotion, Dad's eyes fall to his hands as they rest open on the table, drawing my attention to the calloused, wrinkled skin.

Years of fighting show in the countless white scars etched on his knuckles. Each one represents a memory—a win or a loss. The thick calluses are from the years of hard manual labour he endured with my grandfather, building houses for countless years while he worked for the money to buy his gym. Rampage.

"The gym isn't everything, Braden." He uses his thumb and pointer finger to smooth out his scrunched brows. "I hope that someday you'll be able to see that."

I'm saved from this conversation by the ringing of my phone. Sliding it from the pocket of my jeans, I see a name on the screen that doesn't surprise me in the slightest. I'm surprised Tyler waited this long to call me. Dad must have told him that he would be talking to me this afternoon. The asshole's probably been waiting all day to call me and gossip.

"Need to answer that?" Dad asks. He stands up and moves to get rid of his still half-full bottle of warm piss. I know my dad well enough to tell when I'm being dismissed, so I swallow down the rest of my questions and take a steadying breath to keep myself in check.

Following his lead, I silence my phone and stand up. "No. I do have to leave though. I'm sure we'll talk about this again later."

I stay in the kitchen long enough to catch his barely-there nod before heading for the front door. After slipping my sneakers on, I throw a pained goodbye in his direction and rush out of my childhood home feeling more fucking weighed down and pissed off than I have in a long time.

My muscles ache. They're on fire, throbbing deep to the bone, a clear warning that I've spent far too long in front of a punching bag. Still, I haven't even *begun* to touch on the feeling of rage that's been swirling my insides around with a hot poker since I left my father's house.

I still can't believe it. Moving across the country for some ditsy Barbie Doll that he hasn't even known for a year?

I've been replaying our conversation in my head for hours. *The gym isn't everything, Braden.*

That's bullshit. Maybe he's happy to give it up, but I'm not. This gym—boxing at this gym—is all that I have. I gave up the only other thing in my life that has ever made me happy to help run this damn place. I threw away what could have been a professional career in hockey for this place. For him. And he's just going to leave it all behind. Like it's nothing but a speck on a map of his past. A *blip*. Vancouver is our *home*. I'll be damned if I let him leave it all behind just to chase some young tail.

"You don't think he's actually serious, do you?" Tyler mutters gruffly, his swift punches not faltering as they make the swinging leather bag cry out in pain. I know he's hurt by our dad just as much, if not more than I am. And he has every right to be.

Whereas I grew up with our dad, he wasn't so lucky. He grew up only knowing his abusive piece of shit stepdad and drugged-up mother. The same mother who kept both Tyler and our dad in the dark for twenty years.

It's almost a sick joke, really. I've known him as a friend for five years, and only as my blood brother for two of them. His mother dropped the bomb on all of us the night she disappeared from his life. She wasted no time in hightailing it out of Vancouver after finally spilling the beans about my father's secret love child. It was the definition of a mic drop moment.

But more than anything, it was a punch to the balls. For Dad especially. He knows it wasn't his fault that he missed out on so many years of Tyler's life, but that doesn't make it any easier a pill to swallow.

Ever since that night, Dad has been trying to make up for his absence whenever possible. Until now, I guess. Now the girl clawing on his arm is more important than his damn family—his *kids*.

"I think he's dead serious," I spit. "He wouldn't have brought it up if he wasn't."

"I don't see how he could expect us to follow him out

there. I would rather chew off my own tongue than play for Toronto's hockey team," Tyler grunts while wiping a towel aggressively down his face, leaving the skin red.

"I'm sure Lana would be your number one fan." I nearly choke on her name.

"I don't understand. Vancouver is our home. Gracie would feed me my own cock if I even considered uprooting us."

That has my scowl cracking. Talk about a sight I would pay a hefty penny to see. Gracie Hutton may be small, but damn she's vicious.

"I don't care how hot the girl is. Nobody could make me leave Vancouver," I say.

Tyler remains silent for a long moment, and I have a feeling he's going to tell me that that could change someday, but he doesn't. I don't doubt for a second he would follow Gracie to fucking Mars if she asked him to. But Tyler and Gracie are different. They're the closest thing to soulmates I've ever seen. There's nothing odd or abrupt about their love and adoration for one another. It's pure and raw.

"I don't think he'll do it. What about the gym?"

Tyler takes a drink from his water bottle, looking around the gym. It's closed to the public right now, so it's just us. Technically, we should be open, but I couldn't risk anybody hearing about Dad ditching out on us. It would have opened a can of worms that I don't have the strength to pry back shut right now.

This gym is home to the majority of my childhood memories. The good, the bad, and the fucking ugly.

I spent more time here than I did anywhere else. Hell, during my rebellious teenage years, I practically slept here. These chipped brick walls and cushioned floor mats kept me sane during a time when I feared I would never be able to get a grip on my angry at the world attitude.

I was pissed off at my parents for splitting and not being able to keep it civil between them, even at the best of times, not even for me. It took years for me to get my head out of my ass. And even then, I was still an asshole most of the time.

I knew that Dad was aware of the fights held behind his back, but he still let me get my ass beat time and time again without so much as a shrug in my direction. He never mentioned them when I came home from the gym to shower and sneak food from the fridge with bloodied knuckles and bruised eyes, or when he would drop me off on the curb outside of my grandma's house.

He didn't say anything when I wandered into his office requesting the first aid kit after getting absolutely rocked by a guy three times my size. And he definitely didn't offer me any sympathy when I broke my nose for the third time in a year because I refused to wear headgear out of pure stubbornness.

At the time, his lack of attention to my dangerous hobby served as a catalyst, encouraging me to keep going and going until he finally acknowledged the fight I had inside of me. With every win came a sense of hope that I wouldn't be as invisible to him as I thought that I was. I wanted him to be proud of me. I craved it with every fibre of my being.

With his time spent between a divorce lawyer, financial meetings regarding the gym, and training a full list of aspiring boxers, the only time I saw him was right before I left for school.

He would be leaning against the countertop with a steaming cup of black coffee in his hands when I came to grab my lunch. I would get a brisk wave and a tired grunt. Then we would go our separate ways until I saw him at the gym after school.

Now that I think back on it, I realize he was just trying to teach me a lesson. I was never invisible to him. He was going through a hard time too. I could never excuse the shit that happened between my parents during their divorce and the years that followed, but I can give them some leeway.

Every loss I took taught me the benefits of not giving up when shit got hard. My body hated me for it, but I'm not sure that I would change much from back then if it came down to it.

My stomach pitches as I turn back to my bag and swing at it. My arm locks due to my lack of concentration and I hiss from the burning pain that explodes through my shoulder when I make contact with the punching bag.

"Fuck!" I shake out my arm and rip my glove off, tossing it a few feet away.

"Told you to stretch," Tyler sings, earning himself an eyeful of both my middle fingers.

"And I told you to stop being such a loser, but here we are," I shoot back, trying not to cringe from my lame insult. I massage my shoulder and grit my teeth when it begins to throb.

"Wow, good one. What are you, ten?" Throwing off his own gloves, he grabs his water bottle and squirts a stream of water over his torso.

"Are you leaving now? I'm nowhere close to done and you're just pissing me off."

He rolls his eyes. "You need to go home before you hurt more than just your shoulder." He's right. I have a match in three days. Getting injured is not in the plans.

"I can't handle Clayton right now."

"Okay, so go somewhere else. Just not here. I can't stay here all night and babysit your raging ass."

Sierra's bright smile dances through my head, grabbing at both my chest and my groin. She would tell me to grow the hell up if she saw me right now. Her smile would be there, though, teasing and distracting me. I wouldn't be able to keep my hands off of her, seeing her in my domain, having her watch me do what I love.

"Ah, there it is," Ty chuckles, tossing his gloves in his bag before zipping it up. "Anything I should know since we last talked?"

"Huh?" I clear my throat, focusing on him again.

"Are you really going to keep pretending with me? I've seen that look before. *In the mirror.*"

"She's just a friend." The words feel wrong in my mouth.

"Right. Have fun with that then." He laughs to himself and tosses his bag over his shoulder. "Just be careful, Braden. I thought it meant nothing when I was just sleeping Gracie too. The next thing I knew, I was telling her I loved her while standing butt-ass naked in her living room. It sneaks up on you and knocks you on your back."

"Well, I'm not you." I paint on a fake smile. This is not a conversation I want to have with him right now. Everything is still so new to me, I'm not ready to admit my feelings to anybody else yet.

"Alright." He throws his hands up in surrender. "If you're so sure she means nothing to you, then I believe you. Just figure yourself out and calm down. Have sex or get drunk, I don't care. Just don't hurt yourself." He moves toward me and punches my good arm, saying, "Call if you need anything."

I punch him back. "Will do."

21

Braden

I DON'T KNOW WHY I TEXTED SIERRA, BEGGING HER TO LET ME come over, or why I'm knocking on the front door knowing how close I am to the edge of losing my sanity, but here I am. And I'm dying to be inside of her.

Sierra pulls open the door wearing nothing but a loose-fitting pyjama shirt that falls mid-thigh. Her hair is thrown up in a messy bun and there isn't a speck of makeup on her face. She looks stunning.

Magnificent, really.

"Is everything okay? Your text worried me," she mumbles, inviting me in and shutting the door softly behind me. I walk inside without muttering a word, kick off my shoes, and turn to face her.

Her concern for me is written all over her face. I rasp, "Come here."

She doesn't hesitate before walking straight into my chest, wrapping her arms around my middle as I pull her flush against me, sighing out in near instant relief. My hold on her is tight, like I'm terrified she'll run and leave me here. But she doesn't. Instead, she relaxes in my arms, strong puffs of air fanning across my chest as we stand in the middle of her apartment, neither of us wanting to let go.

My eyes close when she starts running a hand up and down my spine, warm fingers soothing the ache in my chest. A moan of appreciation falls from my mouth, and I kiss the top of her head, keeping my lips there for a few seconds, not wanting to lose the contact so soon.

With a reluctant sigh, her grip loosens the slightest bit and she leans back, looking up at me with worried eyes. My immediate reaction is to pull her back into my chest, but I loosen my hold on her with a soft sound of annoyance.

"Are you okay?" she asks gently. "Talk to me. I'm here for you."

The hand that was rubbing my back slides around to my front before climbing up my chest and gripping my nape. She gives it a slight squeeze, and smiles a small, toothless smile that fiddles with my chest, unlocking something she wasn't planning on letting me keep away from her for much longer. I try to be upset with myself for letting her get so close, but can't find it in myself to do so. Not right now, at least.

"Let's sit down, yeah?" I wince at the emotion in my voice.

She drops her arm from my neck and grabs my hand instead, leading me into her lamp-lit bedroom. "The couch is super uncomfortable. I picked it up at a thrift store downtown after . . ." She hesitates for a moment, chewing on the inside of her cheek before straightening her back. "I got it after I moved out of the apartment Logan and I shared. All of the furniture was his when we were living together, so I had to stare over. I didn't mind because the last thing I wanted was a reminder of him and my ex-best friend having sex on the couch. You know?"

I don't bother hiding my surprise. "He cheated on you

with your best friend? If I would have known that, I would have hurt him worse for you, fighter."

She lifts a shoulder in a shrug before sitting down on the edge of the bed and tapping her fingers on the white duvet.

"I was upset for a long time. It was more betrayal than anything else."

"How long were you together?" I would rather swallow gravel than think of her with anyone else, but I'm too curious to stop asking questions. I want to know her. I almost feel like I *need* to.

"Four years. I only had one boyfriend before him, and none after. I guess the idea of trusting someone again has never appealed to me."

"Or maybe you just haven't found anyone worth trusting."

She seems to gnaw on that for a while. "Or maybe I have, but I'm exactly sure what to do with him yet."

Surprise collars my throat and threatens to toss me off a tall cliff.

My mouth is dry as I try to pull together a reply. She doesn't let my silence bother her, though, as she says, "Your turn. What made you come here tonight? And don't tell me it's because you missed me."

She meant it as a joke. But I did miss her. It wasn't the reason for the aching pain of betrayal or the sharp burst of pain in my shoulder from behaving carelessly in the boxing gym, but it is the reason that out of any place I could have gone to try and get myself back under control, I'm here. With her.

The fear of being open and honest with her about how I'm feeling is numbing. I've always prided myself on being confident and fearless. I almost feel like I've let myself down in some way by not taking a risk that could end up paying off in the end out of fear of the unknown.

Maybe if I knew exactly what I wanted from her, I would be able to articulate that to her, and maybe it would put us both at ease. But I'm like a fish out of water here. I don't know my head from my ass. The only thing I know is I can't get enough of this woman, nor do I want to anytime soon.

I'm in front of Sierra before she has a chance to be surprised, gripping under her ass and hoisting her up. Her legs wrap around me without hesitation before she presses against me with a heavy sigh and a roll of her hips. Needing to taste her, I take her mouth in a heated kiss that I hope allows her to feel the ache that's settled beneath my rib cage, only calmed by her.

My tongue slips between the seam of her lips before working deep inside her mouth, possessing her in a way I've never craved before. I taste the mint-chocolate chip ice cream she must have been eating before I arrived, mixed with the pure, addictive taste that belongs to Sierra and groan. She swallows the sound.

We both need to breathe, but neither of us are willing to break apart. I'm a man possessed, too utterly captivated by the feel of her plush mouth moving against mine with a familiar possessiveness to think of my own needs.

With another roll of her hips against me, I jerk my hips and brush my cock against her underwear-clad pussy, relishing in the feeling of warmth radiating from her. I drag my open mouth across her flushed cheek and under her jaw, nipping on the skin before tugging on her ear.

"I need to be inside of you, baby."

"Then take me. Please."

"That's a good girl," I growl, sucking hard on her neck before pulling back and crawling on the bed, keeping her tucked beneath me and holding her to my chest as I do.

Only once I've moved us to the top of the bed do I release her, watching as she falls to the bed, a toothy grin looking up at me. There's a shatter in my chest as she breaks me open again and slithers farther inside the crack, owning me in a way that should have me terrified.

Slim fingers begin pushing my shirt up my torso, and I yank it over my head before removing the rest of my clothes.

"Take it all off, my little fighter. This is going to be hard and fast. I don't have the patience for slow and steady right now. Have to fuck you."

Need to own you like you do me.

She does as I say with lust-blown pupils and swollen lips. As soon as her shirt hits the floor and her bare flesh is right there in front of me, I curse.

"You have the most gorgeous tits." I suck a rose-tipped nipple into my mouth with a moan, flicking it with my tongue before letting it slip from my lips and blowing on it, watching as it grows needy for me. I pay the same attention to the other one, but bite down on it gently before pulling back and sucking on the skin beneath her breast, marking it.

She cries out when I reach down to cup her and feel the smooth, wet skin beneath my palm. "*Shit.* Jesus Christ. How long have you been this wet, baby? You're soaking my hand."

Her head falls back against the pillow, and she arches her back, pushing against my hand with a twist of her hips. I slide a finger through her slit and curse as it sinks inside her tight hole with no resistance.

With my thumb pressed to her clit, she cries out. I slide in a second finger, jack-knifing them when I feel her begin to pulse around them. Desperate noises spill from her pretty mouth as she grinds against my fingers, needing release.

I only plan on having her come around my cock tonight. Not my fingers, and not my tongue. She can soak my face in her cum when I take her again later. I need to feel all of her right now.

She sobs with frustration when I slide my hand from her

pussy and grip myself with it instead, using her wetness to cover the throbbing length. I give my shaft a couple of hard pulls as I watch her catch her breath—thighs spread wide to reveal glistening pink flesh.

The tightness in my spine lets me know that I won't be lasting long tonight, so I don't wait any more time before rearing back and burying myself deep inside of her, feeling fingernails rip into my back as Sierra cries out with the sudden fullness.

I reach up and grab the headboard, squeezing my eyes shut when I thrust into her again, cursing under my breath as she tightens around me like a fucking fist. I'm barely holding on as I thrust ruthlessly, slapping my hand on the headboard over and over again.

"Braden!" she cries as she comes quivering around me, scratching at me like an animal.

Grabbing the back of my neck, she tilts my head down, forcing me to watch her fall apart. The unguarded affection in her silver eyes has a piece of me shattering, crumbling into a pile of dust laid at her feet as I fall right there with her. I grab both of her hands from around my neck, sliding them down my skin and dropping to my elbows before intertwining our fingers together beside her head. My thrusts become sloppy, and I shoot deep inside of her with a mangled grunt.

Our chests rise together rapidly, both of us falling into a dark, dangerous pit that I don't ever want to crawl out of.

I collapse on top of her with her name on my lips.

Where it belongs.

A clang sounds from the kitchen, jolting me awake.

The bed is cold, hauntingly so as I notice the other half of my blankets are pulled up and tucked under the barren pillow. The unmistakable scent of Braden still lingers on the sheets, providing a thick sense of comfort that I didn't know I needed.

Standing up with the comforter wrapped around my naked body, I suck in a sharp breath at the sharp pain between my legs and carefully walk—or waddle, more like it—to my closed bedroom door. With my heart thumping nervously, I slowly twist the knob and pull the door open an inch.

A shirtless Braden stands fumbling with the frying pan I see resting on the stove. I can hear the quiet grumbles of a few incoherent words as he slides a flipper under a frying egg and attempts to flip it.

A girly giggle I hardly recognize slips through my grin, catching his attention as he jumps back from the oven. He spins around on his sock-covered feet wearing a nervous expression on his handsome face that I find utterly adorable. My grin doesn't dare falter as I open the door fully and walk toward him.

"Did I wake you up? Shit. I tried to be quiet," he rambles, a tinge of red moving up his neck.

Woah, is the great and mighty Braden Lowry blushing? At something I said? I don't know what universe I woke up in, but I don't think that I ever want to leave.

"Nah, I was already up," I lie.

He brushes off my fib. "Are you hungry?"

The fire alarm begins blaring through my apartment, no doubt waking up my neighbours, but I could care less. I catch sight of the large puffs of grey smoke floating behind Braden's broad shoulders and rush past him. A small flame singes the corner of a hand towel, one that he has left resting directly on the burner. I burst out laughing before I can stop myself.

"Were you planning on serving me this for breakfast?" I ask, quickly grabbing hold of the burning cloth before dumping it in the kitchen sink and turning the tap on. After the flames are extinguished, leaving nothing more than burnt fabric behind, I spin around to see Braden's rigid figure, waves of annoyance radiating from his shoulders, and a scowl on his mouth.

"And now I'm never cooking again."

"If that's how you cook, then I must agree with that brilliant idea." I giggle again, a sense of happiness falling over us and filling my belly with warmth.

"You didn't have any toaster waffles or I would have just made those."

"It's okay, Braden. Everybody has flaws," I tease, loving the way his eyes narrow at my subtle insult. I kiss away his pout.

"Careful, Sierra. Don't test me when I'm tired," he replies slyly, pulling me back to his chest and holding me when I go to step back.

I don't mind being held so tightly to this strong man, especially after the sweet gesture he just made, so I cuddle into him, pressing my cheek to his chest. "When did you get up, anyway? It's still really early."

"I couldn't really sleep. Too much on my mind."

"Oh, okay. I know that we didn't really get a chance to talk about what upset you yesterday, but I'm here if you want to talk abou—"

"No. I'm okay. Thanks, though." His voice is hard, the complete opposite of earlier, but I try not to let it weigh on me.

I'm not surprised by the change, but I can't help but let his quick rejection tear at my chest—even just a little bit.

Especially after I shared a piece of my past with him last night.

I pull away again, and this time he lets me. The simple brush-off has my throat tightening as I turn back to the sink and nod before my face can betray me.

I want to give myself a shake at the way this makes me feel. He's nothing more than a mindless screw. I can't afford to let myself feel anything for him. It won't end well. He's not somebody that can give me what I need. Whatever that may be.

Awkward silence envelops the kitchen, only intensifying my annoyance with myself. Just say something. *Get out of this situation.* "Well, thanks for breakfast any—"

"Do you want to go get some food?" He cuts off my rambling with his own, taking me by surprise. I think I even gasp. "I mean since I almost burnt your house down. It's the least that I can do."

Is he asking me on a date? Or is he just starving and doesn't want to go alone? Shit, why does it matter?

"Sure," I reply, spinning back around and shrugging as if his offer doesn't affect me.

He scratches his forearm and forces a smile.

"Okay. Uh, did you want to shower?" His eyes widen immediately and I nearly swoon from how nervous he is. "Not like . . . together, right? I mean, unless you want to? It's not like we haven't done everything else under the sun." His shaky, booming laughter is enough to crack through the awkward tension.

"If we shower together, we won't ever make it to breakfast. Let me go first. I don't trust that you won't use all the hot water." I rush past him.

He stops me when I get within an inch of him by grabbing my wrist and tugging me to his chest. "You're not going anywhere without kissing me."

My stomach swirls as I hide my burning cheeks by reaching up and gently pressing my lips to his, smiling to myself when he does the same. His thumb brushes my warm skin before he pulls away, clearing his throat.

"I'll be back!" I squeak and beeline for the bathroom. I'm about to close the door behind me when I hear him scolding himself.

"What is wrong with you? Focus, dude."

What's wrong with *you*, Braden? More like what's wrong with *me?*

I'M RUNNING a brush through my wet hair for the final time when Braden strolls inside my room with nothing but a Sierra-sized towel wrapped around his hips. A strong sense of need sweeps through me, making my legs shake as I take in the strongly carved muscles that cover his entire torso.

Small droplets of water linger on his tan skin, slowly slipping beneath the towel. My mouth dries as I beg for the towel to drop.

Seemingly reading my thoughts, Braden doesn't give me as much as a sliver of a warning before the towel falls to the floor, exposing every inch of him to my greedy stare.

"What are you doing?" I breathe, raising my hand to shield my eyes when he starts walking to the pile of his clothes from yesterday.

A ridiculous throb beats between my thighs at the pure masculine energy radiating from his shoulders. It's addictive, drawing me in until I drown beneath it. A morning beard covers his jaw, and I ache to run my palm across it, to feel the prickling against my skin.

"Crap, I guess I have to go commando," he sighs, ignoring

my question altogether when I hear the zipper of his jeans rattling around.

"You're ridiculous."

"You've never minded looking at my cock before, Sierra."

I can hear the smugness in his voice as he pulls a tight, grey short-sleeve shirt over his stomach.

"I guess things change."

"Oh?" He cocks his brow and lets his darkening eyes slither up my body. "Is that so?"

"Mhm," I hum.

"What was that?"

"Oh, screw off." I shake my head at his cockiness and anxiously smooth down my hair. His bottom lip juts out in a sudden pout that has me fighting back a grin.

"I don't think so, buddy. I'm hungry for this breakfast that I was promised."

"I'm hungry too, but not for breakfast." His handsome face has become serious and hard, amber eyes blaze with want.

My lungs fail to bring in enough of the thick air around us when he starts moving toward me, his stance suddenly becoming predatory. With wide eyes, I gulp and mutter, "The only way you're getting anything is if you feed me. With *food*."

His deep chuckle meets my ears as I pull my eyes to his and take in the easy expression he's now wearing, blessing me with a dimpled smile that has my cheeks beating with heat.

It's rare and even more unbelievably beautiful.

22

Braden

Morning-after breakfasts have never been my thing—clearly. But seeing the shine in Sierra's eyes when the waiter brought her stack of strawberry pancakes to our table seemed to be enough to drag me over to the dark side.

I'm sure her hands would have been clapping in front of her when the plate was pushed across the table if it weren't for the several eyes roaming carelessly around the restaurant. She would hate to draw attention to herself, although I'm not sure why.

Most of the gorgeous women I've met have loved attention. Maybe that's one of the reasons that I find myself so drawn to Sierra. She's the most beautiful woman I've ever met, but she doesn't let it define her. It's sexy as hell.

Her megawatt smile punches me directly in the chest as she looks up at me from her stack of pancakes. My lips lift in a lazy smile, and I lean back against the booth, tilting my head slightly.

Her long hair is pulled up into a lump on the top of her head again, allowing me to soak in the full extent of her natural beauty. I've always been a total sucker for freckles, and of course, she has plenty speckled across her porcelain skin.

She raises a curious brow when she notices my intense staring. "You know, food is way better when you eat it while it's still warm."

I look down at my plate full of assorted meat. "Might have a point there, baby. You do know your meat." It's a ridiculous, child-like tease, but when she rolls her eyes and her shoulders shake with a silent laugh, a strong sense of pride swells in my chest.

After a few moments, she's back to eating her pancakes, and I'm watching her again, content with just sitting here, soaking in her presence.

"I didn't know that you loved pancakes so much," I say, and shove a piece of crispy bacon in my mouth.

She swallows her mouthful and slides her tongue along her bottom lip to clean off the blob of red syrup that I can't seem to take my eyes off of. I watch her tongue disappear again before she speaks.

"My sister used to make me a stack every Sunday morning. It was our thing."

"You have a sister?" And why haven't I asked about your family before now?

"Yeah. Clare is a few years older than me. Her daughter, Lizzy, is the cutest thing ever." Sierra smiles wide, stabbing another piece of pancake. "My parents weren't really around when I was young, so Clare went out of her way to be a mother figure for me in a way. We're really close. Best friends, I guess you could say."

"She sounds great. You'll have to introduce us sometime."

She seems as shocked by my offer as I am, but recovers quickly, nodding once. "She'd like that. But what about you? Do you have any siblings? Or is Clayton your loaner brother?"

Laughing lightly at that, I grab my glass of orange juice in my palm and gulp down half of it while staring across the table. "Clayton could only be so lucky as to call himself my blood brother. My actual brother, Tyler, is the opposite of Clay in almost every single way."

"Isn't that a good thing?"

"Depends on what type of guy you like, I guess. Clayton is loud, obnoxious, and judges people before getting to know them like the little shit he is. Tyler is the silent broody type who doesn't care enough to judge you. The only people my brother has let get close enough to judge would be his wife, myself, and a select few friends."

Sierra nods, her brows scrunched as if she's thinking hard about something. It makes me nervous, and I begin to feel desperate, not wanting her to shut down and run out of here.

"What else should I know about you, my little fighter?"

"Like what? I doubt you want to hear about my hobbies." Her forced, mocking laugh stings worse than I care to admit. I try to push off her backhanded insult with a tight smile.

There's no way I'm going to let her stop me from finding out everything that I can about her. She's got me too interested now. I can't keep being held at arm's length.

"And if I do? Don't be shy, Sierra. Tell me something interesting."

"Alright then," she hums and taps her chin. "I started a new job at a decent-sized marketing firm pretty recently. I think that I might actually have a chance at getting somewhere in my career for the first time in what feels like forever."

I find myself enthralled with the way she speaks about it with such confidence and pride. It makes me grin.

"That's great," I praise, reaching across the table and covering her hand with mine.

The shock that flashes across her face has me coughing

awkwardly and pulling my hand back, shoving it in my lap as the unfamiliar burn of rejection scalds the palm of my hand. I want to have the right to hold her hand whenever I want to, and I don't do well with rejection.

I'm not sure what I was hoping for when I asked her to go for breakfast with me, but I know that I didn't want to leave her so quickly. I needed more time with her. It didn't matter what we did or where we went. I just needed to be with her.

I've been going around and around with my feelings for weeks, tearing myself up inside over what I wanted to do with them. But I don't think I want to keep fighting them anymore. Not if fighting them means dealing with the constant pain in my chest that only Sierra's presence can soothe.

I don't know what this all means, or if she feels even slightly the same in her feelings toward me—if there even are any beyond our shared lust for one another—but I can't stay away from her anymore. That much I do know. I would rather take my chances than keep torturing myself.

"Have you always wanted to do that?" I ask.

"Yeah. I've worked really hard to get where I am."

Her words make me think of her boss and my jaw tightens. I think he would love for her to work just a little harder—

As if sensing my discomfort, she swaps the attention to me. "What do you do? You've never talked about your work."

"I train and fight at my dad's boxing gym. I don't do anything as glamorous as you."

I crave to feel the same amount of pride in what I do as she does. I'm not ashamed of my job, but I can't help but feel like it pales in comparison to hers. When it comes to being even merely successful, I left that up to everybody else I know.

"That explains Logan's broken nose. You have one hell of a punch," she giggles, eyes sparkling. My chest puffs at her compliment before deflating just as quickly. "Maybe I could come watch you sometime?"

Her question takes me off guard. She wants to come watch me beat someone up? She doesn't seem like the violent type, although she did enjoy watching me hit Logan. But isn't that different? He at least deserved that. The guys that I fight do it solely because they love the feeling of it. There are no chances to back away once the beating starts. They're stuck there until the pain brings them to the brink of surrender.

"I never took you for the violence type," I tease. "But if you really want to go, I have a fight tomorrow night. I can get Clayton to pick you up."

"Oh, you wouldn't be picking me up?" Sierra doesn't meet my eyes when she asks, and the pink colouring her cheeks has me grinning so wide that I'm sure she thinks I'm a lunatic.

"I'll be at the gym too early getting everything ready. But I promise Clayton will take care of you. He won't spend another day on this earth if he doesn't."

Sierra seems happy enough with my answer, her eyes burning brighter than a few minutes ago. The way she's looking at me has my breath catching in my throat as I struggle to swallow back the urge to jump over the table and sit down beside her. I want to pull her tight enough that we could be super-glued together.

The waiter returns and slides his eyes over Sierra's empty plate of pancakes before asking, "Everything going good over here? I would say so."

He's teasing her, but I know immediately that I don't like it. I want him gone ASAP. Especially when Sierra flushes with embarrassment and drops her eyes to her lap.

No, I don't think so. Nobody embarrasses Sierra but *me*.

Grinding my teeth together, I push my plate toward him, letting it scrape across the table to grab his attention. I speak when his eyes finally fall on me. "I want the bill."

His chin dips in acknowledgment while he reaches into his apron and pulls out a piece of paper. After he places it down on the table, I swipe it with a forced smile.

"Thanks, Wilson." I scowl, eyeing the shiny name tag on his chest.

"I'll be back in a few minutes with the machine." I don't acknowledge him, and he leaves without another word.

"You don't have to pay for my food." Sierra reaches across the table and attempts to grab the bill from my hand. I pull it to my chest before she has the chance.

"If you want it so bad, you can always come and grab it." I cock a taunting brow, daring her to try.

She huffs. "You're a child."

"Not the first time that I've heard that, sunshine."

"Sunshine? Really? Is little fighter not good enough anymore?"

"Are you saying that you like it when I call you my little fighter?" I smirk, obsessed with the way she can't help but fight me on everything. I sit further into the booth and cross my arms for a few seconds, waiting for her to push me on it but she doesn't. "That's what I thought, baby."

"Where is that damn waiter? It's been longer than a few minutes," she rambles, physically flustered.

Her fingers brush at her hair, toying with the fallen ends. She slips her lip between her teeth, chewing on it anxiously.

Oh yeah, I got her right where I want her.

23

Sierra

"JUST OPEN THE DAMN DOOR, SOPH. I'LL BE OUT IN A MINUTE!" I shout from my bedroom, annoyed with the incessant knocking that's been going on for the past minute.

The knocking finally stops as I'm shrugging my jean jacket over my shoulders. My reflection in the stand-up mirror on the wall makes me cringe. I spent three hours getting ready, and this is what I managed to come up with? Black skinny jeans and a light washed jean jacket? Jean on jean?

There's no way that Sophie will ever let me out of the house in this.

"We needed to leave five minutes ago, Sierra!" Sophie's voice carries through the closed door.

I rip the jean jacket off and throw it across the room, watching it smack against my desk. Why does it even matter what I wear? It's not like Braden will even see me in the crowd full of people shouting and cheering, pushing their way around the fighting ring like a possessed mob. Okay, that might be a bit of a stretch.

Boxing has never been anything that I've really cared

about nor watched before. I have no idea what to expect once we get there.

The almost inaudible dinging of my phone grabs my attention. Picking it up from its spot on my mattress, I feel my lips lift in a small smile.

Braden: Wear something gold.

Gold? I don't think I have anything gold. Wait, how did he know I was struggling with what to wear?

"Sophie!" I shout seconds before footsteps pound against the floor outside of my room. The door flies open, and Sophie's grin aggravates me instantly.

"I see you've been talking with the half-wit out there," I growl, folding my arms.

"Heard that!" Clayton shouts from somewhere in the living room.

"Don't care!" I shout back and look back at Sophie, sighing, "I need something gold. Help me." I mumble the words.

"Got it." She marches toward my closet and starts tearing through the rows of clothes. Hums and haws make their way from the closet and clothes start flying around the room. The telltale sign of a migraine blurs my vision and I groan, long and heavy. Massaging my temples, I flop down on my bed.

"Please tell me that I have something to wear," I sigh. "I hate that I care this much about this. Who am I, Sophie? You?"

She slings me a glare over her shoulder before returning to the clothes. "You like him."

"I do," I mumble before I chicken out. "Is that stupid?"

"Absolutely not, S. Didn't I tell you that friends with benefits never works?"

I don't answer. I refuse to give her the satisfaction.

"It's okay. I know the truth. That's enough for me," she adds before I hear a few clangs from across the room. I keep my eyes on the ceiling. "Yes! Now we're talking."

Keeping my hands pressed flat on the bed, I push myself into a sitting position and watch Sophie pull a metallic gold, off the shoulder top from a hanger before tossing it to me. The tag pricks my finger before I rip it off and quickly tuck it under my pillow, feeling only slightly embarrassed that I didn't even remember I bought it ages ago. It's stunning, so it was probably one of my impulse buys.

I run my fingers along the silk like material and begin to feel nauseous, nerves burning a hole in my stomach. Most of the time, I avoid unfamiliar places and situations. Fear of the unknown is real, and it sucks. But there's no way I'm going to let fear ruin this for me. Not this time.

I want to put myself out there and experience something new and thrilling. And I guess I have Braden to thank for that. He makes me want to slip out of my comfort zone and breathe in new experiences. It's one of the reasons why I think I'm so addicted to being in his presence.

So, I'm going to let go, at least for tonight. The world can go back to normal in the morning.

"Thanks, Soph."

"Yeah, yeah. Just get changed so we can go," Sophie replies. She sits down on the bed, eyeing me curiously.

"You're not going to leave so I can change?"

She looks at me with pleading eyes. "Please don't make me go out there again without you. Clayton is driving me crazy."

"Fine." I nod with understanding and take the shirt to the bathroom to change.

A few minutes later, we're all situated inside Clayton's Jeep. To say I was surprised to find how absolutely pristine he keeps the interior is an understatement.

The smell of leather and cologne is thick in the air, but I can't say that I mind it much. There's not a single wrapper or fleck of dust anywhere that I can see, and I've snooped through the backseat after letting Sophie take shotgun, much to her frustration and Clayton's pleasure. I can tell that it doesn't bother him much having my best friend sitting so close to him, unable to run and hide from his ridiculous puns and that damn attentive stare that makes a girl feel like she's been placed under a microscope. Sophie, on the other hand, looks like she might jump out of the moving vehicle at any given moment.

"Please tell me we're almost there," she begs.

The street lights move over the front seats every few seconds, shining enough light for me to catch the daggers she's shooting in the side of Clayton's head.

"Oh, please. I can list at least five girls who would love to be sitting where you are." Clay clicks his tongue while strumming his hands against the steering wheel.

"Yeah, right," she scoffs.

"You don't have to be jealous, gorgeous."

"Fuck you."

"You always could."

"In your dreams, asshat."

With a quiet sigh, I lean my cheek against the cold window and tune out their pointless bickering. My eyes slide shut, letting the darkness calm down my jittery nerves.

I'm not sure what to expect tonight. The only thing I expect is to see a completely different side of the laid-back, quick-tongued playboy that I've come to know.

When he first told me that he boxes for a living, all I could think about was seeing him break Logan's nose, and suddenly I couldn't stop myself from asking to go watch him. I'm way more excited than I originally thought I would be to watch Braden in his element. Maybe if I had been spending more time getting to know what makes him *him,* instead of just how he works his dick, I would have been able to realize he was a fighter to begin with.

The scar through his eyebrow and the fresh ones over his knuckles seem more important to me now, like pieces of the puzzle I swept under the couch and forgot about. Even the way he walks—completely confident in himself and his ability to drop anyone who so much as thinks of making a wrong move without breaking a sweat—screams fighter.

I always assumed it was just his ginormous ego that called to me, making my clit swell with need with the briefest flash of his smile. But maybe it was his strength and power instead. They both radiate from his broad shoulders like sound waves, calling to me at a frequency that has my head doing a doubt take, not grasping as to how this man has such easy control over me.

"We're here," Clayton grumbles. We come to a jolting stop as he slides the Jeep into park and whips open his door, walking into the dark. I look at Sophie, my eyes wide with surprise when he slams the door behind him.

"What did I miss?"

"Nothing. Let's just go before he abandons us."

I nod quickly and open my door. The noise hits me like a freight train as soon as I step outside. There's no music playing, the noise comes solely from shouted voices, the clear aggression behind them taking me by surprise. I grab hold of Sophie's hand and squeeze when she steps out and gasps.

"We're going to die," she groans, eying the bulky guys standing in front of the front door, chatting with Clayton. There's a glowing red sign above the door that spells Rampage. "I pissed him off so badly he wants to have us killed."

"We're not going to die." I hope. "Come on." I gather up my confidence and pull her toward the men.

"About time!" Clayton yells when he notices us slowly creep up to him. "This is Roy." He points to the taller but leaner of the two men and I get a grin of welcome from him before we're moving onto the bulkier man. "And this is Brooks."

Gulping, I force my lips to spread in a welcoming smile. "Nice to meet you. I'm Sierra."

They both return my smile with more genuine ones. The shockingly handsome, much stronger looking one—Brooks, I think, offers me his hand. I'm taken aback by the strength of his grip when I place my hand in his, shaking it before dropping it back to my side. I eye him curiously, focusing on the familiar, thick bushy brows, prominent cupid's bow and amber-coloured eyes that I could have sworn I've looked into quite a number of times.

I nearly sputter an embarrassed laugh when he winks at me, informing me subtly that he caught on to my gawking.

"I've heard all about you, Sierra. The pleasure is all mine," Brooks says in a low rumble.

My cheeks burn as I grow confused. Heard all about me? From who? Clayton? I go to offer him a forced smile, but he's already moved on, slinging a massive arm around Clayton's shoulders. *Okay then.*

"And I'm Sophie." I hear from beside me, the voice suddenly entirely at ease. When I catch the slight flutter of her eyelashes as she stares up at Brooks, I know that it's time to go.

"Hello, Sophie," he chuckles, shaking her hand like he did mine.

"Should we go? I think we're already late, Clayton." I expel a heavy breath of relief when he turns to me, nodding. He says his quick goodbyes to the two men before pushing open the door and holding it for us.

"Come on, Soph." I grab her hand again and yank her past Roy and Brooks, forcing her to follow Clayton inside. When we finally make the front doors, she turns to me, visibly annoyed.

"You're such a pussy block, S."

"I spotted a few grey hairs in that man bun. He's way too old for you," I mutter.

"Whatever."

Our shoulders knock together when we're brushed off to the side by a couple of dominant looking women shoving their way through the growing crowd around us. Panic slices up my spine as we become surrounded with large, sweaty bodies.

Steeling my spine, I refuse to let fear rule me tonight. So, with a shake of my head that I hope is enough to clear out my worries, I turn my attention to the view in front of us and steady myself.

Oh, shit. I definitely wasn't prepared for this.

24

Sierra

THE CROWD IS TERRIFYING.

Countless loud voices scratch at my eardrums as we slowly venture further into the gym, Sophie's hand still clasped in mine.

The cement floor looks cold, but the air is hot and sickly humid. I feel too exposed in my current clothes. My skin crawls as several pairs of eyes drag their way up my body when we begin pushing our way deeper into the mob.

We follow Clay as best we can, but it's hard to keep him in focus while being shoved around. At this point, the only thing keeping me from turning around and running away is that Braden wouldn't have been okay with me being somewhere I could get hurt. Or I hope not, at least. He has faith in me and the people here, and I hold onto that like a lifeline.

Sophie gives my hand a hard squeeze, and after a quick look around, I realize we've lost Clay in the mess of people around us.

Slipping my lip between my teeth, I attempt to stand on my toes and search the gym. It's not so easy, though. Not in an entire building full of mostly tall, brown-haired men. Searching for Clay is like searching for a needle in a haystack.

"Just keep going straight!" Sophie shouts.

Her eyes are wide as they move over the people pressed up against us with seemingly no sense of personal space. With a huff, I stick out my elbow and push, leading us even further into the crowd. I duck my head down and yank Sophie's hand, forcing her to follow me. It works like a charm until a tree-truck-sized arm pushes out in front of me, nearly hitting my cheek. I freeze. The arm presses against my collarbone, forcing me to stay still.

My heartbeat picks up, and nerves start to twist my stomach into a boulder-sized knot. I follow the length of the arm until I find a sharp jaw. The thick scar trailing the length of the bone only fills me with even more unwanted fear.

"Are you lost?" the stranger asks, his voice so hoarse it causes a shiver to run up my spine.

"No," I respond quickly. The stranger's dark eyes light up with humour as I lie to him.

"You sure?" He looks past me to ask the question to Sophie this time. Her grip on my hand tightens.

"We're fine. Thanks."

He cocks his brow, serving me with a look that makes me feel like gum beneath his shoe. "Let me take you—"

"Fuck off, Tavares. They said they're fine," a different voice says. The rumble comes from a stern-faced, tatted-up man.

The arm drops from in front of me as the asshole takes a step back, jaw clenching fiercely. Clearly, he doesn't like to be told no. Fancy that.

"Always walking around like you own the place, Tyler," he spits.

The two brawny men stand firm and broad in front of

each other, but I don't miss the way our tattooed saviour shifts himself in front of me.

"Always walking around harassing women, Tavares," Tyler replies, not taking his narrowed gaze off of the guy.

Thankfully, Tavares doesn't seem to want to make a scene and spins on his heel with a mumbled curse before walking off.

"Where the fuck is Clayton?" Tyler moves to face Sophie and me, growling a curse under his breath while running a large hand through his head of short black hair.

I shrug both shoulders. Tyler's towering height, slim waist, and wide back instantly remind me of Braden, and I nearly smack myself upside the head when I remember where I've heard his name before.

"You're Braden's brother, right?" I ask him. The knots in my stomach begin to unravel.

Tyler dips his chin and smiles, looking as if the past few minutes have already been forgotten. He's happy to be introduced as Braden's brother. I think I like him already.

"You're Sierra and Sophie, right? I know that my brother may be a fucking idiot most of the time, but he wouldn't be stupid enough not to have somebody here with you. So, tell me where Clayton is, and I'll knock him around a bit for the lot of us."

"That's us. And I wouldn't fight you on that one. We're lucky that we ran into you. It's insane here. Is it always so crowded?"

He tilts his head side to side in an "eh" gesture. "Mostly just when Braden fights. The guy's got quite the fan club."

For some reason, I expect to hear jealousy in Tyler's tone but am relieved when the only thing I pick up on is pride. Knowing that Braden is surrounded by people who care for him so deeply spears me with a warm and fuzzy feeling.

"As great as it is to meet you, Tyler, I would really love to get out of this crowd," Sophie cuts in, a note of frustration in her voice. I'm reminded of where we are and wince, taking a step closer to Sophie and clutching her elbow.

"Follow me," Tyler says with a firm dip of his chin.

I watch in awe as the crowd parts for him, leaving more than enough room for us to catch our breath.

He leads us through a vast archway that separates the front half of the gym from the back half. There are two men standing in front of the entrance but they let us through with a quick nod in Tyler's direction.

A gasp gets stuck in my throat as I take in the new space. It's much bigger and darker than where we just were, making it more difficult to see the giant, elevated boxing ring that's been placed in the middle of the room. There's an empty hallway to the right of us that I assume leads toward a locker room, and two others, each one on the opposite side of the ring. There are large square lights around the platform that are turned off, leaving it dark.

Anger sizzles in my blood when I spot Clayton leaning against the thick velvet ropes lining the edges, his cell phone pressed to his ear. His body is completely relaxed, not a care in the world as to where Sophie and I may or may not have ended up as he continues chatting with whoever's on the other end of the call.

"Forget something, Clay?" Tyler asks, stalking toward him with a thick sense of power.

I snicker when Tyler brings his hand up and smacks it against the back of Clayton's head. The angry man seems to pull Clayton's head from the clouds as he spins to look back at us, eyes wide with worry.

"Yeah, or maybe a couple of somebody's?" Sophie hisses. I can tell she wants to walk over there and beat some sense into him, so I tighten my grip on her elbow and ignore the glare beating into my temple when she whirls to face me.

Clay stays silent for a few seconds as if he's running through every possible reply for the one that will piss us off the least. But unfortunately for him, there won't be a good enough answer when it comes to a pissed-off Sophie. Or me, for that matter.

"See, what happened was I had to take a piss and the bathrooms up front are always so dirty, so I had to use the ones back here, and then by the time I was on my way back out, I saw that Tyler had you—"

"You didn't even give it to her either, you dumbass," Tyler grunts, snapping his attention to my bare neck before pinning Clayton with a deadly glare.

My brows pull inward as my eyes dart between them. "Give me what?"

It's Clayton who answers me, wearing a sheepish smile that looks completely out of place on his clean, sharp features. "Braden's lucky chain. He gave it to me this morning and told me to have you wear it tonight. I meant to hand it off to you in the car, but Sophie distracted me."

My lips part. There's a warm, buttery feeling wrapping me up in a tight embrace while doves take flight in my belly, their wings flapping so hard I nearly reach down and place a hand on my stomach to see if I can feel them from the outside.

"Oh," I breathe, flushed all the way to my toes. "Can I still wear it? I mean, if it's not a big deal?"

Holy shit it's hot in here. Am I sweating?

I thought I had a greater understanding of the extent of Braden's feelings, but I apparently highly misjudged the depth of how much he cares for me. I expected to find him swimming near the top of the ocean, not deep enough that his stomach could brush the sand. The realization has my heart thumping to an off-tempo beat.

"He would string me up a pole by my balls if I didn't let

you wear it," Clayton snorts, reaching into the front pocket of his jeans and pulling out a thick silver chain.

The silver is dull, worn, and well-loved. Something that feels a hell of a lot like love swells inside of me before I shove the feeling out of sight.

With tentative fingers, I pluck the chain from Clayton's outstretched hand and hold it gently, like I would a piece of my great-grandmother's fine china. I let it fall from one hand to the other, shivering as the cold metal tickles my palms.

The return of voices has me closing my fist around the chain and spinning around. I watch the crowds begin filling in around the ring, the excited whoops and hollers making me tense up.

"Let me put it on you before you drop the damn thing and lose it," Sophie murmurs, the pitch of her voice slightly higher than normal.

Eying her with a scrutinizing look, I see the swoon in her eyes and breathe a laugh.

After I've dropped the chain in her open palm, I feel the cold bite of it over the burning skin of my throat before she quickly clasps it and moves to my side again. "There. Now let's find somewhere to stand before we're stuck sandwiched between a bunch of sweaty old men."

Tyler nudges my arm and points to the empty space a few feet down the ring, directly underneath one of the giant lamps that have turned on sometime during our exchange of Braden's chain. The reminder has me reaching to the hollow of my throat and toying with the silver chain between two fingers.

Sophie and I follow after Tyler and Clayton as they lead the way before stopping and moving so we're sandwiched between them. The protective stance has me smiling.

In all honesty, it's a relief having these two as our bodyguards for the night. Even if Clayton isn't exactly the ideal candidate.

It only takes a few minutes for the building to fill. Hands and arms push against my back, pushing and pulling me as best they can before they're shoved back by either Clayton or Tyler. I can tell that the two men are becoming frustrated, but they try not to show it, keeping their mouths shut and their bodies tight.

It's not until the ceiling lights transform from a bright white to a mesmerizing, shimmering gold that they break out in beaming smiles. A brick drops in my stomach as excitement begins to buzz under my skin.

Smoke crawls over our feet, slowly rising in the air until it toys with the bottoms of my leather pants. It swirls higher and higher before spilling over the edges of the boxing ring. I spot Brooks beside the entrance to the hallway closest to us and nearly choke on a breath when a massive, shirtless figure begins moving toward him. The voices around me get louder as the seconds pass.

Suddenly, two rows of beaming white teeth come into focus, and I smile too, completely enamoured by the stunning confidence behind the star-studded smile. It's a smile that breeds a sense of victory and worship.

There's a deep, husky voice shooting through what sounds like a microphone, but I ignore it, too busy watching the way Braden's massive biceps stretch above his head and toes tap the floor with a sort of grace that I never expected from such a big man. It probably sounds ridiculous, considering boxers have incredible balance and control, but seeing the fluid way he moves his body has my mouth gaping in surprise.

Fingering the chain around my neck again, I watch Braden as he finally makes his way into the shimmering light. A shiny black robe hangs loosely from his shoulders, leaving his defined chest bare for all to see. My mouth waters as the individual muscles flex on their own accord, almost as if to torture me.

An unmistakable itch of jealousy worms up my body at knowing that his miraculous body is on full display. It's a ridiculous feeling, considering he isn't even mine to begin with, but that doesn't help settle me as much as I wish that it would.

Forcing my eyes to move from the solid abdomen in front of me, I drop them to the gold, mid-thigh length shorts that fit snugly to his muscular legs. The material stretches tight as he expertly hands his robe over to Brooks, who I'm beginning to piece together might be his father, and pulls open the velvet ropes to climb inside the ring.

My eyes become saucers when I steal a glance at my gold attire, finally feeling the pieces fall together.

Well played, Braden. Well played.

He raises a fist in the air as the excited hollers continue to praise him, no doubt adding to his already enormous ego. I can't find it in me to care, though. I'm too busy letting a heavy sense of pride shine in my eyes as I stare at him, not daring to move my gaze from his handsome face.

A cheek-splitting smile spreads across my face as soon as his wandering eyes clash with mine, brimming with so much emotion. A beyond obvious, cheesy wink from my playboy boxer is all it takes to forget about everything and lift my own arms in the air to join in the excited cheers, happier than I have been in years.

25

Braden

Dad leans back against the wall with a deep scowl, his arms crossed hard enough for the skin to bulge. "You ready?"

I slip the smooth black and gold robe over my shoulders and give a cocky grin to my reflection in one of the wall-length mirrors hung along the locker room wall.

"Always."

Boxing matches are a more common event in Rampage now that we spent the money updating and expanding the building to accommodate a separate fighting ring and more people. The renovations wouldn't have even been a possibility without my brother loaning us the money, but we've more than paid it back over the past year by hosting these matches. They bring in more cash than we expected. Especially once the high-rollers get interested.

Everything went as planned today while I was getting the usual last-minute jobs done, but I felt the pressure harder than most days. It was easy to recognize why.

Tonight is special. Not because I get to show up countless fighters with my well-worked-for skills, but because for the first time ever, I have someone out in the crowd that I'm actually trying to impress. I don't want Sierra's first experience watching me fight to be a disappointment. My pride couldn't take it.

Usually, I'm too concentrated on the guy in front of me to care about the pussy I'm going to be getting once I step out of the ring a winner. But this isn't just any ordinary pussy out there tonight. This is Sierra we're talking about. Just the thought of demeaning her to the word pussy has my throat burning with the threat of throwing up.

"I ran into Clayton earlier. He introduced me to a couple of his friends," Dad says, accusation flickering in his voice. My brow raises, pushing him to elaborate. "I'm assuming that they're also your friends?"

"Happy you picked up on that, old man." I snort. "Yeah, Sierra's mine."

His eyes widen slightly and he chokes on a laugh. I don't know why, but the reaction has my face hardening to stone. "She's *yours*?"

My eyes narrow into slits. "Yeah. What about it?"

His hands come up in front of his chest, held out in surrender. There's a curiosity behind his calm composure that has me sliding an invisible guard up.

"I didn't know you were dating anyone. That's all."

"Dating?" I choke on the word. "I wouldn't go that far. We both know that I wouldn't even know what to do with that sort of label."

Dropping his arms, he moves toward my locker and grabs my gloves before offering them to me. I take them with a bit more force than necessary and stretch out my wrapped hands, feeling the black material stretch around the knuckles.

"Relax, buddy. Honest mistake." He laughs. "So, you're just friends, then?"

Just friends? Somehow that label is even worse. "Ah, slow down there. I never said that."

Shaking his head, he sits down on the bench in front of me and clasps his hands in his lap. He looks like he feels out of place with his twiddling thumbs and clouded eyes floating around the room. Dad hasn't fought in a long time, not after he tore his rotator cuff one too many times. He misses it. I hate that he has to sit back and watch me, unable to feel the liberation and freedom the way that I do.

"Just don't get distracted out there. You don't get days off for any of the injuries you're going to get trying to impress one of the girls you're banging."

"The only girl I'm banging," I correct him, feeling the need to clarify it for him. For a guy deciding to get hitched to someone half his age, he's immensely judgmental of everyone else's relationships. Although, does what he thinks really even matter?

"Do you really think so low of me?"

"Yes," he replies without hesitation. I inhale sharply, my mouth dropping into a frown. "Sorry. Of course not, Braden. My perfect child. The poster child for monogamous relationships. I must be thinking of my other son who was sneaking girls into my house in the middle of the night since he was fifteen. Oh wait, my other son is happily married."

Ignoring the hurt spearing my stomach from his low opinion of me, I slip my gloves on and strap them like always.

"Okay, okay. I get it. Point taken."

"Just stay focused on the fight. If Sierra really is the only girl you're seeing, maybe she should come around the house sometime. I'm sure Lana would love to cook for her," he offers.

"Sure. If that'll get you to lay off, then consider it set in stone," I reply, although I have a feeling that Sierra would rather eat rocks than what Lana calls cooking.

The surprise in Dad's eyes is evident as he watches me,

intent on making me squirm and admit that I would rather spoon out my own eyes than go for another awkward dinner with Lana. But when I keep my mouth shut like a good little boy, he gives my shoulder a squeeze.

"Jesse lacks stamina. Strike first and the win is yours. Good luck."

"Thanks, Dad." I grin and his hand falls from my shoulder. As he makes his way to the entrance, I start to bounce in place, shaking off the nerves. The cheers reach my ears and I know that it's time.

Any prior thoughts that I have disappear as I shake out my arms and walk down the hallway. The usual fog begins to crawl up my legs as golden light pours over my shoulders. Screaming voices pierce my eardrums as I confidently shrug out of my robe and hand it over to Dad.

I pull at the velvet ropes and step inside the ring, basking in the adrenaline and screams of encouragement from the crowd. My feet repeatedly tap the pad as I let my eyes start sifting through the crowd, desperate to find my golden girl. And when I do, my arm shoots to the ceiling in a victory-like celebration.

She wore what I asked. Pride surges through me when our eyes meet, my lungs constricting in a way that has me wanting to clutch my chest. I fight off the feeling and let a smile light up my face, aching to scream a hurray at the ceiling when she smiles back, shining from head to toe with pure, unfiltered bliss. The gold top clinging to her skin is a near-perfect match to the colour of my shorts and gloves. She looks exactly how I pictured her.

I swear my heart slides to my throat when the light catches on the silver chain wrapped loosely around her dainty neck, the shine capturing my attention and holding it hostage as the room blurs behind her.

There was a part of me that didn't expect her to wear it. To snuff it up to her pride and refuse to wear something of mine when I haven't even told her how I feel. But she *is* wearing it. And I don't think that I ever want it back. The rush of contentment that falls on my shoulders fills me with more than enough confidence to make this a quick, easy fight. I've never wanted to bail on a fight so bad in my life. I need to touch her, tell her that she's mine and there's no longer any room for discussion.

When I hear my opponent's name being called out, I force myself to pull out of the trance and collect myself. After shooting her a cheesy wink that has her throwing her arms up to cheer me on, I finally turn my attention to Jesse.

He makes his way through the ropes, meeting me in the centre of the ring with an icy scowl that I can't wait to sink my knuckles into. He's about an inch or two shorter than me, but wider. Much wider. If it weren't for the constant drug tests we run before matches, I would assume that he's become good friends with a performance-enhancement drug named Steroid. His size doesn't shake me, though. I've trained and fought bigger guys than Jesse. He might be stronger, but I *know* that I'm faster on my feet.

Keeping my eyes from drifting to where I know Sierra stands watching is a new form of torture. *No distractions, Braden. Forget she's there.* The reminder has me shaking my head as if the simple movement would somehow do what I've been unable to do for weeks now.

My dad has moved to the crowd now, and I spot him holding my mouthguard from between the ropes. I slip off one of my gloves and pop in the guard, gnawing on the silicone out of habit. It's always driven my dad crazy, but the fear of pissing off the old bastard has never stopped me from doing anything.

I slip my glove back on before tapping my hands to Jesse's extended ones. Taking a step back, I raise my arms to protect my chest seconds before the round begins and Jesse throws the first punch.

As THE HOT, thick air starts to fill my burning lungs once again, I let my arm hang from the hand of the referee in celebration of my hard-earned win. It only took six rounds for Jesse to give up a win that he was never going to get, but it was a hard, exhausting six rounds. I'll be sore tomorrow for sure.

I know Dad's waiting outside the ring—having seen him take off in that direction as soon as I claimed victory—ready to collect my exhausted body in case I drop dead any minute. Which, if it happens, I wouldn't be surprised.

Jesse deserved way more credit than we gave him. He was faster than I expected for being so massive, and more domineering, too. But sloppy with his tells, like a rookie. Like Clayton. That's what cost him the round, not my speed or experienced throws.

As soon as my arm flops back against my side, I carry myself to the edge of the ring and let Dad help me through the ropes and back to the locker room.

"I hate you," I hiss when he doesn't make enough room for both of us to fit side by side through the entrance. My side bumps the door handle and I wince, gnashing my teeth.

The locker room has never looked more inviting as I fall onto the wooden bench and squeeze my eyes shut, trying to ignore the throbbing coming from the left side of my face.

"You didn't strike first," Dad points out. He sits down beside me with a large medical kit. I have no clue when he went and got that, but I don't give a rat's ass as long as it helps with this fucking pain.

"Oh fuck off, you old shit."

"That was insane!" A shrill voice bouncing off the walls only deepens the throb in my forehead as I throw my hands over my ears.

"Your eyebrow!" Sierra gasps, pushing her way past an exhilarated Sophie to crouch in front of me, concern swimming in her silver eyes.

Suddenly the only touch I feel is hers as she drags her thumb above what I can only assume is a decently split brow. My eyes close at the gentle touch as the throb becomes a thing of the past.

"How bad do I look?" I grit out, flinching at the sting in my bottom lip as I speak.

"You've definitely looked better," she says. Her beautiful face is all scrunched up with concern. I want to reach out and grab onto her, but her fingertips leave my face before I can, and I'm left with a raw feeling of disappointment.

"Here, let me," I hear her tell my dad before he's getting up and leaving the locker room.

"You want me all alone, huh?" I ask, watching her with an intensity that I'm sure she feels in her gut. She scrunches her lips to the side as she focuses on what she'll need to use to clean me up.

"Obviously," she teases.

After a few silent seconds, a wet towel is pressed to my brow, bringing a burning sensation with it. There's an unguarded sense of worry on her face, and I would be lying if I said it didn't fill me with pleasure to have her want to fix me up. I want to bottle up the look in her eyes and keep it for a bad day.

"Your concern is adorable, baby. But I always thought our first time roleplaying nurse and patient would involve a bed, not a wooden bench."

She replies by pressing down *way* harder than necessary on the cut, laughing lightly when my features twist in pain.

"Hey, hey. Take it easy. I'm wounded." I grin, ignoring my sore lip and reach up to wrap my fingers around her small, dainty wrist. Her skin is warm and soft and I want nothing more than to go home and feel every inch of it pressed against mine. "I'm just teasing, my little fighter. I really do appreciate your help."

She seems pleased with my more *sincere* words as she pulls the cloth away from my face and nods. "You shouldn't need stitches, but I'm guessing you already knew that."

I did, but it's adorable that she still felt the need to tell me. "You know what I do need, though?"

She cocks a brow, entertaining the question.

"A celebratory kiss. I did win for you, after all."

Sierra rolls her eyes, only making me inch closer to her, not buying the uninterested facade. I slowly grab the wet fabric from between her fingers and set it down beside me. Her cheeks darken, eyes wandering off behind me.

"Shy doesn't suit you, gorgeous," I mumble, gently pulling her attention back to me. My fingers itch to touch her warm cheeks, to run them down the soft skin that her long lashes flutter against like the wings of a butterfly.

I watch as she rolls her lips, almost as if the voice in her head is telling her the same thing as mine. *Calm the fuck down.* It's an impossible task on most days, but as I fall from an adrenaline high with Sierra knelt in front of me, her concentration so focused on fixing me up and making sure that I'm okay, impossible has taken on a whole new meaning.

"You neither," she counters. "If you want something, why don't you take it? The Braden I know would rather be castrated than let his nerves sho—"

"Is that a challenge?" I cut her off, sliding my fingers from her wrists to her elbows before gently pulling her from her kneeling position and onto my lap.

"Does it sound like one?" she breathes, wiggling her ass on my thighs. My eyes darken, heat flaring in my groin as she rubs against my hardening cock with a knowing smirk.

"You're playing a very dangerous game, fighter." My gaze is hungry, primitive as I become transfixed on the way her chest rises and falls so quickly, her attraction to me so obvious. It's like looking in a goddamn mirror.

Two small, warm hands fall to my shoulders, fingers slightly kneading at the sore muscles. "Sorry," she whispers.

I let out a content sigh and press my forehead to hers, basking in the charged energy that's begun to circle us. With a large open palm, I hold the side of her face, my eyes anchored to hers as I trace the shape of her lower lip with my thumb. Sierra tugs it up in a smile that I easily return before sliding my hand to her nape and pulling her toward me. My eyes slide shut and our lips brush, the touch so gentle that I struggle to catch my breath. My pulse is fast and thumping like a kick drum. *Fuck*. It feels like I've just run a marathon.

Suddenly my hand on her neck isn't enough, and I'm gripping her hip with a splayed palm, kneading it and using it to pull her closer. A groan slips between us when her leather-clad centre slides against my cock, our clothes the only thing keeping me from taking her right here.

"Braden," she whimpers, the sound so soft, like a desperate plea.

Her fingers move from my shoulders, finding purchase at the back of my neck a moment later. I wish that I didn't love the sound of my name on her lips as much as I do. It only fuels my need to hear it fall from those pretty lips that much more.

"I knew we should have just waited in the car," my best friend grunts, joining us again. The locker room door slams shut a few seconds later. Sierra jumps away from me at the sound of his voice, struggling to stand on her own feet, and leaving my lap unbearably cold.

Annoyance slithers under my skin but I try to ignore it, not wanting to piss Sierra off.

But one look at Clayton's arrogant smirk and my attempt at calmness crashes and burns. "Clay. Can you please get the *fuck* out of here?"

The prick turns to point at the blonde beside him. She's already glaring at him, arms crossed firmly. "Wrong person, brother. Take it up with this one. I wanted to go, but she refused to leave without Sierra."

"Which clearly was the wrong decision," Sophie speaks up, embarrassment flushing her cheeks. Her eyes flick between Sierra and me with a fierce sense of curiosity.

"I'll take good care of your friend," I promise her before straightening up beside my girl and properly introducing myself. "It's nice to officially meet you. I was afraid Sierra was going to keep me hidden in her closet of dirty secrets forever."

With a pinch to Sierra's waist, I kiss the top of her head and pull her back flush to my front, wrapping my arms around her as my light laughter brushes her hair.

Sophie's nose crunches in evident disgust as she watches us. "I bet. Anyway, I'm out of here. Call if you need me, Sierra.

Without sparing either of us a second look, she clutches Clayton's hand in hers, taking him by surprise, and heads for the door, letting it close behind her.

I'm not sure what the two of them have planned tonight, but I'm glad I won't be finding out. Clayton hasn't gotten laid in a very, very long time, and if Sophie is anything like Sierra, she'll eat him alive.

I stare at the woman leaning back against my chest and

smile, feeling completely at ease. With a sigh, I slide my thumb under Sierra's shirt and rub the smooth skin above her pants. "You jumped away from me pretty quickly back there. You don't happen to be embarrassed by me, do you, baby?"

As if commanded by my words, she spins around in my arms, placing her hands on my chest to steady herself. "Why? Would that manage to chip away at your giant ego?"

"No." I shrug. "But it would make what I have planned for you later a bit more interesting."

Her eyes double in size, and I don't miss the way her throat bobs with a massive swallow. The thought of taking her home and hearing her scream my name while I fuck her against every surface in my apartment has my cock hardening, pressing into her back. Mental pictures become a distraction. I'm more than happy to take her to my place and keep her in my bed for hours—days even.

"Who said I was coming home with you?" she croaks, pushing back against me just enough to let me know that she can feel exactly what she does to me.

"Me."

"Always the gentleman," she scoffs but nods toward the heavy gym bag resting a few feet behind me. "Let's go then. I work tomorrow morning."

With a helpless grin that has me feeling like a little boy, I push myself off the bench and collect my shit. Pulling open the locker room door, I wait for Sierra to walk past me before letting my right palm connect with her ass. Her shriek is immediate, bringing a chuckle up my dry throat as she spins around with her eyes narrowed.

"My God, you're an actual teenager."

"You say it like it's a bad thing. We both know you love it."

"Just shut up and take me home."

"Yes, ma'am."

26

Sierra

"KNOCK KNOCK."

Peeling my eyes off my computer screen, I blink past the burn from staring at the bright screen for hours and see Cole leaning in the doorway to my office. He's wearing a light grey suit today with the sleeves uncuffed and rolled twice, paired with shiny black dress shoes. His aura is confident and arrogant, like he knows some big secret that nobody else does.

I haven't had to spend too much time alone with Cole over the past two weeks, but this is the first time that he's come across this way. Most of the time, he's too concerned with trying to butter me up to let his true colours show. But I've always known this arrogance would make an appearance sooner than later.

Most men like him have a strong arrogant side, one that doesn't usually appear until they have you wrapped around your finger, unable to let their true personality turn you away, already too enraptured by them to care.

"Hi, Cole. What can I do for you?" I clear my throat and plaster on a smile.

Cole was the last person I was hoping to deal with today.

It's just past lunch, and having been plagued with a killer migraine this morning, I skipped it, not trusting my stomach to handle anything other than a glass of flat Ginger Ale.

"Let me start by saying you look beautiful today," Cole says.

Right. With my finger-combed hair and wrinkled clothes, I look ridiculously unprofessional. But after being woken up in the early morning with Braden's tongue between my thighs, I fell back asleep way too late and slept past my alarm. It's a miracle that I even made it today in the first place. I can't say that it wasn't worth the risk, though. Because it definitely was.

In the past two weeks since my first boxing match, Braden's only managed to slither farther under my skin. When I'm not at the office, I'm with him. And in the moments that we're not together, the thoughts of him consume me. I *let* them consume me. I should be more frustrated with how far inside my chest he's managed to bury himself, and I hate that I ache for him to stay there forever.

My house, his house, dinner, the movies, we've been doing it all. I feel like a teenager again with all of this so-called "dating." At least, I would consider it dating. I know that Braden does too.

We haven't exactly put a label on what we're doing, but he's been adamant that he hasn't been seeing anybody else, and I haven't even thought about anybody else since we first met. I'm sure that if I asked him for a label, he would give me one. But what pisses me off the most is that I can't get myself to ask.

Labels bring something heavy and expecting to a relationship. The word girlfriend comes with the expectation of putting your partner above and beyond everything else. And I can't do that. I can't promise that I'll put my life, my *career*, on the back burner for him if he asked me to. The ugly sinking feeling taking up shop in my stomach is exactly why I refuse to label our relationship. It would ruin what we've built. I know it would.

I turn back to Cole with an ache in my chest. My boss seems to think his compliment permits him to drag his eyes down my torso in a way that leaves me itching to wrap myself in a blanket. I swallow the wad beginning to form in my throat and stiffly say, "Thank you."

"I also wanted to stop by to personally escort you to the meeting happening in the boardroom in just a few minutes. It's going to be a jaw-dropper."

His words bring back the confusion that I felt when I opened up my emails this morning to see a meeting with the entire firm scheduled for today. It wasn't posted on the calendar Friday, so it had to have been added over the weekend, although it's highly unusual for such a big meeting to be planned on such short notice. A Monday no doubt.

"A meeting, right? Did I miss an email about it? It wasn't on the schedule before I left on Friday and I wasn't told about it until a couple of hours ago in your email."

"Oh, no. The meeting was pushed up a few weeks. I understand your confusion, but I promise it'll make sense soon. Are you ready?"

It's weird but plausible. The tension drains from my muscles at the realization that it wasn't my fault. After working at my previous job and missing the due date of our marketing pitch for one of my boss's highest-paying clients, I now make sure to check my calendar twice a day, terrified of making the same mistake. That mishap cost me a shit load of respect and nearly my job altogether.

With a reluctant nod, I stand and brush my sweaty hands down my skirt. Cole's excitement is borderline revolting as he watches me closely, not moving from his spot in the doorway until I'm mere inches in front of him.

"Let's go then." He holds out his arm for me to take and with hesitation, I do.

Luckily, the board room is only a few doors down from my office, leaving only a couple of minutes of awkward silence between us. I can tell that he wants to talk to me, but I avoid him as best I can while being so close to his side. His good looks don't have the same appeal as they did just a few weeks ago. It's like someone has reached inside my brain and flipped off the *Cole is attractive* switch. And if I were to guess who that somebody was, I'm sure that I would be right.

When we reach the glass door, I peer in and wince. A room full of people packed in like sardines waits a few feet away. Some sit, some stand, but the one thing everyone has in common is the confusion etched on their faces as they look toward the front of the room. Clark Brenton stands stiffly at the head of a long, dark table, assessing each and every person with a scrutiny that has my skin itching.

It's so quiet that you could hear a pin drop when Cole opens the door and leads us inside. Heads turn and curious, maybe even envious eyes observe me. When Cole turns to face me, I let my arm fall limp to my side. I flinch when he pats my lower back, his pinky brushing the top of my ass.

He mumbles quickly, "Have a seat and enjoy. I look forward to talking to you afterward."

I manage to nod before moving to the lone empty chair that rests against the back wall. Clark's voice echoes with authority as he begins to speak. A shared sense of nervousness floats along the room, sitting heavy and thick. Looking from one set of rigid shoulders to the next, I realize that I'm not the only one who has no idea what this meeting is about. None of us do.

A gorgeous blonde sits with perfect posture on the left side of the table, two chairs down from where Clark stands, his thin lips moving as he addresses the room. A sleek, well-ironed navy pantsuit covers the woman's athletic build. It matches the colour of her eyes perfectly. I notice that after they've narrowed in on me, lit with barely controlled anger.

The intensity has me swallowing an invisible lump. It's then that I begin to feel watched. Turning my head slowly, I see several sets of eyes on me. They all look at me like they've found me tossing kittens onto a busy highway.

The intensity of their sudden hatred has me touching the base of my neck, feeling my raging pulse beneath my fingertips. Suddenly freezing, a shiver racks down my spine.

"The expansion in Toronto will only push our clientele to the next level. And with the team management selected, I have no doubt we'll be up and running in no time," Clark announces.

A list of several names appears on the screen at the same time that my hand flies to my mouth. Mine rests five spots from the top.

Sierra Caster - Marketing Manager

What. The. Fuck?

I meet Cole's eager stare from across the room, fully aware that my jaw hangs unhinged, but not giving enough of a shit to reattach it. This is some sort of ploy to get into my pants. It has to be. I haven't earned this job. Hell, I haven't even been here long enough to earn my choice of fancy coffee creamers in the staff lounge.

It feels wrong—*dirty* even. Like I slept my way to a promotion when I haven't done anything of the sort. Everyone has to be thinking the same thing. I can feel it in the way they look at me, like they're disgusted by me.

Women shouldn't need to sleep their way to the top of anything, let alone a job. Every feminist bone in my body is snapping right now while trying to convince me to throw two middle fingers into the air and scream *fuck you*! It's what I should do, right?

The boardroom is silent, everyone either staring at me or pretending they're not while they are. It's brief, subtle flicks of their eyes or full-blown stares. Nothing in between. And as soon as Clark dismisses the meeting, promising to set something up for the members of the Toronto team this week to discuss the job, there isn't a moving limb in the room.

I feel like the walls are closing in on me. The longer I stay here, facing more judgment than ever before, the harder it is to breathe. The panic in my chest has my breath catching with every inhale. I start to cough as I fumble out of my seat on wobbly knees.

Need to get out of here. Need to breathe.

Grasping at my chest, I sprint to the door and shove it open, the cold air on my face sticking to tears that I didn't know were there. My fingers fumble in my pocket until they grip my phone, pulling it out as I dial the number of the only person I need right now.

With a shaky hand, I lift the phone to my cheek and listen to the dial tone. I brace myself along a dark, quiet hallway and choke back a sob.

"Well, if it isn't my favourite girl. What do I owe the honour?"

Braden's voice is like a wrecking ball, smashing apart the last remaining columns holding me up as I crumble. I can feel the tears streaming down my face, scorching the skin where they fall.

"Baby," he whispers, and I hear something like protectiveness in his voice. It settles down on me like a weighted blanket, comforting me in a small way that I didn't think was possible. "Where are you? I'm coming to get you."

My head falls to the wall behind me as I place a hand over my mouth and try to silence my cries, suddenly overwhelmed with shame. My next words come out watery and weak. "Work. Brenton Marketing. It's downtown. I'm in a dark hallway on the third floor."

I hear him shout something to someone and then the slamming of a door before he speaks again. "I'm on my way, sweetheart, and I'm going to stay on the phone with you until I get there. You don't have to say anything if you don't want to, but there's no way that I'm hanging up this phone knowing how upset you are. Got it?"

I nod, regardless of the fact that he can't see me. "Got it."

The burn in my eyes doesn't let up, even when the ridiculousness of the situation starts to settle in. I should be embarrassed to have called him, but I'm not. He won't judge me for this, and the need to have him here, holding me against that strong chest of his is enough to ward off any more of those thoughts.

Inhaling a shaky breath, I slide down the wall, sitting my ass on the cold floor. I put my phone down on the floor beside me and pull my knees into my chest, tucking my head between them and wrapping my arms around myself until I form a ball. Quiet, subtle sounds come from the phone as Braden drives. I'm not sure how long I stay there, crying silently into my legs, but by the time my cries have turned into small sniffles, I hear footsteps thumping down the hall.

I lift my head slowly, feeling the tense muscles pull, aching from being stuck in the same position for so long. A watery smile forms on my lips when I see Braden running toward me, hair dishevelled, eyes wild as they roam my face and body, like he's searching for even the slightest injury. I think he becomes even more worried when he sees that I'm not physically injured.

A squeak escapes my dry mouth when he bends down and swiftly lifts me off of the ground, holding me tightly against his chest like he's trying to protect me by shoving me inside of him, someplace nobody can hurt me. My back touches the wall, and I wrap my legs around his waist as he holds me, one arm looped beneath my butt and the other in my hair, his face in my neck.

I press my wet face to the soft cotton of his t-shirt and breathe him in, letting the scent of laundry detergent slither under my skin and calm me. We don't speak for a long time, too busy soaking in each other's comfort.

"What happened, sweetheart?" Braden's fingers tighten in my hair and his nails scratch at my scalp, the sensation making me whimper.

"It's not as bad as it seems. I just . . ." My vocal cords are scratchy and hoarse as I trail off, unsure of how to describe what really upset me. He probably won't understand why being given such an amazing position pulled this sort of reaction from me, and if the roles were reversed, I'm sure that I wouldn't understand it either. But my pride is too big for me to appreciate it when I know that I haven't earned it.

"I don't like handouts," I mutter. "And I especially don't like them when what's expected of me in return is something I'm not comfortable with."

I whisper a curse under my breath when Braden turns to stone against me, the arm beneath me bulging and beginning to shake. If I didn't know better, I would have mistaken his rage for the inability to hold up my weight much longer. Lifting my head, I look at him through damp lashes. The way that he glares at the wall behind me has a ball of emotion clogging my throat.

"What do you mean by that, Sierra?"

I swallow thickly while touching his scruffy jaw. Suddenly, his cold brown eyes move from the wall to me, pinning me with a look tainted with the desire to punish.

"Did somebody say something to you? *Fuck*. Did somebody *touch* you? I'll kill them." He spits the words like he's disgusted by them. I flinch, and his eyes soften slightly, his grip on my hair loosening.

"Nobody touched me," I promise him. "I was handed a promotion. One that I'm certain I got because of my boss's attraction to me. I don't want him to expect me to want to owe him for it, but I think that he will."

"He can't have you. Tell me what you need me to do and I'll do it. That pompous prick won't know what hit him."

"I don't know what to do," I whisper.

"We'll figure it out. I promise. That bastard won't be getting anything from you."

Braden pushes me further against the wall while moving impossibly closer to me, as if he needs to reassure himself that I'm really here. The possessiveness that he's showing sags in my stomach before settling between my legs. I tense around him, my thighs beginning to shake.

Embarrassment and shame are two feelings that I should be feeling while I attempt to dry hump Braden in a dark hallway at work, tear stains on my cheeks and snot stuck to my nose. But lust and an aching appreciation have taken over, blinding me.

Braden's face falls in my neck again and he shutters a breath against my skin, thrusting up slowly between my legs. "We need to go home, baby."

I nod quickly, anxiously, unable to pretend like that's not exactly what I want. "Then take me home."

27

Braden

"Almost there," Sierra sobs, clenching her thighs tighter around my head.

The reflex encourages me to suck harder on her clit, knowing that's all it takes to send her flying into oblivion. Her squeak of approval echoes in my ears and makes me grin against her wet flesh, pushing my fingers deeper and faster inside of her before curving them inward and pressing against the place that sends her to space.

"Braden!"

Her back arches away from the shower wall, water cascading down the valley of her chest from the shower-head above her. When her fingers release their grip on my hair, and she gifts me a lazy smile, I slowly lower her legs from my shoulders and stand up. Her pupils are blown as I push against her, moulding her body to mine.

"That never gets old." I smirk and push my hair back and out of my face as the water falls directly on top of me.

Gripping her waist, I take a step back, pulling her under the water, savouring the moment her eyes flutter shut when the warmth runs over her goosebump-covered skin. The way her features relax makes me smile, and I find myself counting the freckles that splatter across her pale skin like the softest brown paint flicked from a brush.

Two, ten, fifteen. Moving from her hairline, down her small, button nose, to the tiny triangle above her top lip. I lose count of them the second her eyes open, transfixed on me in a way that has my breath catching.

"Stop staring at me," she murmurs.

"I like looking at you." Her gaze falls to the water beneath our feet and I raise my brow. "That surprises you?" It shouldn't, and if it does, I've clearly been doing a shit job of making her feel as good about herself as I thought I was.

"No," she rushes, but her stiffening posture says the opposite. With a shake of my head, I have my finger under her chin, tilting her head up.

"Look at me," I plead. She swallows quickly but does as I say. "You're stunning. I don't know how you don't already know that. I'm sure you hear it all the time. And I have no idea how you ended up with me."

When she doesn't reply, I feel my stomach start to churn. Maybe that isn't what she wanted to hear. Fucking shit. My lips roll and I pull back into myself, wanting to hit my head against the shower wall.

"Braden," she calls quietly, attempting to reel me back in when I let my hands fall to my sides. With what little confidence I have left, I nod and open my mouth to take back my words, but her lips are on mine before I have the chance.

With wide eyes, I watch as her hand moves to cup my face. Her touch is gentle, almost impossible to feel as her palm presses against my stubbled jaw.

"I have heard it before. Just not from you."

I CONTINUE to drag my nails up and down Sierra's back as she rests her head on my chest and a flat palm near my collarbone. Her body curves into mine like it belongs there. She's much calmer than she was a few hours prior, and I find myself finally able to relax.

I'm not sure what exactly happened in that shower, but I have to admit that I feel pretty good about it. What I don't feel good about is what happened earlier—when I picked up my phone only to hear her heart-wrenching cries and how broken she looked when I finally got to her.

I expected the worst. The entire drive to that fucking building, I was preparing myself to find her in a state that would test me in ways that I've never been tested before. The imprints of my fingernails on my scalp are probably still there, forever scarred from the aggressiveness of each hand I ran through it, of every clump yanked out of worry.

I knew that I would have done anything she asked me to right then. There wasn't a single unforgivable crime that I wouldn't have committed for her.

But then I saw her there, not a scratch on her body, and felt my heart stop. Somehow, knowing the damage was invisible was worse than anything I had prepared for. With no injury, there was no easy way that I could have patched her up. The damage was inside, damaging her beautiful soul.

I had never felt as helpless as I did right then, with her in my arms, clutching onto me just as tightly as I was clutching onto her.

Cole Travis painted a bullseye on his own back. And I plan on being the one that takes the shot at it.

"You awake?" I whisper.

"Mm," she moans, rubbing her cheek against my peck.

I hate that I'm about to poke and prod at something that I should leave alone so that she can rest, but if I don't get more information soon, I think I'm going to damn near explode. "You wouldn't happen to want to tell me more about what happened earlier, would you? I'm going out of my head here."

"No. I'm sleepy."

"Sierra," I sigh, wrapping my arm securely around her waist and tugging her so her stomach is pressed flat to my side, eliminating all distance between us. "At least give me something."

"Fine," she mumbles. "Work sucks. Are you happy now? Can I go to bed?"

I pinch her side. "No. Not good enough. What was the promotion you got? Why do you feel like you didn't earn it? Is it that much of a career boost?"

My muscles tense at the idea of her being anywhere near her boss after this. I don't notice that my grip on her side has tightened until she gently peels away my fingers.

"Relax, Scrappy." She pushes out a laugh and drops my now relaxed hand back on her waist. "It's pretty much what I've been working for since I graduated. It's not my end goal, but it's a giant step in the right direction. They offered me a marketing manager position, which is what I was close to earning at my old job. But I was there for *three* years. Yeah, it was a harder company to work for and I didn't have half of the opportunities that I've been given here, but maybe that was the first red flag that I missed.

"Cole took an immediate interest in me, and I was so excited about the fancy office and client opportunities that I became naive. I didn't realize that being so appreciative toward him would be taken as something that it wasn't."

"Don't blame yourself for the actions of a man who has

tried to use his power to take advantage of you. No woman, especially one as intelligent as yourself, should need to bow to the feet of a man just to feel like a person. It's incredibly revolting to me that you have had to worry about a smile being taken as something more than you intended it to, and that showing appreciation for being treated like a decent human being at work could lead to you owing somebody something. It's not fair, baby, and I'm so fucking sorry that you've been dealing with that."

She's silent for a few seconds, but the arm laying across my chest tightens. "They want me to move across the country."

"Across the country?" I mutter. Fear spears my insides before collaring my throat, squeezing and squeezing and squeezing.

"The promotion is for a job in Toronto. The company is expanding. I would be going with a small team."

The hand I have on her waist slacks. I want to jump up and run, but my limbs are too heavy. The thought of leaving right now and not knowing if she'll be here when I get back makes me gnash my teeth together.

The weight of her admission falls heavier than it would have had my father not been leaving too. Toronto, Toronto, Toronto. Everything is about fucking *Toronto*. What a coincidence.

I feel betrayed, even though I have no right to feel this way. There's something much deeper, more unforgiving that flares under my skin and sizzles in my veins, boiling my blood. *Abandonment*. A feeling that I buried a long time ago, back when my parents decided that I wasn't enough to heal the broken bridge between them. A feeling that severed my relationship with my mother for years, and still crackles in the air when a disagreement gets a bit too loud and out of hand.

A young boy can't even begin to understand how fractured and broken a marriage has to be for vows to be broken and a single piece of paper to be signed. All of the shouting and the screaming doesn't make sense. The countless nights spent at a house that's not his, just so that he can escape the angry voices don't, make, sense.

All it takes is for those memories to come swinging back for me to roll out from under Sierra and sit on the edge of the bed, my back to her.

"Toronto is shit," is my only reply. The words are rough and emotionless.

"Wow, thank you for your helpful input." I can hear her moving around on the bed. "I don't know why you bothered asking if you were just going to be a dick about it."

"Give me a break." I laugh humourlessly. "What do you want me to say? Break a leg? Enjoy the weather?"

She inhales sharply before I hear her feet hit the ground and begin stomping around the floor. "I don't know what your deal is, Braden. You asked and I answered. You're being ridiculous."

"When are you going?" I grind out, staring at my bedroom door as I debate storming out like a child.

"A few weeks maybe. I never really stayed around to listen to the fine details, in case you forgot."

The only words that register in my mind are the first three.

A few weeks. *A few fucking weeks.*

That's all I have left.

28

Braden

I WASN'T SURPRISED TO FIND SIERRA GONE WHEN I WOKE UP THIS morning. Shit, I was surprised that she stayed the night at all after the way we ended our conversation. I was spiteful and she didn't deserve my harsh comments. So when I said I was going to sleep on the couch, she didn't fight me on it. I was too grateful that she was even bothering to stay to try to push my luck of sleeping in the same bed as me.

But just because I wasn't surprised that she had snuck out in the middle of the night—no note or anything—doesn't mean that I'm not disappointed. Running away from our problems isn't going to work for me. Not anymore.

I slide my phone back into the pocket of my jeans and wait anxiously for the elevator doors to open. It's uncomfortable being stuck in such a tight space with a bunch of pricks wearing expensive suits, everyone pretending to listen to the lame elevator music to avoid an awkward conversation. But that doesn't matter. I'm here for Sierra, not to make small talk with a bunch of businessmen.

A sigh of relief pushes past my lips when the metal doors slide open with a brief *ding*. The space is somewhat familiar, but not enough that I know where I need to be going. I was too busy searching for Sierra yesterday to really take much else in.

I do remember how the white tile flooring sparkled from the sun's reflection through the tall windows, the potent smell of coffee that reminded me of being stuck inside of a Starbucks, and how out of place I felt wearing sweaty gym clothes in such a professional building. But come to think of it, it probably wasn't my choice of attire that had me feeling so out of place.

It was quieter yesterday, with not a lot of chatter or shoes clapping on the tile like there is now. But I tune it out, knowing that if I let myself start thinking about anything other than seeing Sierra, my first stop would be Cole Travis' office.

The woman working the desk gets more familiar the closer I get before I realize that she was here yesterday. Her hair is almost so platinum blonde that it looks white, greyish even, and her otherwise pretty blue eyes are incredibly dull as they stay strained on the thin computer screen.

Clearing my throat, she looks over at me, blinking slowly while assessing me. "How can I help you?" she asks slowly.

"I'm looking for Sierra."

The woman blinks slowly again and raises her hand to point to the hallway to the left of her. "Third door on the left."

"Thanks." I head down the hallway at a quick pace before stopping in front of Sierra's closed office door, my fingers twitching restlessly at my side. I swallow the ball in my throat before rapping three times.

It takes a few seconds before I hear her soft voice. "Come in!"

Turning the doorknob, I push open the door and grin. Even hunched over and frustrated, she looks gorgeous. Her tired eyes fall on me when she lifts her head and quickly brushes a few stray curls out of her face. With her lips slightly parted in surprise, she blows out a harsh breath.

"What are you doing here?"

Okay, not the welcome I was hoping for. "Hello to you too, fighter."

"I'm serious. Why are you here? I don't have time for your games today," she snaps at me, and I know that I deserve it. The purple bags under her eyes make me wince. Did she sleep as badly as I did last night?

"Look, I'm sorry for being a total ass last night. You just took me by surprise."

"What am I supposed to do without my favourite lady?"

Her eyebrows scrunch before she stares at the pile of papers on her desk. "I haven't even made my decision yet."

"I know. Which is why I owe you an apology." I clear my throat. "I also came by to ask you something. It's the worst possible time to ask you this, but just know that there's no pressure or anything." It's now or never.

"Okay." She says it without sparing me a glance.

"My dad's getting married this weekend, and he won't stop bugging me about asking you to come. Something about him not wanting his son to show up alone and all that. I don't know. It doesn't have to be a date or anything. You could come as a friend or somethin—"

"What day is the wedding?"

"Saturday. You wouldn't need to be there until after the ceremony. Dad and his fiancée are keeping the ceremony really small. Just them, her parents, Tyler and me. I could pick you up as soon as it's over if you want." I scratch the back of my head nervously and fight off the urge to kick myself in the ass. I feel like I'm back in middle school asking a girl to sneak away at recess and share a yogurt with me.

"You can pick me up after the ceremony is done. Just let me know what time I should be ready." She's finally looking at me again, her beautiful face beaming with mischief. "But you have to promise me something."

"Anything."

"You have to dance with me."

I throw my head back and laugh. "It's funny you think I'll be doing anything but."

Sierra

"So, it's a date," Sophie states as casually as ever while continuing her aggressive search through the endless racks of clothes in the third boutique we've stumbled into. We have yet to find a store that has the "perfect" dress, and my feet are beginning to throb.

"It's not a date. Braden just needed someone to go with him." At this point, I don't know who I'm trying to convince more—her or myself.

Braden never said it was a date, he actually was pretty adamant on it *not* having to be one. But I want it to be. I don't particularly like being introduced to a casual fling's family and friends. Why bring other people into a relationship that isn't going anywhere? I don't see the point.

The entire situation with Cole and Toronto has created a crack in our relationship, one that I don't think can be fixed simply with apologies and hot make-up sex. Braden is hard to understand at most times, but now more than ever. I'm terrified to tell him that I've made the decision to go to Toronto. He won't give me a chance to explain myself before he runs without giving me a chance to explain myself.

"You're ridiculous," Sophie scoffs. Wrapping her fingers around the metal rack she was just sorting through, she turns to me with a heavy scowl. "Clearly, you're into him. And boy, does he do an awful job of hiding his feelings for you. He never takes his damn eyes off of you, always watching like if he looks away for a second somebody else might snatch you up and steal you away."

I stare at my bare toes as they stick out of my strappy sandals and shake my head, flushing. "It doesn't matter, Soph. I'm leaving, in case you forgot. I told Clark this morning after I got off the phone with you. I shouldn't even be going to this wedding. It's going to make telling him that much harder."

Her eyes nearly pop from their sockets. "He doesn't know yet? Dammit, Sierra."

I divert my gaze, shame falling heavy in my stomach. "I would have told him today, but you should have seen how nervous he was when he showed up at my office. It would have ruined everything." I drag my fingertips down a mauve-coloured velvet dress before clenching it in my hand, fighting off the sting in the back of my eyes.

"Oh, you silly girl. I told you that this would happen. Friends with benefits doesn't work. Haven't you learned that from the thousands of movies about it? The couple always ends up in love."

"I don't need an 'I told you so' lecture right now, Sophie. I don't know what to do." I tip my head back and blink at the ceiling, pushing back the guilt-laced tears that have begun to collect in the corner of my eyes.

"Are you finally going to admit to yourself that you have real, big girl feelings for him? That's probably a good place to start."

My voice is small and chalked full of regret. "I already have."

It was impossible not to. I did an awful job of keeping the lines drawn between love and lust, and now I'm going to break my *own* heart. And Braden's. He doesn't have to tell me how he feels, I already know. He's done just as awful of a job hiding how much he cares about me as I have.

Friends don't act the way we do unless they feel something beyond an ache between their legs. They have to feel one in their chest too. One far stronger, impossible to ignore.

I wanted to say no to this promotion, to moving to Toronto. But regardless of how I got it, I couldn't turn it down. I promised myself that I wouldn't let anything get in the way of my personal successes. Of my career. Cole is just one boss of many, he won't be around forever. He'll get bored of me once he realizes he won't get anywhere with me. He'll move on and back off. But an opportunity like this may not come around again. I would be stupid not to take it.

The thought of leaving Clare and Liz makes my stomach hurt to the point that I want to kneel over and scream. They're the only family I really have, and I don't want to leave them. But when I drove to Clare's last night with a bottle of cheap wine and tears in my eyes, she was persistent that I go. That I stop worrying about them so much.

She pulled me into her arms and hugged me like she used to when we were kids. We cried together, and then we laughed to the point of crying again. It was the first time that I felt like this might be the right decision. And I've been clutching onto that feeling ever since, too terrified that it will disappear if I let it go.

I have all of my ducks in a row. All but one.

Sophie touches my arm, pulling me out of my head. "You need to tell him, S. And not just about Toronto, but also how you feel. It isn't fair to him if you don't."

"I know that I do. Shit, I hate that he doesn't know that I'm crazy about him. Even when he makes me want to yank my hair out piece by piece." I smile for a second before it slips away again. "The thought of leaving him here hurts more than I was expecting."

With all of the sleepless nights spent with my legs tangled in his, our belly-aching laughter that kept Clay up night after night, and the helpless fluttering of my heart with every whisper of my name on his lips, I never stood a chance. I have no idea how I'm supposed to go back to how my life was before eating Italian takeout on the floor between Braden's legs, watching reruns of Law & Order became what I looked forward to at the end of the day.

"Have you thought about asking him to go with you?" Sophie asks after a minute of silence, her lip tucked between her teeth. She watches me nervously.

"Yeah, right." I snort. "Braden isn't the type of guy to chase after a girl he isn't even officially involved with. And his entire life is here. I could never ask him that."

Sophie doesn't reply with words, only a simple nod of her head as she turns back to a rack of cocktail dresses. I didn't mean to come off harsh, but that idea isn't something I want taking root in my mind. There's no need to make this any worse than it's already going to be. I won't be able to handle it.

29

Sierra

Holy. Shit.

I don't know whether to get down on my knees for this man right here in my apartment hallway or throw myself at him, knowing that he'll catch me without hesitation. The way my heart thumps so rapidly against my chest bone is terrifying, but I revel in it. Heated amber eyes burn into my skin as he looks me up and down, striking a match to the arousal in my blood and setting my insides on fire.

My stare carries the same intensity as his, if the groan that rumbles in his chest is anything to go by. I ache to reach out and touch him, but force my hands to stay by my sides as I soak in the model-worthy image in front of me.

A navy-blue suit jacket stretches across his shoulders, and the top three buttons of his white dress shirt are unbuttoned in that sexy *I don't care* way. His thick thighs push the boundaries of his slacks, and I begin to wonder if they would rip if he bent down. Giant biceps swell within the tight restraints of his suit jacket when he places two hands on the doorframe above me, swallowing the space between us.

Moving my gaze, I stare at the hands gripping the doorframe and swallow, feeling my underwear grow damp. The veins in his hands seem more prominent to me tonight, thicker, sexier even. An array of simple black rings are placed neatly on three of his five knuckles. It's a different look for Braden than I'm used to, but I would be lying if I said that I wasn't curious as to how the cold metal would feel pressed against me while he's knuckle deep—

His hips push against me and for the first time tonight, I meet his stare. My lips part at how softly he's looking at me, as if he wasn't just eye-fucking me a second ago. It brings a chill to my skin, and I shiver against his chest. If there wasn't a familiar hardness pressing against my stomach, I would have assumed that I imagined the past few minutes.

"Maybe we don't have to go to this wedding after all." His words are gruff, raspy and thick with need.

"Would you prefer that I change?"

I hear a low chuckle and warm breath fans my face as he moves closer until short beard hairs scratch the underside of my jaw. One hand moves from the door frame to settle on my hip, the heat from his palm soaking through my dress, warming my skin.

I suck in a breath, my eyelashes fluttering when he rubs his nose against the beating skin of my neck, nipping at it gently before darting his tongue to the sore skin, lapping at it with a groan that falls between my legs. He backs away too soon, and a finger is placed under my chin, tilting it upward until our eyes meet again.

Braden softly mumbles his next words as if he isn't sure of them. As if he doesn't understand them himself. "The dress is perfect. *You* look perfect."

I get lost in the way he looks at me—like I'm *his*. Like he'd tear apart anyone who tried to come between us. My heart swells to ten times its size.

And just like that, both of his hands touch me, one

palming my hip, burning a hole through my dress while the other plays with the thin strap on my shoulder, his thumb slipping beneath it and rubbing slow circles into my skin. He licks his bottom lip and tilts his head to the side. "I just don't know if I want anybody else to see you like this. I want this to be for me and *only* me."

"It is all for you." My breath catches in my throat when his hand moves up my side, cupping the side of my breast and squeezing. "Thank you. For the compliment. I wish I would have known that you had a blue suit because I would have gotten a blue dress. But I guess a dress is a dress, right?" My cheeks flame with embarrassment, nerves sizzling under my skin.

"Relax," Braden whispers. He's right there, so close that I can taste the bubblegum he must have chewed on the way here. My nipples harden and push through the tight material of my dress. I arch my back so they brush his chest, whimpering from the contact when they do, but needing more.

Braden shifts the hand massaging the side of my breast before gripping the full weight of it. "Tell me, baby. Did you skip the bra on purpose? Were you hoping that I wouldn't be able to keep my hands off of your perfect tits?" He squeezes the heavy breast in his hand before dragging his thumb across the nipple. "That I would have to have a taste before I paraded you around, letting other men see how fucking amazing you look in this dress?"

My knees threaten to buckle, his words like a zap to my swollen clit. I open my mouth but no words come out. I try again, but cry out immediately when the top of my dress is yanked down and my nipple is sucked between Braden's lips. His tongue moves in slow, teasing strokes before flicking at it. He feasts on the sobs that follow every strong suck and groans in approval when I wind my fingers in his hair, pulling every time his teeth brush the sensitive tip.

His mouth leaves my skin with a *pop* and I gasp at the sudden coldness that envelopes my wet breast. "We can go inside," I mutter, almost adding a please before I think better of it.

The grin that spreads across his face is evil, maniacal even. "No, my little fighter. From now until the end of the night, I'm going to be a *perfect* gentleman, and you're going to keep those soaked panties on so that you remember exactly who you're coming home with tonight. I can't have you forgetting who it was that made that pussy so wet, now can I?" He clicks his tongue to the roof of his mouth and winks.

I blink twice, wishing that I was angrier with this show of possession than I really am. But no. Instead, my panties only become damper, causing them to stick to the slick flesh beneath them.

Pushing up on my toes, I grab his jacket by the lapels and gently press my lips to his. He responds quickly, like I knew he would, but only with a light caress of his mouth, nothing more. A sigh escapes me at the sudden change in tempo.

I pull him closer, just needing to feel his body against mine, and grin into the kiss when he does the same, palming my cheeks in those big hands, making me feel dainty and small.

If only he knew just how much of me he really did hold in his hands, all of it so easily breakable.

We break apart after a few more seconds, my breath escaping in one big puff while he simply laughs, eyes bright and sparkling with mischief. "My, my, Sierra. Are you trying to trick me into breaking my own rules and having my way with you in this hallway? Who knew you were so naughty."

"You say it as if it's a bad thing," I tease, dropping my hands with a step backward.

"It couldn't be farther from a bad thing, sweetheart," he says while I grab my clutch from inside and lock the door.

When I return, Braden extends his elbow toward me and I take it, letting him guide us outside and into his car.

It's not exactly a horse-drawn carriage, and I'm not wearing glass slippers or a dress made just for me by my fairy Godmother, but the man on my arm could very well be my Prince Charming.

BRADEN and I have just walked hand-in-hand through a wide, pink daisy-covered archway when I hear a cheerful, vibrant voice yell, "Well if it isn't my handsome brother-in-law!"

The welcome comes from a petite blonde with a gorgeous sparkling silver, knee-length strapless dress fitted tightly to her slim figure. As she hurries toward us from inside the ballroom, I notice Braden's brother, Tyler, following closely behind her, his head shaking as he watches her.

"And he brought a date!" the woman shrieks. The striking blue in her eyes contrasts against her silver dress effortlessly. It isn't until she turns to the side, briefly stealing a glance at her husband as he settles beside her that I see the protruding baby bump. I want to congratulate her, but decide to do it later.

"You act like I didn't tell you that I was, Gray," Braden replies with a chuckle while snaking an arm around my waist and pulling me close. "Sierra, this is Gracie. Gracie, this is Sierra." He introduces us just seconds before I'm tugged away from him and enveloped in her small arms.

My body tenses for a small moment before I laugh and return the hug. "It's nice to meet you."

Gracie pulls back but keeps her hands on my shoulders, holding me in place as if to inspect me. "Are your eyes naturally grey? Or are they silver? Either way, they are gorgeous!"

Her outgoing, sweet-as-honey personality takes me by surprise in the best way. Tyler seems like such a hard person to get to know, so I think I just assumed that maybe his wife would be the same. "They are both grey and natural. I used to hate them when I was a kid." I laugh nervously.

"I hope you don't anymore! They're *so* unique," she gushes.

"Thank you."

"Okay, princess. Don't scare away the only girl that can stand Braden's presence," Tyler half-heartedly scolds, placing a kiss in her hair and rubbing her swollen stomach. "Let's go find our table before the reception starts."

Gracie rolls her eyes but agrees anyway. Her reaction has Braden laughing, his palm now comfortably resting against my lower back.

"Fine. But I'm so not done with you, Sierra. We'll see you in there?" she asks, her tone hopeful.

"Where else would we go?" Braden teases, earning himself a smack on the arm that has him wincing.

"Alright, smart ass." She gives him the finger before turning back to me. "I'll see you soon."

As we watch Gracie wrap her fingers around Tyler's forearm and nearly drag him back into the ballroom, I let out a small giggle.

"Something funny?" Braden asks, flashing me a beaming white smile.

"I like her."

"Yeah? She's definitely something."

"I found it refreshing. She seems genuine." Like the type of person who knows exactly when to be warm and compassionate, but also cold and merciless when she needs to be. She reminds me of Clare. Maybe that's why I like her so much already.

Braden nods in response and turns us so we face each

other. Lines form across his forehead as his mouth turns down, a heavy feeling twitching in the air. "She's the reason for my brother's happiness. It's hard to think about where he would be right now without her." I grab his hand and squeeze as he clears his throat along with all of the worry that was present just seconds ago. "Anyway, we should probably head in. You ready?"

"I think so. I used to love weddings as a kid." There was something magical about watching two people announce their love for one another so publicly. It gave me butterflies and only grew my obsession with fairytales as a little girl.

"It's been a long time since I've been to one. I'm glad you're here with me." Braden presses his lips softly to my forehead and I lean toward him, closing my eyes.

"Me too," I whisper before he pulls back and interlocks our fingers. "Lead the way, handsome."

30

Braden

I've never been a fan of weddings. But that's probably because I don't ever want one.

Weddings are pointless, futile. They're an excuse to spend thousands of dollars on the idea and hope of forever. You invite hundreds of people, some of whom you probably haven't seen in ten, fifteen years, and stand in front of a priest just to proclaim a love that you already know you feel. The day is over before you know it, and life carries on like it did before you were handed that flimsy piece of paper. The one that tells you that you're tethered to someone for the rest of your life. For better or worse, right?

But what happens afterward? After the honeymoon phase washes away and you realize there's no going back. The years go by and you begin to hate the way your partner handles stress, or maybe they work too much and are home too little. You realize that you're not happy, but that damn piece of paper says you have to stick it through. You have to grow to hate each other before the topic of divorce is brought up.

That nasty seven letter word still makes my skin itch.

Divorce. Even years later I remember exactly how it felt when my mother sat me down at the kitchen table and told me that her and Dad were getting a divorce.

"We're just not happy anymore," Mom had said, as if I hadn't already known that. As if I hadn't spent most of my life watching them grow to hate each other.

There was a reason I immediately understood why she had chosen a night that he was out of town fighting to deliver the news to me, her things already packed. They hadn't been alone together in the same room for months, too busy ripping each other apart, so why would I have expected that night to be any different?

She dropped me off at my grandmother's that night and I didn't see her again for two years. It was two years that I spent confused, hurt, and worried. I didn't know where she was, or who she was with. Dad would let me know that she was alive and well every few weeks, saying he had talked to her and that she was fine.

I was seventeen when my mother came back from a two-year trip trekking across Europe with Antonio, her new fiancé. It turned out that they met in Italy, at some hole in the wall bistro or something like that. He was visiting his family for a few months, and as my mother would say, *the rest is history*. It took me years to forgive her for leaving, too betrayed to hear her out.

And it wasn't until I saw how easy it was for my mom to move on and be happy once the chains of marriage were broken that I promised myself that I wouldn't make my parents' mistakes. That I wouldn't marry someone just to lose them a few years down the road.

I don't need a piece of fucking paper to tell me that I'm going to spend the rest of my life with someone. That's not how it works.

I have no idea why my dad wants to get married again, let alone throw another huge party. But I've tried not to spend much time thinking about it. If he wants to keep making the same mistakes, then who am I to stop him?

It's Sierra that brings me out of my head, her voice putting me at ease. "This really is beautiful. Did they plan it themselves?"

I turn in my seat until our knees brush. Her eyes are already waiting for mine. I reach over and place my hand on her thigh, squeezing the bare skin over her knee where the dress has ridden up. Toying with the hem, I smile, happy to have her with me.

Fuck, she's a sight for sore eyes. All warm, pink cheeks and bright eyes that hold the power to consume me with a single look.

"I can only assume that Lana hired someone to do the work. She seems like the type," I mumble and pull my attention to the tacky vase placed on the centre of our table. The number of frilly, pale-pink flowers peeking out of the top makes me cringe. Talk about overkill.

"Braden," Sierra scolds, placing her palm on top of the hand I have wrapped around her leg in what seems like an attempt to pull me back. "I'm sure if she did hire someone that it was for a reason. Some people need help planning something as big as a wedding. If this is just the reception, I can't imagine how beautiful the ceremony must have been."

It was definitely something. "You're lucky that you weren't there. I almost fell asleep at the altar."

Huffing, Sierra removes her hand from mine and wraps it around her wine glass instead. "You're helpless."

"Weddings aren't my thing, babe. I'm not going to apologize for it."

"You don't have to apologize. But you don't need to be a

dick either," she scoffs before taking a sip—or more like a gulp—from the crimson liquid in her glass. "I actually happen to love weddings. A wedding is supposed to be one of the best days of your life," she sighs, the faint ghost of a smile on her lips.

I sling my arm around the back of her chair and lean in so my mouth brushes her ear. "Let me guess, you've been planning yours since you were a little girl? Did you used to dress up in one of your mom's dresses and pretend you were a bride?"

I meant for it to be a joke, but I sound more mocking than I intended to, and when hurt flashes across her face, I know that she caught it too.

Her smile falls and she begins looking around the room to avoid looking at me. Guilt falls like a rock in my gut. "If you don't like weddings that's fine, but don't be a prick to everybody who does. This day isn't about you and your arrogance, it's about your dad and his new wife," she replies after a few seconds, her words muttered low enough to only be heard by the two of us and not the entire table.

Thank God for that. Gracie is already pinning with me a glare that has my blood cooling.

Suddenly, a hand is placed on my left shoulder, causing me to flinch in surprise. With an uncomfortable cough, I turn to see my mom, her attention glued onto the annoyed woman beside me.

"We didn't know that you were here yet, Braden. And with a guest at that," she half-scolds. If it weren't for the slight smirk on her lips, I would have assumed that I was about to receive a lecture.

Sierra jerks beside me as she takes in the woman beside me before introducing herself. "You must be Braden's mother. I could recognize those timeless cheekbones anywhere. I'm

Sierra." She extends her hand confidently as she slips into business mode.

I register her compliment and smirk. So, she thinks I have timeless cheekbones, eh? Can't wait to tease her about that later.

Mom's eyes widen for a split second, a clear response to Sierra's outgoing, genuine gesture as her grip on my shoulder tightens ever so slightly and her other hand grabs Sierra's.

She's happy with the compliment, although I'm not sure why she's surprised by it. My mom's features really haven't aged over the years. She isn't old by any means, but she definitely doesn't look fifty. I don't think that she's ever even found a gray hair among all of the chestnut brown.

"Please, call me Tia." She grins. "I can't say that I have ever had one of Braden's girlfriends make me blush so easily. Thank you, Sierra. You are just lovely."

When Sierra's cheeks darken to match Mom's, I step in with a chuckle. "Okay, I get it. Sierra's special. How about we don't scare her away."

There has to be a thousand questions running through my mom's head right now, considering that there have only ever been two past girlfriends in my life, and I would never have taken either of them to such a family-filled event. Not willingly, at least.

"I'm sorry, Sierra. I have loose lips." Mom laughs with a slight roll of her eyes. "I'll leave you two for now. But I'll be back. Don't disappear before I have a chance to chat with you some more."

"Wouldn't dream of it, Tia," Sierra replies, flashing her a genuine smile that has my heart thumping a bit too heavily.

"Well, alright." My shoulder is squeezed once more as breath tickles my ear. "I like her," Mom whispers and walks away, leaving my chest filled with pride.

Me too, Mom. I really fucking like her.

Sierra

"Did I tell you how beautiful you look yet?" Braden asks, the words kissing the skin of my shoulder seconds before his lips do. I tighten my arms around his neck and hide my growing smile in his dress shirt, welcoming the familiar smell of his cologne.

The music playing around us has been slow for the past few minutes now, seeing as we're one of the only pairs left on the dance floor. Most guests left when Braden's dad and the new bride did, but some hung around, revelling in the classy music and free bar.

I didn't mind staying and surprisingly, neither did Braden. We've just been hidden in our own little world, swaying slowly to the music, clutching each other like we fear the other might vanish in thin air if we let go.

"You did. A few times." Heat warms my cheeks as I pull away just enough to stare up at him.

There's an unmissable playfulness in his eyes, one that always sparks when he's happy. *Really* happy. The thought alone of him feeling so lighthearted and giddy while in my presence makes me feel prouder than I probably should.

"Well, I'm going to tell you again," he murmurs, kissing my hair. "You look stunning."

"You're feeling generous tonight."

"You have no idea."

"Is that so?"

Much to my surprise, Braden has kept to his word all

night, never touching me in anything but a gentlemanly way. But as nice as it's been, there have been a few times that I've wanted nothing more than for him to reach under the table and slide a hand up my dress. I'm pretty sure that that's just my hormones talking, though.

"Give me one more dance. Then I can show you what I mean."

"I already know what you mean," I poke, loving the way his lips tug to the ceiling when I tease him. "But I'll give you the pleasure of one more dance."

He doesn't reply right away. He pulls me closer instead, close enough that my chest moves with his with every sharp inhale. "Did you have a good time? I know that Gracie can get a bit nosey."

"It was great." I press my palm to his chest, directly over where his heart beats. "And you really love to rile her up. Poor girl."

"Poor girl? Did you forget what she did to me tonight?" Braden looks traumatized as he gags. The repulsion in his eyes makes me laugh, choking on air mid-laugh.

The pissed look on Gracie's face when Braden gave her a noogie will be forever in my memory. I was genuinely surprised when she didn't try and attack his balls as payback. That's usually my go-to revenge move.

However, Gracie preferred a much subtler form of revenge. She had the chef swap their plates before they were brought out, making Braden choke down whatever vegan meat she ordered while she pretended to dig into his steak. How he didn't notice the difference in texture or smell is beyond me. But the way he struggled with the silent retching while gulping down mouthfuls of water straight from the pitcher was hilarious.

"I don't think I could ever forget." My forehead falls to his chest as my body shakes with silent laughter. There's no point in holding it in, Braden can pretend that he's still annoyed but I know that he loved the whole thing. His playful nature is too strong to be wounded by some fake veggie steak.

Braden's hands move from my hips to my sides before his fingers are digging into them. I shove away from him, squealing and swatting at him. "You think it's funny that I nearly threw up all over the table? Wait until I get you home, little fighter. You won't be laughing then."

"Stop! Stop!"

His head falls back with a loud laugh, his eyes twinkling beneath the party lights. Tears blur my vision as my abdomen begins to ache. Our eyes meet and my belly fills with warmth.

A portrait of pure joy is staring right at me in the form of a truly beautiful man. One with bushy, scarred eyebrows, eyes the same shade as expensive whiskey, and a smile that could turn even the most ruthless of people into a puddle of goo at his feet. Braden is protective in the best ways and also playful enough that in those few moments where you find yourself stuck in the realities of being a grown-up, he can make you feel like a kid again.

He's everything that I've been needing and begging for.

"You're really beautiful," I choke out before my eyes bulge and then shut. Our laughter slowly dies, and the air begins to tighten.

His mouth falls, and he lets out a wavering exhale. "I will never hold a flame to your beauty, baby. I promise you that."

I STIFLE MY YAWN. "How far are we?"

We left the reception a few minutes ago, once the music cut and the few stragglers left. The blisters on my feet made it impossible to walk to the car without limping, so of course, like the gentleman he promised to be, Braden swept me off of my feet and carried me the rest of the way. I think it made me fall for him that much more—that much deeper.

It also makes my telling him about Toronto that much harder.

The car comes to a jolting stop, my body lurching forward and the fabric of the seat belt digging into my skin. With wide eyes, I turn to see Braden already undoing his seatbelt, turning the headlights off, and sliding his seat back.

"Are you okay?" I shriek, looking through each window in an attempt to find a reason as to why we're currently stopped on the side of an empty street instead of at home.

"I'm way too horny to be driving right now," he groans and I watch him palm the thick bulge in his slacks.

"You're kidding," I scoff and push out a relieved sigh. "I thought you were having a heart attack or something, jackass."

"A heart attack? Do I look like someone that would be having a heart attack? I'm healthy as a horse, sweetheart. Don't worry about me," he boasts and pats his thighs. "Now come over here."

I stay in my seat. "You want to have sex here? On the side of a road? What if somebody sees?"

"Who cares." Lifting a shoulder, he starts to unbutton his dress shirt, revealing a sliver of his taut chest. "Don't tell me you're too chicken, Sierra."

I narrow my eyes. "I'm not chicken."

"Then come over here and ride my cock."

My clit swells at his dominant tone, my panties becoming damp. Swallowing, I watch his fingers skim expertly down his shirt before pulling it open. I itch to reach out and feel the familiar ridges covering the tanned skin, craving the heat of him beneath my fingertips. But I keep my hands to myself, wanting to watch him first.

He reaches for his pants now, fiddling with his belt buckle until it flaps open and pulling down the zipper of his slacks. My thighs clench together as I try to soothe the throb between them, keeping my eyes trained on Braden so he can see just how desperately I need him.

It feels impossible to keep from touching myself. My nipples swell behind my dress, and I can't help but palm my breast, whimpering when my inner walls pulse in response.

His eyes meet mine as he lifts his hips and pushes his pants and boxers down his legs. My lips part when he grabs his hard cock with a tight fist. He gives his shaft a few slow, hard strokes before swiping the bead of pre-cum away.

"Well? Do you want an invitation, Sierra?" His voice is gravelly, raw.

The arrogant question slides off my back as I unbuckle my seatbelt and climb over the centre console. With my thighs pressed to the outside of his, I sit down on his lap and nearly cry out when my core brushes the hard ridge of his cock.

My teeth sink into my bottom lip as my hands find purchase on his shoulders for balance. A firm hand grips my face, squeezing my chin and tilting my head down. Braden takes my mouth in a desperate, dirty kiss, sucking the air from my lungs. My tongue licks the seam of his lips and he parts them for me with a throaty groan that I feel vibrating deep in his chest.

I've never been so attracted to somebody in my life. Braden invokes something carnal in me, something that's been hidden for as long as I can remember. It makes me desperate. It's scary, even a little terrifying. But I've begun to harness those feelings, using them to take control over this man in a way that I never thought was possible.

Our kiss is frantic, *hungry*. It's as if this is the last time his lips will taste mine and we both know it—a thought that I don't let poison my mind as I grind against his bare shaft, searching for the release I need so desperately.

I feel him reach between us and pull my panties to the side, exposing my drenched pussy. My head falls back with a curse when he cups me, pressing his palm against my clit.

"You're always ready for me."

I suck in a sharp breath and buck against his hand, my hips swirling. One long finger teases my entrance before sliding inside, agonizingly slow.

"More," I breathe, twisting my hips again as blinding lust heats my blood. My nails dig into his shoulders, and I press my face into his neck, pressing my lips to his pulse point and sucking on the racing beat beneath it.

Two more fingers thrust inside of me, swirling and bending to hit my sweet spot before retreating fully with a wet, sloppy sound. "If I don't get inside of you right now, I might fucking die, baby," Braden grunts before I feel the swollen, wet tip of his cock press against my entrance. He coats himself in my wetness before slapping my clit with the head, my thighs shuddering as I struggle to hold myself up.

The heat in his amber eyes has me unable to look away and watch him as I lower myself onto his shaft, sinking inch by inch until I've taken all of him.

I feel so desired, so beautiful that I can't catch my breath. My throat constricts, tightening to the point I have to gasp, as if an invisible hand is collaring it, choking me until black rims my vision and the world stops. But there's nothing there. Nothing but bright, world-burning, unadulterated love for the man in front of me. A stinging sensation builds behind my eyes, my vision blurring.

I love him.

But I have to leave him.

"Braden," I whimper, sliding the dress shirt down his

shoulders and gripping the muscles resting there in an attempt to ground myself. Something warm and wet slides down my cheek, and I swipe it away quickly, hoping he didn't notice. I refuse to cry right now. This might be the last time . . . *no. Don't think about it.*

With a throaty groan, he grips me tighter and thrusts his hips, burying himself so deep I cry out. My head falls back and I close my eyes, blinking back the blinding pain that ricochets through my chest.

Braden's hands slide through my hair, gripping it tightly like he always does when he uses it to move me how he wants me. Closer, farther, it's his choice. Just how he likes it. I don't put up a fight, too utterly weightless.

"Tell me that I'm the only one who gets to fuck this pussy," he orders, thrusting into me relentlessly while shoving my dress down my shoulders and rolling my left nipple between his calloused fingertips.

A sob tears up my throat when I feel the familiar pull in my stomach. "You're the only one."

Lifting my hips, I take back control and begin to ride him. I try to memorize how it feels to be filled with him, the smooth, thick size of him pulsing as he gets closer and closer to his release. My nipples drag against his bare chest as I arch my back and place my palms on his thighs, using him to increase our pace.

His large hands cup my face and I'm right there, shaking in his lap like a leaf in the wind as tears scorn my cheeks, falling to his chest. Those amber eyes fill with something broken, something too heavy to carry as his thumbs begin to catch my tears, wiping them away frantically as he says my name like a curse.

He drives inside of me hard one last time before stilling, my walls continuing to pulse around him, the last of my orgasm draining what little energy I had left. "You're mine, Sierra. *All mine.*"

I nod over and over again and collapse against him, seconds before his arms wrap around me, holding me to him like he's scared I'll open the car door and run. But I can't. Not right now.

31

Sierra

"You're absolutely ridiculous," I squeal, attempting to hide my smile in Braden's shoulder as he carries me bridal style down the hallway to his apartment.

There was no way that he was about to let me out of his sight after what happened in the car—which thankfully, he hasn't mentioned since—so I wasn't surprised when he insisted that I stay the night with him. There wasn't any way that I was going to say no either.

This is exactly where I want to be.

"I think you mean absolutely jaw-droopingly handsome, sweetheart," he mumbles, kissing my head.

Keeping me held firmly in his arms, he manages to use his key to unlock the door before pushing it open with his foot.

Loud voices erupt through the doorway, and I lift my head in search of the culprit, hoping that we didn't walk in on something that's going to be burned in my memory for the rest of my life. But when I find Clay lying outstretched on the couch, feet hanging off the edge, a box of half-eaten pizza on the coffee table, and a horror movie playing on the TV screen, I laugh.

"Why aren't you gone?" Braden asks gruffly.

Clayton shoots up and reaches for the remote, turning the sound down a few notches before resting his eyes on the two of us.

"Well, if it isn't the two lovebirds. Finally home, are we?" He drags his attention to the clock above the T.V. "It's two in the morning, in case you forgot how to read a clock."

"And?" Braden shoots. His eyes drop to mine, sending me a warning before my feet are placed on the floor. "I didn't know that I had a curfew, Dad."

After pulling my dress further down my legs to avoid giving Clay a view of my goodies, I cross my arms and pin him with a look. "At least we were out doing something. What's your excuse?"

"Plans changed. Figured I would save my liver for the night and watch a movie."

"Smart." Braden snorts. When he laces his fingers with mine, I look up and see him already staring down at me with soft, muted eyes. "You tired yet?"

My mind screams yes but I shut it up, shaking my head instead. "I can stay awake for a while longer."

With as little as a nod in my direction, he pulls me behind him to the living room. And when Clayton makes no move to share the couch, Braden sits down in front of it, his back leaning against it. Grinning, I watch him pat his lap and hold his arms out in front of him. I settle on his thighs without hesitation.

He bends forward and presses his mouth to my ear. "Keep your hands to yourself, yeah? We have company."

A shiver racks through me at the thought of trying anything while Clayton sits only a few feet away. Braden's hands wrap around my waist and pull me as far against his chest as possible.

"I will if you will."

"Best behaviour, baby. Scouts honour." He pats my sides.

Clayton turns the volume back up, cutting our conversation short as we turn our attention to the young woman screaming for help on the screen. I attempt to ignore the consistent flutter in my chest with every soft stroke of Braden's thumb against my side but fail miserably. His body heat wraps around me tighter than his arms do, and I find my eyes starting to droop as his heart beats quickly against my back.

There's only one thing that runs through my mind before it all goes dark.

In just a few days, this is all going to disappear.

Braden

The bed is cold when I wake up, my least favourite feeling as of late. I don't have time to get frustrated by Sierra leaving because I hear her voice in the apartment, muffled by my closed bedroom door. The sound makes my lips lift in a smile as I sit up and stretch my arms behind my head. I look down at the pink pillow resting beside my black one and gnaw on my lip.

I've never been the guy to let a girl so much as keep a sock at his house, let alone half of the kind of shit that I find littered around here now. There's no room that's safe from the Sierra invasion, but I can't find it in myself to give a shit. It's so natural to me now seeing an extra toothbrush on the bathroom counter or a pair of booty shorts in my laundry basket.

Maybe that makes me a pussy-whipped loser. Who the hell knows.

Reaching down beside the bed, I stretch my arm out to

grab a t-shirt from the floor but freeze when my nightstand starts buzzing. As I move to pick up the vibrating phone, I hesitate when I notice it's Sierra's.

Do I, or don't I? Is there a rule that says I can't pick up her phone when it rings?

With a shrug of my shoulders, I grab it and flip it over, raising my brows at the caller ID on the screen. My pride gets the better of me and I answer the call with a clenched jaw.

"What do you want?"

"Who is this? Is Sierra there?" Cole asks, his tone cautious. *Good, he should be nervous.*

"It's her boyfriend," I all but growl at him, surprising myself when I use the title. We've never really discussed placing a label on our relationship, but this fucker doesn't need to know that.

"Right." He clears his throat. "Well, is Sierra available to talk? We need to discuss her flight times."

My eyes narrow as my stomach clenches, worry building in my spine. "What do you mean, flight times?"

"Yes. Flight times. For her move to Toronto next week," he says.

"She hasn't decided if she's taking your creepy ass offer yet, dickbag," I grind out, gripping my jaw tightly. "You're messing with the wrong fucking girl, Cole Travis. Don't think that I won't break you in half just because you're my girl's boss. I promise you that she would not sympathize with you in the slightest."

"Is that so?" He sounds bored. And fuck does that piss me off. "I'm sorry to be the one to inform you, but she has actually taken my offer. Maybe you should have a talk with your girlfriend before throwing such careless threats around. It seems that you're not on the same page. Please make sure you tell her to call me after you have your much-needed *talk*."

The dial tone rings in my ear after he hangs up on me. I

squeeze my eyes shut and dig deep for any ounce of calmness left in my ice-cold body.

I know that I haven't exactly been the most open about what exactly I wanted from this relationship, but I assumed she knew me well enough to know that I didn't think of this as a fling. I might not be ready to offer her a future of forever, but I would *try* and give her something close if that's what she wanted.

The thought of not having her anymore is like being stabbed from back to front with a serrated knife only to have it ripped back out again. The mere idea of it makes bile sting my throat.

After spending the past couple of months getting to know each other, I would have hoped that she would have told me about something as big as her taking a job across the country. If not for her own conscience, then for me. Because if she is planning on leaving, then I don't know why the fuck we've been wasting our time together, building something that would only burn to the ground.

With a fire raging in my chest, I toss her phone on the bed and stand, nearly ripping my door off its hinges as I open it. I spot her leaning against the kitchen counter wearing a baggy shirt and pyjama pants as she laughs at something Clayton must have said.

Unable to hold myself back, I yank off the Band-Aid without warning. "When were you going to tell me that you took that fucking job?"

When she spins to stare at me, wide-eyed and tense, I know that Cole was telling the truth. That fucking weasel was telling the truth and she's been lying to me for *days*. What a slap to the face.

"Brade—" she squeaks, but I cut her off with a dark chuckle.

"I never took you for a liar, Sierra. It definitely doesn't suit you."

"I never lied to you. I hadn't decided yet," she mumbles, staring at her toes, her neck a dark shade of red.

Guilt flows off of her in waves, but I don't let it affect me. I refuse to back down from this.

"That's not an excuse. You had plenty of time over the past few days to tell me. I've been with you constantly. But you were going to wait, right? Until when? The day you left? Well sorry to ruin all of your fun, but I know now and I'm done wasting my time."

"Wasting your time? Nice," she scoffs, looking at me again with narrowed eyes.

"If I would have known that you would be leaving, I wouldn't have bothered letting you meet my parents or leave your shit all over my house! You made everything so much more complicated," I hiss, running a hand through my hair and pulling at the ends.

"Well, it's great to know that it's so easy for you to throw me away and move on with your life. It's not like I'm moving to another country! We could always try to make it work."

"I'm just going to go," Clayton mumbles, earning himself a glare from both of us as he scurries off to his bedroom.

When his door shuts behind him, I spin back to Sierra, a dangerous mix of betrayal and hurt building deep in my chest.

"Try to make *what* work? As much as I love fucking you, I'm not going to fly across the country to have an endless tap of your pussy." I laugh humourlessly, ignoring the ache in my chest when I see the new shine in her silver eyes. My protective walls slide back up, where they should have been the entire fucking time. I was a helpless idiot to think it was okay to let them down.

"Good to know," she whispers, shoulders dropping before she's walking to the front door, not sparing me a second look.

I'm hot on her heels, aching to push her against the wall and fuck this decision right out of her. I don't want her to leave, but the words won't stop flowing from my fat mouth.

"I wish you the best of luck. I'm sure Cole will be there for all of those lonely nights," I say.

She slips her shoes on quickly and opens the door, hesitating in the doorway. "I knew that you wouldn't come with me. That's why I didn't say anything. I knew that telling you I took the job would have meant the end of us. I should have told you; I know that. I just wanted more time."

And then she's gone, stepping into the hallway and disappearing from my life.

I can't find it in myself to chase her or so much as close the door once she's gone. Instead, I send my fist through the wall and watch the drywall dust float in the air, too numb to care that my blood now drips on the floor.

32

Sierra

My feet ache and my arms feel like warm string cheese. The box I'm holding wobbles as I attempt to move it from my bedroom to the living room. To some, it might seem pointless to move a singular box from one room to another just a few feet away, but with the number of boxes cluttering up my bedroom, I'll take whatever free space I can manage.

Waking up in the middle of the night to go to the washroom, only to end up stubbing your big toe on a heavy box and falling on your ass isn't how I would like to spend my last two nights here.

My sigh of relief replaces the sound of my laboured breathing when I finally place the collection of picture frames on the floor. The glass clatters as the poorly packed frames bang around inside the box.

Too drained to care, I just stretch out my cramped arms and kick the mess of broken glass away.

That's a problem for another day. And it's not like I have many family pictures inside that box, anyway. Most of the frames are filled with lame quotes that at one point in my life, made me think that I could take on the world. At this point, I don't think that I could take on the world even if I woke up gifted with every superpower known to man.

I head for the fridge in desperate need of some water. The cold fridge air makes me sigh with a weird mix of relief and pleasure. My eyes burn from exhaustion as I fight to keep them open, knowing full well how nasty my under-eye circles must be by now.

I haven't slept more than three hours a night in the past three days. Since leaving Braden's house, I've been lost in a sea of regret and confusion, unsure of where to go now. My future is flashing in front of me in the shape of a giant question mark.

I don't know if I've made a huge mistake, or taken a risk that will end up paying off in the end. I'm sure if my mother knew what I did she would praise me up and down, so proud of me for putting my career before anything else.

Is that what I want? To have made a decision that would have pleased my mother of all people?

The bottle of water meets my sweaty palm as I unscrew the lid like a maniac and finish the contents in a few gulps. The plastic crunches when I twist it and throw it toward the recycle bin, not bothering to look if it ended up on the floor or not.

Three light knocks on my front door have me smiling, knowing exactly who's on the other side.

"Coming!" When I pull open the door, my smile pulls into an even wider grin.

Clare stands with Liz on her back, legs wrapped around her waist in a bear grip. Both girls radiate happiness and love. It's an addicting, nearly overwhelming aura that I still haven't been able to fully comprehend. How could I? The only time I've experienced a bond even remotely the same is with my sister. And even then, it's not the same as what she has with her daughter.

"Auntie!" Liz shouts and jumps down from Clare's back. She rushes toward me and hugs my leg tightly before pushing her way inside and heading for the colouring book and crayons I left out for her on the couch.

"She'll be busy all night now. Smart move." Clare steps inside, shutting the door behind her. "It looks awful in here. Are you sure you're leaving in two days?"

"Don't remind me," I sigh and walk to the kitchen. "Want something to drink? I have water or wine."

"Go easy with all the options, sis." She laughs. "Did you leave any glasses unpacked or are we drinking it from the bottle?"

Pulling open my cupboard door, my lip slips between my teeth when I realize I haven't been drinking from a glass for a few days now. "Bottle?"

"From the look of your overflowing recycle bin, it looks like tonight isn't the only time this week you've been drinking straight from the bottle," she says, attempting to hide her curiosity with an otherwise harmless poke.

"You caught me." I shut the cupboard again before pulling a mostly full bottle of red wine from the fridge and sucking back a few sips.

"On second thought, you can enjoy that on your own."

I try to find the judgment in her voice but come up short. Not that I'm surprised. My sister is the least judgmental person I know. If anybody is going to understand my sudden obsession with booze, it's her.

"Thanks." I wipe my mouth with the back of my hand and hold the bottle by my side.

"Wanna talk about it?" Clare pulls a barstool away from the small kitchen island and sits down, her brows pulled in tight, round eyes locked on mine.

"There isn't anything more to talk about." I sit in the seat beside her. The bottle rests on the countertop as I lean forward on my elbows and close my eyes.

"That's a lie," she scoffs. "Have you talked to him since? If you leave without at least trying to talk to him you know that you'll regret it, S."

Right. I forgot that she was the one who brought me home Sunday morning. There was no way that I could have avoided explaining the situation to her after I started sobbing in her SUV.

"He doesn't want to talk to me. He's probably banging someone else as we speak."

The thought alone of another girl in his bed makes my skin burn and my top teeth scrape the bottom ones in an almost animalistic action. I know that I lost the right to care about who he spends his nights with, but I can't help that I still care. I care way too much, and I have no idea when or *if* I'll be able to stop.

His words still echo in my ears, burning fresh in my mind when I try to fall asleep at night. *"As much as I love fucking you, I'm not going to fly across the country to have an endless tap of your pussy."*

The crack in my chest deepens, my love for him burning a hole inside of me. I hoped that he had felt even relatively similar feelings for me, but I know that it was a far-fetched idea. We were never meant to be forever. I was just a step in the right direction for him. A reminder that he doesn't always have to hide that big heart of his behind that playboy facade.

"I doubt that." Clare's soothing voice breaks me out of my jumbled thoughts. "If he felt even remotely close to what you felt for him, I guarantee he's wondering how to reach out to you."

A laugh breaks through my frown. "You don't know him. He's not the type."

"No?" she asks, lifting a brow. "Well, I know *you*. And

there's no way you were spending your time and effort on someone who didn't deserve it. That fact alone makes me believe that he isn't as bad as you're trying to convince the both of us he is. I don't need to know him to know that."

My eyes bulge as I stare at my sister, a feeling of gratefulness swelling behind my chest bone. What happened to the thirteen-year-old girl who spent three hours on hold with the oven company because she couldn't figure out how to turn the oven on and *needed* to bake me a birthday cake? Or the seventeen-year-old who went to the drugstore in the middle of the night to buy me a pack of pads when I got my first period because "every grown woman should have her own set of hygiene products."

I would do anything to go back and relive those moments.

"I always forget how old and wise you've gotten," I grumble.

She shrugs away my compliment. "Sometimes people surprise you, Sierra. You have to at least give him a chance to."

"Even if he did, it wouldn't matter. I would be setting myself up for an even worse heartbreak down the road. I want to get married someday, Clare. He doesn't believe in that sort of thing."

Clare surprises me by laughing.

"What's funny about that?" I narrow my eyes and tilt my head.

"You love him, right? And don't lie to me."

"I do," I reply softly. There's no doubt about it. If I didn't, losing him wouldn't feel like having my heart wrung out like a wet towel.

"Then don't be ridiculous. Men don't know what they want half the time. Not until they grow up and find the right person. How do you know that you aren't Braden's right person?"

"I don't know."

"It wouldn't be easy, but at the risk of sounding incredibly cheesy right now, nothing worth the risk is ever easy."

"That *was* cheesy," I agree. "But also very wise."

Lifting the wine bottle to my lips, I let her words marinate in my mind and the liquid slide down my throat. My immediate response is to tell her that she's right and promise to go see him. To make things right. But the fear of rejection is overwhelming. It looms over me like a rain cloud.

I hate that I've been wasting my last few days in Vancouver locked inside my apartment packing things that I don't even care to bring with me.

I should be with Braden.

I want to be with him, but does he care for me enough to want to try and make this work, knowing how complicated it could be? We both deserve closure, though. How am I supposed to move away, not knowing if we were ever really, really over? That there might have been a chance but I was too stubborn to take it?

Shit. Why is loving somebody so damn hard?

Braden

"Holy fuck!" I spit through a clenched jaw. My stiff body slides into the ice-chunk-filled bathtub and I start shivering instantly. Squeezing my eyes shut, I let my ass smack the bottom before unclenching my legs and pressing my heels to the metal sides.

"Did you expect it to be warm?"

I peel my right eye open and watch Tyler snort his reply from the row of lockers in front of me. He rips his locker door open and grabs his bag, tossing it to a bench before sitting down beside it.

"Hurry up and go home." I let my neck fall limp and my head sags forward, my eyes closing again.

"Someone's exceptionally touchy today."

"In case you haven't noticed, I'm a little sore," I grunt.

"That's what happens when you get your ass beat for the second time in two days by someone out of your weight class. I told you not to fight that guy."

The locker door slams shut and I clench my sore jaw. The last thing I want to hear right now is a fucking I told you so. Especially from my brother.

"Do you have anything useful to say or are you just going to continue to lecture me?"

"I'm not lecturing you. I just think there are better things that you can be doing with your time right now. Like trying to find a place to live in Toronto."

My eyes pop open instantly before narrowing on his shrugging shoulders. "Not going to happen."

"Was worth a shot," he sighs, leaning back against the metal locker with crossed arms.

"Was it?"

"It was. Not like it pulled your head out of your ass at all, though."

"Like I said. You can leave anytime now."

"You know that hurting yourself won't make you feel any better or bring her back, right? There's only one way to do that and you seem too stubborn to dump that damn pride of yours to do so."

I lift my right arm out of the ice water and place my palm on the edge of the tub, gripping it so tightly that the cuts on my knuckle begin to pool with blood again. "I don't want her back. I was the one who ended things with her."

I'm not sure if I'm more upset with myself or Tyler for

bringing her up right now, but in all honesty, it doesn't matter. I was thinking about her long before he brought her up. Like I have been every fucking day since I've last seen her.

It's been three days since I've touched her, kissed her, and felt her body against mine. I haven't heard her laughter or felt the lurch in my chest that comes along with each smile she gifts me. I'm pissed off at the world, just like I was when I was an angsty teen. It's ridiculous.

"Yeah, because you're an absolute idiot," he says and moves toward me. "It runs in the family, don't feel too embarrassed. It takes a lot of missed shots and sleepless nights alone, but it is possible to learn how women work."

I roll my eyes. "It took Dad a divorce to learn how."

"Your parents didn't get divorced just because Dad didn't know how to treat your mother, Braden. You know that." He flashes me a pointed look. "Plus, just because Dad was divorced, doesn't mean we're all doomed to the same fate. *I've* never been divorced, nor do I ever plan on it. You just have to realize what you have to lose and whether or not you're willing to lose it. It took me far too long to come to that realization, brother."

"You and I are *very* different, Tyler Bateman."

"So what?" he asks stiffly, *aggressively*, like he doesn't like me calling him by his mother's surname.

I did it to put some distance between us, feeling too exposed under his expert stare. We've known each other too long for him not to be able to see right through me, but it still pisses me off.

"So, one of us is meant for a real relationship while the other is not. You, my dear brother, are the one that was destined to be a husband and father. You believe in the *happily ever after* bullshit. I don't. I don't want to have someone rely on me that heavily. I don't want that sort of pressure." I don't know if I would be able to stand beneath the weight of it.

"So, you plan on living the rest of your life in a different pussy every night? Give me a break."

"If that's what happens then sure. I could think of worse ways to live." Lifting my arms above my head, I stretch out the numbing ache in my shoulders. "Hand me a towel, would you?"

Tyler tosses me one, tenser than a stretched elastic band. "You can't fool me with this tough guy shit, Braden. You miss her and you're too stubborn to tell her that. You're going to regret letting her leave."

My teeth scrape the inside of my cheek as I get out of the tub and step onto the cement floor. I wrap the towel around my wet underwear, water pooling at my feet.

I don't just miss her. I'm way beyond that, and I'm sure the purple crescents of exhaustion beneath my eyes make that more than obvious. The bed doesn't feel the same without her warm, smooth skin or clumps of brown hair that almost always wind up in my face as I sleep.

"It doesn't matter what you think. I'm going to be fine—she's going to be fine, we're both going to be *fine*. We weren't even that serious."

Tyler bursts into a fit of laughter, gripping the side of the bench and keeling over dramatically. My anger begins to bubble under my skin the longer I watch him put on a show.

"Right," he chortles. "Let me ask you a question."

I blink, not trusting myself to speak.

"If you weren't serious, then I don't suppose it would upset you to think of her being swept off of her feet by some big-time successful hotshot in Toronto? It doesn't make you angry in the slightest to think of him bending her over their shiny kitchen countertops and having her scream his name, begging for more of his coc—"

His words stop short when I shove him against the lockers, my forearm pressed tight even against his throat so that he feels the weight of it against his windpipe. With a tilt of his head, he grins, eyebrows dancing with amusement. "Exactly."

With a grunt, I release the pressure on his throat and place my palms on his chest to shove myself back. My nostrils flare as I shove my hands through my hair. "You have a fucking death wish."

"Call it whatever you want. But you know that I'm right. You can't have it both ways. If you let her go because you refuse to stop letting the past live in the present, then you'll lose her. You can't live your life out of fear, Braden. You'll end up living it alone."

"Thanks for the advice." There's only a tiny note of appreciation in my tone. The reality of his words sits heavy on my chest, pressing down on top of me like a cement block.

I know that my parent's marriage screwed me up, I've never denied that. But my feelings toward relationships and marriage aren't going to change just because of one girl. It doesn't matter how much I care about her. There's no knowing if we would even be happy together somewhere that's not here. I would be risking my entire life in Vancouver over a pipe dream and a beautiful woman.

We could spend years together, but once it came to marriage, I would never be able to give her what she wants. I would only be delaying the inevitable heartbreak that we would be facing years down the road.

Staying away from her is the smart thing to do. And for once, I'm going to do the right thing, for both of us.

"Just think about it, Braden. She doesn't leave until tomorrow. You still have time."

Deciding to just give him what he wants, I nod my head, clearing my throat. "Okay."

Tyler grins and straightens his shoulders. "Okay? Like you'll think about it? You're not just saying that to get me to drop it?"

"Yeah. I'll think about it. Just for you."

"I'll take it." He laughs and tosses his bag over his shoulder. "Now get dressed so we can leave."

With a fake salute, I snicker, "Aye aye, captain."

33

Sierra

The desk drawer slides shut slowly, almost as if I'm trying to delay the inevitable. Which I totally am.

I wasn't in this office for very long. Definitely not for as long as I had anticipated. But given that it was the very first office I've ever had all to myself, I'm going to miss it. Even if it was *way* too close to the men's washroom for my hearing pleasure.

I never even had time to hang my degree on the wall. But the Devil is in the details I suppose. From the pictures Cole sent me of my new office in Toronto, I think it's safe to assume that I'll have more than enough room to do so this time around.

"You really pushed it to the last minute, I see."

Looking up from the sleek black desk, now completely bare of anything but the medium sized box packed with my few personal belongings, I see Cole leaning arms crossed in the doorway. There's a typical teasing glimmer in his eyes, one that pairs almost too well with his sinister grin. He smells like trouble today, and that makes me nervous.

"I suppose I did," I reply tightly. I was hoping to make it

out of here without having to deal with him anymore than necessary. I'll already have far too much Cole time once we arrive in Toronto.

"Is everything else ready? Did you end up deciding on an apartment?"

"I did."

It only took a week and three Skype calls with the landlord, but I move into a new construction, two-bedroom condo the day after tomorrow. In a perfect world, I would be handed the keys as soon as I land in Toronto tomorrow afternoon, but with such short notice, I'm lucky to be moving in just a day late. Plus, who would say no to a free, company-paid hotel room for a night? Not me. I'm looking forward to spending far too long in the hotel spa. Maybe I'll even book an acupuncture appointment. There has to be a nerve that can be poked and prodded to clear Braden from my head.

"Excited?" Cole asks, dropping his arms and moving further into the room.

Of course, I am. But I would describe the cluster-fuck of emotion's inside of me as more so terrifying than anything else.

"It's going to be a big change," I say.

"One that I hope you're ready for?" The questioning edge in his words rub me the wrong way, but I shove my feelings to the side and bite my tongue, deciding to be the bigger person.

"If I wasn't ready, I wouldn't be going. You can trust me on that." Now please leave before I scratch your eyes out and feed them to a stray cat.

His smile is back as quickly as it had faded, and with an almost missable wink, he says, "See you tomorrow then, little worker bee."

I nearly puke.

"YOU WANT me to go to a club and get wasted with you the night before I hop on an early morning flight across the country?" I scoff, squeezing my phone between my shoulder and ear as I open my apartment door and drop the contents of my desk on the counter. "Is this payback for something?"

Re-adjusting the phone, I put the call on speaker and place it down beside the box so I can unbuckle my strappy heels.

"You so owe me this, Sierra. You're about to make a bunch of new fancy friends and forget about me while I eat cookie dough ice cream by myself and miss you," Sophie wines.

"I'm not going to forget about you, Sophie. You're my best friend," I promise her, hating that she's doubting that for even a second.

"Okay, well come anyway. It'll be our last hoorah. Don't miss out on our final girls' night because you're scared of a tiny hangover."

I lean my elbows on the counter and let my head fall until my forehead touches it. I love Sophie to death but I was really hoping to just spend my last night here, curled up on the couch, eating my feelings in deep-dish pizza. But as hard as she tries to understand everything running through my mind these last few days, she really has no idea how I feel. I don't blame her for that, of course, but when she pushes these things on me it becomes more exhausting than helpful.

Besides, the only thing alcohol has done for me lately is make me unbelievably horny. Although, I do partially blame that on the fact that before this week, I wasn't going more than a single day without having sex. Braden is to blame for that. He completely ruined my single-girl routine.

"Fine. What time?" I rub my temples.

"I'll come get you at ten! Love you, gorgeous." She hangs up on me before I reply, leaving me confused and a little annoyed.

"Whatever," I whisper to myself and comb my fingers through my hair. Looking at the time on my phone, I'm grateful that I still have a few hours to relax before going to completely destroy my liver.

Now I just have to decide which one of my TV boyfriends will keep my company until then.

My head bobbles as another hard chest pushes against my back. Sweaty hands cup the skin of my waist through the cut-outs in my uncomfortably tight dress. Sophie's choice, of course.

My thoughts are cloudy, tongue way too numb to tell whoever this guy is that I'm fine on my own. I let my eyelids slide shut as the neon lighting becomes too much for my throbbing head. In an attempt to collect myself, I lean against the body behind me, just for a second.

The man smells like cheap body spray and orange juice, a combo that makes my nose crinkle and my stomach churn. Just a little bit longer, Sierra. Then you can hop in a cab, sleep for a couple of hours, and wake up, ready to start your new life.

Sophie and I got here about two hours ago, give or take an hour, but I haven't seen her for at least half of that time. My anger toward her lack of company probably explains why I drank so much so fast, and why the earth is doing the wave.

Hot breath crashes against my exposed neck, and I tilt my head to the side, as if on instinct. I'm too drunk to feel embarrassed for not pushing this guy away. And hopefully, tomorrow will just be a blur when I wake up.

I feel the stranger pull away from me and shrug my shoulders, muttering something unintelligible under my breath. Straightening my spine, I palm my thighs and start to walk off the dance floor, but stumble backward when another set of hands grab me. My skin sizzles where we touch, and I gasp.

The stranger's chest is hard but welcoming, and it moulds against my back in a way that I can't comprehend. His jaw is rough and covered in stubble. He brushes it against my cheek, nudging my head to fall to the side to allow him to run his nose along my racing pulse.

"I saw you all the way from the bar. You're impossible to miss. Just like you were the first time we danced like this."

My eyes close when I hear his voice, my entire body becoming a burning ball of fire and melting away the ice I let build up inside my chest. Whatever was left of my guard is dropped as I turn around and reach for him. My palms lay flat on his rising chest and I swallow the boulder in my throat before raising my gaze to his, eager to see what's waiting for me behind those amber eyes.

"Braden," I choke.

The smell of whiskey is strong on his breath, reminding me that the sheen in his gaze probably matches the one in mine.

When he doesn't respond, I suck in a sharp breath and drop my gaze to the black t-shirt that looks as if it was painted on his model-worthy chest.

Jealousy—one of the most unwanted emotions—claws up my skin as I think of every one of the other girls in this club that probably caught his eye tonight. Did he look at them the way he's looking at me? Like he could take me right here, right now, and not care who watches?

"Why are you here, Sierra?" he slurs, voice rising to be

heard over the bass thumping around us. "You shouldn't be here. Not dressed like that."

His possessiveness sends shock waves directly to my clit. "What should I be doing then?"

His bottom lip slides between his teeth. "Anything. You prefer staying in, wearing those tiny little cookie monster pyjamas and drinking all of my orange juice. Why not do that?" He sighs heavily and moves his hands up my body to cup my cheeks.

"I didn't want to come here either. But I'm starting to think it was a good decision." I lean into his touch and close my eyes, practically purring while attempting to think of my next words carefully. I don't want to scare him away.

"Stop thinking. Just let me kiss you before you leave. One last time." He's begging, not bothering to try and hide it. It makes my heart soar, knowing how desperately he needs me. Even if it's just for right now. Because I need him too. So much it fucking hurts.

I've barely nodded before his lips are on mine, pushing against them with an unspoken goodbye. A goodbye that makes my eyes burn with the fear that I've made a mistake. One that I'll never be able to come back from. He takes my mouth and owns it, pushing forward a million different emotions and feelings that have my entire body in a disarray.

He pulls back slowly, eyebrows scrunched with curiosity, eyes focused on my cheek. It's not until I feel the wetness on my cheeks that I realize I've been crying, and that he's been brushing away every single tear with his thumbs.

"I love you," I whisper, unable to take the pain of holding back any longer. My voice is so quiet, so broken. The only thing that lets me know he's heard me is the instant look of fear that spreads across his handsome features.

Noise has never felt as silent as it does right now, as he drops his hands, almost as if my skin has burnt his fingertips.

His head shakes, lips parting before meeting again, over and over until he jerks back, nearly tripping over his own feet.

"Fuck. *Fuck.* I'm sorry," he sputters, jaw tensing as his eyes harden to stone. "I need to go."

I stand frozen, my feet glued to the dance floor of the place I can never come back to. I watch him turn from me and walk away with an urgency that has my chest splitting wide open and my heart slipping to the ground, two severed pieces laying at my feet.

34

Braden

"WHO'S HANGING A FUCKING PICTURE?" I GRUMBLE, MY TONGUE dry as all shit.

The incessant knocking reverberates through the apartment, yanking me from my restless sleep. My hands press to my eyes until I see static.

When the knocking shows no signs of stopping, I grind my teeth together and slowly open my left eye, ignoring the blasting burn in my retina.

"Clayton!" I yell before a throb in my forehead scolds me. A tingle in my arm makes me attempt to shake it out from underneath my head, and I cringe at the pain that shoots through my shoulder at the movement.

It's not hard to tell the more I wake up that I'm not laying in my bed. And as my vision becomes less and less blurred, I make note of the bathtub and toilet. With a humourless, dark laugh, I drag a hand down my face.

I didn't even make it to my room last night. What a fucking accomplishment.

My short temper—my favourite side effect of drinking myself into a vomiting mess—begins sparking as the knocking continues. With a hiss, I push myself up off the floor and stand with a slight wobble, my jaw aching as I grip the counter for balance.

Ripping the bathroom door open, I shrink away at the brightly lit apartment with an immediate scowl. My attention moves to the front door when I realize the knocking is coming from behind it. With a huff, I look down to double-check to make sure I'm not stark naked and stalk to the door.

"Relax already! Jesus Christ," I grunt, unlocking the door.

I don't even have the door pulled open an inch before a red-faced blonde is shouldering her way inside and pushing at my chest. She shoves me for a second time, and I take it, not lucky enough to have forgotten the reason that she's here.

Sierra. It's always Sierra.

I force myself to stand tall, even when I want to collapse to my knees and beg her to help me go get my girl. My head is pounding, and my thoughts look a lot like scrambled eggs, but the picture of Sierra, so broken and helpless, remains untouched, standing among the mess like a prized possession. It makes me sick, so beyond disgusted with myself.

Instead of doing what every fibre of my being wants and needs me to, I harden my features and with my tone like ice, say, "Get out of my house, Sophie."

My words seem to piss her off even more, just like I knew they would. With a look that probably could have tossed me six feet under had I not already felt like death, she stabs a finger into my sternum. "You have some nerve, jackass."

"What the hell did I do to you?" I swallow past the bile in my throat and move away from her, closing the apartment door with more force than necessary. My fingers curl into fists that I want to throw through a wall, but I choose to bang them against my thighs instead.

"You did everything!" she spits, glaring so hard it wouldn't surprise me if she burst a blood vessel in her temple. "Do you have any idea the damage you've done? Or do you just not care?"

"How I feel isn't any of your concern. Now get out." I gesture to the door with as much arrogance as I can muster up through the growing knot in my stomach.

If only Sierra could see me now. She would have wished that she kept those pretty words inside her mouth and saved them for somebody deserving of them.

"Isn't any of my concern? Sierra is the only person I give a shit about in this world. And I was the one who took her home crying last night after you shattered her to pieces. I've never seen her that way before. So fucking lifeless, like the light was snatched right out of her soul."

I push back the wall of guilt rising in my chest before forcing myself to shrug. My insides are screaming for mercy as they're torn apart by the reality of what happened last night. Of what I *did*. My next words sound as weak as they feel. "Sierra is strong. She'll be fine."

Sophie barks out a humourless laugh and takes a brave step closer to me. "You're even dumber than I thought you were, you know that? I hoped you were more than just a pretty face, but turns out you're even less."

"I don't care what you think of me." I can't even keep eye contact with her.

She wears her disgust for me with pride, and it carves into my back deep enough to scar. Sophie doesn't know me, and I don't know her, but we used to share something so fucking deep, something that made us connected on some weird, spiritual level.

We don't like each other—I'm pretty sure she would volunteer *my* name as Tribute if given the chance—but we did respect each other. Now, though? There's no respect there, not on her end. And I can't blame her for that.

"What kind of person walks away from someone when

they tell them they love them? You can't honestly want me to believe that you don't love her too. I've seen it!" She ridicules me fearlessly, not backing down an inch. There's a warrior inside of this tiny girl. One that doesn't know how to tell when the battle has already been lost.

"I don't give a shit what you believe, trust me." I snort, crossing my arms across my bare chest and digging my nails into my biceps.

"You keep saying that but somehow, I don't believe you," she nearly sings, a cockiness flooding her confident tone that has the same effect on me as nails on a chalkboard. "We both know that you could have easily thrown me out by now if you didn't want to hear what I had to say somewhere very deep in that bitter, frozen chest of yours."

I narrow my sharp gaze. "Get out. This is the last time I'm going to say it."

"She's leaving in four hours. There's still time to tell her how you feel before she's gone."

My breath hitches before I shake my head shutting that hope right down. "She'll have fun in Toronto."

"You have got to be the most stubborn person I have ever met," she groans. "You're lucky I care enough about Sierra to even waste my time standing here arguing with you."

"Feel free to leave. I've only told you to do so a hundred damn times." I gesture to the door again with a pointed look.

"That's not what I'm trying to—" she cuts herself off by sucking in a dramatic breath and closing her eyes briefly. "You have one last chance, Braden. In four hours, you lose that chance. The chance to ever see her again. To ever hold her or see her smile again. Is that what you want? Because I know that's not what she wants."

Her gorgeous smile flashes in my mind, making my lungs tighten to the point of near suffocation. The urge to tear at my chest becomes overwhelming as I attempt to ignore the regret swarming my head with every flash of her tear-stained cheeks. The unmistakable taste of metal rings in my mouth as I clamp down on my tongue, her words playing over and over in my head like a broken record.

I love you.

Three words turned every inch of me stone-cold without warning. Three words that I should have said back to her, but couldn't—*wouldn't.* Not when I knew they would have come with the plea of asking her to stay. To give up the chance of a lifetime, one that she deserves more than anything because I'm too much of a chicken to take the chance on her and me.

"It's too late. I can't drop my entire life on a pipe dream."

"Braden, if I had someone look at me the way that you look at Sierra, I wouldn't doubt love—real, passionate love—ever again. Don't give that up because you're afraid. We're all afraid. But sometimes it's worth the fear of the unknown. And I think you two *are* worth it. Don't you?"

"What would I even do? Stop her at the airport without a working plan as to what happens next?"

"You can figure that stuff out after you tell her how you feel. Don't let her leave thinking that all she was to you was a fuck buddy—a way to pass the time until you found something better. She deserves better than that."

"I know that, Sophie!" I curse, yanking on the messy hair flopping in my eyes just to feel the sharp pain. "This is too complicated."

"What's complicated?" Clayton asks, eyes droopy and bloodshot as he stumbles in through the front door, shirt hanging around his neck. I can feel my guard rising again as I straighten my back and shake my head, refusing to look at the hopeful glimmer in Sophie's eyes.

"You look like shit." I force myself to laugh.

"Ditto," he replies before turning to Sophie curiously. "What are you doing here? You two didn't . . ." There's something dark in his voice, something that he's attempting to hide.

"Hell no. You're disgusting," Sophie gags.

"Then what are you doing here?" He's too curious.

"She was picking up the rest of Sierra's shit before she leaves town," I rush, nodding to the small collection of clothes piled up outside my bedroom.

Realization flashes across his face as he nods and breaks into a smile. "In that case, wanna join me for breakfast, gorgeous?"

"No thanks. I have to get those clothes to Sierra. She leaves in four hours." Her last sentence is shot toward me, and I hate that I'm going to pretend like I never heard this entire conversation as soon as she leaves.

My gaze drops to the floor when she bends down to grab the last remnants of Sierra, and I keep it there until she says goodbye to Clayton and leaves.

It isn't until I hear the front door click shut again that I look up and clench my fists until my knuckles are white.

Sierra

The back of Clare's SUV sags as I place the last of my bags inside. I never thought I would find myself relating to an inanimate object, but I feel pretty saggy myself right about now.

I can almost feel the curiosity radiating off my sister as she remains eerily quiet and stands on the road behind me. When I step to the side, out of the way, she doesn't hesitate to reach out and close the trunk door with a forced smile.

"Is there something you want to say, Clare? You're

creeping me out with the whole quiet thing. It's a bit out of character," I sigh, a ghost of a smile on my face that I know looks ridiculously fake.

"What? No." She laughs quickly. "I'm just excited for you. It has nothing to do with the puffy eyes or the fake smiles that I've been getting since I saw you this morning."

Even though I pushed, it still sucks to hear that I have done a shit job at keeping my feelings hidden. I didn't need to be dealing with this on the day that I'm supposed to leave and start over.

"Do you want to talk about it? Liz tells me that I'm a good listener."

"Can we go first? I don't want to miss my flight," I mumble, playing with the uneven strings on my baggy hoodie.

"Of course!" She nods and moves quickly toward her door.

As she gets inside, I let out a slow breath and look back at the plain brick building that I called home for such a short time. I always thought that I would be here longer, that I would create memories here that I would carry around with me. But the only memories I have in the empty walls of my old apartment are ones that I never plan to revisit again.

The sting building in my eyes is enough to push my feet toward the passenger door. I open it and quickly crawl inside, almost as if I'm running away from something. Which, I guess I am. Or more so running toward something else. Something far from here.

Clare starts driving as soon as I buckle up.

"Thanks again for driving me. I could have called a cab."

"Of course. I wouldn't make you take a cab. Plus, it gives me a little more time with you."

My heart warms. "What am I going to do without you?"

"Honestly? I have no clue. Probably end up trapped somewhere or losing your mind because you can't find something that's been sitting in front of you the whole time," she teases.

"Wow!" I suck in a breath. "You're feeling ruthless today."

"It's true. You're a damn mess sometimes, S. But I love you anyway."

I give my head a shake and shove her arm. "I wish I could argue with you on that."

"It gives you spunk. Nobody can be as perfect as me." She winks.

"You wish."

She's quiet for a minute as she fiddles with the radio controls, browsing through them. I lift a brow when she ends up letting the original station play. "So, everything is taken care of here then? No unfinished business? I would hate for you to leave with any regrets."

"Regrets?" I ask, folding my arms across my chest. It's easy to realize where she's going with this. "Unfinished business?"

"You know what I mean," she hums.

"Do I?"

"Stop answering all of my questions with questions," she groans. "You know exactly what I'm talking about. Or *who*, I'm talking about."

"Nope. No idea."

"Braden? Super-hot, super buff guy who you've been spending every minute of every day with for a couple of months now? I'm assuming it is him that's behind the puffy eyes and lost sparkle?"

"I'm just tired," I lie. "Sophie made me go out with her last night. I didn't get a lot of sleep."

"It looks like you didn't get any at all, S."

That's because I didn't. The only thing I saw every time I closed my eyes was the fear in Braden's eyes when I told him how I felt. I don't think I'll ever be able to sleep again.

"I got a few hours," I lie again.

"Come on. I know you better than that. I'm your big sister. And big sisters know everything."

"There's nothing else for me to take care of here. Trust me."

"Why not? Is he coming with you then?"

Her question makes a rough laugh rip up my throat and her eyes widen in shock. "I'm going to take that as a no?"

"Not in this lifetime, Clare. He doesn't feel the same way I do. That's all. Can we just leave it?"

"There's always more to it than that," she pushes, not dropping the subject. "Men just need a bit more of a shove than women do."

"I don't think that's the problem," I sigh.

"Then what is?" she asks. "I've never met the guy, but from what you've told me, he's just a hard shell to break. The typical fear of commitment and inability to open up type of guy."

"That's an understatement." A heavy one.

"He makes you happy though, right? I've seen it. It's been *nice* to see it. Really nice."

It's been nice to be happy. Refreshing, almost. But that's done, and I'm going to be happy again. Just in a different way. I don't need anyone to make me happy. Just myself.

"I can make myself happy," I reply confidently, nodding to myself and smiling slightly when I see the airport standing in front of the rising sun.

"I have no doubt about that. But maybe don't give up on him yet. He could always surprise you."

"Yeah, okay," I agree half-heartedly, my attention resting mostly on the excitement and nervousness I feel as we pull up to the drop-off lane in front of the airport. Butterflies swarm in my stomach, forcing me to swallow nervously. It's now or never.

As soon as the car comes to a stop in the drop-off line, I'm hopping out and moving to the back. Pulling open the trunk, I collect my bags before dropping them on the pavement and turning to see Clare standing off to the side. My heart lurches when I see the unshed tears in her eyes, hiding behind the pride I see there as well.

"I'm so proud of you, Sierra. Don't forget that. And don't forget to come visit us sometime. This will always be your home," she says, voice wavering.

I move to hug her quickly, wrapping her up tightly and nodding into her sweater. "I love you so much. I'll come back as soon as I can, and we'll FaceTime every single day," I whisper, sucking back my sniffle.

She pushes me back but keeps a firm grip on my shoulders as she says, "I love you too. Now go get 'em!"

I nod quickly, smiling for real this time before grabbing bags and heading to the sliding doors, not daring to look back and risk changing my mind.

35

Braden

"THERE'S STILL TIME TO STAY HERE," I MUTTER, DROPPING A newspaper-covered plate into a small moving box.

Dad's scowl is immediate as he rolls his eyes and continues folding fuzzy pink towels before packing them away neatly. "You don't have to help me. Tyler and Gracie could have."

"And miss out on this amazing bonding time? Yeah right."

My attitude has only gotten worse the longer I've been at my father's house, but as much as I'm dying to get the hell out of here and drown my feelings in whiskey, I would regret not spending every chance I have left with him. God knows I only have a few chances left before he runs away with his child bride.

"Attitude like yours is meant for a teenager, Braden. Not a grown-ass man."

"Don't lecture me, Dad." My shoulders tense and I place the glass I'm holding inside the box harder than I probably should have. Lucky for me, it doesn't break.

"If you want to act like a kid then I'm going to treat you

like one." He lifts a shoulder, sending me a fleeting look. "Can't you just drop it for a few hours?"

"Yeah," I grumble, leaving it at that. I don't have anything else to add. If he wants me to pretend that I'm okay with him leaving then he's being an even bigger idiot than usual. I'll never be okay with this.

"Do you want to talk about how you're feeling? Will that help? I'm ready to do just about anything so we can move forward. This is exhausting, Son," he sighs, shoulders sagging in defeat. "You don't have to like the idea, but I would appreciate it if you would just accept it and stop being such an ass about it so we can all move on. Lana isn't going anywhere."

"Right," I chortle.

"What?" he asks, brows lifted with an unspoken warning. "Spit it out."

I lean forward on the leather couch and grip my knees, meeting his pointed look with my own. "You expect me to believe that this marriage will be any different than your last one? You and Mom couldn't even make yours work and you had a little kid to think about. Not like that made a difference. You both dragged me into the middle of your gigantic shit storm instead of making it work."

The shock that crosses my dad's face nearly makes me proud, but I shrug away the feeling before it has a chance to fester.

"We never meant to drag you into anything," he whispers, eyes dropping to his sock-covered feet.

"Well, you did. Over and over again until Mom took off to travel the fucking world. Neither of you cared enough to hide your problems from me, and now you want me to believe that you'll be able to actually keep this one around?" I ignore the hurt in his eyes and continue, the built-up feelings crashing into me like a wave that I can't hold back. "I love you, Dad, but you both fucked up. And you fucked *me* up."

"If this is about Sierra, there's still ti—"

"No, there's not still time!" I'm shouting now, my skin burning under my fingertips when I rub my jaw and stand up. "She's gone and it's your fault! If my idea of love hadn't been so fucked up, maybe I wouldn't have let her leave me. Maybe I could have said it back instead of letting my fear destroy us! You should have seen her face. I *can't* stop seeing it."

"Braden," he chokes out, my name sounding muffled. "We never meant for you to carry our problems with you. If I could go back and change how we acted, I would have. You didn't deserve to witness that. Especially not at such a young age."

"Well, there is no going back. It's too late. It's too late for everything."

My hands slide in my hair, yanking on it in an attempt to distract myself from the burning in my chest, a feeling I never used to be used to, but have quickly grown to hate. I've been sucking these words in for years, way too many years. They keep sliding out like my tongue is covered in soap, and as hard as I try to feel guilty for saying them, I'm not.

"Your mom and I weren't meant to be together, Braden. We were just too young and naïve to realize that. We ignored the red flags, and we paid the price—*you* paid the price. That doesn't mean that you and Sierra would have made the same mistakes we did. You can't let that ruin your happiness," he says gently, standing in front of me now, sunken eyes dull and glossy.

"The way you light up when you see each other and grin until your cheeks hurt, that's how you know you have something special. Please don't give that up. Especially not because of your mother and me," he continues.

I squeeze my eyes shut and sigh heavily. "I love her, Dad. I love her more than I thought I could love anything or anyone and I hate it. I fucking hate knowing that to be with her, I have to give her the power to hurt me. How is that fair? How am I supposed to want to do that?"

"Nobody wants to give somebody else power over them. But we do it because we would rather have them for a short time than never at all. That's what you want, isn't it? To at least have the chance at real happiness with her? Even if it doesn't last forever?"

Is that what I want? Are a few more weeks, months, or even years with her worth the chance of it crashing down on top of us? By the way my stomach lurches as I ask myself that question, I think I know the answer already.

"What if she doesn't want me anymore? I wouldn't even be able to leave here for a few weeks. There's too much to do." I swallow, nerves starting to coat my skin.

"I don't think you have to worry about that," he chuckles. "As far as arrangements go, I know that Tyler wouldn't mind helping you. He acts like he owns the gym anyway. I'm sure he would love to be the real one in charge for a change. You can figure out the rest *after* you go tell her how you feel. The last thing you want is her boarding that plane thinking that your balls aren't in her carry-on."

A rough laugh tears up my throat before I look at the grandfather clock pushed to the corner of the living room and feel my mouth fall. Her plane leaves in an hour. She has to be at the airport already. "I'm not the guy that runs through an airport to make some intense, movie-worthy love confession, Dad."

He grips my shoulder in a tight grip and squeezes, staring at me with a look so intense my eyes widen. "Tough shit, Son. Today, that's exactly what you are."

My heart pounds against my rib cage, adrenaline beginning to burn beneath my skin. "Look," I say guardedly. "About what I said before—"

"Don't apologize," he cuts me off, voice heavy with authority. "You should never have had to feel like that in the first place. I'm sorry."

"I know. It's okay." I let my lips lift somewhat before I'm pulled into a rare hug. I know that the awkwardness I feel is shared between the two of us, but I try to ignore it and enjoy the moment.

"Okay." He clears his throat. "Now let me drive you to the airport so you can go get your girl."

My smile grows into a full-fledged grin as I nod twice and straighten my back with a new-found sense of confidence. It feels like I can breathe again, my head clear and body at the ready. There's a glimmer of hope on the horizon, one that I can almost taste.

It won't be easy, I know that. But I have to hope that she'll at least hear me out and understand where I was coming from. I still can't promise her forever, or that I'll be completely confident in handing her the reins and letting her lead me through the unknown, but she already owns me in a way that terrifies me the shit out of me. Why not offer her my heart on a silver fucking platter while I'm at it?

I look at my dad and say, "Let's go."

CAR HORNS BLARE and police lights reflect off the glass windows of the building beside us. My legs shake as I try Sierra's cell phone again and get her voicemail. I hang up without leaving a message, not trusting myself not to blurt out that I love her. She's not going to find out how I feel through a voicemail, that's for fucking sure.

"Can you not get around them?" I snap at Dad, unable to keep my calm.

"No." He's frustrated, like me. The four-car pile-up ahead has the entire highway backed up. We haven't moved in twenty minutes.

With the car in park and the knowledge that there's no way of getting out of here anytime soon, I push open the passenger door and get out. I face the car and slam my palms on the roof hard enough for the sound to echo through the street.

"Fuck!" I shout, feeling the weight of the past week fall heavy on my shoulders, threatening to crush me like a bug under a boot. I welcome the feeling, knowing that all of this is my fault, my doing.

If I had just let the past go and focused on the future I could have had with Sierra, none of this would have ever fucking happened. We would be on that plane together right now, her head on my shoulder, my arm slung around her. I wouldn't be here, in the middle of the highway, banging my fists on the roof of a car and shouting like a maniac.

She left thinking I thought so little of her. Thinking that she was just some woman I chose at a bar to keep my bed warm until I found something better. But there is nobody better for me than my little fighter. The woman with all the answers all the time, a witty sense of humour that keeps my heart thumping and my dick hard, and a drive for success that has me wanting to do and *be* better.

She excites me, tortures me, and pisses me off like nobody I've ever met. We're such opposites that to most people, we don't look like we would work. But we do. We really do. Our chemistry is beyond anything that I've felt with anyone else. We fit together like we were made to do so, and just the thought of never having her in my arms again has my chest feeling so tight that every breath I take is like tiny razor blades tearing through my lungs.

I feel a hand on my back and flinch, tensing my body like

I'm attempting to protect it from an outside invasion, as if the real monsters weren't already inside.

"You should call Sophie," Dad says behind me.

I nod, feeling too numb to do anything else. Sierra's gone, her plane already boarded and getting ready for takeoff. I only had an hour to get to her, and we've been stuck here for too long.

My cell phone is placed in my hand and I call Sierra's best friend. She answers after the first ring, alarm evident in her voice.

"Braden? What's wrong?"

"I was too late."

The seconds pass slowly as she breathes heavily into the phone. When she finally speaks, I almost fall to my knees.

"No, you weren't. I'm going to help you fix this."

EPILOGUE

THREE WEEKS LATER

Sierra

"SEE YOU TOMORROW, SIERRA!"

Spinning on my heel, I stop and throw a wave at our sweet-as-honey receptionist, my lips forming a genuine smile.

"Have a good night, Gretchen," I reply, laughing lightly when she throws me a wink and nods, her tightly bound red curls bouncing around her head.

I've grown to care for the outgoing redhead over the past three weeks. It's been seriously hard not to. Her charismatic energy and warm smile always give me the warm and fuzzies. It's also been awesome having someone to talk about TV dramas with on slow days. It helps with how much I miss Sophie and my sister.

With a pep in my step, I pull my knee-length coat tighter across my chest and continue walking through the office building, giving the security guard a smile when he pushes open the door for me.

The smell of fresh garlic bread makes my mouth water the second my heels connect with the pavement, courtesy of the small Mom and Pop Italian restaurant a few buildings down. As if on a timer, my stomach growls, reminding me that I forgot to plan dinner tonight. I groan, fully aware of the extra weight I've packed on since moving to Toronto.

Pizza again it is. Or maybe Chinese. Eh, either work. *Stay focused, Sierra.*

There's still no snow on the ground yet and the temperature isn't too low, so I can still walk to and from work without getting too cold. I'm grateful for the moderate weather. I can't even imagine the nightmare it would be trying to find parking outside of our downtown office every morning. Plus, I really like walking to and from work. It gives me some much-needed time to relax after a busy day.

The only downside to walking everywhere every day is having the giant Toronto crowds of businessmen and women, bikers, and impatient teens all trying to do the same thing, pushing past you as if you're invisible. Which I guess to them, you are. It's not always so bad, but some days I think I might prefer the struggle of trying to find a parking stall. Emphasis on *some days*.

A grateful smile pulls on my slightly wind-bitten cheeks when I come up to the obscenely tall, forty-story condominium. I fiddle with the keyring in the pocket of my jacket, pulling out my fob and unlocking the doors before walking inside.

After greeting the concierge, I get into the empty elevator, and lean my head against the wall, closing my eyes as exhaustion washes over me. The ride up to my floor is a lengthy one, and I sometimes debate whether or not a power nap on the way could be warranted. The idea is quickly shot down when I imagine stopping to pick someone up on the way and being seen with drool running down my jaw.

My phone starts vibrating in my pocket, and my heart soars when I pull it out and see Sophie's name flashing across the screen.

"Hello, gorgeous," I sing. It's only been two days since

I've spoken to my best friend, but in my opinion, that's two days too long. It's been hard adjusting to the distance, especially when I first moved here, but every day gets a bit easier.

"Hey, baby cakes. Did I catch you at an alright time? Are you on your way home?"

"Yep. I'm in the elevator. I'm surprised there's enough service here to talk, actually."

She laughs, the sound awfully nostalgic. "That's what you get when your rent is more than what I make in a month."

"How is work going? Have the kids driven you insane yet?"

A week after I left, Sophie got a job teaching kindergarten at her old elementary school. The previous teacher had quit midway through October, and they had been in the middle of looking for a replacement when Sophie's resume came up. This is the first steady job that she's had since we graduated, and I couldn't be happier for her.

"I had one kid throw a used Kleenex at me yesterday, but other than that it's been really great."

"Good, Soph. That's *really* good." I toy with the ends of my hair. "Have you seen Clayton lately?"

She sucks in a sharp breath. "Yeah. But what you really want to know is if I've seen his roommate, right?"

I chew on the inside of my cheek. Yeah, that's exactly what I want to know. But I don't ever ask directly. Just the sound of his name has tears welling in my eyes. Even after not seeing him for three weeks, his name remains branded in my soul.

"I haven't seen him in a week, S. Clay told me that he moved out of the apartment."

I stand still, frozen in time. I hate the way my heartbeat skyrockets, imagining all the reasons as to why he would have done that. But I shut down all of the what ifs before they grow into something too big and hopeful.

"Oh," I mutter, watching each floor the elevator passes light up in front of me.

Several voices are muffled through the phone before Sophie rambles, "I'm sorry to cut our convo short but I have to go! Call me soon! Love you." she hangs up before I answer her.

The dull sound of the dial tone leaves a bad taste in my mouth. Her swift dismissal after dropping such a bomb on me confuses and hurts me at the same time. It's not like Sophie to leave like that.

A few seconds later the familiar *ding* rings through the air and I hurry through the opening metal doors. The entire journey toward my condo is spent avoiding my thoughts and picking at the skin beside my nails to keep busy. It's a quick walk, but when I reach the door, it feels like I've been walking forever.

As soon as I slide my key into the lock on my door, I freeze, my mouth dry. A bright blue sticky note is stuck above the gold-plated numbers on the centre of the door. My eyes remain scarily wide as I read the sloppy writing scrawled across the paper.

There's no me without you anymore baby. I'm sorry it took me so long to realize that. Meet me on the roof. I know that you know how to get there. Blame Sophie. I'll see you soon.
P.S if you forgot about me in the past 3 weeks, I'll spank your ass so hard you won't be able to sit for another 3.

I HADN'T EVEN REALIZED that my hands had begun to shake until I lift one to my lips. Shock, fear, anger, and happiness are among the feelings racing through my veins as I re-read the note, not believing that he could be here. Especially not for me. Not after this long.

I knew that he tried calling me the day that I left, but when he didn't leave even a single message, I assumed they were an accident. He never called again, so neither did I. I learned to wake up every day and accept that we were over, as best as I could. I never thought that there was even the slightest chance that he was thinking about me, let alone planning on coming here.

I have no idea what to do. Do I go? Do I stay?

Shit, it shouldn't be this complicated. My chest is pounding and my stomach feels like it could fall to the carpet at any second. Oh, fuck it. I won't be able to forgive myself if I don't at least go and see what he has to say.

I pull the note from my door and slide it into my pocket before heading toward the maintenance door a few doors down. Yeah, it's kind of weird that I found myself compelled to open a maintenance room door one day, but I was bored and when I found out what it led to, I was happy that I did. If I hadn't snooped, I wouldn't have figured out that it was really only there to hide a stairwell that takes you up to the roof of the building.

The view is incredible. You can see the entire city. It's become my secret spot where I can go to simply hide from the world. But tonight, it's the place where I can finally get the closure that I've been needing.

I get to the door at the top of the stairs way faster than I expected. And now that I'm here, I want to puke, nerves unlike any I've ever known spearing through me. With a deep, shuddered breath, I grip the door handle and twist, half expecting it to be locked and for this to be some cruel prank.

I toy with the buttons on my jacket before opening the door and stepping outside. The wind nips my cheeks as I search for him, my knees threatening to buckle at what I find.

My lungs give out and I gasp for a lifeline, tears blurring my eyes. I stare at the several strings of fairy lights strung from the tall poles scattered along the roof, and the thick flannel blanket resting a few feet in front of me, covered in an array of pizza boxes and tin containers like they're the most beautiful things I've ever seen.

But then I see him—leaning back against the railing, hands shoved in the pockets of a tight pair of blue jeans, and that signature, cocky grin pulling at the dimples in his cheeks —and nearly jolt back at the pressure that builds in my chest.

My battered heart calls out for him, beating against my rib cage like maybe he'll be able to hear it and come running. Warmth flows through me like molasses, emotion clogging my throat.

I take a step forward, and then another, and when he opens his arms out in front of him, staring at me like he loves me, I'm running, colliding with his chest as the dam crumbles and the tears begin to fall.

"Hey there, my little fighter."

This is not The End.

TAMING *the* PLAYER

HANNAH COWAN

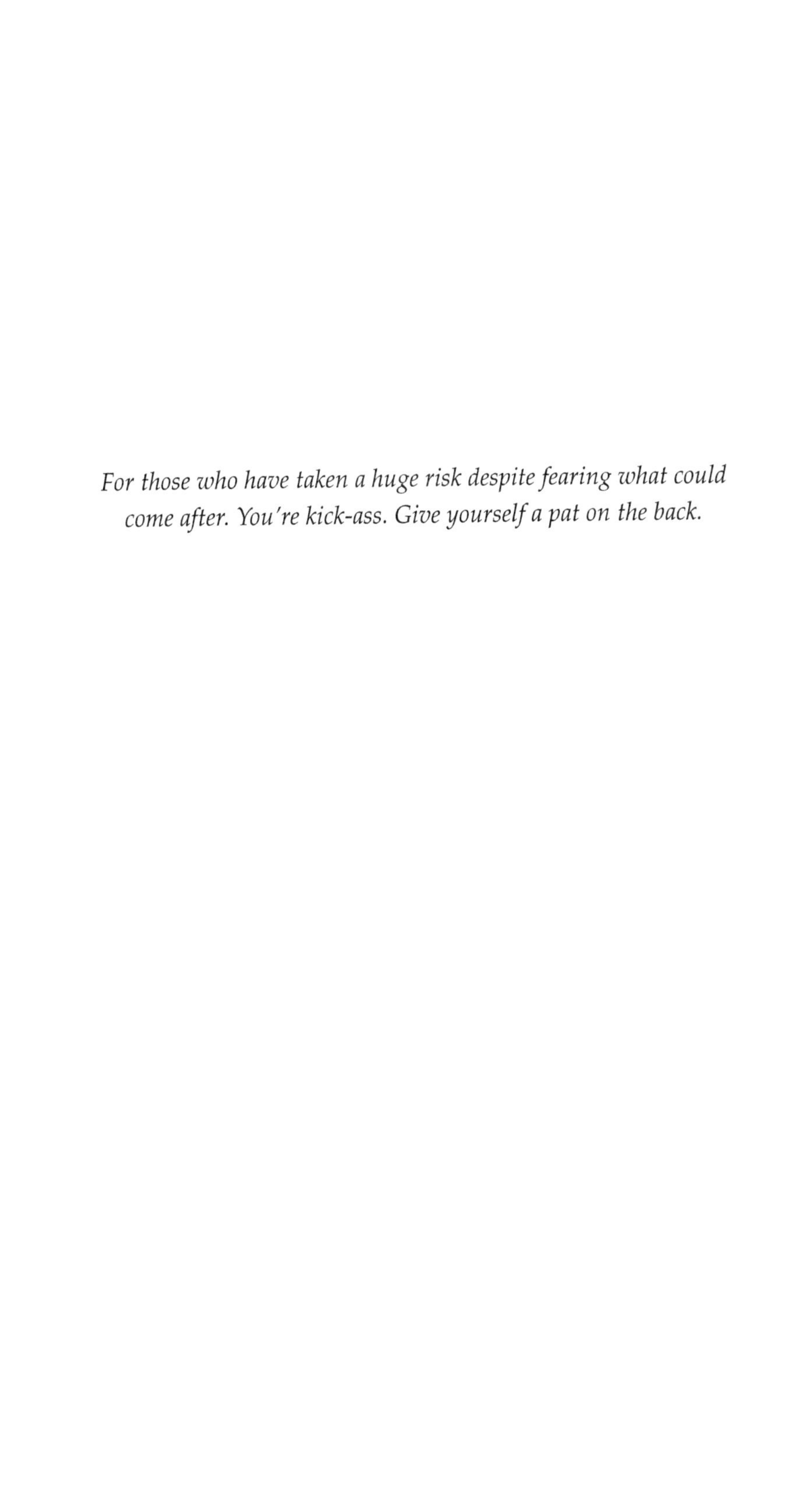

For those who have taken a huge risk despite fearing what could come after. You're kick-ass. Give yourself a pat on the back.

PROLOGUE

THREE WEEKS AGO

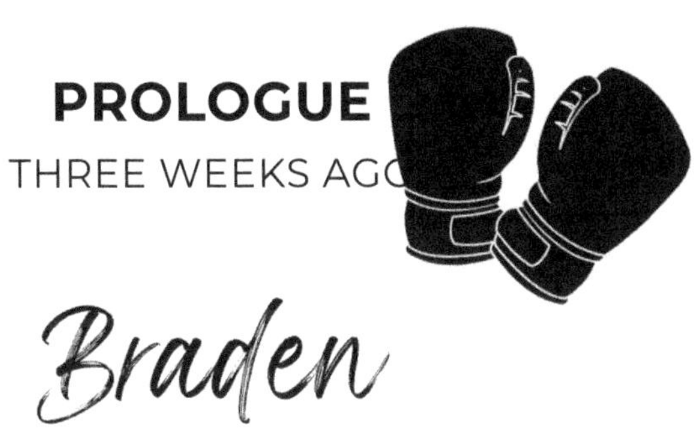

Braden

Sierra's gone. Her apartment is empty, her car is in storage. All I have left of her are a few hair ties on my bathroom counter and the smell of her shampoo on my pillow.

My chest feels hollow. Like she took my heart with her and left me an empty husk.

Tyler sits across from me on my unmade bed. A thick stack of papers rests between us, a blue pen placed on top. He's saying something, but I don't listen. I'm too far inside my own head, lost in a colossal mess of potential plans and self-deprecating thoughts that I've been tormenting myself with.

Sophie's voice plays on repeat in my thoughts every time I pull one of those potential plans out and focus on it. *"I'm going to help you fix this."*

I hear it over and over again but don't reach out. Don't ask for her help. Without any plans of my own, there's no point. It's only been a day, and I feel the heavy weight of defeat on my shoulders.

Tyler snaps an impatient finger in my face, and I blink a few times, clearing my head. "Yeah?"

He sighs, annoyed. "Did you hear anything that I just said?"

"No."

With a roll of his eyes, he picks up that thick stack of paper and holds it up in front of me. Narrowing my eyes, I focus on the word *sale* written across the top before looking at him.

"What is this?"

"It's a plan. One that's going to get your ass out of this room and on a plane."

"Don't be vague." I can't handle the false hope right now.

"Alright, I won't." Setting the papers back down, he hands me the blue pen. "Sell me the gym. Take the money and buy something in Toronto. Start a new life there with your girl. Let me make this happen for you."

"*What*?" I ask again. "I'm not sure that I heard you right."

"Sell. Me. The. Gym."

"It's not mine to sell." I swallow the lump in my throat. "It's Dad's."

The corner of Tyler's mouth tips up. "It was. Until he suggested transferring ownership to you."

I scoff. "Why the hell would he do that?"

Tyler stares at me with a look that says, *You're an idiot.*

"Because it's been yours, more or less, for the past ten years. Dad's old. He doesn't want it anymore. He wants to close this chapter of his life and start a new one with Lana. This is the easiest way to do that. I had my lawyer draw everything up. We just need you to get on board. Accept ownership, sell it to me, and then take the money to start something new."

"You're crazy." A warped laugh escapes me.

This sounds fucking nuts.

"Maybe." He shrugs. "But it's a damn good plan. Stop letting this goddamn city hold you back. Take the money from the sale and create a future for yourself somewhere else. If it doesn't work, you can always come back. It's not life or death. You'll always have a place here. But don't miss this opportunity."

"It's not going to be that easy," I say.

"So? Is that supposed to mean that you shouldn't do it? That's pussy mentality, man."

He has a point. I'm being handed the perfect opportunity here. A chance to get my girl back. I would be an idiot not to take it. But doubt is a nasty bastard that loves to play mind games. What if I do this and she turns me away? What if there's no second chance for us?

I can barely think past the raging sound of my own heartbeat in my ears.

Opening my own gym . . . fuck, I don't know if I could even do it. It could either be the biggest mistake I've ever made or the best decision of my life. But I won't know until I actually take the jump and risk landing on my face.

When I don't reply, Tyler says, "I've seen the way she looks at you. It will take some time and a fuckton of work on your end, but she'll forgive you. She loves you just as much as you love her. Just take the fucking chance."

His words light a match inside of me, and before I realize it, I've grabbed the pen.

"Where do I sign?"

1

THREE WEEKS LATER

Braden

The door behind me creaks open slowly, tentatively. The *click-clack* of high heels on the roof drowns the thumping heartbeat in my ears. With my shoulders pulled back and my confidence teetering on the edge of completely fucking imaginative, I turn around and smile, any previous thoughts clearing from my head like a break in a heavy fog.

"Hey there, my little fighter," I say through an emotion-clogged throat. It's only been a few weeks, but seeing her in front of me again is enough to cut me down at the knees.

My fingertips tingle in the front pockets of my jeans. I want to close the distance between us and take her in my arms. The need to promise never to let her escape them again is earth-shattering, nearly debilitating. My ego is a thing of the past, nothing but a memory of the terrified little boy I was before Sierra stormed into my life like a category five hurricane. Fuck pride. I want her to know exactly how badly I've missed her. Rejection be damned. Anything would be better than living every day with broken pieces and an ache that only she can soothe.

Sometime before she left, Sierra managed to pry her

perfectly manicured, french-tipped nails deep into my chest cavity and grip my beating heart with punishing strength. What she didn't know before hopping on that plane was that I would have held her wrist and helped her yank the bloody thing from my body with the promise of forever.

If she had known how I felt, maybe she wouldn't have left without me. And maybe I wouldn't have let her go, my heart tucked unbeknownst in her suitcase. But she didn't know how much I love her, and I've spent the past three weeks planning how to fix what I broke between us.

Everything inside of me is begging me to storm over to her and feel her soft skin against my fingertips. To kiss her lips and breathe her in. But I know I can't push it. Can't push *her*.

The ball in my throat threatens to cut off my air supply seconds before her feet move, jerky at first before forming a desperate stride in my direction. I catch her easily when she jumps into my arms, fitting perfectly against me like she always has, even when I wished she felt wrong. My hands grab her thighs as they lock tight around my waist, keeping her as close to me as possible. A gush of air is pushed from my mouth as relief flows through my tight muscles, relaxing them.

"You're here. You're in Toronto." Her words kiss my throat, dripping with surprise. The arms she has looped around my neck loosen. Her face leaves the crook of my shoulder, and shining silver eyes fall on my face, wide, familiar, and so fucking warm.

"I'm here, baby."

I hope to God she can see everything I haven't said yet in the way I devour her with my stare and press my forehead to hers. My chest is tight, so full of unspoken truths and feelings, but my tongue lies limp in my mouth.

"How are you here?" she asks a heartbeat later, watching

me, her expression so full of hope yet dampened by something I can only assume to be heartbreak and fear.

Sweat breaks out on the back of my neck as I drop her to her feet and push my hair back for no good reason, instantly regretting letting her move from my arms. I play off my nerves with a sarcastic reply that I realize right away she doesn't appreciate.

"A plane."

Her eyes harden, jaw setting. I want to tell her everything that's happened in the past three weeks. Every tough decision and goodbye. She deserves to know what led to this meeting, but will she forgive me afterward for everything that came before?

"*Why* are you here? Why now?" Her words lack emotion, but I'm not surprised nor offended by it. She has every right to keep me at arm's length.

My hands shake at my sides, but there's no stopping what comes next. Fear be damned.

"I should have been here three weeks ago, Sierra. I know that. I should have told you how desperately in love with you I was in that fucking bar and never let you leave me in the first place. But I was a coward, baby." I grab her face in my hands. There's shock in her eyes, but I beg her to stay silent with the look in mine.

"I don't deserve your love, but I'm a selfish bastard who's going to take it all anyway. Every single last fucking ounce of it until there's none left. And I want you to do the same with mine because there's so much of it that I felt like I was going to explode these last three weeks with nobody to share it with. I love you so goddamn much, my little fighter. And as long as you'll have me—*if* you'll have me—I'll be here."

Sierra blinks, lips slightly parted. I'm winded, overwhelmed with relief and a hint of nausea sparked by her silence.

A thousand questions tumble through my head, making me wonder whether or not I should have waited to tell her how in love with her I am, if I'm too late, or if, by some fucking chance, there's someone else in the picture now. If there is, it's absolutely a test from God. One that I'll fail with a smile when I kill the guy who thought for even a second that he could have my girl and dump his body in the ocean.

Shark food, Sierra. Don't test me.

My thumb runs over her bottom lip, pressing gently. The adoration I feel for her is written all over me; I know from the way she's watching me, like I'm a creature she can't quite figure out but desperately seeks to. There isn't anything that I wouldn't tell her right now when she's looking at me like this, all wild-eyed and flushed. I would allow her full access into my head and let her sift through my thoughts for anything she wanted to know.

It's a dangerous, terrifying realization, but one I've prepared myself for.

"Say something," I whisper softly.

"I don't know what to say. I'm so surprised that you're even here, let alone saying all of this," she finally says, sounding just as out of breath as I feel. For some reason, that thought helps calm me. "I've wanted to hear you say all of that for weeks."

"And do you believe me?"

She doesn't hesitate. "Of course I do. You're not exactly the most outspoken about your feelings. I can't see you lying about them."

A breath of relief escapes as I nod, my gaze unwavering. A warm feeling settles in my stomach as my heart rattles my ribs like the bars of a prison cell, desperate to burst through my chest.

There's a spark of doubt, though, somewhere deeper in my mind. "I sense a 'but' coming." The words taste rotten.

Sierra's the first to break eye contact, heaving a sigh. She turns slightly to the left, toward the blanket laid on the rooftop. The sudden movement forces my hands to fall back to my sides, and the warmth that once filled my stomach turns to lead, sinking deep.

It was Sophie's idea—the romantic gesture, that is. I've never done anything romantic a day in my life. I don't know my head from my ass when it comes to romance, so I didn't argue with her when she said I should go all out. So I spent far too long this afternoon hanging twinkly lights and ordered too much food for the both of us.

I can't be sure if it helped any with getting me back in Sierra's good books, but it was worth a shot anyway. Even if it makes her feel appreciated and not want to gut me like a fish for the slightest moment.

"I believe that you love me. I think I always knew that you did, you just weren't ready to accept it. But how are we supposed to do this? You've already made it very clear that long distance won't work. So what? Now it will? You haven't reached out to me in three weeks and what? Now you're ready for a relationship? I'm confused, Braden."

I can't blame her for being frustrated. It was *my* fuckup and inability to open myself up to the possibility of a future with her that planted the seeds of doubt inside of her head. I let her feel unwanted and like she wasn't worth it. I'm the one who told her she was nothing more than a fuck buddy when she was always so much more than that. Even when I was incapable of seeing it.

There's only one thing I can do now that has a chance of helping anything, and that's to tell her the whole truth about why and how I'm here.

Closing the distance between us, I grab both of her small hands and squeeze them before bringing them to my chest, desperate for her touch. Her breath hitches while she presses her palms against my pecs and stares up at me with guarded eyes.

I have to fight back the urge to curse at myself for being the cause of the wall she's put up between us. Shoving away the anger that's started heating my blood before I let it show on my face, I grip her hips and pull her body flush to mine.

"Sit and have dinner with me, and I'll tell you everything about how and why I'm here. I'll answer any questions that you have. I promise."

I'm pleading with her, but I'm too antsy to care. I'm aware of how small my window of opportunity is here.

Sierra isn't the type of woman who needs a man. If she doesn't think I'm worth it, she'll toss me out on my ass with both her middle fingers raised. I know how well she's been doing for herself out here, and the last thing either of us wants is to ruin that.

She lifts a brow and looks between me and the food that's in desperate need of being reheated with a strong sense of contemplation. I can practically hear the gears turning in her head as she thinks about whether to tell me to fuck off and never show up here again or take the chance on dinner.

Luck seems to be in my favor tonight because she nods and says, "I'll have dinner because I'm starving and you brought enough food to last me the entire week. But as pretty as it is up here, we're not eating in the cold."

I almost bend down to kiss her before thinking better of it, opting to grin and squeeze her hips instead. "Done. No eating outside."

"I would say that you can follow me down, but it seems Sophie has already taken care of letting you know which apartment is mine."

I gulp before Sierra shakes her head and smiles softly to herself.

"I prefer to follow you. The view is better that way."

She steps back and looks away in an attempt to hide her blush from me, but it only makes me feel a heavy sense of pride to see that my words still affect her just as strongly now as they did before. Nothing has changed in that regard.

"Help me pack this up," she mumbles before rushing to collect the containers of food and placing them in the basket I set off to the side of the blanket.

Her thick pink coat covers her thighs, resting just above her knees, but paired with her skirt and thin black tights, it leaves her lower body completely bare to the early December chill. I scowl but decide not to chastise her for walking home in the low temperature without proper clothes on and help her collect the food in silence instead. She won't be walking to and from work alone anymore now that I'm here anyway.

Usually, I would have pushed my luck, unable to keep myself from poking at her, but this is just yet another reminder of how badly I need this night to go well.

Sierra has to forgive me. I don't want to think of what I'll do if she doesn't.

2

Sierra

After three weeks of silence, Braden told me that he loves me. Yes, *loves* me.

Talk about a shock to the system. The last thing I expected today was to find the man who hasn't made a single effort to reach out to me after discarding my heart like a dirty sock on my roof with a grand romantic gesture and a love proclamation. I'm still trying to catch my breath.

His presence presses against my back, warm, heavy, and confident despite the nerves I noticed on the roof. Nervous. Braden was *nervous*. I'm not sure whether knowing that I brought out that side of him should make me feel proud or guilty. Considering it's nearly impossible to catch a glimpse of that part of Braden through the heavy armor of arrogance he wears on the daily, I should feel accomplished seeing him sweat. But at the same time, my damn feelings for him have my stomach in knots at the mere thought of him being upset.

My apartment in Toronto is only a bit bigger than my old one in Vancouver, but more expensive considering the location is in the city centre, only a few blocks from work. With two bedrooms, one bath, and a small yet open-concept kitchen and living space, Braden's presence is nearly suffocating.

The living room seems to shrink in his company, forcing me to feel closer to him than I really am from my place on the couch. Braden sits with his legs splayed out on the cushion closest to me, refusing to move to the far cushion like the stubborn ass he is while I sit with my legs tucked under my body, chewing on a bite of chow mein.

It's hard not to see the similarities between us before and now, with the scattered tins of Chinese food on the coffee table and the feelings threatening to pop like an overfilled balloon between us, but it's different now. That's why I didn't let him turn on *Law & Order* after we sat down, opting for the evening news instead. I won't be able to stand my ground if I let us fall back into that routine. *Our* routine. The memories of past nights spent together have my throat tightening and an unsettling feeling coiling in my stomach.

With that thought, I'm putting my food down on the table, not hungry anymore.

I avoid looking at Braden, knowing that he's been watching me slither back in my head to hide. But it's his hand on my thigh—the touch so gentle and reassuring—that sends me over the edge. Suddenly, I can't see past the unshed tears blurring my vision or breathe past the thick lump in my throat.

The hollow ache in my chest that I've fought so hard to dull comes back with a vengeance. My heart splits again, both halves too fragile and sore this time around to stick together by more than a frayed string.

"Fuck, baby," he curses before eliminating the distance between us and pulling me into his lap. He binds his arms around me and holds my body so close to his that I can feel his heartbeat against my cheek when I press my face to his hard chest.

I welcome the familiar smell of his cologne, and a shudder racks through me at his next words.

"I tried to get to you the day you left. I was too late, though." A large palm traces the ridge of my spine in soft strokes, not stopping even when I grow rigid beneath it, my breath catching. "I was with my dad hours before your plane took off, trying to convince him not to move away with his new wife. It was such a jackass thing to do, but I didn't care. The only thing I could think about was making him stay. I was terrified of how lonely I would be without him. Without *you*."

Braden's heartbeat keeps thumping away in my ear, and I find myself rubbing my cheek against his chest, as if that would somehow help calm him down and help him continue his story. It's rare for him to open up like this, and regardless of how I feel about everything that's happened, I want to help him in any way that I can.

"I was a pretty lonely kid my whole life, but especially after my parents divorced. They hated each other for the majority of my childhood. The fights were ruthless, both of them so angry with each other for things I never understood. I was hardly even a teenager when my mom took off for two years. She barely waited a day after the papers were signed before she went to 'find herself' in a completely different country. My dad didn't know how to deal with me on his own, so we barely spoke.

"I spent the rest of my teen years getting my ass beat in fights and doing the stupidest shit. I was so desperate for my dad's attention that I would have done anything to get it. It wasn't until I graduated and started university that I grew out of it. Once I became an adult, it was easier for my dad to talk to me. I wasn't as hotheaded and dramatic as I was as a kid. We got along."

"All kids are attention seekers, Braden. Even more so when they feel invisible to the people they care about. There was nothing wrong with how you reacted to something so drastic and life-changing." Leaning back in his arms, I slide my hand up his chest to hold his jaw. The skin is prickly under my fingertips, showing his lack of shaving as of late.

He leans into my touch, eyes clouded and dark with something that looks a lot like regret. I want to smack him for carrying this feeling of self-loathing with him for so many years.

"Don't feel bad for me, Sierra. That's not why I'm telling you this."

I glare, pinching him in the side with my free hand. "I'm allowed to feel bad for you. I know you're not telling me this so that I'll pity you. But I'm not going to pretend that I agree with the weight you've been carrying all these years."

He sighs and turns his head to kiss my palm. "I was an awful son to him when he met Lana. I didn't understand their relationship—hell, I still don't—but I took it too far. I didn't realize that until I found myself in his exact position. I spent months criticizing something that I didn't understand until I met you."

My stomach flutters before I can control my reaction. "What are you talking about?"

His stare is so intense I feel it everywhere. It steals my breath, holding it hostage. "My dad was willing to risk everything to follow the woman he loved across the country. He was planning on following Lana here, to Toronto. For months I told him that he was making a mistake. That no girl was worth leaving everything you've ever known behind. But I was so fucking wrong, Sierra. Even after flying all my shit out here and renting an apartment that is honestly pretty embarrassing compared to this one, I still can't believe how wrong I was."

I suck in a sharp breath, tears welling in my eyes for the second time tonight. They spill when I shake my head and raise a shaking hand to my chest. "Don't lie to me right now, Braden. It's not funny."

He laughs, rough and familiar, and swipes my tears away with his thumbs. "I'm here to stay as long as you'll have me. There was nothing keeping me in Vancouver, not after you left. I was fucking blind not to see that earlier."

"What about your brother? Clayton? Boxing?" I push at his chest and stand, my fingers winding through my hair, scratching at my scalp. *Distance*. I need distance to think.

I start pacing around the living room.

He didn't really move out here for me. There's no way. He's about to be an uncle—now isn't the time for him to be making rash decisions. His family is going to need him. I can't stand back and steal him from his family. Even if his dad is moving out here for his wife. Tyler is going to need him. His mom—regardless of how close her relationship is with her son—will need him. Right?

There's movement by the couch, but I avoid looking toward it, scared I'll completely lose it once I look into those brown eyes I love so much.

"Dammit, Braden. Why did you do this?" I spin around, my arms flailing in the air before coming down on a hard chest.

My eyes widen in surprise when I register Braden's closeness. I exhale slowly and curl my fingers into the soft material of his sweatshirt.

"Relax, fighter," he coaxes, his strong hands rubbing my shoulders and upper arms in soothing motions. "You need to calm down before you have a panic attack."

My eyes narrow. "Don't tell me to calm down right now. And don't call me that. This is serious!"

There's a twitch in his brow as he watches me with heated eyes. It's like he wants to pick me up and toss me on the bed so he can fuck my worries out of me. Usually, that would have worked, and I would have let him without a second thought. But not now.

Sex is completely off the table. Even if I'm so completely sex deprived that the thought of being punished by Braden has me rubbing my thigh together.

"Do you not want me here? Is that it?" The heat in his eyes is washed out by something deeper, anger maybe.

"Of course I do! I've been asking Sophie every single day for three weeks for updates on you and your whereabouts. But that doesn't mean that I'm not worried. I can't just not worry about something so monumental just because you tell me everything's okay, Braden. That's not me."

"I know, and I don't want to change that about you. I'm just asking you to trust me when I say everything will be okay. Better than okay, actually."

Sliding my hands to his shoulders, I press my forehead to his chest. I'm being weak, I know that. I should be putting up a bigger fight, kicking and screaming and telling him how badly he hurt me. But instead, I whisper, "Tell me how you know everything will be okay."

His arms engulf me like my own personal shield. "The flight time from Toronto to Vancouver isn't even five hours, sweetheart. It won't be impossible to fly home and visit. Not to mention Tyler will be playing here a few times this season. I know you're worried about me not seeing my niece or nephew, but I will. If it makes you feel better, I promise that I'll go home after Gray gives birth and stay with them for a few days.

"Clayton is a big boy. I wouldn't worry about him. I'm

sure Sophie will keep his ass in line for me. And as far as boxing goes, you'll just have to believe me when I say I have it figured out. That's all you're getting from me right now."

His tone is final, and I find myself nodding. I know better than to push my luck with him, even if the mere thought of not knowing absolutely everything settles in my stomach like a puddle of vomit.

The tension leaks from my muscles as I replay everything he just said. He's right about the distance not being as big of a barrier as I thought. But I can't help but wonder why he's okay with being away from them but not me. I mean, he *moved* here. He very well could have just come back for a weekend and tried to get me to agree to a long-distance relationship after telling me all of this. He didn't have to get up and move here for me. Especially knowing that he did it with the chance I could tell him to leave me alone for good.

A gentle finger is placed under my chin and tilts my head so I'm forced to meet Braden's stare. It's like he's in my head, reading my thoughts. I don't have a chance to tell him what's bothering me about all of this before he's speaking.

"I know exactly where you're taking this conversation, and I'm putting an end to it right now. If you think that I would be content with seeing you merely a few times a month, not touching or witnessing with my own eyes that you're okay and happy, you must have forgotten who you've fallen in love with. There was nothing but an old boxing gym tying me to Vancouver. I had no plans, no dreams, no fucking anything."

He bends down, hovering his mouth over mine. We're close enough that I can feel the brush of his lips but so far that I can't taste him like I'm dying to after weeks apart.

With eyes unwavering, he says, "The weeks without you were hell on fucking earth. I'm not doing that again. Ever. You're mine, little fighter. And you have no idea what you've gotten yourself into. I've never done relationships before, but that changes right now. With you. You're never going to be free of me again."

His words crash into me like waves on a cold, windy day. They knock me over and drag me under. No matter how hard or fast I swim, I'm stuck under their pull, drowning beneath them as they force me to surrender.

And I do surrender—mind, soul, and definitely body as I push up on my toes and connect our mouths, stealing from him like he did from me. He's gentle, but I'm rough, desperate, *hungry*.

He tastes me while I devour him.

The heaviness of how sudden the roles have reversed doesn't go unnoticed. If anything, I focus on it, taking my fill while I have the chance.

My hands grasp his nape and hold him to me. I'm overwhelmed with the sensations swirling in my veins and clawing at my insides. It's intense, almost too intense as I lose my balance and lean against him, stabilizing myself.

He catches me with ease and holds me tightly against him before pulling back. Braden's pupils are dilated, the black nearly engulfing all of the warm chocolate brown. His breaths are hot puffs of air on my pulsing cheeks.

"Things are going to be different this time, Sierra. If I'm going to get another shot at this—if you'll give me one—I'm going to do it right. And fucking you on the floor of your living room after a reheated dinner and an emotional talk is not what I had in mind when I came here today."

I stare back at him, trying to blink away my surprise. He shakes his head and laughs, grinning so wide his dimples show on both cheeks.

"I'm going to go back to my apartment before it's too late, and after I'm gone, you're going to go to sleep and dream of me. I'll be back in the morning to walk you to work, and you can let me know what you've decided then."

I hold my breath as he places a kiss on my cheek, followed by one on my lips, and walks to the front door. My first instinct is to ask him to stay, not wanting him gone again after finally getting him back, but I push back that urge. If he were to stay, we wouldn't make it five minutes without having sex.

If Braden of all people wants to give this a real try, I'm going to at least *think* about it. Everything that he's done to win me back has to count for something. I mean, he moved across the country for me, knowing that I might never forgive him.

If I were a different person, someone less hard-headed and stubborn, maybe I would have forgiven him the moment I saw him on the roof. But that's not me, and I can't find it in me to hate myself for it.

Over the past weeks, I've hated him, begged for him, and mourned the future we could have had if things had gone differently. But still, after the tears and anger fade, I can't deny that being with Braden is still something that I want, crave, and sometimes feel like I *need*.

Love doesn't disappear overnight, not when you feel so strongly about somebody. But it does take shelter, hiding from anything that could possibly shred it with unforgiving claws again.

Love becomes wary, fearful after heartbreak. It doesn't throw out forgiveness or second chances. It has to be earned, and if Braden is willing to work for it, I'm not going to tell him no. Although, if I'm being completely honest with myself, I don't think that I ever could.

"So, you want to be my boyfriend now or something?" I ask, watching him slip his sneakers on.

He shoots me a proud wink and opens the door. "Or something. Boyfriend doesn't even come close. But I'll take it until I can think of something better. Oh, and wear pants when you walk to work from now on. It's cold out. Good night, my love. Dream of me."

"Good night," I mutter, holding a hand to my chest as he leaves, shutting the door softly behind him.

I'm in a state of shock as I do as he says. I get ready for bed before crawling under my sheets, falling asleep quicker than I have in weeks, and dreaming of what the future could hold for us. All night long.

3

Sierra

True to his word, Braden shows up at seven thirty with a Christmas-themed Starbucks cup in his hand and a thin coat stretched across his shoulders.

His smile burns bright as he stands on the other side of my door, foot tapping the carpet, oblivious to my peeping. I'm grateful he hasn't noticed that I'm currently peeking at him through the tiny peephole in my door instead of inviting him in and examining him face-to-face. I have no doubt he would tease me for it if he did.

Blowing out a breath, I step back and wipe my sweaty palms down my thighs.

There was a part of me that didn't believe he would actually show up this morning. I mean, it's easy to make promises in the heat of the moment just to realize after a good night's sleep that maybe you shouldn't have.

I don't want to have doubts about his intentions or spend the time preparing myself for the possibility that once he leaves my side, he won't come back, but once trust is broken, the scar left behind never fully fades.

I don't know how long it will take for that trust to grow again, if it ever will.

"Are you going to let me in anytime soon? I don't have a problem with waiting, but your coffee is going to be cold, and I know how much you hate cold coffee," he calls through the door, a hint of amusement in his voice.

My lips tug up at the corners with the knowledge that he remembers something as small as how I like my coffee. Maybe that's ridiculous—okay, it totally is.

"One second!" I flatten the hairs at the top of my head, button up my jacket, and slip my work bag over my shoulder before opening the door.

Braden's presence is commanding and intimidating as it swallows me. The way he carries himself even in unfamiliar territory has always made me jealous. He has the type of aura that you either gravitate toward or get owned by. Depending on the day, I've done both.

Today, it owns me.

"Good morning, gorgeous." He extends the Christmas cup toward me. I grab it eagerly, stepping into the hall and taking a sip of the latte.

"Good morning. I suppose I should be thanking Sophie for making sure you got here on time? It was her that told you when I leave for work every day, right?"

His grin is wicked. "You're not wrong."

I lock the door behind me and raise a brow when I catch Braden's heated stare on my legs.

"You're wearing pants." It's a statement, one full of something dirty and knee locking. I'm proud to have received such a reaction from him. Bringing a man like Braden to his knees over something as small and ridiculous as wearing pants just to appease one of his concerns is enough to make a girl too cocky for her own good.

Snapping my attention to the legs I purposefully covered in fleece-lined leggings, I nod. "It's cold." *And you said to wear pants.*

He brings his eyes to mine, and I shiver from the heat flaring in them. My chest rises and falls rapidly, and I squeeze my coffee cup tighter.

Familiar tension crackles and sparks in the air between us. The feeling grabs me by an invisible, silky thread and pulls, attempting with every bit of its strength to make me tumble into him even as I straighten my spine and repeat the word *no* in my head.

Braden steps toward me, and I step back, my back pressing against the door. He places a hand beside my head and leans forward, kissing me softly before pulling back, eyes still closed.

"That's my good girl."

My eyes nearly roll back in ecstasy. With legs like Jell-O, I focus on keeping my balance and my heart from fluttering out of my chest. "We need to leave. I can't be late for work."

A hint of a smile pulls at his mouth before he's kissing me a final time, this one hard, possessive, and *final*, leaving my lips buzzing with the feel of him when it's over.

"Let's go, then."

I wait for him to back up, to give me room and air to breathe, but he only watches me with lust-drunk eyes. It's like he's trapped in my atmosphere just as much as I am his.

Thankfully, he doesn't make me beg and steps back after a few more seconds, leaving me with just enough room to slide around him and lead the way to the elevator.

His stare is a brand on my back the entire way to the elevator. It's not until the doors slide open and we're caged inside the metal box, side by side, that he looks elsewhere. I don't torture myself by trying to find what now holds his attention.

"How long have you been in Toronto?" I ask after a few silent heartbeats. My fingers tap the strap of my bag resting on my shoulder as I watch the numbers light up with every floor we pass on our descent.

Without hesitation, he says, "A week."

"A week?" I gulp. "Has everyone known, then? That you've been here?"

I look at him and frown, recognizing the look on his face: contemplation and a flash of fear.

"I asked them not to say anything."

It shouldn't bother me that his arrival was kept a secret, but Sophie should have told me. As my closest friend, she should never keep secrets from me, especially not ones containing info about my . . . ex? Whether he asked her to stay silent or not, it shouldn't matter. She knew how devastated I was. The rejection and self-doubt that I was living with every day.

Betrayal winds in my gut regardless of my inner pleading.

It took every sliver of my self-control not to respond to her calls or texts after Braden left last night, not wanting to give her any sort of false hope or talk about feelings that I couldn't even figure out myself. Now, after finding out that she knew about his surprise arrival all along, I'm glad that I didn't.

If she had lied to me last night, I don't think it would be as easy to forgive her.

"Don't, sweetheart." His voice rips through my head, yanking me from my thoughts. I blink back my hurt and cock a brow. "If you're going to be upset with anyone, be upset with me. Not them, and especially not Sophie."

I square my shoulders, lifting my chin. "You don't get to tell me what to do. Not anymore."

He grimaces but nods in agreement. "You're right. I just want you to know that even though Sophie kept this from you, she's also the reason that I was able to get here so quickly. Without her help, I probably wouldn't have made it here for at least a few months."

"I don't like secrets."

"I'm sorry." Braden swallows thickly, his Adam's apple bobbing.

It looks like he wants to say more, but the opening of the elevator doors has him choosing to drop the conversation. His hand falls to my lower back as he leads me silently through the lobby and into the nipping winter wind.

A shudder moves through me, the surprisingly low temperature chewing through my jacket and brushing my skin. It's not even a second later that a heavy arm drapes across my shoulders and pulls me close to a warm body.

"You need to start driving or taking a cab. It's fucking freezing." It's almost a scolding yet somehow carries a flicker of amusement.

"Are you telling me this jacket isn't warm enough for you?" I bite back my laugh and grab a handful of Braden's thin, army green bomber jacket. "You're dressed for mid-fall Vancouver, not for early winter Toronto."

A flick on the arm makes me squeal.

"Keep it up, little fighter. Keep it up." His voice rumbles, deep and strong.

"Was pulling me close to keep me warm or you?" I flick him back, grinning when he winces. "Or neither?"

I know that I should stop teasing him. Stop playing everything off as back to normal, but it feels too good, too *natural*. It seems almost criminal to stop in hopes of keeping up a rough exterior.

Besides, playing with him is harmless. It's something that we used to do back before it became more than just sex. It doesn't have to mean anything more than what it is.

"What if I said both?" he asks. I lean my head against his bicep and shiver when he places a kiss on my hair.

"I would say that you're pushing your boundaries."

"That so?"

His eyes burn into me from above.

"It just seems like a very . . . boyfriend-y thing to do." Can he hear how fast my heart is beating?

"Yeah, it does," he says confidently, not even a flicker of indecision in that raspy voice of his.

Blushing, I drop my eyes to the sidewalk, watching my feet tap the concrete with every step. Braden's huge feet somehow match my pace. I swallow my laugh.

I wonder how hard he's trying to slow his stride and walk at the speed of my much smaller legs.

Braden clears his throat, and I shove the stupid thought from my head to look up at him. "This is it, right?"

Turning, I realize we've made it to our destination. The towering forty-storey building that now houses the new offices of Brenton and Thompson is, in simple terms: really fucking intimidating.

I remember standing in this exact spot and nearly painting my brand-new pair of open-toed heels in vomit on my first day.

Maybe the intimidation stems from the new territory or from the fact that none of us have yet met the infamous Mackenzie Thompson, the new second half of Brenton and Thompson.

From what I've gathered, Mackenzie was in Vancouver the day the announcement of an expansion was made, having just finished signing all of the legal crap for the joining of companies. He was expected to make an appearance but decided to fly back home instead.

Clark and Mackenzie—according to Gretchen, Mackenzie's receptionist and my newest friend in this still-unfamiliar town—grew up together in Toronto before Clark moved to Vancouver after graduation. Clark built Brenton

Marketing while Mack attempted to build Thompson Marketing.

Clearly, one fared better than the other.

I assume that it was Mack's idea for us to expand and merge companies here after he nearly went bankrupt on his own just a few months prior to our merger announcement. Again, office gossip and rumours. I'm not sure that I'll ever know the full story, nor do I really care to.

I'm here for one reason. Experience in a more decorated position that under different management, I may never have gotten this quickly.

As soon as I've spent enough time working under Cole Travis to fill that empty space on my resume, I'm gone.

Hasta la vista, baby.

See you *never*.

"Would you like me to walk you in? Or is that too boyfriend-y for you?"

I snort in the most unflattering way possible but can't find it in me to shy away.

"I can walk by myself," I reply, grinning at the humour twinkling in his eyes before gulping back the majority of my warm coffee.

"Fine. I'll be back at five thirty to walk you home."

My breath clots in my throat when he pulls me into his arms, our chests pressed firmly together and my empty coffee cup mashed between us. Then he claims my mouth in a kiss that should belong solely in the bedroom.

I let my eyelids slide shut and focus on the feeling of his lips on mine, so warm and familiar. They're as addictive and thigh clenching as I remember them to be late at night. When I'm alone, two glasses of wine deep, and can't help but think about him.

Braden draws out a breathy sound from deep in my chest

while branding his name on my mouth in an invisible claim that I'll have no choice but to carry with me all day.

His hand slides up my back to cup my nape and tilt my head. The move drips of possessiveness in a way that has my mouth opening for him, as if he just commanded me to allow his tongue to stroke mine. And when it does, he groans, the deep, strained noise shooting like a zap of electricity to my clit.

We separate when the honk of a car horn blares somewhere close by, reminding me that we're in front of my work and, in fact, *not* in the bedroom.

Fuck.

Suddenly deadly aware of what I just let happen—*again*—I push at Braden's chest and stumble backward. "I have to go." The sense of déjà vu is sickening.

I swallow when I meet his stare and see the utter frustration etched in the smooth edges of his face. No doubt my rejection scratches at his pride.

But just as quickly as it appeared, the frustration is gone, replaced by a mask of easy confidence that I recognize quickly. Too quickly.

"Text me if you get finished early. Please don't walk home without me."

Simply knowing that he worries so much about my safety is enough to have me agreeing to just about anything that could come from his mouth, but I don't say that. Knowing Braden, he would hold that against me for as long as possible.

Braden waits for me to acknowledge him with an easy nod before he's gently grabbing my wrist and tugging me back toward him. I don't fight him when he kisses my forehead or lingers a few seconds longer than usual before pulling back and walking back the way we came, hands tucked away in the pockets of that stupid jacket. I watch him, laser focused on the quick stride of his legs until he turns the corner and disappears from view.

Sucking back a few deep breaths, I dump my empty cup in a nearby trash bin and head inside Brenton and Thompson.

4

Braden

I HATE WATCHING SIERRA PULL AWAY FROM ME—BOTH emotionally and physically.

The realization and regret that filled those big beautiful eyes seconds after we broke apart might as well have been the nails in my fucking coffin.

There's no mistaking who should bear the fault for those walls she's rebuilt around herself, but they still act like a dagger to the gut regardless. I desperately want to go back to how things were before shit hit the fan, but with every conversation we have, I feel the weight of my mistakes heavier than the last. At this rate, it won't be long until I'm crushed beneath it.

My apartment is not much warmer than the air outside as I slam the front door behind me and lock the three separate locks.

Dad hasn't stopped digging into me about my choice of housing—given the sudden influx of zeros in my bank account—but I began viewing anywhere without Sierra a formality a long time ago. Plus, I've been crashing in his new house every night for the past week while it sits empty, waiting for their arrival.

I imagined my first few days here to be lonely and quiet while I got everything figured out, but although it was lonely, it was a far cry from quiet.

The new Lowry boxing gym, while still an empty, nameless shell, has begun to take shape and for the past week has occupied ninety-nine percent of my spare time. With buying a completely empty building in a new construction area, we're starting from scratch, but it'll be worth it, however long it takes.

That doesn't stop me from thinking about how permanent this all feels now, though—owning my own gym in Toronto. All too quickly, I have something else tethering me to this city. Something that I won't be able to just up and leave behind, regardless of what the future holds.

Sierra was the reason I came here, the reason I pushed myself so far out of my comfort zone that I couldn't climb back in no matter how hard I tried. But it's quickly become deeper than that. I can only hope that when I show her how serious I am and that I'm not going anywhere regardless of if she forgives me, that that damn armor of hers will slide off her shoulders and bare her to me again.

There is no going back for me. I just have to convince her of that.

My phone sings in my pocket, drawing me out of my head. I cringe when I realize that I've been standing by the front door in my snow-soaked jacket and shoes that began making awkward squelching sounds on the way home.

Kicking off my sneakers, I shrug out of my jacket and answer the phone, tucking it between my shoulder and ear. "Hey."

"Please tell me that you've gotten back in Sierra's good

graces because her demon twin is going to be the reason I become a liquor store regular."

I sputter a laugh at Clayton's venomous words. "Sophie is not that bad."

"Not that bad?" he echoes incredulously. "She broke into my car and dumped glitter all over the seats, Braden. It's been a week and I'm still picking glitter off my pants every time I get out. How old is she? Twelve?"

"You spied on her date with that Jarod guy and then told him that she had genital herpes."

"I didn't spy on them. I was picking up food for my mother."

"At a Thai restaurant? Your mom hates Thai food. She told me it gives her heartburn."

He's silent for a few seconds before he grunts, "It doesn't even matter. Point is, I need her to leave me alone, and until you fix your relationship, I'm stuck with her coming around, bugging me for updates. Actually, why don't you just text her yourself? Last time I checked, I wasn't a messenger pigeon."

I fight the urge to tell him that I do, in fact, text Sophie updates and have been for the past few weeks because I don't want to fall in the middle of whatever game these two are playing.

If I didn't know better, I would have started to think that they were into each other.

"I'll text her later," I choose to say instead. My breath escapes in a *whoosh* when I flop down on the cheap couch I found on Kijiji.

"Thanks. But really, how is it going? Did she kick you in the balls?"

I scoff. "No. She didn't."

"But?"

"But it's going to take time. Like I told you it would before I left. Sierra is almost as stubborn as I am. I told her that I wanted a real relationship, and I saw how that affected her. She wants it too, but she's hurt. *I* hurt her."

"I'm surprised she even let you speak. I owe Sophie twenty bucks."

"You bet against me?" I gasp, although I feel anything but surprised by that.

Clayton abandoned me to join Team Sierra after the whole club fiasco, alongside pretty much everybody else I know. Their side swap didn't hurt me in the slightest, but it did make asking for help a bit harder. Clay was the easiest to convince, though, considering I was offering him something he wasn't expecting.

The entire apartment to himself.

"Technically, I suppose," he replies. Something clunks around in the background, sounding like somebody banging pots together.

"If I was a lesser man, I would be offended by your betrayal."

Clayton laughs loudly. "If you were a lesser man, I would have bet more than twenty bucks."

"Careful, you'll make me swoon." My eyes fall shut as I rest my head against the back of the couch.

The moving boxes that I know are still lined up along the walls of the living room make the place feel almost claustrophobic. It's usually stuffy on a good day, but my skin almost feels slick with sweat as I sit here.

I need to go work out, maybe run a few miles to burn off some energy before I combust and destroy the place. I've fallen off my training with everything going on, and while it doesn't look like it, I'm definitely beginning to feel it. I'm embarrassed to admit that I got winded after running up the stairs the other day. Dad would never let me hear the end of it if he found out about that.

There's a loud bang that shakes through the call. It has me

pulling the phone from my ear and wincing. Clay's shouts follow close after, the octave they hit surprising me.

His next words are rushed. "I gotta go. Keep me updated, and text Sophie. Stay positive."

The call ends before I can reply, so I throw my phone down on the cushion beside me. Groaning, I run a hand through my hair, slightly pulling on the ends before standing.

I know full well that I won't be staying here tonight, so I spend the next few minutes collecting another few days' worth of clothes from packed boxes and shoving them in my duffel bag. After the bag is full enough that the zipper barely holds together, I sling it over my shoulder and head back out into the cold.

Growling under my breath at the cold, I make a promise to myself to buy a fucking winter parka and slide inside the first cab that I can find.

5

Sierra

Toronto is a gorgeous city. More so after the sun has set and the buildings light up the dark like stars do the night sky. My heart skips a beat each time I see the skyline—an unfortunately rare occurrence—and the bright streaks of colours that reflect off the water like melted crayons on a black canvas.

While I know how to appreciate it, art was never my strong suit. It still isn't. Not in the generic sense.

I was never creative enough to create something beautiful out of lead and paper or paint and a blank canvas. I remember the art projects we used to do in school and how I dreaded every single one of them.

My silhouettes looked like blobs, my landscapes wince-worthy at best. I didn't have a real passion for anything back then, but I knew art was a definite no go.

The only thing I gave a shit about back then was the sometimes overwhelming need to get the hell out of Parkridge High and the plan to use the next four years at Vancouver University as a reason to piss off my parents, even if the thought of marketing classes had dread hovering over me like a dark storm cloud preparing to piss rain.

Imagine my surprise when I began to enjoy the marketing classes I took each day enough to look forward to them every day. It wasn't exactly the art that I thought I *should* love, but art nonetheless.

Suddenly, I was coming up with themed advertisement ideas and logo designs that filled countless notebooks to the point half my minuscule paychecks from my part-time job at a local college coffee shop went toward new ones.

As my grades rose, my enthusiasm skyrocketed. By the time four years had passed, I was attending interviews with a dozen firms willing to give me even five minutes of their time. More than half of them were just being nice, I realized later on, but by then, I had already accepted the job working for Julia Stroll. The woman I thought would help me reach my potential, but instead ripped my confidence to shreds before feeding it to her stupid little dog that she brought to work with her every day.

I was naive when I worked for Julia, and even more so when I started with Clark and that man whore Cole.

Some days, I don't know what would have been worse: staying to work with Julia and being treated like a rabid dog or working with Cole and being treated like a piece of property that he can't wait for the sale to go through on.

"Knock knock, baby doll. I brought lunch," Gretchen says from the doorway to my office, her thick curls a vibrant shade of red.

Her mossy-green eyes hold a heavy sense of calm that settles me the moment I look her way. She reminds me of home in ways that have helped tremendously during this move. It's almost like Clare is here with me.

I close my laptop and grin. The white takeout bag from our favourite sub shop rests at her side.

"Meatball?" My stomach growls audibly.

"With green peppers and extra mozzarella."

Slim fingers wrap around the back of one of the plush grey chairs in front of my desk as she pulls it back and sits down. A white-wrapped sub is placed in front of me alongside a bottle of Pepsi, and my mouth waters instantly at the smell of food.

"Mack let you go for lunch early today? I thought he was still being a massive alphahole," I mumble, tearing through the wrapping of my sub before taking a massive bite. The moan that escapes me would usually embarrass me, but for some reason, nothing I do around Gretchen makes me feel embarrassed or weird.

She rolls her eyes at the topic of her boss. "His mother came by and stole him for the afternoon. I made the executive decision to take an early, long lunch break as a reward for entertaining her until he finished up a meeting. If he has a problem with it, he can take it up with me later."

I shake my head, smiling at her confidence. If anyone can grip the balls of a man who believes he's larger than life, it's Gretch. Although, I'm sure it helps that she's actually held Mack Thompson's balls in her hands before, but that's a story she doesn't like retelling unless she's wine drunk.

"He's lucky to have you. You deserve a lot more than a long lunch break considering everything you do for him," I say honestly.

Gretchen snorts. "You're right. Maybe one day he'll realize that."

"Maybe he does and he's just picking on you like schoolboys do to the girls they like," I tease.

"Then he's got another thing coming because that shit has never ever worked." She takes a bite of her sandwich, glowering at me from over the top of the bread.

"I would say to tell him that, but it's probably safer if you don't say anything. Knowing you, you'll end up handing him his ass, and I can't risk you getting yourself fired. There's no way I could deal with Cole without having you to vent to afterward."

"That's because Cole Travis is a pig, Sierra. If you went to HR, you could probably get him fired. I would go with you if you wanted."

The food in my stomach turns to lead as I set my sub down on the wrapper and take a large gulp of my drink, desperate to wash away the spoiled taste in my mouth.

The reminder of Cole's hands on my ass, gripping and pulling at it like it was his to touch, makes everything I've eaten today threaten to come back up as I pale and exhale shakily. "You don't really think that they would believe me over him. It would only make things worse."

The frown on Gretchen's face is prominent as the sad reality of how the world works sets in. "We won't let him get away with how he's treating you, Sierra. I promise."

I don't want to talk about it anymore, so I nod in agreement. The bile burns in my throat as the smell of food continues wafting around me. With sweaty hands, I push my office chair away from my desk and stand on wobbly legs.

Gretchen is following suit before I have a chance to excuse myself from the room like I planned to, saying, "Let it out now, and then lock that shit right back up. Don't let him see that he has any effect on you."

Arms wrap around me, and the smell of greasy meatballs is replaced with eucalyptus and mint. My stomach settles slightly, and I allow Gretchen to hold me tight, to become my shield from the world for just a few moments.

"I saw Braden outside this morning," she whispers, tightening her grip on my shoulders briefly before pulling back and running her hands down my arms. "When did he get here?"

I swipe away a stray tear and take a step back, steadying myself. She must have recognized him from the pictures she saw on my phone. Yes, the ones I couldn't bring myself to delete. What can I say? I'm a glutton for punishment.

Her sudden interest doesn't sneak by me, however. She's far too clever.

"Don't even think about it, Gretch. He can't find out."

The idea of Braden finding out about Cole's behaviour since I arrived in Toronto is enough to strike fear deep in my bones. But it's not fear for myself or for Braden. It's fear for Cole.

There is not a sliver of doubt in my mind as to how Braden would take care of him. It would be cruel, painful, and *bloody*. The worst part is that if it came down to it, I would stand back and let him do whatever he saw fit to that asshole. That's why I can't give him the chance in the first place.

"How long is he here for?" she asks after a long pause.

"He said for good."

Her eyes bulge almost comically. "Oh, wow."

"I know. I was up all night replaying our conversation. When he showed up at my apartment this morning to walk me to work, it really threw me for a loop. He told me he was going to be there, but a part of me didn't believe that he would actually show up." That's an understatement, and the bags under my eyes would agree.

"That's a good sign, right?" she asks. I nod, and she blows out a dramatic breath and wiggles her brows. "The pictures didn't do him *any* justice, by the way. How do you plan on staying strong when the guy wanting back in your bed looks like that? I couldn't do it. I would let that man break my back right in half and thank him afterwards."

A smile breaks out on my face as I throw my head back and laugh. "I actually *did* try to get him in my bed. But in my defense, I've been so damn horny lately, and Braden has some weird juju claim on my vag that makes it nearly *impossible* not to want to jump his bones."

"Juju claim?" she sputters, looking like I just called myself the queen of fucking England before pouting and adding, "I'm jealous. I want a man to own me like that."

"It's not exactly ideal when falling into bed so quickly is exactly how we started and ended up in this mess in the first place. We need a new beginning. Even *he* wants to start fresh. Do this the right way, you know?"

She stares at me sympathetically but not in a way that makes me feel pitied.

Gretchen doesn't know everything that happened between Braden and me, but she knows the most important parts. She was the one rubbing my back and sliding scoops of ice cream in my mouth while I sobbed over the loss of someone who I was never even able to fully claim as mine.

"Then that's what you do," she says, ever so confident in me. "No more screwing that god of a man until at *least* the third date."

Third date? I can do that. That's how normal people date, right? Shit, I don't even remember how to date.

I've gotten over my initial surprise of him turning me away last night and have quickly sunk into a small pit of embarrassment when I think back on it.

I couldn't have done anything more desperate than practically climbing him like a tree before we had even managed to have a decent conversation about the future. But I was just so happy to see him, so overtaken with the need to be close to him again, to touch and feel him, to think of anything but doing just that.

He was right to stop us when he did. Everything he said about starting over and doing this the proper way was exactly what we should do. Regardless of what happened before I left, I can't pretend that my feelings aren't there, that

I'm not head over heels in love with him when I so obviously am.

We didn't do things right the first time. We were both too stubborn and jaded about the idea of love and relationships that by the time we both got there, it became too much too soon. For Braden especially.

I don't know exactly what it was that seemed to pull Braden from that noncommittal fog of his, but I plan on finding out. I plan on learning *everything*.

We have a second chance here, something so many people don't get. And I plan on doing right by it.

I owe it to myself to at least try.

Who knows what I might be giving up if I don't.

6

Braden

I STRETCH OUT MY FINGERS IN THE POCKETS OF MY NEW JACKET AS I wait for Sierra to finish work. It's just after 5:00 p.m., but with how dark it is, it feels way later.

The whole Christmas vibe going on downtown is eye-catching, I'll give it that. With the yellow lights wrapped around the lampposts, freshly fallen snow, and wreaths hung on seemingly every business' door, it looks like the setting of a Hallmark movie.

Christmas was never a huge event when I was younger. Mom became a modern-day Scrooge after the divorce, forcing us to spend Christmas eating pasta at Antonio's restaurant like any other day, while Dad was too emotionally closed off to offer me much more than a brief "Merry Christmas" and a bowl of bland oatmeal.

And while it's still a little over two weeks away, I want to know what Sierra does to celebrate. Was it a big deal for her as a child? Does she have any traditions that she's held on to over the years? We're here together now, and there's a giant piece of me that wants to spend the holidays stuck to her side like a damn leech.

Lana and Dad won't be here until a few days before Christmas, but I know that my new "mommy" will want to do something to celebrate her first major holiday as an official member of the Lowry family. I just have to cross my fingers and hope that Sierra will join me and save me from a few hours of Lana-induced torture.

I hear Sierra's laugh before I see her. She's the first through the door, jacket hugging her body like a glove, that fucking gorgeous smile of hers beaming right at me. I ache to have her in my arms and have to fight to stay where I am on the sidewalk so that I don't up and steal her away.

Her eyes, so warm and gentle, are locked on mine as she lifts a hand and waves almost shyly. I'm no longer surprised to find myself missing her whenever we're not together. It's become like second nature to me, and I don't hate it either.

It isn't until the person beside her waves a hand in her face that she looks away from me, shaking her head and saying what I can only assume to be an apology. The woman beside her has flaming orange hair that's whipping furiously in her face as the wind picks up. She's small in size, almost elf-like. I could easily bench-press her without breaking a sweat.

Both of them turn to me then, and Sierra's small friend eyes me threateningly yet carefully, like a predator does its prey. It's like she's assessing me, learning the best form of attack to cripple me in one go. I feel a sense of approval toward her, knowing that she's protective of my girl. That she's looking out for her when I'm not around.

They both head my way soon after, their cheeks already pink from the cold.

"If it isn't the infamous Braden Lowry," the redhead says, crossing her arms and pinning me with a glare. "I have to admit you're shorter than I expected."

Well, that's a blatant lie. I cock a brow. "Sorry to disappoint. I'll try better next time."

I feel Sierra's warmth against my side and wrap my arm around her, pulling her as close as possible. I grin when she doesn't fight me on it but relaxes against me instead, like being held in my arms is exactly where she wants to be.

Fuck, that makes me happier than it probably should.

"Braden, this is Gretchen. Gretchen, Braden," Sierra introduces us with a wave of her hand and a stern look shot at her friend, almost like a warning.

"Gretchen," I echo, biting back a snort. "Like from Mean Gi—"

"If you say *Mean Girls*, I will cut you," Gretchen cuts me off, her words like a whip. I blink a few times, too stunned to speak.

Sierra steps closer and places a hand on my chest, laughing under her breath. I look down, sucking in a breath when I find her already staring at me. Her eyes are my favourite shade of melted silver. The intensity in her stare hits me low in the stomach.

"You got a new jacket," she states on a breath, fiddling with the bottom hem. Her fingers have always been slim and dainty, but for some reason, it's more noticeable to me now.

My attention becomes laser focused on the slight shake of her hands and how red they've gotten from the cold. I immediately grab her hands in mine and bring them to my chest, brushing her knuckles with my thumbs. "I did."

She swallows. "It looks good."

I smile at the compliment. "Thank you, beautiful."

Gretchen's snort reminds me that she's still here.

"Ready to go?" I ask Sierra, tucking a piece of her unruly brown hair behind her ear. "You're already freezing, and we still have to walk."

As if she's just remembering the time and place, her eyes

widen slightly, and she nods, turning to her friend and wishing her a quick goodbye before I do the same.

Once we're alone again, I tuck one of her hands into her coat pocket, keeping the other linked with mine and sliding them into my pocket. I set a mental reminder to bring her gloves tomorrow morning.

We walk for a few minutes in comfortable silence, both of us trapped inside a web of our own thoughts. It doesn't last for long, though. Mostly because I don't want to waste my time with her not speaking.

"How was work?" I ask, immediately cringing at how fucking lame I am.

Thankfully, Sierra doesn't seem to mind because she replies without hesitation.

"Frustrating. One of our newer clients is refusing to raise their advertisement budget regardless of how many times I tell them that what they're offering isn't enough to get them anything better than a bus stop ad in a low-density residential area." The last sentence comes out in a grumble that has me fighting back a smile.

"What is the product?"

"Pine-tree-scented men's soap."

I can't hold back my laugh before it escapes me, loud enough that it draws attention from the people around us. "You're shitting me."

Sierra's annoyance is gone just as quickly as it appeared as she says in a voice far too deep, "Are you ready to find your inner lumberjack?"

Fucking brutal.

My chest shakes as I pull my hand from her and maneuver us around a group of men. Throwing my arm over her shoulder, I pull Sierra closer. "Was that slogan your idea?" I already know that there's no way in hell she came up with that lame-ass jingle, but I won't miss a chance to poke at her.

Sierra plays along. There's no way that she doesn't know what I'm doing.

"What if it was?" she throws back with ease, peeking up at me through long, snow-coated lashes. A lump gathers in my throat, and everything dims around her.

I wait for a halo to appear above her head and wings to spread at her back.

Sierra is an angel made of everything pure and fucking holy, and I'm more than ready to finally get down on my knees and worship her.

My next words come out with enough sincerity to shock me.

"Then I've never heard anything better in my entire goddamn life."

Sierra

My breath catches at the way Braden looks at me. Like I'm the most precious thing in the world to him. It should hurt—how deeply he's dug himself beneath my skin—but all there is is a searing bliss that I can't seem to get enough of. He managed to get deep enough to wrap himself around my soul and brand his name on it, and I wouldn't have it any other way.

As quickly as someone taking a hammer to a brick wall, I crumble beneath the love I see bleeding from his stare. Love for me and what I hope he imagines our future could hold.

"Then you'd be a liar," I tease lightly, grabbing his side when a shoulder knocks mine on the crowded sidewalk and I stumble slightly.

His hold on me becomes stronger, like an anchor. "Meh, it would be worth it. At least you'd be happy."

The heaviness of those words hits me harder than I expected. I hide my blush behind the collar of my jacket. "Stop saying stuff like that."

"Why?"

I know that he's looking at me. His curiosity is a heavy weight between us. I look straight ahead and say as calmly as I can manage, "Because you're making me want to skip the first three dates and invite you upstairs."

A giddy laugh escapes me when he scoops me up and takes off down the pavement. I bury my face in his shoulder to keep the wind away while he laughs, the rough sound of it making me shiver.

"What are you doing?" I shriek.

"What does it look like? I'm taking you home, my little fighter."

7

Sierra

My giggle can be heard for miles as Braden fumbles with my keys, trying to unlock the door to my apartment. I don't tell him that sometimes it gets sticky and you have to jiggle the key at a certain angle to get it to work because watching him get flustered is far too entertaining and rare of a chance to pass up.

"Stop laughing at me and help," he grumbles, attempting to sound annoyed with me but failing miserably. I couldn't pretend not to notice that smile on his face, even if it wasn't one of the most beautiful things in existence.

I palm his jaw—the rough stubble bringing back memories that make me rub my thighs together—and force him to look at me. His lips part, nostrils flaring, and I know that he can see the heat in my eyes and flush on my cheeks. "Hurry."

Half expecting him to set me down on my own two feet so that he can concentrate, I'm surprised when his grip only tightens as a new look of concentration washes over him. It's only a few heartbeats later that my door flings open and he walks us inside.

I vaguely hear the door shut behind us before I'm on my

feet and pressed against a wall, gasping. My eyes zero in on Braden, on his intimidating presence that has wetness pooling in my panties and eyes so dark with his want for me that I subconsciously lick my lips in a silent invitation.

He watches my tongue slip back inside my mouth and groans so deep that I feel the vibrations of it in my stomach.

I want him closer, pressed against me so that I can feel his heartbeat. Has his chest ached like mine? Did his heart break like mine did?

"Every single day without you was torture," he admits, his words like gravel.

My breaths are shaky, weak. I'm aware of the way my palms are pressed to the wall when they become slick with sweat. Braden takes a step toward me, followed by another, and another, until his warmth wraps around me like tendrils of smoke.

Fingers brush my cheekbones, and I arch my back, desperate to feel more of him as he murmurs, "So beautiful."

With shaky fingers, I unzip his jacket and slowly push it off his shoulders, feeling Braden's stare like a brand on my skin. When the jacket drops to the floor, neither one of us makes a move to pick it up.

Braden simply moves it aside with his foot and closes in on me, so close that I can't help but look up and meet his soft, unwavering stare. I swallow the emotions bubbling up before they overwhelm me.

His fingers drag from my cheek to the pulse thumping in my throat. They dance over the smooth skin before dipping lower to the collar of my jacket. Braden toys with the lining for far too long, almost like he likes the way I'm growing more and more anxious too much to stop.

Just as I'm about to say something, he's unbuttoning my coat with a surprising swiftness before sliding it down my shoulders and tossing it away. I'm left in my peach blouse and these damn fleece leggings that I put back on in exchange for my pencil skirt before leaving work.

He pinches the silky material of my blouse with a reluctant sigh before saying, "I'm sorry."

I don't have a chance to ask what he's apologizing for before he tears it open, the buttons scattering along the floor. *Holy shit.* Need rages inside of me like rough, windy waters as I grab him by the front of his shirt and pull him toward me, close enough that I can kiss his waiting lips.

He doesn't waste any time before responding, kissing me back roughly, so desperately that my knees shake, seconds away from giving out completely. Like he already knows, Braden grabs me by the back of my thighs and lifts me. I tighten my legs around his hips and cry into his mouth when he thrusts his erection between them.

"Do that again," I gasp, running my hands all over him, taking my fill. Taking and taking and taking. He presses against me harder this time, sending my eyes rolling back at the friction.

The ache between my legs is all-consuming. I'm hyperaware of my breasts in my bra, how my nipples swell and harden, scraping against the material. I feel like a starving animal, and Braden is my next meal.

"*Fuck.* Look at you," he says while leaning down and nipping at my throat before soothing the sting with his hot tongue. "You're soaking, aren't you, baby? Does your pussy ache for me?"

There's no point in lying. I'm too far gone for that. Nodding frantically, I whimper, "Touch me. Please."

Cold air nips my back as he pulls back and moves us around before dropping me on the couch. I sit there in front of him, my sore lips puffed and eager and my chest rising and falling rapidly as he watches me with a look of pure savage hunger.

My head hits the back of the couch as I wait. Each second that passes by is pure and utter agony. Thankfully, he doesn't wait long before dropping to his knees in front of me and taking hold of my thighs in large, warm hands, kneading the skin and muscles with powerful fingers.

Suddenly, I realize that in these moments, when all of Braden's walls are down and he's baring himself to me completely—jaded soul, wild heart, and all—I fall even deeper in love with him. So much so that I know without a doubt that I would do anything *for* him and anything *with* him, by his side.

The sharp edges that protect that mushy, warm centre of his don't scare me anymore. Not when I know that he won't allow them to touch me.

It's times like this when I'm reminded of the way he keeps himself hidden from others. Right now, I see the side of him that would rather cut himself open and bleed himself dry just so the person he loved could see that giant heart of his without risking them so much as pricking themselves on his serrated exterior.

The weight that I've been carrying on my chest evaporates, taking with it the fog in my mind. There's a rattling behind my rib cage as my heart acts like a bird trying to take flight. I suck in a confident breath and speak without hesitation.

"I want to do this. Us. I don't want to waste any more time," I say frantically. His surprise is written all over his face, but I don't let it affect me or keep me from saying what I need to. "I know that we did this backwards, and that as much as we both want it to, it might not work out anyway. But I also know that I love you. And I don't want to throw what could be our only remaining chance away because of hurt feelings and a messy past."

My cheeks are on fire by the time I finish baring my heart

. too aware of Braden's firm grip on my thighs and . way he hasn't so much as blinked since I began speaking. The weight of his reaction—or lack thereof—is hung above my head by a thin wire just waiting to be cut loose and crush me to a pulp.

He must finally register the alarm on my face because he pulls his hands away from my thighs and places them on my cheeks instead, leaning into me with a look of complete bliss.

His eyes search mine, for what I'm not sure, but when his face fills with my favourite dimpled grin, I know that he's found whatever he was looking for.

"I'm so fucking happy to hear that, Sierra. But now I really, really need to kiss you."

"Kiss me, then, Braden," I whisper.

He does without hesitation. His mouth takes mine in a kiss so powerful I feel it as an ache in my bones. I wind my fingers in his hair and attempt to pull him closer, to take back some of the power I can feel him stealing from me, but he nips at my bottom lip in response, like a punishment.

I break our kiss with a near painful gasp when his fingers brush my hardened nipple through my bra. The sensation is heightened tenfold by how turned on I've been the past few minutes, and I wonder if I could come like this, with nothing more than his fingers brushing my nipples. By the state of my underwear, I'm not sure if I'm willing to rule out that possibility yet.

He discards my shirt and pulls my breasts free from my bra. The peaks of my chest tighten and swell under his stare before he's pinching the left one. I whimper his name, my head falling back again.

"I won't let you leave again, baby," Braden groans, the words heavy with lust and a promise that doesn't slip past me. He twists and pulls my nipple between his thumb and forefinger. "I couldn't let you go again even if I tried. You're fucking mine."

Nodding, I arch into him, desperately trying to get more contact. My brain is short-circuiting, and every fuse inside of me blows, leaving me desperate for more.

"I still have some apologizing to do."

I hear the words but don't register them, too far gone to even begin trying to understand. My head shakes furiously, though, as if it knows what to do all on its own. "No."

"Yes." He presses his face in my neck and kisses my flushed skin, inhaling deeply before leaning back and sucking my nipple into his mouth. My fingers find purchase in his hair, scratching at his scalp when his teeth close around the sensitive flesh and bite down just hard enough for me to feel the throbbing increase between my legs.

My nipple is wet when he releases it with an audible *pop* before nipping at the other one, making my toes curl.

"Braden." The word is nothing short of a plea for more. More friction, more of the feeling flaming inside of me.

His hands fall to my thighs again before he pushes them apart. "I'm going to make it up to you, my little fighter. But first"—he slides his fingers under the waistband of my leggings before yanking them down swiftly—"I need you to come on my tongue."

8

Braden

Sierra's muscles quiver beneath my fingertips. They actually quiver, and fuck if that doesn't make my already aching cock throb and push against the zipper of my jeans. I can feel the wetness collecting on the tip, wetting my underwear, and it only makes me want to yank it free of its restraints that much more.

My dirty words have her whimpering and grabbing at me like I'm a tall glass of water she's finally found after being stuck in the desert for days. I love it when she gets like this. All wild eyes, flushed cheeks, and no inhibitions. Like she's completely let go and has handed over control of her mind, body, and soul to me and me alone.

Swallowing a possessive growl, I remove her leggings from around her ankles, dropping them beside me. I squeeze her thighs one final squeeze before trailing my hands upward, stopping just before my fingers make contact with her panties.

Biting down on my tongue, I stare in absolute awe at the simple white underwear and how they've become so wet they stick to her pussy, exposing how swollen and ready she is for me.

"Just like I thought. You're soaked," I say breathlessly, my voice thick with desire.

Sierra nods again, like that's the only thing she's capable of. She's too turned on and lost in the feelings that we undoubtedly share to even attempt to speak.

I swipe a finger along her slit and unleash the groan that I've been trapping down when my finger meets the slick material. She shivers, sucking in a sharp breath when I tug her panties to the side and expose her glistening pink pussy.

My dick is so hard it physically hurts as I take my fill of her, but I don't make any move to touch myself and alleviate the pain. In all honesty, I deserve it. I deserve a lot worse.

Right now, this is all for her. I wanted to worship her, and now I have my chance.

Already on my knees, I lean further between her legs and spread her with two fingers. A string of curses slips from my mouth before I press my tongue flat against her heat, slipping it between her folds and circling her entrance. She bucks her hips at the sudden intrusion, gasping a string of breathy words that I can't understand.

I raise my eyes to watch her, expecting to find her staring up at the ceiling in bliss, but find her staring at me instead, eyes burning so bright that I feel their heat licking my skin. The urge to take a picture of her so that I can have this image with me whenever I please beats at my chest, but I shove it aside and slide a finger inside of her instead.

"Braden," Sierra chokes, gripping my hair and arching into me again, stronger this time. I press a hand on her hips and hold her still. "Please."

"I know, baby. Just a little longer. I haven't had my fill yet."

Her clit must be throbbing horribly by now, with how I've

been ignoring its presence, licking and sucking everywhere else, knowing that she'll come the moment I touch it. She's on the edge already from all of the teasing earlier, so I know that it won't take much more to set her off. But I want to delay her orgasm as long as possible. It'll make it that much more explosive, that much more *memorable*. Maybe that makes me selfish, but I don't give a fuck.

I trace circles around her swollen clit with my tongue, continuing to tease her. My face is soaked in her arousal as I replace my finger with my tongue, fucking her with it. I use my wet finger to continue circling her swollen bud at a quick pace.

Her grip on my hair becomes painful, letting me know that she's close.

"I need you to come for me now, Sierra." I'm sucking her clit between my lips and shoving two fingers inside of her as soon as the words hit the air. Her walls grip me like a fucking vise, and her clit begins to throb as she cries out for me.

"Braden. I'm coming! Oh my God, *Braden*." Her legs tense and lift from the couch. I remove my hand from her hips, letting her press up against my mouth.

"That's it," I hum in approval, lapping at her entrance and revelling in the way she quivers around my tongue.

Sierra rides her orgasm beautifully for a few seconds before her legs fall limp and the fingers in my hair relax, leaving behind a dull ache. There's the slight sheen of sweat on her forehead that makes her hair stick to her flushed skin, and her bare chest rises and falls at a speed that at any other time would have had me worrying.

She looks well and truly sated.

"Are you okay?" I ask, fighting back a grin as I sit back on my heels and use the bottom of my shirt to dry my face.

A flicker of amusement passes across her face as she wipes

the hair from her forehead and exhales slowly, nodding once. "More than."

I nearly beat at my chest like a fucking gorilla but opt for a crazy grin instead.

She must notice my confidence rising because in Sierra-like fashion, she half-heartedly scolds me in an attempt to keep my head from inflating too much.

"You're ridiculous."

"That I am, little fighter. You should have hidden while you had the chance."

She contemplates my words for a few seconds, like I've just spoken some riddle that I want her to solve. Her brows furrow as she asks, "Would that have stopped you? If you didn't know where I was?"

I don't have to think about it.

"No. I wouldn't have stopped looking until I found you." I'm moving closer and holding her face in my hands now, my thumbs brushing across her lips. "I might have gone crazy, though. Depending on how long it took me to find you."

Molten silver eyes blink back at me, eyelashes sweeping across the skin beneath them that hints at several sleepless nights. A sharp pain grows behind my ribs at the knowledge that she hasn't been sleeping. I wonder how long it's been since she's had a good night's sleep. For me, it's been weeks.

Those same eyes travel across my face, searching for something. The possibility that I'm lying, maybe. Whatever it was, she doesn't seem to find it.

"As opposed to what? How crazy you already are?"

I shrug. "Crazy for you, yeah."

Her mouth falls open, a loud laugh falling between us as she shakes her head and pushes at my shoulders. I take the hint and pull away from her again, even as every fiber of my being scolds me for it. She reaches down to fix her underwear.

"What are you? A teenage boy?"

I smirk. "Fuck, I sure hope not."

Her lips twist to form a scowl, and she gestures for me to get up. "We need to work on your after-sex talk."

"If I remember correctly, you were the one who insulted *me*."

Holding out my hands, I help her off the couch.

"Somebody has to keep you grounded," she states like it's common knowledge.

When she tries to pull her hands free, I tighten my grip on them, not ready to let her go just yet. The minute that I do, it'll sink in that I need to go home. That I need to leave her here alone. A muscle ticks in my jaw, and before I can hide it, Sierra's kissing me.

The kiss surprises me so much that I don't respond for a few seconds. She threads our fingers together and squeezes, finally drawing a response from me. I pull our joined hands so that they rest against my chest and kiss her back, trying to shove my thoughts toward her as if our minds are connected by an invisible thread.

Her touch calms me, my frustration slipping away. I want to wrap myself in this feeling, want to curl up in her arms and stay there forever. But that's not taking it slow.

She might have agreed to give me a second chance and to do this over again, but that doesn't mean that she's ready for everything that I'm ready for. We need to move at her pace, and I plan on respecting that.

Gently pulling away, I let go of her hands and tuck her hair behind her ear. "I should go."

"Okay," she whispers, watching me with a sadness that acts like a dagger between my ribs.

"I'll be back in the morning. Please try and get some sleep." I sweep my thumb beneath her eye, on the blue-tinted skin. "Call me if you need me."

She nods, swallowing so hard her throat bobs.

"I mean it," I push. "Doesn't matter how late it is."

"Are you okay?" she asks cautiously. Sierra knows me better than she probably thinks she does. I used to see that as a threat, but now I recognize it as a blessing. She understands me completely. There's no reason to hide anything from her.

"I don't like leaving you. Not normally, and sure as shit not somewhere I'm not familiar with. Call me overprotective or whatever you want, but it's true. Toronto is new territory for me. I'm going to start worrying about you as soon as I walk out that door just like I have been since the minute I left you in that stupid fucking club." The words come out in a rush. My cheeks burn. I'm fucking embarrassed.

Sierra's eyes soften instantly. "I'll call you if I need you. I promise. Plus, my building is incredibly safe. You really don't need to worry so much."

I roll my eyes and pull her in for a hug. "Tomorrow morning. Check the temperature before getting dressed, would you? Or should I take a cab here instead?"

"I'll let you know." Her laugh vibrates along my skin, permanently marking itself along my body like a damn tattoo.

It's not long after we pull apart that I'm kissing her goodbye and walking back out the front door. A familiar sense of excitement—like the one I get before every fight—dances in my stomach, buzzing in my ears like a swarm of angry bees when I think about seeing her tomorrow.

The last thought that I have before I leave is that I never want this feeling to go away.

9

Sierra

The clock on the wall shows that it's just past 10:00 a.m. Eleven past ten, to be exact. The time is a heavy weight in the room as the realization continues to bounce off my office walls.

Mack Thompson was supposed to be here, in *my* office, eleven minutes ago.

My new boss—the one who seems to have been avoiding everyone and everywhere except his own office for weeks now—is supposed to be standing just a few feet from me, for a meeting that *he* called, but is nowhere to be seen.

It's irrational for me to be worried and annoyed after only eleven minutes, but with every tick of the clock, I grow more and more anxious. My brain is bursting with questions and sizzling with paranoia.

I haven't been stood up, have I? By my own boss at that. How utterly mortifying that would be. Gretchen would wring his neck once I told her. No questions asked.

My brows come together in thought as I collapse on my fancy leather chair. Dropping my elbows on the desk in front of me, I shut my eyes and groan.

There's no way Gretch would have worked for Mr. Thompson for so long if he was a complete and total asshole. She might act as if she can't stand him, but I think that has more to do with their unresolved sexual history than his behaviour at the workplace.

If she truly thought he was that bad, she would have jumped ship the minute Mackenzie Thompson's firm tanked, not stuck around to see if there was a chance to save it.

A small sound of surprise escapes me when a rough chuckle echoes through my office. My attention snaps to the owner of such a gruff laugh—one that sounds as if it hasn't seen life in years—while I slide my sweaty palms down my navy blue dress pants and rush to stand.

He stands in the open doorway, a slight sheen to his dark brown skin. It looks as if he had chosen to run up all twenty-seven flights of stairs instead of taking the elevator up. "Are you okay, Ms. Caster? You seem a little . . . agitated. Should I come back in five minutes with a latte?"

I gape at who I can only assume to be Mackenzie Thompson and the way he holds his large, suit-tailored body with such ease. He's unfamiliar yet speaks to me as if he already knows me. Either he's just very confident, or he knows more about me than I thought.

A lightbulb goes off in my head. *Gretchen*.

Clearing my throat, I round my desk with an easy smile and extend my hand. He takes it without hesitation. "Mr. Thompson, I'm assuming?"

"Oh God. Call me anything but Mr. Thompson. Mack or Mackenzie works fine." I attempt to hide my surprise, but he notices, adding, "The only two people who call me Mr. Thompson are my assistant and my mother. Both opting to do so only *after* I've done something to piss them off."

"Gretchen may have mentioned that that is a very common occurrence." I laugh and make note of the way his emerald-green eyes spark at the mention of my friend. "Would you like to sit?"

Stray pieces of thick black hair fall to his forehead as he nods and sits down in one of the two leather chairs opposite my desk. "You're probably confused as to why I asked for a meeting."

"More curious than confused," I reply, settling back behind my desk.

"Gretchen tells me that you're working on a difficult project at the moment."

It's a statement worded like a question, so I reply as if it were the latter. "That's right. I am. There have been a few snags along the way, specifically regarding money on their end, but I'm hoping to have that resolved by the end of the week."

It's a pipe dream, in all honesty. It's already Wednesday, and the Waterton Brothers have no intention of giving me what I have assured them over and over again that I need for all of this to succeed. They might be content with having their advertisements plastered on broken bus benches and shattered store windows, but our company is not.

There's no way that I can run this by anybody above me as a serious option without it looking horribly on my reputation and future here. Not to mention Cole would use it to his advantage. A shiver racks through me.

Mack scratches at the dark stubble covering his jaw, looking as if he's fighting back a smile. My face pales, and I know instantly that Gretchen has told him far more than I initially thought. *That damn traitor.*

"You can be honest with me. I'm the last person who would think less of you because of an idiot, tight-pocketed client who thinks they live above reason. We've all had them." He pulls at the knot in his tie and sighs in relief when it loosens slightly. "If I'm being honest, I did request this meeting because Gretchen asked me to help you, but I didn't come here planning to do so unless I thought you deserved it. I don't put my back out for many people, let alone a new hire who I have never met and certainly don't trust."

Sweat breaks out on the back of my neck as I register his words. It would seem that my dear friend has a lot more pull with her boss than she let on. I'm not sure whether to be grateful for that or a bit embarrassed that she felt the need to ask for help on my behalf. I know that it wasn't with ill intent—quite the opposite of it, actually—but I'm not somebody who is overly happy looking like a helpless puppy in the eyes of my superiors.

The way Mack is looking at me right now doesn't scream pity or disappointment, though. If anything, he seems to be . . . curious? Maybe a bit cautious?

It's clear as to why Gretchen has deeply scarred feelings for this man. Some reasons are the same as to why I love Braden. There's something undeniably sexy about a confident, straightforward man. They make you weak in the knees and your heart flutter wildly like a baby bird trying to learn to fly. It's nearly impossible to get over them once you offer them a piece of you.

"Okay." I straighten my back and meet Mack's confident stare with my own. "What do you want to know?"

Approval flashes across his face before it fades away to nothing. "I'm assuming you have plans—ideas, and a way to execute them. So tell me what you need from those buffoons, and I'll get it done."

I blink once, twice.

His pink lips part with a grin. "That surprises you?"

"I thought you said that you didn't know whether or not I deserved your help."

"I did. And I've decided."

"So quickly?"

He chuckles, pushing back the hair that continues to flop across his forehead. It's cut in a way that would hint at a daily use of hair gel. I'm assuming he skipped that step today.

"Is that a problem, Ms. Caster?"

"No," I rush out. "I'm just surprised. I figured that you weren't awfully involved around here anymore." Wincing, I tell myself that I should have stopped while I was ahead.

The amusement I watch flicker to life in his eyes has me floored.

"All of you transfers seem to have the impression that I either don't know how to do my job or that I simply hate it."

"Is that why you haven't been around, then? The judgment?"

He seems to like it when I'm blunt, because his smile reaches his eyes, and the skin beside them crinkles, making him look older than I first thought. Maybe late twenties or early thirties.

"I'm far past caring about other people's judgment, darling."

My eyes narrow as I say, "Then why not introduce yourself sooner? It would have been nice to receive some sort of welcome when we arrived."

I scowl as I begin to recognize how the bitterness toward this move, and what it cost me is clouding my judgment. Being a bitch to the one person here who wants to actually help me—favour or not—isn't going to get me anything but fired. When I turn back to look at him, I find him in thought, as if he's silently chewing on the words I've rudely spoken.

"I can see why my assistant is so fond of you, Ms. Caster." Mack's face is stoic, yet his words are almost tender. It's a weird paradox that I don't understand, but I smile anyway. "Do you have my email?"

Is that a serious question? "I do, yes."

"Send me everything in the Waterton Brothers file, and I'll look it over tonight. It was nice to meet you."

He gets up and leaves without another word, the reality of the situation really dawning on me for the first time.

First, I just met Mack Thompson. And second, he's going to help get my ass out of some serious hot water. After I chew her ass out, I definitely owe Gretchen an endless tap of tequila for this.

10

Sierra

"I've never been so turned on in my life as I am watching you eat those noodles," Braden says, his body shaking beside mine on the couch. He's laughing, nearly in full-on hysteria as he watches me with glittering eyes.

The Chinese food that we ordered after work is nothing but empty boxes stacked between us. The TV plays a Hallmark Christmas movie with a cowboy and a wedding planner returning to her hometown. The originality of it was what sold me. *Not.*

In all honesty, I nearly turned on one of my recorded episodes of *Law & Order* before I caught myself and gripped the remote so hard the buttons left imprints in my palm. I didn't feel like opening up that can of worms and digging into all the reasons as to why I haven't been able to watch the stupid show in the past three weeks.

"Keep making fun of me and I'll kick you out in the snow." I wipe away the grease on my cheek before reaching across the chow mein box in my lap to swat him in the arm. Swallowing the rest of the food in my mouth, I narrow my eyes on his dimples.

Braden cocks a daring brow while setting his food down on the coffee table. Patting his spread thighs, he says, "Try me, fighter. I'll go willingly if you can get me off the couch."

"Having me splayed across your body isn't much of a punishment, now is it?" I laugh before shoving the last forkful of noodles and chicken in my mouth.

I feel his smile deep in my chest.

"Fuck no it isn't. Having you on my lap and in my arms is a fucking reward, never a punishment."

"Then no." I place the empty box beside his on the table before moving to sit back down. My eyes fly toward him when he grabs my wrist and pulls, sending me toppling toward his thighs. "Braden!" I squeak. He ignores me but drops my wrist, giving me false hope before he's gripping my hips and situating me so my legs hang on either side of his.

His body heat wraps around me, his smell flooding my senses. I place my hands on his shoulders and watch through thick lashes as his warm eyes slither over my torso, snagging on the white scar I know lives along my left collarbone.

"I fell out of a tree when I was ten," I murmur, shivering at the feeling of his calloused fingers rubbing the bare skin above my hip where my shirt must have ridden up. His eyes meet mine with an intensity that nearly steals my breath. "There was a big oak tree in front of our house, and Clare double-doggy-dared me to climb as high as I could. I only made it a few feet before I slipped and fell. I broke my collarbone pretty badly, and they had to stabilize it through surgery. My mother was livid. She grounded us for two weeks and called some guy to come and cut down the tree the next day."

"She grounded you for falling from a tree?"

I smile sadly and press my thumb to the creases between his brows, trying to smooth them out. "That's my mother for you. If we were having fun, we were being too rowdy, and if we were too quiet, we were being sneaky and deceitful. There was never a middle ground. I learned young that it was impossible to please her, yet I couldn't help myself from trying."

The fingers on my hips tighten their grip and guide me further up Braden's thighs until I'm so close to him that my nose brushes his chest, and I can feel the bulge in his pants brush my centre.

"Your mother sounds awful," he says, voice full of gravel. "What about your father? Was he just as bad?"

I shake my head but frown. "He loved to play games with us when Clare and I were younger. Hell, he encouraged us to laugh and yell when we were having fun. But then he started letting Mom walk all over him. He never told her to back off or that we should be allowed to act like kids."

"You resent him for that." It's not a question, and there's no judgment in his words. Nodding, I close my eyes and try to think about where to start.

I want to deny it, to stand up for my father in ways he never thought to do for us as children, but I do resent him. I blame him for never being around the same way that I blame his job for taking him away so often. Hating a job, an organization, that does so much good in the world never fails to make me feel like a piece of old gum underneath a running shoe, but I won't torture myself by forcing myself to feel differently.

My parents spent their lives helping other people's children while their own grew up alone. It's a sick twist of fate, I guess.

I think the worst part of it all is that we could have dealt with the distance between us, the lack of family dinners and no "I love you's" at night if they had both cared enough to try when they weren't away working. Even when the distance was no more than a few feet, my sister and I ate alone before it was her that tucked me into my bed at night.

There are so many questions that I want to ask them but never have the guts to do so. Did they even want kids? Were we really a burden that they didn't want to feel the weight of? Is that why they found a job where they could pretend we never existed?

A soft touch on the wet skin of my cheekbone pulls me from my thoughts. I open my eyes, realizing through blurred vision that I've started to cry and that Braden is wiping the tears away.

There's a thick ball in my throat that I try to swallow past. "I'm sorry."

"Don't apologize for things you can't control, Sierra. And never for how the actions of somebody else affect you. Your parents let you down. It's as simple as that. You don't need to feel guilty for being upset about the way they've treated you."

I exhale slowly. His eyes narrow and blaze with something that looks a lot like anger and frustration as he watches me fight a silent battle. The way that he can tell exactly what I want to hear has me wondering how he knows all of this. I want to ask if he's speaking from personal experience or if he's just become incredibly wise over the past few weeks.

Almost like he can read my thoughts, he says, "You're not the only one who's spent years resenting your parents, baby."

I want to push him, want to tear open the small hole he's exposed in his close-kept past for me, but fight against the urge. If I touch that opening, he'll stitch it shut before I have the chance to mangle together an apology.

Instead, I slide my hands to his trim waist and hold him, pressing my cheek to his chest. I debate on whether or not to say anything but decide to keep quiet and hand the invisible reins over to him.

His heartbeat quickens beneath my cheek, and I recognize the way it skips and rams against his rib cage, trying to burst free, because mine does the same all too often.

Fear is an all-encompassing emotion. It fills your stomach with acid and spikes your blood with adrenaline. Fighting against fear is like going up against the boss at the end of a video game without actually playing a single level.

I tighten my grip on him and kiss the centre of his chest, then the burning skin beneath his Adam's apple. He shudders, breathing deeply and licking his lips.

"I didn't grow up around love. I grew up with two parents who fought so often they forgot what it was like not to fight. When I was ten, I watched my mother throw an empty bottle of vodka at the TV after Dad got home too late from work."

My sharp inhale is obvious enough for him to briefly pause and drop his chin to the top of my head. I squeeze him in response, and he continues his story.

"My mother disliked vodka the way she did my dad—with a passion that burned so bright the line between love and hate often blurred. She didn't drink often, but when she did, you wouldn't dare reach for her glass in fear of how deeply it would upset her. It was the same way with my dad. When she cared for him, he would be the only one she could see in a crowded room. But when she hated him . . . he learned over time to try and keep a lengthy distance between them.

"It never worked when he would stay away, though. It was like she craved the high that came with winning a fight between them and always sought him out just to have a go at him. It was impossible to understand why my parents went from smiling and laughing one second to cursing and screaming the next. To this day, I still remember begging Dad to make it stop. He was tucking me into bed the night that I told him they were tearing me apart. Two days later, my mother told me they were getting a divorce."

"Do you think that he told her what you said?" I ask gently.

Braden nods once, and a strong breath of air ruffles my hair. "Yeah, I do. They never told me what the final straw was, but I've always thought that it was what I said that night."

I think back to the night of Brooks' and Lana's wedding and how different Braden's relationship with his mother looked than how he's describing now. From what he's told me, it's been over ten years since she left him behind and took off to Europe, so I suppose I shouldn't be surprised. I for one know how hard it is to continue holding a grudge against someone that you love so deeply. It's the reason I struggle so badly with the relationship I have with my dad.

There's a pang in my chest at the heavy sadness that's found a home in his words. If I could shoulder the hurt and betrayal that he's felt for the past decade as my own, I would. The decisions that he's made in our relationship are starting to make more sense to me as the different parts of himself that he's shown me form a much clearer image. It's still fuzzy around the edges, but progress is progress. Especially when it comes to someone as steel-walled as Braden.

I nuzzle my face against the spot in the centre of his chest and ask, "How is your relationship with her now? It seemed good at the wedding."

"I love my mother, I do. And we're much better off now than we were a few years ago. But it took me a long time to forgive her for everything that happened to our family and how she decided the only way she could repair what was broken inside of her was by abandoning me for two years. My father was far from perfect in their marriage, but it's no secret between both of them that I chose his side, regardless of what feelings I held against him and his part in everything."

The warm breath on my head becomes laboured slightly, so I look up, my stomach turning sour instantly. I'm not surprised to see the guilt that's sunken deep into his features, but it still upsets me nonetheless.

"The last thing that you should feel is guilty, Braden," I say, a bit harsher than I intended, but I don't dare take it back. I don't want to. "You were a child forced to watch the two people you love destroy each other. Choosing a side was inevitable, especially when you had to choose between someone who had stayed with you and somebody who had left."

Braden's lips part, and his eyebrows stitch together. I watch something dangerous, something tipping on the edge of becoming out of control, spark in his whiskey-brown eyes seconds before he takes my mouth in a searing kiss.

The kiss doesn't last long, but it leaves my insides simmering by the time he pulls away to mumble low words across my lips.

"Thank you."

11

Braden

I've been here in Toronto for just over three weeks now, and although my gym is still nameless, it's no longer empty. The training equipment was brought in yesterday, and the crew finished up the locker room this morning. We're still a few months away from opening to the public, but it's progress.

It doesn't matter how much time I spend here, I still can't believe how far this place has come in such a short time. I'm incredibly grateful. Each day that passes is another day that I have to bite my tongue to avoid telling Sierra about this place.

It's not that I don't want to tell her; it's that I don't want to tell her *yet*. Not until it's finished. I want her to see it for the first time with just me. Just us, alone. Is that stupid? Probably. But I'm selfish that way. When her pretty pink lips part in shock and she turns to me with surprise in her eyes, I want to feel that same rush too. In private, with the girl that helped me realize I'm capable of doing something bigger.

For now, she knows that I've started working at a local

boxing gym. It's not technically a lie, but it still makes me feel a bit guilty regardless. *It'll be worth it*, I remind myself.

I'm flipping my newly built desk over onto its legs when I hear a set of familiar, low voices carry to the room that will soon be my office. Dropping the screwdriver that I borrowed from one of the crew members out front, I push my hair out of my eyes and head out to meet the guys.

When Tyler called me yesterday and told me the Vancouver Warriors would be in town for their last game before Christmas break, he pretty much invited himself over. I didn't mind, seeing as how I've actually missed the asshole, but I will admit that I got a bit nervous. It was Tyler's money from the sale of the old gym that helped make this possible in the first place, so I guess I just don't want to disappoint him. If he knew that I was thinking this way, he would undoubtedly kick my ass—or try anyway.

It doesn't help my nerves any that he also invited his brother-in-law and team captain along. Oakley Hutton has seen more athletic gyms and training centres than most people ever will. It's not shocking, considering he's the face of the professional hockey league, but it still makes my small, unfinished gym feel tiny and forgettable in comparison.

I'm still trying to shake off my nerves when Tyler pops out from behind the small wall separating the front entrance from the main gym, spotting me at the same time that I do him. He doesn't exactly grin, but he smiles in that familiar half-assed way while bumping Oakley on the shoulder.

The move pulls Oakley's eyes from their intense sweeping of the gym as they land on me. "Well, well, well. If it isn't Braden fucking Lowry. Long time no see, buddy."

"You're telling me," I reply while eating some of the distance between us and pulling them both into quick hugs. "How was the flight?"

"Restful. Slept the whole way." Oakley says, squeezing the

brim of his hand between his hands. I could count on one hand the number of times I've seen him without a hat on and messy brown hair peeking out from beneath it.

"Snored like a fucking pig too," Tyler grunts.

I slant my brother a look. "I have it on good authority that you snore loud enough to make Gracie contemplate buying earplugs."

"She said that?"

I toss him a wink.

"I believe it. She used to complain every morning about my snoring when we were growing up." Oakley chuckles.

My grin is evil. "At least I know what to get her for Christmas."

"Has anyone ever told you that you're an asshole?" Tyler asks, scowling right at me.

"Once or twice." I shrug. "What time is the game tonight?"

"Eight. You want tickets?" Tyler asks.

I shake my head. "Nah, I already have plans."

"Speaking of," Oakley says, the corner of his mouth twitching. "When are we gonna meet these 'plans'? Gracie's been going on about your girl since they met at your dad's wedding. It's made my wife incredibly jealous."

Tyler snorts. "It's not Gray's fault that you've been too busy to meet her."

Oakley pins my brother with an exasperated look before turning to me again. "This guy hasn't invited us either."

"I've only been here for three weeks." Throwing my hands up in front of me, I shake my head and scowl.

It's Tyler that speaks next while patting me on the shoulder with fake sympathy. "Plus, he's been grovelling for those three weeks. I doubt Sierra would have agreed anyway with how bad Braden fucked up."

I want to step into a pit of quicksand and let myself get

pulled under. Talking about my rocky relationship with Sierra is not how I planned on starting this reunion. It's not a conversation that I had planned for today at *all*.

The past two weeks have been anything but easy. Sierra and I have made leaps and bounds in our relationship, but trust takes time to rebuild. I've walked her to and from work every day, and each night she invites me inside for dinner. We talk about things so trivial and childish while learning about each other in ways that I never wanted to learn about somebody before.

I know the way she likes her eggs in the morning—runny and drenched in ketchup—how she only wears mismatched socks because "the dryer eats the matches," and what three things she would take with her on a deserted island. She looked almost giddy when she told me her list.

"Obviously a water bottle for water, a magnifying glass to help start a fire, and a black Sharpie."

When I asked why she would bring a Sharpie, she said, "So that I can draw a penis on your forehead and laugh to distract myself from the fact that we're going to get eaten by animals and die on a stranded island."

I didn't tell her, but the fact that she imagined herself there with me kept me up all night with a smile on my face.

There's still that same buzzing attraction between us that seems to only intensify as time goes on, and every night we fight it like high school virgins scared of our parents catching us making out on the couch.

We eat whatever takeout I've ordered before picking her up, or if she's not too tired, she'll teach me how to cook something easy that won't lead to me burning the house down. Then we cuddle up on the couch and watch TV until she passes out in my lap, and I carry her to her room before letting myself out.

It's become a routine, something that I look forward to

every day after working at the gym. I can almost see the broken pieces of our relationship gluing themselves back together. If I wasn't terrified of speaking anything into existence, I would say that we might be even better than we were before.

I fall back into the conversation happening around me when Oakley throws a teasing dig at my brother.

"He's not the only one of us that's fucked up something great because his head was in his ass, Ty." Oakley chuckles before adding, "At least he didn't sleep with her best friend."

"He's got a point," I say in easy agreement, ignoring the evil side-eye from Tyler.

Gracie kicked her ex-best friend/roommate out of their shared apartment the same day that she found out about her secret one-nighter with my brother. It had happened way before Tyler and Gracie got together, but it caused quite the ruffle between them. The fight didn't last long, though, before Ty was declaring his love for her and promising a happily ever after.

"Whose side are you on?" Tyler asks, still glaring at me.

I sling my arms around both of their shoulders and tighten my grip. They both stiffen but don't fight to break away as I say, "Whoever's paying for pizza."

"Who said anything about pizza?" Oakley ducks under my arm before tilting his head to the side, cracking his neck.

Tyler shoves his elbow into my ribs, forcing me to let him go and clutch my side with a pained wheeze. "Can you even have pizza, Lee?" He flicks his amused gaze to me. "Oakley here is on some fucking vegan diet now. Can't even have real cheese anymore."

My nose scrunches. "You're kidding."

Oakley rolls his eyes, as if he's already tired of this conversation, and casually lifts one shoulder. "Some of us actually listen to our trainers."

Tyler scoffs, and a muscle in his jaw pulses. "Here we go again. I'll continue to eat my real fucking food and avoid becoming a scrawny shit like you."

"You're no bigger than me. If anything, you're smaller. I have at least two inches and ten pounds on you. Plus, that's not how it works. You don't just get skinny because you choose not to eat real dairy or meat products."

Tyler's scowl only gets more intense. "Keep telling yourself that, string bean."

My brows are raised as I watch the two guys, bemused by the sibling-like bickering going on between them. Tyler may be my blood, but they're just as much siblings as we are. It gives me some sort of peace knowing that he has a family that loves and cares for him outside of just Dad and me. He damn well deserves it.

"Do you guys want a tour?" I ask, hoping that my suggestion will help draw their attention away from whatever argument I can sense brewing. If I had to guess, I would say Tyler's asshole ego has been getting him into trouble at work. It wouldn't be the first nor the last time.

Their attention snaps away from each other and falls on me. Excitement passes across Tyler's face, and I'm happy when he doesn't bother hiding it from me.

Oakley smiles wide, nodding. "Please."

I lift my arm and gesture for them to follow me as I move us away from the front doors and past the hallway leading toward the two large locker rooms and my office. Coming to a halt where the old tile flooring meets the newly laid laminate, I look toward the empty open area bordered by floor-to-ceiling mirrors with a prideful smile. Soon this entire room will be fully equipped with the array of workout equipment we got this morning, punching and speed bags, and a training ring.

"There will be a room for those who want to train

privately as well. The goal is for anyone to feel comfortable working out here, not just boxers," I say, looking at them from over my shoulder.

"How many trainers are you considering having?" Oakley asks as he steps up beside me, his arms crossed and eyes carefully working their way across the room.

"Two boxing trainers other than myself and one personal. Right now, it's hard to tell how many I'll need. I don't have any clients here yet," I answer. There's a subtle hint of nerves in my voice that I try to ignore.

"And when are you estimating you'll open? February? Early March?"

It's Tyler who speaks next, sneaking around me and walking toward the tape stuck to the floor where the training ring will eventually sit. "It was March, right?"

I nod. "Yeah. There's only a few more cosmetic things left before the ring can be placed. The equipment will be moved in soon."

"I think you should look at hiring a few more personal trainers. I know a lot of the guys train with a bag but not in a ring. They don't wanna take the risk."

"Bunch of pussies," Tyler grumbles.

I ignore him as my brows stitch together in confusion. "What guys?"

Tyler simply laughs at me while Oakley slaps my shoulder, saying, "I've been talking you up to Kyle Davies, and he said that he and a few other guys from the team might be interested in swapping gyms. He wants to come check it out before opening."

"Kyle Davies as in the captain of the Toronto Timberwolves?"

"Yes. That is if you want a bunch of puck-twiddling assholes in your gym," he replies, squeezing my shoulder before dropping his hand and joining Tyler by the ring markings.

"Adam has a few past clients from WIT that live here now too. He told me to tell you that he can send you their numbers anytime," Tyler throws in.

One of our college friends, Adam White, owns an ice hockey training arena in Vancouver. I'm not surprised in the slightest that he has clients way out here. He's made quite the name for himself after graduating college. Especially when it comes to players in the hockey world.

Adrian Loskowski, the first pick of the draft this past season, spent the last four years of his junior-league career training alongside his coach *and* Adam at White Ice Training.

"I'll call him today," I reply, still a bit dumbstruck. My stomach is twisted and knotted to the point I'm beginning to wonder if I'll be able to undo all the damage.

"You've done a great job, Braden. This is going to be huge." Tyler's tone is so light and airy that I nearly stumble backward in surprise. His pride is openly scrawled across his features, like he couldn't hide it even if he wanted to. I soak it up, knowing that it's a rare occurrence.

"Toronto was the right move, buddy. You're going to make a name for yourself out here," Oakley chimes in, wearing a similar look to Tyler's.

"Thank you. Both of you." My chest is tight, nearly painful even. I rub my palm above the ache before I can stop myself.

"Okay, let's go eat before we all break down into fucking tears," Tyler grunts as his mouth forms its usual scowl again.

I can't help but laugh and nod in agreement. It will be a cold day in hell before the three of us snuggle in a circle and let our walls down enough to cry together. But fuck, our joint laughter is more than enough.

12

Sierra

"Come to dinner with me on Christmas Eve."

I lift my eyes from the bowl of spaghetti in my lap to stare at the giant man stretched out on my couch. Braden's watching me intently, cautiously, as if he really believes there's a chance that I'll say no to him.

Setting my bowl down on the coffee table, I readjust myself so that I'm facing him on the couch, my legs tucked under me, knees brushing his thigh. "You know, usually the guy *asks* the girl to have dinner with his family, not orders it."

He visibly winces, and an apologetic smile pulls at his mouth. Clearing his throat, he asks, "Would you like to go to my father's for Christmas dinner with me?"

"I would."

My insides turn to mush when he grins so wide his dimples pop. He looks like a kid in a candy store, and it amazes me that it was me that put that look on his face.

Before Braden, I viewed dating through a black-and-white lens. There were set criteria and a list of do's and don'ts to follow before you could consider yourselves a society-approved relationship.

Obviously, having sex with a stranger and then falling in love with them in three months was not a part of that plan.

I never would have thought that I would be so eager to spend a holiday with a guy and his family after only being on a single date, but here I am, completely accepting of the idea —excited, even.

Braden and I didn't spend time at restaurants and bowling alleys getting to know embarrassing childhood memories or our biggest pet peeves before deciding whether or not to continue a relationship. Instead, I learned how easily Braden falls asleep when I play with his hair and how he drinks his coffee black and piping hot in the morning.

As time went on, I started becoming proud of him over small things and frustrated for him over others. It didn't take baring my soul and all of its dark secrets to get to that point. It just happened.

We didn't fall in love the "right way" when it comes to society and its standards, but we did it *our* way—tangled up in sweaty sheets and drowning in denial.

"Okay," Braden replies, almost to himself, before setting his bowl on the table and grabbing my hands in his. "Okay."

"How are they settling in?"

Brooks and Lana only arrived in Toronto three days ago. Five days later than what they were hoping. Turns out Lana's modelling career is a bit more serious than I previously thought. Serious enough that she got called for a shoot in Vegas the morning before their original flight and had to postpone the next one for four days later.

A familiar stiffness pulls at Braden's shoulders, and I know right away it's because the topic of his new stepmom isn't his favourite one. Not by a long shot. His attitude toward her has definitely gotten better—more accepting and less cruel—over the past few weeks, but it's going to take a while for him to fully accept her into his family. Nobody, not myself, his father, or anybody else, can judge him too harshly for that.

"It looks like they've lived there for weeks already. Lana didn't waste any time."

His thumbs roll circles on the top of my hands as he rests his cheek against the couch, watching me with a calmness that I welcome wholeheartedly. I want to curl up beside him, so I do just that. Scooting closer, I press my front to his side and lay my cheek on his chest.

Expelling a quiet puff of air, Braden drops my hands and grips my thighs, laying them over his lap. It's only after I'm as close as possible that he wraps an arm around my back and asks, "Is this good?"

"Very good," I hum in satisfaction while looking up at him through a curtain of mascara-coated lashes. The idea of having to get up and leave the warmth that is Braden just to take my makeup off makes me want to throw a fit like a small child.

"Are Clare and Liz still coming on Boxing Day?" Braden asks, tracing designs on my hip with the calloused fingers that I've grown to love so much.

Excitement blasts through me at the mention of seeing my niece and sister for Christmas. We've never not spent the holidays together, and although I offered numerous times to be the one to fly back home, Clare was insistent that she and Liz needed a change of scenery. Whatever that means, I have no clue. But I'm sure I'll find out.

"They are. I'm excited for you to meet them." Probably a bit too excited, but oh well.

When I first asked Braden whether he would want to meet my family over the holidays, I was pleasantly surprised when he said yes, not a twinge of hesitation in his voice. In a way, it also helped reassure me that I made the right decision in giving our relationship another shot.

"I'm excited too, fighter. And pretty scared, if I'm being honest. I can barely handle one Caster woman, let alone three."

My eyes roll. "I would be more scared of Clare's cooking than anything else. She hasn't been able to perfect a meat dish in her entire life. So I hope you like overcooked, rubber-like turkey."

Braden doesn't have a chance to reply before my body is flushing cold, and sweat breaks out on my neck and chest. I push away from him, swatting at the warm hands wrapped around me and placing weak legs on the ground. One hand flies to my mouth while the other presses against my stomach, eager to calm the churning sensation I feel forcing my dinner back up.

"Sierra? What's wrong?"

That stupidly warm hand touches me again before I'm pulled against an equally warm, if not hotter, hard body. I shove at Braden again, but it doesn't do anything. I'm too weak to fight him as he guides my hunched-over body to the bathroom.

"Jesus Christ," he mumbles. His voice sounds higher-pitched than usual.

"Get out," I groan before sinking to my knees in front of the toilet bowl. Reaching behind me, I wave my hand in the air. "Go."

He doesn't listen, and before I can protest again, my throat is contracting and my dinner is coming back up. I heave into the toilet bowl, my arms shaking and nose burning.

"You're okay, baby." Braden's presence moves from behind me before I hear the sound of drawers opening and closing. I shiver when fingers brush the back of my neck and my hair is pulled back into a loose pony.

He rubs circles on my back until the nausea passes, and I fall back onto my feet, my head lolling to the side, hitting his chest. A shaky breath escapes me as I wipe my mouth with my arm and attempt to climb to my feet before swaying too much and sitting back down.

"Let me help you," Braden orders gruffly, flushing the toilet. He moves behind me and slips his arms beneath my armpits before pulling me up easily, like I weigh nothing at all. "Do you want to shower?"

I debate saying no, but the thick layer of sweat covering me makes me reconsider. "Yes. But I can do it myself. Go. I'm disgusting right now."

"Stop telling me to go, Sierra. I'm going to fucking help you whether you like it or not."

"But you don't need to. I'm more than capable of showering myself."

He sighs, exasperated. "Let me help you, dammit. I *want* to help you."

"Fine," I snap through gritted teeth. Pulling free of his supportive grip, I sit down on the toilet, shooting off a quick, silent prayer that the seat wasn't up. I've been embarrassed enough for one night without adding falling into a toilet bowl to my resumé.

Braden doesn't say anything else as he moves around the bathroom, his shoulders and back tense, brows pinched together in concentration. He turns the shower on as hot as it can go and digs through the cabinets before finding fresh towels.

I'm being a complete bitch right now, but the part of my brain that would usually tell me to suck it up and accept the help seems to have been brought up with tonight's dinner and flushed down the toilet.

"Let me take off your clothes," he orders in a rough tone, daring me to argue. I don't have the energy to fight him on it anymore, so I don't.

I dip my chin and stand. "Okay."

With my approval, Braden drops to his knees in front of me. The backs of his fingers brush my knees and the tops of my thighs before he's reaching for the waistband of my sleep shorts and swiftly pulling them down to my ankles. I step out of them and watch him drag his intense gaze up my bare skin before he presses a soft kiss to the inside of my thigh. My chest throbs at the gentle gesture that I wouldn't have expected from him a few months ago.

I want to tell him how much those little things mean to me, but when he backs up quickly and rises to his feet, I keep my words to myself. He's silent as he removes my tank top and drops it beside my shorts.

Braden moves to the shower and tests the water as I wrap my arms around my naked chest and watch in slight wonder at the way he so easily fills the small bathroom. When he stops a few steps in front of me and starts taking his clothes off, I blink at him.

"The tub is smaller than both of our old ones," I mumble half-mindedly, too busy staring at the strong rippling of his thigh muscles as he lifts one leg at a time and steps out of his pants. "I doubt you'll fit."

His grin is crooked and beautiful. "Have a little faith, sweetheart. It might be tight, but I'll fit."

I release a puff of air and smile slightly, meeting his glittering stare. "Does your head always go straight to sex?"

"You're almost naked, Sierra." He shrugs, moving his eyes along my body. I'm fully aware of how my nipples tighten beneath my arm and goosebumps slither up my bare skin. "But you need to get in the shower before you pass out. Up," he orders before reaching for my hands and pulling me up.

The sigh that escapes me as soon as I step under the water is one of pure relief. My arms hang limp at my sides, and my forehead touches the tile while the hot water pelts my neck and upper back, seeping deep into the tight muscles.

I feel Braden step in behind me before the shower curtain slides shut. Fingers brush my spine, moving higher and higher until strong hands grip the skin of my shoulders. "How are you feeling?" he asks in a deep, gravelly tone that makes my belly tighten. I can feel him completely bare behind me, so he must have shed his boxers after I got in.

"Tired," I reply, my voice a bit strained. Tipping my head back in the water, I reach for my shampoo, but my arm stills in the air when his fingers close around my wrist.

"Let me."

Blinking a few times, I drop my arm.

More than a few moans spill beneath the water when he slides soap-lathered fingers against my scalp and massages my head for probably far too long before nudging me forward to help rinse it out. I fight back a whimper when he coats my loofah in bodywash and moves it along my body in a way that I'm positive isn't intended to be sexual but feels incredibly intimate. By the time I shut off the water and we step out of the tub, there is way more than a slight tingle between my legs.

Tucking in the end of the towel I just wrapped around myself, I walk the few steps to the sink and grab my toothbrush. After squeezing out a hefty amount of toothpaste on the bristles, I shove it in my mouth and meet Braden's eyes in the mirror. They're dark, half-lidded. The toothbrush in my mouth feels unnaturally heavy as my stare travels down his bare, damp chest, past the collection of dark hairs gathered in the middle of his Adonis belt, and falls to the thick, hard cock between his legs.

I quickly look away and force myself not to gulp, spitting a mix of toothpaste and drool into the sink instead. His presence behind me couldn't be any harder to ignore than it is right now. If I didn't consider myself totally unfuckable tonight, I would have already dropped this stupid towel and let him have his way with me.

I hear him moving around behind me before the bathroom door creaks open and his footsteps fall on thick carpet. With a shake of my head, I'm pulling myself back together despite the ache between my legs. *Get it together, Sierra.*

Braden doesn't return from whatever he was doing until I'm dressed in a baggy shirt and plugging my phone into its charger by the bed.

"Is there anything you need before I leave?" he asks, fully dressed in his hoodie and jeans from earlier. Suddenly, a feeling of dread hits me. I don't want him to leave. I haven't wanted him to leave a single night since he's been back but haven't found it in me to ask him to stay. Before tonight anyway.

"Stay," I blurt out. "If you want to."

Lines stretch the length of his forehead when he lifts his brows. "You sure?"

"I'm sure." I pull the comforter back and slide into bed.

Braden's surprise doesn't last long before he's shedding his clothes again and joining me. He's warm, like always, but instead of turning to his side and curling around my body the way I became accustomed to in Vancouver, he stays on his back. If I had to guess, I would say that this is his way of being respectful and not stepping over the boundaries he assumes I still have in place.

With a small smile, I make the move and turn to him, resting my head on his chest and sliding my arm along the hard grooves of his stomach. Tapping my fingers against his side, I tilt my head and press my lips to his jaw.

"Thank you for taking care of me. I don't know what the

rules are when it comes to what we're doing, but I love you. Good night, Braden."

His swallow is audible as long, strong fingers intertwine with mine. He dips his chin, and his mouth brushes the top of my head.

"I will always take care of you, little fighter. I love you."

13

Sierra

I'M HAVING A MELTDOWN. A FULL-BLOWN, SWEATY-PIT, stomach-collapsing meltdown. I've burned holes in the carpet from my pacing, I just know it.

Oh my God.

Nothing. Fits. *How* can nothing fit?

My entire closet is scattered across the carpet in my bedroom. Not a single one of my dresses zips up past the middle of my back, and my skirts—even my favourite, five-season-old stretchy one—won't make it up past the ass that has seemingly grown double its size overnight.

I'm too young to be having a heat flash, but I feel like I've been shoved inside of a damn oven. Pulling at the neck of my tank top, I let the cool air hit my damp chest and sigh, tipping my head back.

My panicking isn't helping matters; if anything, it's only making it worse. If I don't calm down, I have no doubt that I'll end up sweating off the entire face of makeup I spent far too long doing this afternoon or yanking out the fancy braided bun I glued to the back of my head with an entire package of bobby pins.

It's Christmas Eve. I can't lose it on Christmas fucking Eve. Especially not when I'm supposed to be spending it with my boyfriend and his closest family members. Not to mention that I can't exactly show up in my underwear and a sweat-soaked tank-top either.

I'm too scared to check my phone to see what time it is. Braden is supposed to be here at four thirty, and I'm almost certain that it's way too close to that time. I've spent at least fifteen minutes just standing here freaking out.

Raking my eyes over the mess of clothes on the ground, I fist my shirt so tight my fingers burn. "Screw it."

The bottoms of my feet hurt as I stomp my way to the closet and pull the accordion-style door as open as possible without ripping it off the hinges. There, hiding behind a bagged pantsuit and the dress that I wore for my high school graduation—not sure why I still have that one—is the only article of clothing that my mother ever gifted me.

A knee-length maroon dress with long, lace sleeves and a plunged yet modest enough neckline that keeps enough chest to the imagination, made by a designer that I've never heard of before.

This dress was my gift for graduating university, and it would have been a great gift had she not bought it a size too big and in a colour that I've avoided like the plague my entire life, knowing how badly it washes out my pale skin. I kept it anyway, since it was one of the nicer gifts she had ever thought to buy me, but it hadn't seen the light of day since it left the store four years ago. Well, until tonight.

Tonight, it's the only thing big enough to fit me. Talk about a blow to the old pride and confidence.

Yes, I tend to wear more formfitting outfits that don't technically leave a lot of room for . . . growth, but it still sucks big-time to try on dress after dress with not a single one fitting the way they used to.

I rip the dress from the fabric hanger and throw it toward the bed before taking off my tank top and dropping it on the floor. The bra I slide on is nude and strapless and matches the plain cotton underwear I've been strutting around in all afternoon. It's not a sexy set by any means, but I'm hoping it won't stay on long after dinner. At least I *was* hoping to have Braden strip me naked and have his way with me as soon as we got home, but that was before I realized I had gained more than just a few pounds of happy weight. Now I'm not sure if I want Braden anywhere near me after I pound back turkey and potatoes and fall into a food coma.

Shit. What has he been thinking these past few weeks? How long has my ass been growing? Also, how is it growing in the first place, considering how sick I've been the past few days?

Stopping my hands before I rub at my face, I pick up the dress, feeling the silky material between my fingers. With one long exhale, I slip it over my head—careful not to wreck my hair—and pull it the rest of the way down. It fits almost perfectly, only slightly loose around my waist and shoulders and formfitting everywhere else.

Three hard knocks on the door have my heart in my throat. With shaky hands, I grab my phone, jacket, and black ankle boots off the bed and stumble over my own feet as I walk out of my bedroom, flicking off the lights as I go.

My palm is sweaty when it closes around the doorknob, and I open the door.

"You really need to give me a key to this building if you're not going to answer your buzzer or cell phone. I had to slide through a closing door after an old couple came inside. I'm pretty sure whoever watches your security feeds has my face plastered on a 'keep an eye out for' poster in their office," Braden says, half scolding and half teasing me. He grins brightly down at me, chin to his chest.

There are big fluffy flakes of snow in his gelled-back hair, and his cheeks are pink, looking wind bitten. Moisture collects on my tongue as I rake my eyes along his body in an anything-but-subtle way. I've seen Braden in dressy clothes a few times, but I can't say that I think that I'll ever get used to how well he can pull them off.

The thick wool jacket stretched across his wide shoulders and brushing the top of his knees hides most of his outfit, but with the top few buttons undone in typical Braden fashion, I can see the hint of a black dress shirt and the knot of a . . . tie? Blinking back my surprise, I lower my eyes to the black slacks and shining black dress shoes peeking out from beneath them.

"Oh crap. I didn't hear anything," I mutter apologetically and start to fiddle with the jacket in my hands. "Are you wearing a tie?"

His chest shakes with a laugh that brushes my warm cheeks. "My dad threatened to beat my ass if I didn't. I had to watch a few YouTube videos before I figured it out."

I'm far from surprised by that. If I was a betting woman, I would put money down on either Gracie or Tyler being the one who tied Braden's tie for his father's wedding.

"I'm sure that he'll be happy you listened to him," I assure him. It's so obvious how badly Brooks wants his son's approval in all aspects of his life, but said son just so happens to be too much of a stubborn ass most of the time to see that.

"You look beautiful, Sierra." He reaches forward and traces the neckline of my dress with gentle fingers. A thick brown brow lifts. "You never wear red. I assumed you hated it."

I hold back a snort. "I do." Confusion twists his features before I shrug and nod to the open door behind him. "It's a long story. We should go."

"Right," he says, like he's just remembering we have

somewhere to be. "The cab driver is a real prick, by the way—just a heads-up in case he's gone when we get downstairs."

I slip into my jacket before picking up the bottle of wine I set by the door and asking, "Wouldn't you be if you had to spend your Christmas Eve driving people around town?"

Braden contemplates it for a second, his mouth twisting before replying, "You have a valid point. I can't say that I feel like testing the bounds of his patience, though. We'll be lucky to get another one here before dinner if he leaves without us."

With my keys and a bottle of wine in hand, I step into the hallway beside him and lock the door before we head downstairs. Braden lets out a triumphant holler when we near a yellow cab waiting by the curb. The passenger window rolls down, and an older man, probably in his late fifties, glowers at my boyfriend as if he just tossed his only child out of an apartment window.

"I leave in two minutes," the driver snaps, frowning in a way that reminds me of an angry man in a cartoon.

Braden must think something similar because he places a hand on the small of my back and laughs a bit too loudly. "Got it, Mr. Fudd."

THERE'S A SLEEK, black SUV with overly tinted windows parked in Brooks' driveway when we arrive. Beside it, an old, lifted truck with chipped cherry-red paint and badly rusted rear wheel wells sits, hugging the pavement with thick, well-treaded tires. I know just about nothing when it comes to vehicles, so I won't embarrass myself by trying to guess what year or model it is.

Catching on to my gawking, Braden presses his fingers a bit deeper into my lower back to get my attention. When I look up at him, he's already watching me with a look of amusement.

"That's Dad's. I swear he loves that piece of shit more than me," he says, humour thick in his words. His fingers slide up and down my back through my jacket, pulling a sound of appreciation from my throat.

"How long has he had it?"

"Since I was small enough to need to be lifted into it."

I smile at the idea of a toddler-sized Braden having to be lifted and set inside of the large truck. "You probably hated not being able to jump in yourself."

His grin is affirmation enough. "I did. But after I pitched enough fits about it, he started carrying a step stool in the box —oh, don't give me that look, babe. The old asshole already has one young woman chasing his heels. He doesn't need another."

I swat at his chest and try to snuff out my swoon. "I can't help it if your dad is a DILF."

Braden's hand stills on my back. My eyes bulge.

There's no possible way that I actually said that out loud. Clearly, I've been on the receiving end of far too many of Sophie's gushing rants about Brooks and how he's complete DILF material. *Oh God.*

"Did you just call my dad a DILF?"

My cheeks have their own heartbeat at this point as I flush from head to toe. Avoiding eye contact with Braden is incredibly hard, especially when he's looking at you as intensely as he is me right now. Rolling my lips, I nod, not daring to move my eyes from the patch of ice below the drainpipe on the side of the house. "Yep. That I did."

Braden hums, deep and loud, as his fingers resume their exploration of my lower back. He's so close to me that the heat from his body soaks into my side. I suck in a breath when his other hand lifts to stroke my jaw and cheek, his thumb tracing the edge of my bottom lip. "I'm not above being jealous of my own father, Sierra. Don't make me put on a show with you."

"What do you mean?" is my reply, although I'm sure I can already guess what kind of show he's talking about. I'm stuck between wanting to laugh at how easy it was for him to believe there's a single man that could compete with him and slapping him silly for it.

One second, we're standing in the open on the sidewalk, and the next, we're hidden between the shadows of the side of the house and the garage, visible only through a small window that I assume leads to a bathroom.

My heart thumps against my ribs when the fingers beneath my chin tilt it up, and he bends down enough to hover his mouth so close to mine, close enough that if I just pushed up on my toes the tiniest bit—

"You're mine," he rasps before slamming his mouth to mine.

I gasp against his lips, and he uses my surprise to slide his tongue inside my mouth, tasting, exploring, taking. My eyes slide shut, and my toes curl in my boots as I respond, turning my body so that my front brushes his front and then moving even closer until we're as good as fused together.

With the hand I don't have clutching a wine bottle, I touch his waist before moving to his back and sliding up to his strong shoulders. The cold bites at the bare skin of my fingers, but I only press them into his well-earned muscles, using them as a way to anchor myself.

There's an audible smack when he pulls his mouth from mine and lets out a long, deep breath that fans across my swollen lips. I'm still regaining my bearings when he says with an obvious promise, "Next time, I won't stop. I don't care where we are."

I blink once, twice, three times before swallowing and

dipping my chin in acceptance. Braden places a soft, quick kiss to my cheek before grabbing my hand and threading his fingers through mine. "Let's go before they send out a search party."

"The SUV in the driveway." I clear my throat. "Are Tyler and Gracie here?"

Braden pulls on my hand lightly and starts walking toward the house. I catch up to him quickly and walk by his side. "Yeah. They got here this morning."

I run my free hand along the top of my head and over the bun in the back to make sure I'm not going to be walking in looking like a mess. When everything is still in place, I let out a sigh of relief. "That's exciting. I thought they weren't going to make it."

Braden makes a sound in his throat. "Tyler didn't want Gray flying out here, but from what he told me on the phone yesterday, she threatened to name their baby after Harry Styles unless he let them come. Her doctor also assured him that she's safe to fly for another few months, so I think that helped."

"She's six months along, right?"

He nods and grabs my forearm to help me up the porch stairs that shine with the look of fresh ice. "Careful." He mutters something under his breath that sounds like a curse toward his father for not salting earlier before swinging open the front door.

Braden ushers me inside the warm home before following right behind me. There's Christmas music playing and voices twirling and mixing together as we shed our coats and shoes in the front entry.

My stomach gurgles at the array of different smells from various foods, but I shove the uncomfortable feeling away. I just have to make it through dinner.

"You okay?" Braden asks quietly, rubbing my arm with one of those large hands of his.

I plaster a smile on my face that I wish was completely genuine and place my hand over his, squeezing it. "It's Christmas. Of course I am."

"If I find out that you're lying to me, I'll spank your ass as soon as we're done here. I don't care if I have to do it in the cab."

"Merry Christmas to you too, son."

14

Sierra

Lana Lowry is a Christmas elf. And I mean that in the most flattering way possible.

From the moment Braden and I were ushered inside—our cheeks beating with embarrassment after Brooks heard his son threaten to spank my ass—and glasses of apple cider were shoved in our open palms, Lana hasn't stopped twirling around the house either singing a Christmas tune, fluffing at her overflowing tree, or passing around plates of homemade gingerbread men.

I've found her love of Christmas quite adorable, seeing as how I've never witnessed anyone with so much holiday spirit that hasn't been on a television screen before. Braden, on the other hand, looks like he hasn't gone to the bathroom in a week.

He's seemingly oblivious to the way I'm watching him from where I'm sitting with Gracie in the living room, which is probably why he hasn't felt the need to mask the annoyance written all over his face and body.

Brooks' and Lana's new house is incredibly charming. From the wood-burning fireplace beside me, the original oak floors, and massive windows that must let in so much morning light, I feel rather comfortable here. It's exactly the kind of place I would picture a man like Brooks living.

Lana obviously had some say in the place when it came to decorating. I can't imagine Brooks willingly purchasing a beige, faux-fur rug, a tall lamp with a beaded lampshade, or the painting of the Santa Monica Pier sunset that's hung above the fireplace. They must have compromised, and that makes my heart warm.

"How long do you think it will take before Braden tells her to go stick her head in the snow?" Gracie asks quietly, leaning over just enough to ensure I'm the only one that hears her.

Lana continues to babble on about something, either not noticing the exasperation on Braden's face or just not caring. His hands are shoved deep in his pockets as he leans against the archway separating the kitchen from the living room and mumbles something back to her.

"I'm surprised he hasn't already. I was prepared to jump in five minutes ago."

Laughing under my breath, I steal a glance at Gracie's hand as she rubs soft, slow circles on her swollen stomach. She hums in response to me, but it's clear that her attention has fallen elsewhere.

As if sensing my stare, she turns to me, all blue eyes and slightly flushed skin. "Do you want to feel? Baby hasn't stopped moving since we got here this morning."

I blink at her, taken aback by the offer, before managing to recover with an eager nod. She smiles wide and grabs the hand I don't have wrapped around a glass of water, pressing it down flat on her stomach, just above her belly button.

I nearly drop my glass when something pushes against my palm. My eyes bulge when it happens again, stronger this time, even through her dress. "How is it so strong? You feel that all the time?" My mouth is hanging open when I drop my hand back in my lap.

Gracie laughs gently. "Yeah. Mostly while I'm trying to sleep or after I eat ice cream."

"And you don't want to know the gender?"

She straightens out her back before starting to rub her stomach again. "I did at first, but we've made a bet out of it instead. I'm positive it's a boy, but Ty is certain it's a girl."

I tap my fingers on my thigh before saying, "I'm with you. I think it's a boy. Call it a gut feeling."

Gracie's smile is beaming as she grabs my hand again, this time leaving it where it is but just holding it in hers. I find myself smiling too and give her fingers a squeeze. "You're awesome, Sierra. I'm so happy that everything worked out between the two of you. Braden was absolutely terrible without you—don't tell him I told you that."

My eyes find him again so easily. There's a lurch in my chest when our gazes meet, and I realize that he's been watching me. I smile softly and watch the tightness in his shoulders disappear.

Brooks and Tyler have joined him and Lana, but I know that he would rather be over here with Gracie and me than in the middle of whatever they're talking about. I purse my lips and kiss the air, earning a swift eye roll and wink from him before I turn back to Gracie.

"Was he really that bad?" I ask her, chewing on the inside of my cheek.

I'm not sure why it's still hard for me to imagine Braden struggling so hard after I left. I've heard it from Sophie before and from Gretchen during all of the nights she spent trying to make me feel better. Even from Braden himself. But it feels so much more real hearing it from someone who knows him so well. Someone like Gracie.

Her grip on my hand tightens, a sigh spilling from her

glossy lips. "He got better every day, once he knew that it was actually possible for him to go after you. But he wasn't ever fully himself."

"What do you mean?" I mumble, feeling an ache build at the centre of my chest.

"See, I've only known Braden for five years, but there was never a time where he wasn't wearing arrogance as a shield for whatever parts of him were broken inside. Tyler and Braden are very similar in that sense. It takes a lot for them to open up, and even when they do, it's like pulling teeth out of someone who hasn't had their mouth numbed. I think that's why it hit me so hard when Braden would come to the house and just . . . sit there, silently, like he couldn't be bothered to try and act like everything was fine.

"He didn't even look like himself. I was staring at someone who had lost everything while also experiencing an epiphany at the same time. It all hit him at once. You were gone, he was realizing how in love with you he really was, while also figuring out his past and how to move forward with that."

There's a burn in the back of my eyes that has me grinding my teeth in frustration. Hissing out a breath, I set my glass down on the floor and swipe away the tear that escaped with the back of my hand.

Suddenly, both of my hands are in Gracie's. "I'm sorry," she apologizes quickly. "I didn't mean to upset you."

Her apology only frustrates me more, knowing how ridiculous it is that I'm getting so worked up. The ache in my chest has expanded to my entire upper body now, and my stomach coils around itself. *What is wrong with me?*

Once a sob builds in my throat, I'm pulling at my hands, pushing off the couch with an apologetic glance at Gracie, and heading down the hall to where Lana told me earlier the bathroom would be. I grab at my chest as if I'll be able to rip the ache away before falling into the bathroom and shutting the door with my back.

My breath is shuttered as I rip off a piece of toilet paper and hold it beneath my eye, hoping to avoid ruining my makeup. What a disaster. This isn't me. I don't get so emotional that I go off so easily. Especially not in front of so many people.

Maybe I really am sick. I've been pushing away the possibility due to the fact I hate going to the doctor's office and avoid doing so like the plague. But I haven't been myself for a few weeks now at least. The vomiting I brushed aside as anxiety and moving stress, which I suppose could be the case for my emotional changes as well, but it seems more serious than that.

I jump at the soft knocks on the bathroom door before running furious hands over my hair and throwing away the wet, mascara-stained toilet paper. "I'm almost done," I say, loud enough that it's way too easy to hear the wavering in my voice.

"Can I come in?"

Relief washes through me when I hear Gracie's voice instead of Braden's. If Braden isn't here, hopefully that means that he didn't see what happened. I doubt that he would have let Gracie come see me instead of himself.

Instead of replying, I pull open the door. Gracie's guilt is obvious as she frowns, her blue eyes dull and avoiding mine.

She steps inside the bathroom and shuts the door behind her before turning back to me. The bathroom isn't exactly small, but with one of us sticking out more than the other, it's pretty crowded with both of us. Her belly is only a few inches from brushing mine when she asks, "Can I ask you something pretty personal?"

Swallowing back my fear, I nod once and rub my palms along the front of my dress.

"Do you get regular periods?" Her question comes out of left field, stunning me. I stare at her blankly as she continues. "If you don't want to answer that, I totally understand. I just want to help." She looks just about as nervous as I feel. "Braden called me the other day to ask for advice on what to do to help you feel better when you're sick, and after I asked what was wrong, he told me that you've been throwing up a lot recently."

"I don't get my period anymore. My doctor said that it's because of my birth control," I mumble, my body flushing cold. Sucking in a shaky breath, I tuck an invisible hair behind my ear.

Gracie watches me intently, like she's evaluating my answers and coming up with a hypothesis. That only makes me more nervous.

"Okay," she says, and it's only now that I spot the purse hanging from her shoulder. "I know this is probably overstepping my boundaries, and you can yell at me and tell me to screw off if you want and I won't be mad, but I checked and there's a gas station open a few blocks away. I think we should go get you a pregnancy test."

I barely manage to drop to my knees and lift the toilet bowl lid before I'm heaving into it, tears freely streaming down my face. A hand touches my back as Gracie sits down beside me, staying close but not too close as I lose everything that I managed to eat today.

"I'm going to text Tyler and let him know to keep Braden busy, okay?"

I nod quickly, my throat burning too much to try and speak.

"How long has this been going on?" she asks, and I lift three fingers. "Three weeks or three days?"

"Days," I croak and lean back on my feet, pressing my chin to my chest.

Gracie holds a wet wipe and a piece of gum out in front of me, both of which I accept eagerly. After I wipe my mouth and pop in the gum, she holds out a hand, and I take it, standing up on wobbly legs.

"Thank you," I whisper before washing my hands in the sink. She checks her phone.

"You're welcome. Are you ready to go out there? Tyler has the guys in the basement doing God knows what so we can sneak away, but he insists on driving us. Is that okay? I can tell him to suck it up."

Yeah, right. There's no way I'm going to stand in the way of Tyler's protectiveness over his pregnant wife and unborn baby because of my own problems.

"It's okay," I assure her. "Do you really think I'm pregnant?"

The question sits heavy between us and even heavier on my shoulders. I'm happy that my brain is still playing catch-up and I haven't fallen into a full-blown anxiety attack yet.

She chews on my question for a few seconds before saying, "It's very possible. But we should get you a test before anything else."

And so we do.

SNEAKING out of the house was easy, as was sitting in complete silence as Tyler drove us to the gas station that wasn't even five minutes away. The lack of conversation didn't even faze me. Not when I couldn't bring myself to speak even if I wanted to.

But things only got harder.

I bought three pregnancy tests, a toothbrush, and a tube of toothpaste before carrying everything into a dirty bathroom to avoid having to take the pregnancy tests at my boyfriend's father's house. Then I took each one of the tests, hovering over the germ-infested toilet as I did so before washing my hands until they were raw and brushing my teeth until my gums started to bleed.

Yet that was still nothing compared to now. I stare at the freshly taken tests and wait for the results to show—alone because I'm too stubborn for my own good and refused Gracie's company when she offered it.

Before I got out of the SUV, she told me waiting would feel like an eternity, especially if I stood and stared at them for the entire three minutes, but I'm doing exactly that anyway.

My stomach is weak, still sore from earlier and even more painful now as fear sinks its claws into it and threatens to tear it to ribbons. I've been avoiding thinking of what comes after. What I do or say once the results flicker across the little screen.

I'm twenty-six, far from incapable of raising a child. I have decent savings and a job that I might have a love/hate relationship with but still provides a secure income. My apartment is small, but at least there are two bedrooms.

That's all that I'm allowing myself to think about. Not the fear of Braden's possible reaction or what might come from it. And definitely not what my parents will say.

I will those worries away and force myself to glance at the tests on the counter. My knees buckle, and I have to grab the edge of the sink in a white-knuckle grip to keep from collapsing. My vision blurs as I read the results staring back at me.

Pregnant. 3+ weeks.

15

Sierra

From the moment Gracie, Tyler, and I got back to the house, Braden hasn't left my side. I've taken full advantage of his attention, needing him now more than ever, even if he doesn't know what's weighing on me yet.

With a steadying hand on my thigh, he strokes my skin with his thumb and throws his two cents into one of the various conversations taking place around the dining room table.

My dinner plate is empty besides the half-eaten dinner roll that Braden's been picking at over the past few minutes. He finished eating long before me—even after refilling his plate with overflowing stacks of turkey, potatoes, and a puddle of gravy for a third time—so he opted to help me polish off my food. The same food that now sits like lead in my stomach.

Gracie and her husband have been shooting me cautious, borderline terrified looks ever since I slid into the back seat of their rental car and we drove back in complete silence. I don't blame them for being curious about how I'm feeling about all of this. I haven't given them much to go off, considering how I've taken to hiding behind phony smiles and forced laughs.

This is not the time or place to deal with something this important, and the last thing I plan to do is ruin Braden's Christmas with his family because I can't shoulder this alone for a few hours. We can talk about this when we get home. It won't be long now.

The thought has me pushing out a long breath and reaching for Braden's hand, desperate for his support. His eyes flick to me, and he smiles so sweetly that I can almost feel my blood sugar spike. He makes my worries disappear so effortlessly. It seems borderline unnatural.

"Do you want anything else to drink? It's Christmas, baby. You don't have to drink water," he whispers, leaning over to brush his nose along my cheekbone. His sudden closeness has me shuddering in my seat, a sound of satisfaction daring to claw up my throat.

"I'm good with water" is my fumbled reply. I forget to breathe when his palm slides up my thigh an inch, and he cups my skin like he's scared it'll fall apart in his hand.

He must notice my sudden breathlessness, because he says his next words in a low, husky rasp. "Do you want to leave soon?"

My skin is burning when I nod. As if acting on their own command, my thighs squeeze shut, sandwiching his hand between them. The black rings on his fingers are cool against my skin as he wiggles them between my legs, and his left brow twitches in amusement.

"I hope that you'll consider coming with me sometime, Sierra," Lana says, her high-pitched voice distinct enough to pull me from my lustful haze. I blink a few times as I try to recall what she's talking about.

"Sierra's really busy with her new promotion, but I'm sure

that she'll try, right, sweetheart?" Braden cuts in, sending me a smirk that heats my blood.

I clear my throat and say, "I would love to go," hoping to the gods that I haven't just agreed to spend an afternoon at a tennis club sipping on nonalcoholic martinis or something. I'm atrocious at anything sports related.

The smile that lights up Lana's perfect complexion is enough to make it worth it if that were the case, though. She has a million-dollar smile. One that hits you right in the gut.

"Speaking of your promotion, Sierra. We both wanted to congratulate you," Lana adds. Brooks grunts his agreement, too busy shovelling food into his mouth to speak. I bite back my laugh.

"Thank you." My lips lift in a genuine smile. "It's a definite change of pace."

"I hope you don't mind, but I threw your name out to my modelling agency. I'm not sure if your firm takes on agency clients, but I figured I would give it a shot." Lana mentions it so subtly, so calmly, that I take a second to digest her words.

Of all the things that I was expecting her to say, that was not one of them. My appreciation and respect for her grows tenfold. Every day, it becomes clearer to me just how little you know a person until they do something that takes you by surprise.

After what seems like an eternity later, I respond. "Wow. That's amazing. Since we just expanded into a new city, we're looking for a bunch of new clients. I'll keep an ear out."

She clasps her hands together in front of her. "Perfect."

I sit up straighter in my chair, gasping when fingers travel higher between my legs and knuckles brush the seam of my underwear. I reach beneath the tablecloth and pinch Braden's wrist.

He laughs under his breath and does it again, this time twisting his hand and running a fingertip along my slit, using enough pressure to have my legs begging to open back up. I press my tongue to the roof of my mouth and attempt to calm my racing heartbeat. Thankfully, the conversation has moved on, and the eyes that were just settled on me fall elsewhere.

I wrap my fingers around Braden's wrist and tug, but he only continues to rub at my centre, teasing me to the point my arousal wets my underwear and my clit throbs, pleading for attention.

"Something wrong?" he asks, that stupid arrogance dripping from his words. I want to reach over and smack him but somehow reel the urge back in. "Do you want to go home now?"

"We can't leave yet," I hiss, wishing it was that easy. My head is foggy, my thoughts jumbled. I can't focus on anything but the touch of his fingers between my legs and how long it's been since I've had him inside of me. My cheeks flare at the thought. I wish I had left my hair down so that I could have hidden behind it.

"We can." He toys with the side of my underwear, pulling it to the side before letting it settle back in place. "We've been here for hours."

"Your dad is still eating. And it's rude not to help clean up."

His next words brush my ear. A whispered promise. "The only mess I'm going to clean is the one I've made between your legs, baby. It's up to you whether I do that here or at home. Choose carefully."

I'm shooting up from my seat not even a second later, smoothing down my dress as five sets of eyes fall on me. My fingers shake at my sides as I place one foot over the other and stare down at the man grinning like he won the fucking lottery. "I don't feel well."

His bottom lip slips between his teeth while he watches me with lifted brows. "Really? What's wrong?"

I won't stab him. I won't reach down to my plate, pick up my fork, and stab him in the crotch. I won't do it again, and again either.

My eyes narrow as I glare at him, hoping that every ounce of my anger is clear on my face. His Adam's apple bobs as he swallows, and his grin falls.

"I'm going to take her home," he rushes out, standing up beside me and sliding an arm around my shoulders, pulling me so that I'm forced to lean against his body.

I hear somebody choke on something and see a red-faced Tyler with a fist over his mouth while his wife pats his back, looking just as red. Braden mutters something under his breath that sounds a lot like a string of curse words before I'm being placed in front of him. When I try to turn around to ask what he's doing, I feel it.

He's rock hard, pressed against my hip.

A tidal wave of realization washes over me, and I laugh. I laugh so hard that Braden cups my shoulders and squeezes, trying to get me to stop. He hisses a plea under his breath when I press my cheek to his chest to muffle myself.

"Yeah. We're leaving," he grunts. "Thanks for dinner, guys. It was great, Lana. I promise that I'll come clean the bathroom or something this week to make up for ditching."

"Go. It's fine. Thanks for coming," Brooks says, his voice a little wonky, a little higher-pitched than usual.

Oh, my God. His dad saw.

Braden doesn't even wait to hear what Lana has to say before he's rushing us out of the room, and I laugh again.

"You just showed your entire family your boner, didn't you?" I stammer, trying not to trip with how fast he's pulling us through the house.

"This is never to be spoken of again," he states, stopping so that we can slide our shoes on. "I mean it, Sierra. Never."

Tears leak down my face as I shake my head frantically. "I

can't promise that. No way. This has been the highlight of my life."

He reaches toward me, and his fingers curl into my sides when he says, "Don't make me tickle you, Sierra. I can never face them again. Promise me that this dies here. Tonight."

I squeak in surprise and look up at him with wild eyes. "What do I get in return for this promise?"

"Anything."

I arch a brow. "Anything?"

He dips his chin, looking exasperated. "Anything."

"Take me home."

IT'S easy to forget about your problems when you're lounging in the warmth only true happiness can provide. When what plagued your mind with darkness is washed out by the light that radiates from the person you love. The person who makes you feel content, at peace.

It's a dangerous feeling—letting go. Turning off the switches in your head that allow fear and doubt to grow and fester deep in your belly so that the exact opposite can take shape. Excitement, joy, the good kind of nerves that feel like butterflies flapping in your stomach; they're all good feelings that battle the bad.

Once you shut off the bad—if you can—that's when you're at your best. That's when life seems worth living, worth enjoying. I know that because I'm living with that realization. That reality.

As my mountain of a boyfriend flips on the lights in my apartment, his dark, hooded eyes on me, I feel that excitement, those butterflies in my belly instead of fear nipping at my spine and squeezing my throat.

Right here, right now, he's everything. Braden is my focus, that voice in my head repeating soft, encouraging words. The break in the storm raging inside of me.

He cups my cheeks in his hands and holds me there in front of him, his breath on my parted lips, amber eyes moving from one of mine to the other. I place my open palms against his chest, above the hard, grooved muscles I love so much, before sliding them outward, over his sides, and around his back.

The tension between us makes it hard to breathe. It's like we've been stuck inside of a sealed box for days and have nearly depleted our air supply.

My fingers curl into fists around his shirt as I pull him closer, his hips meeting my lower stomach. I focus on the way his throat contracts with a generous swallow when he tips his head back and a low noise gathers in his chest.

"Sierra," he says, sounding pained in a way that has my knees threatening to wobble. "If you want to wait, tell me right now. God help me, I will turn around and leave this apartment right now if you tell me no. But if you let me kiss you right now, I won't stop until your legs are up by your head and my cock is so far inside of you, you'll feel it for fucking days."

Holy. Shit.

My mouth dries as all of the moisture in my body floods between my legs. I don't bother speaking. I push up on my toes and take his mouth in a brutal, unmistakable kiss of approval.

He responds instantly, sucking my bottom lip between both of his before letting it go and slipping his tongue inside my mouth. Braden kisses me like a man possessed. Like he's spent his whole life not knowing what the inside of my mouth tastes like and is realizing what he's been missing.

His kisses—his *everything*—make me feel utterly desired,

like I'm something he needs to survive. I want to live the rest of my life soaking up this feeling, burying it deep inside of me in a place nobody else will find it and dare try to take it away.

Cool air hits my cheeks when he releases them and slides his hands to the back of my head, trying to thread his fingers through the tied-back hairs. With a curse spilled against my wet lips, he digs through the braided bun holding back my hair and pulls out each bobby pin keeping it in place. One after the other, they hit the floor before my hair falls free, and he wastes no time before taking his fill, scratching and pressing on my scalp. My eyes try to roll back at the sudden wave of pleasure his touch evokes.

Braden shifts his hips, rolling them against me. I suck in a sharp breath when I feel him, long and hard against my stomach.

"Bedroom," he orders, tearing our lips apart. I nod once and grab both of his hands, removing them from my hair and using them to pull him toward my bedroom, even though I know he doesn't need help to find it.

We're silent as we walk. The only noise in the apartment comes from the padding of our feet, the hot air blowing from the vents, and our shuddered breaths.

I keep waiting for the nerves to settle in. For them to throw a ruin in the comfort that I've been soaking in since we got home, but they don't. I'm not sure if that's because of how utterly desperate I am for the man behind me or if I've just accepted the prospect of Braden fucking me into next week. Either way, I'm grateful.

The lack of nerves helps give me the confidence to stop in the middle of my bedroom, not even a foot from the edge of the bed, hold Braden's heavy-lidded stare, and pull up my dress. It slips off before falling to a puddle by my feet.

I'm naked besides a strapless nude bra and matching

panties. But by the fire in his gaze, I could have forgotten that I wasn't standing naked. His usual amber eyes are nearly black, his pupils so large and dangerous that they've overthrown the warm colour. But it's his tight jaw, the muscle fluttering in his cheek, that gives him away.

I shudder under the intensity of his stare and sit on the bed, keeping my feet planted on the floor. He follows me like a bee to honey, stepping between my spread thighs before stopping, his fingers twitching at his sides.

"Don't make me beg," I whisper, pressing my hands flat to the mattress.

Large hands grab my thighs, kneading them and pushing them even further apart. "Maybe I should," he hums low in his throat. "But I don't think that I can wait that long. Not when I can see how slick and ready your pussy is."

His dirty words have me dropping my head back, exposing my throat as I whimper. My nipples pucker, forming hard buds beneath my bra as I arch my back and push toward him like a fucking offering. I'm handing my body over to him on a silver goddamn platter, and he's just standing there, burning holes into my skin with the heat in his eyes.

Frustration blooms deep in my chest the longer I sit exposed, so slick between my legs that I've most likely ruined my underwear. If he thinks he can say such dirty things, things that he knows will have me clawing for him, trying to climb him like a tree and then make me wait, he's got another thing coming.

With a new determination, I reach for his belt buckle, resting my fingers there for just a second before dragging them over his thick, hard flesh and gripping him. He pulses in my hand seconds before thrusting against my palm, a lip tugged between his teeth.

The look of pure need on his face is enough to have me

scooting forward on the bed and tearing at his belt, yanking it from his pant loops and tossing it to the side. His zipper is next. I waste no time in pulling it down, exposing familiar black boxer briefs hanging low on his hips.

With a whimper of need, I shove his pants down over his thick thighs and down his legs before he kicks them away. Towering over me in a black dress shirt and boxer briefs, he's the epitome of perfection. A living, breathing definition of the term.

My heart gallops when I lower my eyes to the massive organ that I know waits behind tight, tight black material. Without hesitation, I reach forward, wrapping my fingers around the outline of him and hearing my breath hitch as clearly as I do his. But it's not enough, and it's with that thought that I'm yanking on the waistband of his underwear and watching with wide eyes as his cock slaps his abdomen, the smooth head red, angry, and wet.

"Fuck, Sierra. Take me in your mouth. Please," he grinds out, his chest heaving.

I want to torture him, to make him feel as helpless and needy as I do, but there's something about the plea in his eyes that has me shoving aside those thoughts and wrapping my lips around him, swallowing as much of his length as I can in one go.

A hand cups the back of my neck as I continue to suck him deep before retreating, flicking my tongue at the head and collecting the liquid pooling there. I wrap my hand around the base and stroke him in time with my mouth.

Two hands get lost in my hair, and his grip becomes more firm, more controlling. His hips thrust in time with every dip of my head, and those fingers dig deep into my scalp. He uses his hold to pull me further down his length with every jerk of his hips. I sputter a breath, spit leaking from the sides of my mouth and moisture collecting in my eyes when he brushes the back of my throat and groans out a noise so raw that I let him continue controlling my movements without complaint.

"You feel so fucking good," Braden growls, continuing to fuck my mouth like a man on the edge of losing his mind. "You're the only one that makes me feel like this."

Tears wet my skin, and my throat burns, but I don't stop. I won't. Not until he rips himself from my mouth and hisses, "As much as I would love to paint your throat with my cum, I need to be inside of you."

16

Sierra

PUSHING BACK ON THE MATTRESS, I PROP MYSELF UP ON MY elbows and lift a taunting brow. His words make my insides roll into themselves. I want him to make good on every promise he's made tonight. My legs up by my head, his cock deep inside of me.

It's been a long six weeks spent full to the brim with insatiable sexual frustration. Every lingering kiss on my neck and brush of his fingers across my chest has made me so high-strung that I worry I'll snap and lose my grip on sanity at any given moment.

I saw it in the way Braden held his shoulders when we got home—heavy like they carried the weight of the world—that he was expecting me to say no and push him back out the door. He has no idea how deep my ache for him goes. But that's going to change. Hopefully, it's already started to.

"Take off your shirt," I whisper while reaching behind my back and unclasping my bra. With no straps, it slides off in one motion, joining the rest of our clothes on the floor.

He unbuttons his shirt with steady fingers, each one exposing a bit more of the brown hair sprinkled across the hard lines of his chest. Dark eyes move over me in a long sweep. They settle heavy on my chest as he shrugs the shirt from his shoulders and sets his knees on the bed, towering over me.

"Look at you," he says through clenched teeth, sounding angry but looking far from it. No, that's not anger. It's unadulterated lust, an undeniable need that I see in his eyes. For me. The realization has me shuddering into the mattress. "You are the most gorgeous thing I have ever seen."

My lungs tighten, capturing my breath and holding it hostage before releasing it in a wavering puff. Tears pool in my eyes at the sincerity in his words and the way they pry my ribs apart and squeeze my heart.

"So are you," I admit, the words so true that the weight of them sags on my tongue. He shakes his head while searching my face with eyes so hot they could shoot fire.

I swallow hard when his hands cup my calves, moving up over my knees and thighs before settling on my hips. He's towering above me now, the scent of his cologne strong against the heat of his body. Slowly, so fucking slowly, his fingers curl beneath the waistband of my panties, and I lift my butt in the air to help him slide them off.

Now bare, I reach out for him, one hand moving to hold his jaw, the other his trim waist. Warm breath brushes my nose and cheeks as he settles between my legs. My breasts touch his chest, hard nipples against hard nipples, when he drops to his elbows beside my head and runs a knuckle across the length of my cheekbone.

I should speak. Should tell him all the words crashing and burning inside of my head and the reality that I'm hiding from right now. But the moment feels too delicate to risk saying the wrong thing.

I'm pulled from those thoughts the moment careful fingers part my lower lips, so slick with my arousal that if it were anybody else, I might have been embarrassed. Braden circles the throbbing bundle of nerves once, twice, three times before sliding a long digit inside of me.

Noises escape my mouth that I don't recognize as I clench around the invasion, wiggling my hips, searching for more—begging for it. Sweat breaks out between my breasts as I arch into him, crushing them against him. I cry out when he adds a second finger, pushing them deeper with each in-and-out motion and groaning in my ear.

"Jesus Christ, Sierra."

His face falls to my throat as I croak, "I need you."

Nodding a few too many times to pretend he's not just as desperate as I am, he slips his fingers from inside of me. The absence of his touch only lasts a second before the smooth, round head of his cock rubs along my seam, coating itself in my wetness. "I need you too, baby."

He enters me with a curse, only sheathing himself halfway before retreating and moving again, this time filling me completely. His pace picks up as I adjust to the size of him, and warm, wet lips mold to my throat, moving along the side of it before sucking and grazing my raging pulse with his teeth. I use the hand gripping his waist to pull him closer, encouraging him to pick up the pace.

"Braden," I whimper, lifting my chin, giving his mouth full access to my burning skin. His groans vibrate along my skin, and his fingers press into my hips hard enough I wouldn't be surprised to see bruises there in the morning.

Our bodies move as one, falling in sync as easily as if we were never apart.

"Legs up," he grinds out, pushing back onto his knees. His hands move to my thighs before he's shoving my legs to my shoulders, sliding his palm down to grip my calves, holding them there.

The new position allows him to push in even deeper,

hitting a spot inside of me that has stars twinkling in my eyes and my throat burning with a hoarse cry. My head drops to the pillow as I lose the ability to hold it up any longer.

"Do you feel that, little fighter?" he rasps, his lips swollen and red. I grip both of his hands where they hold my ankles. "Do you feel how full you are? How fucking good it feels when I'm inside of your hot pussy?"

Braden's words strike a match to my insides. It's impossible to put it out the flames. A raging inferno with no plans of dying. I let myself burn, loving the way it feels. My heart roars deep in my chest, failing to keep up with the lust ripping through my veins.

"Oh God. Yes. Yes." The release I've been chasing is right there, growing and filling me up like an expanding balloon. Without a second thought, I'm letting go of his wrist and dragging my hand between my legs, sliding my fingers in my arousal. I find my clit and pinch it between my fingertips, gasping at the pleasure that sparks and explodes from the motion.

Braden's eyes glaze over when they focus on my hand, on the way my fingers circle the throbbing bud before pulling at it, again and again as he fucks me harder.

"Shit. That's right," he grunts. "Get yourself there. Need to feel you come around me."

With a few more thrusts, I'm there. My vision blackens around the edges as my orgasm rips through me, sending me flying off the side of a cliff. I'm lost to the pleasure zipping through my bones when Braden comes to a stop, buried as far inside of me as possible. He spits words so dirty I clench around him in approval as he spills inside of me, filling me with a warmth I've been without for too long.

"Holy fuck," he breathes, falling toward my chest, still buried inside of me.

"Yeah," I murmur in agreement.

I don't have the willpower nor the want to be separated from him yet, so I wrap my arms around his neck and pull him toward me, letting out a content sigh when he ducks his head to my shoulder and kisses the wet skin. His next words are so soft and pure that I don't bother hiding the tear that slides down my cheek.

"I can't help but feel like I wasted so much of my life being without you. You're everything to me, Sierra. I won't waste any more time."

I press my face to his throat and force a gentle sigh past my lips as tears pepper his skin.

Tomorrow. I'll tell him tomorrow.

As I TIE the strings of my cartoon reindeer–spotted pajama pants tight around my waist, I'm hit in the gut with a punch of appreciation for my family's "comfort over beauty" Christmas rule. And by family, I mean the one comprising Clare, Liz, and me.

Ever since I can remember, we've had a silent agreement to only wear our comfiest clothes on Christmas. Reason being, nobody should have to dress up in clothes that tighten up and tease the threat of suffocation once the turkey settles and your stomach swells up like you've been bitten by an elephant-sized wasp.

My sister and her daughter should be here any minute, and while that would usually fill me with excitement, I'm terrified instead. I stare at the dresser drawer that I know hides three positive pregnancy tests and try to push back the anxiety festering inside of me.

The high from last night disappeared the moment I opened my eyes this morning and reality swooped in just to take a giant crap on my face. The already wavering support beam I had been standing on collapsed without a worry about what might happen to me afterward. Update: I ended up tumbling into a dark, miserable pit and have thus shrunken back behind my protective seal, where I've been hiding since. Despite the obvious effort I've made to avoid his kisses and all eye contact today, Braden, the stubborn man that he is, has refused to take the hint, never leaving my side.

I didn't miss the way his eyes narrowed into slits of suspicion when he tried to follow me into the shower and I refused to let him join me, or the scoff that followed when I offered to be the one to stop by the grocery store to pick up the missing ingredients Clare needed for dinner when he knows better than anybody how much I loathe spending time at the store. I had just wanted distance, and he knew it immediately.

Guilt burns beneath my skin while I lift my hair off my neck and release a stressed breath.

Keeping this a secret from Braden is far from easy. It's not like I want to shoulder this alone because I really, really don't. But I'm also not about to risk anything by telling him about the pregnancy before I've even gone to the doctor and confirmed what the tiny plastic sticks told me.

With Clare here, it'll be easier. We'll sneak away after dinner, and I'll tell her. Then tomorrow, she'll come with me to the doctors and hold my hand while I'm told what the rest of my future holds. If it's true, if I *am* pregnant, then I'll tell him. I'll crack myself wide open and see if he'll yank my heart from my chest or glue me back together.

Come on, Sierra. I need to think positively, which is the exact opposite of what I've been doing.

Braden won't run. He won't realize this is way more than he bargained for so soon and take off in the night. Maybe it won't be with open arms and a smile, but he will accept this. Right? I keep repeating the encouraging words in my head until they echo in my ears, leaving me with no choice but to believe them.

I'm not sure what compels me to walk, but I'm fumbling with the dresser drawer before I think too hard about it. I rifle through the old shirts and gym shorts with the tags still connected from when I made "work out more" my last New Year's resolution before I nearly keel over and die.

I keep waiting to hear a splat on the floor from where my stomach fell out of my ass, but there's nothing but silence. Eerie, skin-crawling silence. Until I hear him and the forced clearing of a throat coming from the doorway. Where the door was just shut.

My eyes slide shut, and I grab the edge of the dresser tight enough to turn my knuckles white, but I don't turn around. I can't.

Instead, I wait for him to speak, to yell and scream at me. But he doesn't. I keep waiting and waiting and waiting for what seems like hours before he breaks the silence with words that reach down my throat and rip the air from my lungs. That leave me gaping and boneless.

"I'm the only man you'll ever refer to as a DILF again. Got that, little fighter?"

17

Braden

If someone had asked me six months ago what I pictured my life to look like at this very moment, my answer would have been so disgustingly simple.

Women, booze, busted knuckles, daddy issues, and a God complex so intense I would have been choking on it.

That's what my life consisted of before I met her. Before I fell in love and found a purpose—a want to do better and actually achieve something worth a damn.

Life was predictable, flat, but still lively enough to keep me from smashing my head against a brick wall. I was under the pretence that I was happy with the way things were. Every woman that I took to bed and every fight that I didn't deserve to win but somehow managed to added another layer of fog to my smoky mirror. Another stormy night camouflaged as a warm, cloudless morning.

It wasn't until I found a goddamn angel in my bed, halo and all, that that mirror shattered and the mirage cleared, leaving me reeling at the reality of the depressing mess my life had become.

With her beside me, it was easier to captain my sinking

ship. I fixed my shit one bucket of water at a time until the deck was dry and I was no longer sinking but merely coasting, swaying gently. Some days I still feel the waves crash against the sides, sloshing overboard and trying to pull me back down, but my ship never fills, never sinks. Not like before.

Six months ago, if I had ever asked myself what I would do if I found out that I was going to be a dad, I wouldn't have had an answer. Actually, I probably would have blacked out and wound up unconscious on the floor of whatever bar I had got shit-faced in.

There's not a doubt in my mind that I would have lost any semblance of reasonable thought and ran once I peeled myself off that floor and was slapped with the reality of it again. I wouldn't have gone too far, or been gone for too long, but I would have run nonetheless. Escape for a little while. I'm ashamed to admit that, but there's no use pussyfooting around the obvious.

Now, I'm no longer that guy, at least not completely. I still have my moments. I'm a fucking far cry from perfect. But as I stood in front of Sierra's dresser this morning—not even minutes after she had left for the store—with one of my old hockey shirts in one hand and a positive pregnancy test in the other, the last thing I wanted to do was escape.

My first instinct was to run *after* her, not away. I wanted to chase her ass down a grocery aisle before throwing her over my shoulder and taking her home. My second was to bend her over the bed and spank her ass for keeping this from me. And my third, well, that one shocked—no, terrified—the shit out of me.

I wanted to sink to my knees in front of her and cry. Not a few silent tears but full-on broken sobs. Fuck, I still do.

Regardless of the fact that my head feels like it's on backward and my chest is so tight that I might as well be wrapped beneath the scales of a giant snake, I can't shake the need to just let it out. My emotions are bubbling up, threatening to boil over and burn everything and everyone in sight.

And it isn't until I stand behind her, watching as she roots through a drawer for something that she won't find, something that currently lives in the pocket of my pajama pants, that I let a string of half-ass flirty words slip from my lips and feel the first splat of that emotion on my skin.

Sierra spins around at the sound of my voice, her expression stricken with surprise and her eyes laced with something that I don't want to admit to myself looks too much like fear.

I can sense it in the air—the moment she realizes what's happening. She starts toward me with hurried footsteps before stopping a breath away, no doubt curling her toes into the carpet in her effort to keep her distance. I shake my head frantically, as if to tell her how stupid it is to keep that fucking space between us when the only thing that I want is to feel her pressed against me, to smell that fresh laundry and men's bodywash scent that clings heavier to her skin the longer I'm around her.

She must understand the urgency in the movement, because slowly, too damn slowly, small arms slide around my waist, and a warm body brushes mine. She holds me like she's scared I'll crumble into a million unfixable pieces if she squeezes too tight, and the thought itself has a muscle in my cheek pulsing in a way it definitely shouldn't.

Expelling a frustrated puff of air, I curl my arms around Sierra and pull her tight, not bothering to brush off how perfectly her body fits with mine, like we're two halves of the same fucking stone. I stopped forcing myself to ignore those things weeks ago, and now it's impossible not to see the spotlights on them.

"I was going to tell you," Sierra whispers.

There's a huge part of me that already knew she would

tell me. That she would sit me down and explain what I could so visibly see torturing her. Despite that, there was still that small, barely there part of me buried deep, deep down that had doubted her intentions, doubted that she would open up to me about this and not carry that weight on her own. Yeah, I hate that part. Fucking detest it.

"When did you find out?"

She stiffens in my arms for no longer than a blink of time. "Yesterday."

"With Gracie." It's not a question, but she nods into my chest anyway.

Now, the missing pieces of the puzzle reveal themselves, slipping into their missing slots and creating a much clearer image for me to dissect. I knew it was weird when Tyler told us he was taking Gracie and Sierra out for a few minutes, but it was my brother, the guy who does nothing without a good reason. The first thing I thought was that his wife got one of her insane cravings. Who was I to argue with that? And if Sierra wanted to go . . . I was too excited at the prospect of her getting along so well with my sister-in-law to question it.

Then they got back, and the shift I saw in Sierra was obvious. But I chalked it up to her being in an unfamiliar place. I didn't want to push her, but I should have. And I sure as shit shouldn't have taken her home and had sex with her.

Fuck. I hate that I can taste the bitter anger and resentment on my tongue. Anger at myself for not recognizing the signs for what they were the moment they appeared, and resentment for not being the one by her side when she found out.

"Did you find out alone? Did you have anyone with you?" I ask.

Who am I kidding? She wouldn't have let Gracie watch her do something so intimate and scary. She did it alone, I'm sure of it.

"Gracie was there before and after," she replies.

An image of a terrified, shaking Sierra staring down at three pregnancy tests with no one there to hold her hand flashes through my mind before I'm gasping for air, truly losing it.

Noticing that my fingers have curled into her shirt, I relax them, moving one flat palm to her lower back, the other wrapped all the way around her shoulders.

"Are you mad?" she asks.

I suck in a breath through my teeth before letting it out gently. "No."

"Are you upset?"

"At you? No. At the fact you have my baby growing in your belly? Fuck no."

She tries to move out of my arms, but I pull her closer, keeping her from looking up at me. "The only thing I'm upset about is that I wasn't there with you. I should have been. Or at least with you after. You shouldn't have come back and sat in silence, Sierra. It fucking pains me to know you were sitting there with me at the dinner table with this knowledge burning a hole in your gut. Fuck, you let me stick my hand down up your skirt while you were digesting this."

I'm the one that pulls back this time, too angry at myself to hold her. There's a whimper of protest from her when I spin around and push my palms into my eyes, rubbing furiously against the static in my vision.

"You couldn't even look at me this morning. Is that why? Did I force you to have sex with me last night?" Bile burns its way up my throat.

I should have waited. I should have said good night and gone back to my apartment after getting her home. The possibility of her hating me for this sits like a grenade in my stomach, the pin already pulled. My hands fall from my face before I set them on my hips and toss my head back.

"No. No, of course not. How could you even think that?"

"How could I think that?" I echo with a humourless laugh.

Sierra's hand on my arm makes me flinch. Yeah, fucking flinch. I'm surprised when she doesn't recoil from that but wraps her fingers around my skin and tenderly pulls me around to face her again. I can feel the burn of her stare on my face, on my scowl and rigid jaw, but I keep staring at the wall behind her, too terrified of what I might see if I look at her.

"Baby," she murmurs while pressing her lips to the place between my pecs. A shiver builds at the base of my spine, but I ignore it. "Look at me."

I can't. I'm furious with myself and how selfish I've been.

More pieces to this unfinished puzzle appear as I start to picture a timeline in my head—our timeline. I was too shell-shocked to notice it earlier, but there was a number on one of the tests. 3+ weeks pregnant. That's what it said.

Apart from last night, we haven't had sex since before she left Vancouver. That was over six weeks ago. My blood freezes. A cold rush slithers up my body. She was either already pregnant when she left or was shortly after.

Fuck, fuck, fuck. What if I hadn't come after her?

I'm suddenly dizzy, my vision spotting for a moment.

"Braden." She says my name firmly, with a sharp edge. Her grip on my arm tightens before she's reaching up and cupping my jaw. "You look like you're going to be sick."

I probably do. I feel sick, but not the way she's thinking. I'm sick with the idea of never having found out, of never getting the chance to be a dad, even if the idea of it has my stomach cramping up and sweat breaking out on my neck. I'm being insane, I know that. There's no way Sierra wouldn't have told me. But I'm not thinking that way right now. Everything is too much—I feel too much.

I sink my fingers into my hair to the point of pain before I finally look at her. There's a look of pure devastation on her face that takes the wind out from beneath me.

I'm being selfish. This isn't about me. This is about her, this baby, and us. Our future. I can't block her out. Not right now, and when she's looking like a visible representation of everything going on inside of my head.

My arms fall to my sides. I walk backward until the backs of my knees hit the mattress. Sitting down on the edge, I press my hands to the unmade bed and exhale slowly. Get it together.

"Come here," I order gruffly. When she doesn't hesitate, a flicker of hope fills me so brightly that I might have squinted on reflex. As soon as she steps between my legs, I'm cupping the backs of her thighs and pressing my forehead to her stomach. "I'm sorry. I'm so fucking sorry, baby."

Gentle fingers run through my hair in slow strokes, nails lightly scratching my scalp. "It's okay, Braden. You did nothing wrong. Not now. Not last night." I shake my head, but she lightly pulls on my hair to stop me and speaks again.

"If we're going to play the blame game here, then I should be the one at fault. I'm the one that didn't ask you to take me to get a test. I wanted your hand up my dress last night just as much as I wanted to be with you afterward. There isn't a thing that happened with you I didn't want to happen."

Her chest shakes against my forehead when she sucks in a long breath. She's upset, but I know better than to interrupt her again.

"I couldn't look at you this morning because I knew that if I did, I would blurt out that I'm pregnant, and I didn't want to do that until I knew for sure. There can always be false positives, and yeah, I know the odds of that are low considering I took three tests, but I needed to be one hundred percent sure. I was going to go see someone tomorrow with

Clare. Braden, even if I wasn't really pregnant, I still would have told you. That's a promise."

I'm nodding before her words have even completely sunken in. And once they do, a massive sense of relief hits me dead smack in the centre of my chest.

The weight pressing down on my shoulders, trying to push me to the ground, eases exponentially as I slide my hands up, up, up, settling them on her lower back. I clutch her tight, tipping my head so that my chin rests on her stomach and our eyes meet.

"I want to go to the appointment with you," I say. The roughness of my voice has me fighting back a wince. "Let me be there. Please."

The way her silver eyes soften at my plea makes my mouth tip up in a small smile. There really isn't anything more that I want right now than to stand beside her through this. I still haven't completely wrapped my head around the idea of us—of me, rather—bringing a baby into the world, but I can't deny the intense zing of excitement in my stomach when I think about it either.

"Yes," she says, a slight flush to her cheeks. "Of course you can come."

My small smile grows into a dimpled grin as I nod once and press my lips to her stomach repeatedly.

I can't believe it. Me: a fucking dad.

18

Sierra

Clare's round eyes have never been so narrowed.

My sister watches the man beside me like a shotgun-wielding father standing at the top of a set of porch steps. Braden's grip on my hand tightens the slightest bit, and I swear I just heard him gulp.

"Clare, this is Braden. Braden, Clare," I speak up, moving the hand Braden isn't using as a comfort device between them. "Liz is the little Devil that just took off behind us."

Soft sounds of excitement come from my spare room as my niece makes herself right at home. The thought has warmth expanding in my chest. I've missed her so much.

"It's nice to finally meet you." Braden speaks with confidence, but I hear the brief tickle of nerves he can't hide from me. He sticks his hand out in the distance between us and Clare and waits, letting it hang there as she stares at it for a few seconds. The hand wrapped around mine begins to sweat.

"I would say the same, but I'm not sure if it would be a lie quite yet," Clare replies in a no-bullshit tone. Braden winces beside me before she finally takes his hand and gives it a firm shake. She drops it quickly. "Do your hands always sweat so much?"

"Jesus, Clare!" I sputter a laugh before shutting myself up with a fist pressed to my mouth. I know what she's doing right now, acting so brash and nonchalant. It's what she's done since the very first time I ever brought a guy home. She came dressed in her big-sister supersuit, ready to put Braden to the test.

When Clare finally turns to look at me, her features relax, Braden forgotten for the time being. With a wide grin, she rushes over and gathers me in her arms. "Oh my God. I missed you so much. It's only been six weeks, but I feel like you've been gone for six years."

My cheek smushes against hers, and her familiar smell mixed with the feel of her arms wound around my shoulders has my stomach clenching with nostalgia. "I missed you too, Clarebear."

All too quickly, we break apart, and I force myself to remember that she's going to be here for the next two days so that I don't break down and start sobbing like a child who's had their lollipop stolen. Clare isn't leaving anytime soon. Now is *not* the time.

As if she can read my thoughts, my sister places her hands on her hips and throws a look over her shoulder to the bags sitting by the door. "Help me bring this stuff in? There's more in the car, but I'm sure Braden wouldn't mind making a trip down. Would you, big guy?"

Braden tosses me a look that says "did she really just call me big guy?" before pressing a quick kiss to my forehead and eyeing my sister. "Of course not. What vehicle is yours?"

"Silver Focus parked three stalls from the sidewalk. Here, catch." A key ring cuts through the air before Braden grabs it in a tight fist. Clare's eyes widen for a moment. "Quick reflexes."

He drips his chin. "Thank you." His eyes cut to me when he says, "Be right back."

Braden is barely through the front door when I shut it behind him and pin my sister with a glare. "You're being mean."

She lifts a shoulder before picking up a black duffel bag in one hand and a pastel blue and yellow backpack in the other and hauling them into my spare room. Hot on her heels, I stand in the doorway with my arms crossed, spying Liz stretched out on the bed with a *Geronimo Stilton* book open in her hands.

"I'm always mean to your boyfriends," Clare replies coolly. She drops the bags on top of the dresser and finally turns to face me. There's something in the way she's eyeing me that makes me feel all twitchy and nervous. I don't like it.

"Stop staring at me like that. And you know what I'm trying to say, Clare. You're being extra mean."

She exhales loudly. "You're right. Why don't we go to the kitchen and pop open one of the bottles of sauvignon blanc I bought on the way from the airport. It's still your favourite, right?"

Something churns in my stomach. Maybe guilt? "I'm not thirsty."

"Are you sure? You probably haven't had it in forever. You've earned it."

Yeah, it's definitely guilt. Or nausea. Possibly both? I run a hand over the length of my ponytail and twist it around my fingers.

"Maybe later," I croak. Good God, could I be more obvious? Just come out and say it, Sierra. *I'm pregnant, Clare. You're going to be an auntie.* Yeah, blunt is good. Blunt is easier. Quick and painless, like ripping off a Band-Aid.

If she's going to be disappointed, there's nothing that I can do about it. She'll just have to get over it and learn to accept that her little sister is having a baby. Of course it will suck not to have her there supporting me through the next several months, but I won't allow her to make us feel bad or like we've done anything wrong.

What am I even talking about? Clare isn't like that. If she's not happy, it won't take her long to get over it. That's how she works. I'm being ridiculous.

If Braden could hear my thoughts right now, he would look at me with that damn stubborn scowl and tell me to knock it the hell off.

My toes are tapping the floor when Clare throws her arms in the air, letting them come down on her thighs with a *smack*. "Oh, good grief! You're pregnant, right? I'm so beyond offended that you thought I wouldn't be able to tell. I can read you just as easily over the phone as I can in person."

What? The world stills for a few seconds.

"You knew?" I wheeze.

Clare's bright blue eyes roll as she reaches for my hands. "Come on. You've been asleep by eight every single night, you've completely forgotten what you were saying in the middle of nearly all of our recent conversations, and you're fucking glowing. Your wine refusal was the last thing I needed to check off before I was completely sure."

"Don't forget the morning sickness that's never actually *in* the morning either," I grumble.

I hear a sharp inhale of breath before soft hands tighten around mine to the point of pain. Smiling sheepishly at her, I let my sister's awed expression drown out all of my previous fears and feelings of doubt.

"You're having a baby?" a soft voice asks, drawing our attention to the little girl watching us gingerly. Her soft eyes peek over the edge of her open book as she continues to hold it in front of her face, using it like a shield.

Something slips between my ribs and pokes my heart. "I

still have to go to the doctor to make sure, but we think so, Lizzy."

Cutting a worried glance at Clare, I lift a brow when I find her already watching me with a similar expression. I don't have time to worry about whether the news has upset my niece before she's very carefully placing her book beside her and hopping off the bed, rushing in my direction. She throws her arms around my waist and lights up with a toothy smile.

"Babies are so cute," she exclaims. A thoughtful look flashes across her face before she crinkles her nose. "But stinky."

I laugh lightly and ruffle her light blonde hair, careful to avoid the red beret pinning her bangs to the side.

"It looks like I missed something important."

Liz jumps away from me at the sound of Braden's deep voice. I have to hide my smile in the neck of my shirt when I catch a glimpse of her pink cheeks before she's flopping on the bed face-first.

Braden sidles up to me, a hand curving around my hip. Jutting my chin in the direction of the door, he takes the hint and leads us out of the room, Clare following closely behind us.

As soon as we round the hallway and enter the open area of the living room and kitchen, I notice the pile of gifts and wine bottles set by the front door. Clare follows my gaze, clapping her hands in excitement.

"I thought we agreed that you guys coming here for Christmas *was* my present, Clare," I scold.

I'm torn between wanting to smack her upside the head for spending too much money and feeling excited. Unlike myself, Clare has always been almost *too* good at giving gifts. Even if she doesn't know you all that well, she always seems to pick out something that you'll love. We've always called it her superpower. Meanwhile, I can't choose a good gift to save my life.

I almost smack her when she swipes a hand through the air, shrugging me off. "Me, not bring gifts? It's your fault for believing that I wouldn't bring my own sister a Christmas present." Turning to Braden, she adds, "Thank you for bringing this all up. I'm just going to pop the wine in the fridge before starting dinner."

Braden acknowledges her thanks with a shaky smile—clearly still feeling nervous talking to her due to her cold behaviour—and runs his hand up and down my spine. With a long exhale, I slip my arm around his waist and cuddle into his side, using his presence as my own personal security blanket.

"Let her spoil you if she wants to, baby. You deserve it."

I try not to let his words affect me as much as they want to, knowing that I'll most likely burst into a fit of tears. "I love you."

His words make the hairs on the top of my head flutter. "I love you too. Now, let's go help your sister with this fucking turkey."

My laugh sneaks out before I have a chance to register it. With a lingering kiss to Braden's jaw, I'm detaching myself from his arms, instantly hating the way I feel without him as I join my sister in the kitchen.

As the day comes to an end, I realize that I should probably tell Braden that my sister is really no more intimidating than a small yippy dog biting at your heels. But watching the most calm, cool, and collected guy that I've ever met squirm beneath the glare of someone so much smaller than him has me feeling a bit smug, like an evil villain in a Disney cartoon. Besides, it can't be long now until Clare gives it up and hugs the shit out of the big man. I'm surprised she's even held out this long.

He's passed her test with flying colours—never getting upset or letting her stare keep him from touching me whenever possible, even if it was just brief squeezes of my hand or a fleeting kiss on the cheek. He hasn't frowned or grumbled annoyed words under his breath. He has, in all honesty, been a *perfect* boyfriend. I'm not sure that I can take any more of it before I end up falling all over myself trying to shoo him into bed.

"I want to tell her that if she doesn't stop scowling, her face will stay like that forever, but I don't want her to strangle me in my sleep," Braden mumbles, quiet enough for only me to hear.

He's watching warily as Clare looks up from her half-coloured picture of a Christmas elf and squints her eyes at him, lifting a brow in a "do you have something to say?" kind of way. I bite back my laugh when Liz pinches her mother right below her elbow and grumbles something while stabbing a finger against her own colourful picture.

"It would be more likely that she would strangle you while you're awake. Clare doesn't leave her bed once she's under the covers unless absolutely necessary," I tease.

Braden's body shakes with a laugh. His eyes warm my face like the sun on a clear day. "Who would have thought that a couple colouring books would have slid me into your niece's good graces. I was expecting to be shooting myself in the foot for not buying her a doll or something."

"You chose well, although you really didn't have to get her anything. She gets spoiled enough as it is. Too many more gifts and she'll start thinking that she's the queen of England."

She truly is spoiled, no question about it. Being my parents' only grandchild and my only niece, she gets more than enough presents on any day that ends in *Y*, let alone special occasions. My parents send gift cards in the mail often —seeing as that's all they can give without having to learn a damn thing about her—and I always tried to bring her something every time that I popped by.

Obviously, I don't have the luxury of stopping by on random days after work anymore—a hard truth that unfortunately doesn't become any less painful as time passes—so I've had to improvise. It's safe to say that she'll be taking home a lot more than she came with.

Regardless of how absolutely spoiled the little munchkin is, I can't deny the way my heart grew double its size and attempted to climb up my throat when Braden pulled a Minnie Mouse Christmas bag out from God knows where and handed it over to her with a timid smile.

Liz didn't hesitate before tearing through the tissue paper and letting out a squeal when she pulled out two holiday-themed colouring books and a set of art supplies. I could see a slight dent in the armour Clare threw up earlier and felt the win for both Braden and myself.

"Does that mean that I shouldn't have gotten *you* anything? Because the way you looked at me with those wild, excited eyes after you opened your present made my cock really hard." His voice drops an octave, and his breath brushes the sensitive skin of my ear. An invisible hand cups the area between my legs before I push them together, fighting off the shiver swirling at the base of my spine.

I want to feel surprised by his ability to turn me into a dripping puddle of lust with just a few flirtatious words, but I can't. I've spent months experiencing how easy it is for Braden to make my underwear feel heavy and create an achy tension low in my belly that only he can soothe. I know that his promises aren't empty, and unless absolutely necessary, he wouldn't leave me high-strung and desperate for relief.

At this point, my body has become his to do with as he pleases, and more often than not, I can't find it in me to care.

Suddenly, a wave of exhaustion hits me, and I snuggle into the warmth radiating from his body. A yawn interrupts my train of thought.

He chuckles under his breath. "Do you want me to stay the night? If not, I should get going before you pass out on me."

"If you left, I would chase you down." The power behind my words has me blinking in surprise before I shake it away.

Braden snakes an arm around my shoulders and pulls me into his side. His cheek presses to my temple. "You say that as if I would make you chase me. I would have turned right back around as soon as I heard you coming after me, sunshine."

"That's good. We both know that I couldn't keep up with you anyway." I lift an arm and flex my nonexistent muscles to prove my next point. "I'm embarrassingly out of shape."

Braden squeezes my bicep and lifts the corner of his mouth. "You know that all you have to do is ask and you can join me at the gym. I promise to take it easy on you the first few times."

It's meant to be a joke, but the thought has me feeling both incredibly turned on and intrigued. There's no way that I could keep up with him, but seeing Braden all sweaty and out of breath . . .

"When do we start?" I ask in a rush, nearly panting like a dog in heat.

"Really?" he asks, looking completely shocked.

I roll my eyes. "You make it seem as if I'm a complete bum. I walk to work every day, jackass."

"You're right." He smooths his palm down up and down my arm. "Just tell me when, baby."

Another yawn rips through my mouth as I scoot closer into his hold, nuzzling my head under his chin. My eyelids begin to droop, feeling like I've glued sandbags to them. Sleep sounds like the most beautiful thing, and I stop trying to fight it. Braden's body wrapped around mine becomes the last thing I think about before I let it take me under.

19

Braden

Is it creepy to watch your girlfriend while she sleeps? Probably. Do I care? Not at all.

After carrying Sierra to bed and making sure the duvet is tucked under her like a cocoon, I take two steps to the door before stalling. I shift on my feet and peer down at her sleeping form, feeling a surge of contentment. There's something about knowing that she'll be waiting for me when I crawl into bed, ready to wrap herself around me, that strips me bare, leaving me way too vulnerable.

If it weren't for the intimidating woman waiting for me in the other room, I would shed my clothes and join my girl in bed right now. There's no place that I would rather be than wrapped around Sierra, but the conversation that awaits me might just be the most important one I've ever had.

With that thought, I'm closing the bedroom door softly and stepping into the lamplit living room.

It's almost like being on the receiving end of a swift kick to the stomach when I spot the simple black picture frame housing the photo of Tyler, Oakley, Adam, and me playing college hockey that Sierra gifted me before dinner. It stands by itself on one of the two side tables, looking as if it belongs there—here, in Sierra's place.

That's a dangerous, dangerous thought. One that I don't have the energy to focus on right now.

Luckily, Clare doesn't seem to be a fan of beating around the bush. Her eyes sweep the room before focusing on me. "Are you going to come sit down? I might seem like it, but I don't bite."

There's a brief moment where my breath quickens before evening out again. This is Sierra's big sister. From what I've gathered, sitting down alone with Clare is the equivalent of having a heart-to-heart with a terrifying father. It's better to just get it over with so that everyone can move on from the awkward tension and the occasional fleeting glare. Not that I have even a fucking sliver of experience in that department. The younger version of myself had never cared enough about any of the girls I dated to even consider meeting their fathers.

Wow, talk about what a great conversation starter that would be.

Fighting back a wince, I dip my chin and take a seat on the opposite end of the couch. To keep my legs from bouncing nervously, I pull one over my knee and hold on to my ankle to keep my hands busy.

Clare is looking far too relaxed with her back to the armrest, body turned to face me head-on, and a completely blank stare. I shiver slightly when I start to imagine all of the personal questions and accusations she must have locked and loaded in that head of hers.

She taps her blunt nails on the tops of her thighs and hums in a way that has my hackles shooting straight up. I'm not sure if she's waiting for me to be the one to break the ice, but I can't even seem to muster up a curse to mumble to myself, let alone a decent conversation starter.

There have only been a handful of times where I've felt as

uncomfortable as I do right now. Once when I told my parents I was dropping out of school, and the other when I told my old hockey coach that hockey wasn't the sport I was planning on pursuing long term.

Clare decides to cut through the tension before I have a chance to rip chunks of hair from my scalp. "I'm assuming you know how close I am with my sister," she starts calmly. I nod. "So you understand why I'm being such a hard-ass?"

"I do."

How could I not? It would feel almost criminal for Clare not to be so protective of Sierra. I'm grateful for that. It's reassuring to know she has someone else watching her back and looking out for her best interests when I can't be.

"When Sierra told me that she was offered a job opportunity in Toronto, I didn't hesitate to tell her to go for it. As you know, my sister is driven by the idea of success and reaching the goals that she's set for herself. It would have been incredibly selfish of me to tell her that in reality, I was terrified of her being so far away and all alone.

"She probably didn't tell you, but I pushed hard for you before she left. I could see the change in her since meeting you, and I wanted her to keep that glow forever. So I kept trying to get her to just *ask* you to go with her, and if you said no, then, well, that's that. At least she'll leave knowing that there wasn't anything else she could have said or done. But of course she refused to. She was adamant that you weren't the type to follow after a woman. That you weren't interested in a happily ever after."

The contents of my stomach curdle at what I know is coming next. While Clare's admission surprises me, it does nothing to stop the lingering guilt from rising to the surface again like a zit that won't clear up.

Clare exhales slowly while running the pad of her thumb between her eyebrows.

"Sierra kept the details of what happened between you two a secret until a few days after she got settled here. It didn't take a genius to know that you fucked up in a big way, but getting her to open up about it was just about as difficult as convincing my daughter that Santa won't come if she stays up all night sitting on the couch waiting. I'm just ashamed of myself for not being able to decipher the root of her hurt before I let her get on that plane. I assumed that she was upset because she had to leave you behind, but I didn't think that something had happened the night before. I didn't think that you would have been so cruel to her. That's my fault, though, I suppose. For not automatically assuming the worst of you when I clearly should have."

Ouch. There's no hiding the way I flinch.

Clare almost looks apologetic when she catches me doing it, but it's a fleeting expression. "I really don't mean to be so rude, Braden. I just want you to understand where I'm coming from."

"No, I get it. I fucked up. You're just looking out for your little sister," I assure her, even though there's a ball in my throat that makes it difficult to speak. "If somebody had hurt my brother the way I hurt Sierra, I would be doing the exact same thing."

I know better than to expect my admission to earn me any respect in her eyes, but hopefully it helps shine some light on a decent side of me that she hasn't seen. We share a similar sense of loyalty when it comes to family. It's probably one of the only things that we have in common besides our love for the beautiful woman sleeping in the other room.

"I need to ask you something, and I'm hoping you won't bullshit me," she states.

Straightening my spine, I nod once. When she flexes her fingers and smooths her hands down her thighs, my gaze is drawn to the tattoo on her left hand—her otherwise bare ring finger, to be exact. I didn't notice the black ink before now, but after spotting it, I can't seem to look away. A set of initials —the letters *MF*—are written in a thin script on the top of her finger, right where a wedding ring would sit.

Her fingers curl under the intensity of my stare, forcing me to look away, knowing that I've been caught gawking like a weirdo.

"When we got married, Max, my husband at the time, and I were too broke to afford wedding rings," she says, surprising me. A light yet almost pained laugh falls between us. "Max and I were together from the moment we realized cooties weren't real until shortly after Elizabeth was born. I would love to say that our marriage was just as perfect as our dating life had been, but I'm not going to lie to you. Clearly, I'm divorced, so it didn't work as well as we thought it would. However, marrying Max remains one of the best decisions that I have ever made. I wouldn't trade all of the good memories for anything. Not to mention I got Lizzy, and she's the biggest blessing I've ever received."

Her eyes shine, the ghost of a frown on her tight features before she steels her expression. "Too much information, I know. This was a great lead-in to what I wanted to ask you, though, so I'll go ahead and come out with it. Are you planning on marrying my sister, Braden?"

If I tried to get off the couch right now, I couldn't. My brain is nothing but a jumble of unplugged cords and blown circuit breakers. That familiar pinch in my stomach that always seems to appear when the topic of marriage comes up returns with a fucking vengeance. Fighting back a hiss, I genuinely consider bending over just to soothe the pain as the blood drains from my face.

"She wasn't kidding," Clare mumbles, not bothering to hide her disappointment. "You look like you're going to spew chunks."

Her statement pisses me off. Not because it's not true, but because it's *too* true.

"I don't believe in marriage," I grind out.

She arches a near condescending brow and leans forward. "No? So what do you believe in, then?"

"I don't need a piece of paper to tell me that I love your sister and will do everything in my power to take care of her and our baby. Sierra means so much more to me than a damn label meant to convince others that we're in love and happy. If there's anything that I believe in, it's exactly that."

"And I'm supposed to just take your word for it?" she counters, not giving an inch.

I suck in a long breath before pushing it back out and letting my crossed leg drop to the floor. Leaning forward, I rest my forearms on my knees and turn to look at my girlfriend's sister—or my fucking executioner, more like it—with my eyes narrowed.

"If I'm being honest, I don't care what you do with it. All I do know is that I plan on loving Sierra for the rest of my life. Whether she's wearing a ring around her finger or not, it doesn't make a difference to me. She's mine, and I don't plan on ever letting her get away from me again. That's a fucking promise that I would die to keep."

The rapid rise and fall of my chest should be alarming, but I'm too tense to care. Too pissed off at myself for not being able to give Sierra's only real family the answers that she wants.

There's nothing else that I can say to convince Clare of my feelings or intentions. The ball is in her court now. Either she can let the past go and stand with us as we move forward, or she can hold on to it and let it fester. I'll continue to respect her either way, but I would be an idiot to not hope for option A.

"What if all of that stops being enough, Braden? What if it's either marry her or lose her all over again?"

I look away, sweeping my blank stare across the room. A muscle in my jaw feathers.

"I won't spend another day without her again, Clare. So if those were my only two options, I would marry her in a fucking heartbeat."

20

Braden

TIME FEELS LIKE IT'S SPED UP SINCE CLARE AND ELIZABETH FLEW back to Vancouver four days ago. Between Sierra's first doctor's appointment that confirmed via pee in a cup that she's really pregnant, the sudden influx of potential client calls I've received for the gym while trying to keep a handle on the renovations and deliveries, and my weak attempts at preparing myself mentally for our first glimpse of our unborn baby, each day has felt more chaotic than the last. I feel like I've been running in place, each day stuck in an endless, chaotic loop.

I try to shake those thoughts away and focus on right now. It's the day of our first ultrasound appointment, and like any commitment-terrified man turned first-time dad, I'm trying not to lose my shit. Not in a generic sense where I've found myself pacing back and forth in this incredibly small ultrasound room with my head in my hands, but in a more internal, hidden way where I can't think of anything but the faint ticking noise coming from the bomb implanted in my stomach as it counts down, preparing for detonation.

We've already been told not to get too excited about the

idea of seeing much today, that this is just meant to give us an estimated due date and to see how far along Sierra is. The lady on the phone who confirmed our appointment made it clear that we won't be able to see anything yet but a small blob, but I don't care. Blob or not, I'm going to see our baby.

"You need to calm down."

Sierra laughs at me from where she sits on the ultrasound table, dangling her legs off the side. She shifts her butt slightly, which in turn has that ridiculous paper under her crinkling loudly.

I watch her from my place directly beside the table, one hand cupping her knee and the other on her lower back. The ultrasound tech disappeared after leading us to our room and has been gone for so long I've considered the possibility that he decided to take a lunch break across town mid-appointment.

"I am calm." I straighten my back. "I told you that we should have requested someone else."

"Right," she muses with an exaggerated nod. "A female tech, of course."

I don't bother hiding my feelings on the matter. "Exactly."

"I wouldn't worry about that guy. He's most definitely married."

"Married, Sierra. Not blind," I tell her like it's the most obvious thing in the world.

In my defense, the guy we got stuck with isn't nearly ugly enough for me to feel comfortable with his eyes on that section of her bare skin. Her arms? Fine. Her legs? We're getting a bit iffy, but depending *how much* leg, maybe. But her stomach? No. I can feel the vein bulging in my forehead already.

"Either way, he's no competition. Although it will be nice to watch you struggle the way I do when I watch you in the ring, all bare-chested and sweaty. I'm positive that wearing a shirt every once in a while wouldn't keep you from winning matches," she grumbles, lifting her chin defiantly.

I'm grinning like an idiot, but I don't care. "I didn't take you for the jealous type, Sierra." Leaning down, I blow on her ear. "It makes my cock hard."

Her body turns slightly toward me. "You're playing dirty."

"As opposed to what?"

I tower over her, soaking up the easy way she fits to the curve of my body, but it's still not enough. It never is. Maybe it never will be. My addiction to her is everlasting, always growing, evolving. If this is the hill I die on, I'll do it with a fucking smile.

Sierra jolts when three knocks echo through the room, and the door opens, revealing a very unappealing interruption.

"Sorry about that," the not-so-ugly technician says, moving into the room and shutting the door behind him. He plops down on the stool placed in front of a small, four-wheeled desk fit with a massive computer screen, a weird keyboard, and a bottle of hand sanitizer before beginning to type in a bunch of stuff I don't understand. The only thing I pay attention to is Sierra's full name written at the top of the screen beside today's date—December thirtieth.

Sierra's hand covers mine, and I look down to see her already watching me nervously. Despite my own nerves, I throw on a confident smile and give her hand a firm squeeze.

The technician—Marvin, the badge clipped to his scrub top says—moves the desk away from the wall to midway down the bed and spins his stool around to face Sierra. "If you wouldn't mind lying back and lifting your shirt up over your stomach for me, I'll ask you some questions, and then we can get started."

I reluctantly let go of her and take a step back as she follows his instructions. Afterward, she rests her clasped hands on her upper stomach and answers a set of generic questions.

"What is your full name?" Marvin asks.

"Sierra Genevieve Caster."

I snort, and when she turns to glare at me, I mouth, *Gwenevieve?* She pinches my arm, and I swallow back my laugh.

"Your date of birth?"

"June eighth, 1995."

The tech hums quietly before squinting at the screen.

"It says here that we don't have a date for your last period, but you have a general idea of a conception date, correct?"

"Yeah. Early or mid-November. It's hard to guess the exact day, though," I answer for her, puffing my chest like a fucking possessive idiot. Sierra shakes her head at me, but I don't miss the smile she's trying to hide.

Marvin just looks unimpressed. "Either way, we'll have a better idea after today. I'll try an abdominal ultrasound first since we're guessing you're already about eight weeks along." He slides on a pair of gloves and grabs the bottle of blue goo that's been sitting at his station. "I'm going to squirt some gel on your stomach now. It will be a bit cold."

Sierra flinches and grabs my hand again. The gel seems to warm quickly once the tech starts moving it around with a round-ended wand-type thing.

"You can come around and watch the screen if you want," he tells me while continuing to smooth gel all over her stomach.

I look to Sierra for confirmation, not wanting to upset her by seeing something that she can't, but she's already looking at me with a reassuring smile. With a final squeeze of her hand, I'm moving around Marvin and staring at a seemingly empty screen.

Even though I have no fucking idea what I'm looking at, I can't seem to look away from the screen. Sierra watches me, most likely trying to read my expression to see if I've seen anything interesting.

Marvin wears a blank expression as he continues to do his job in complete silence. I know without even looking at her that his silence on top of not being able to see what everyone else can is only increasing Sierra's frustration.

"It doesn't look like anything yet, fighter," I say, grabbing her ankle. "It's just a sea of bl—"

Lub-dub. Lub-dub. Lub-dub.

A lump builds in my throat when a steady heartbeat floods the room. Sierra's muscles bunch up so tight beneath my fingertips that I get the urge to crawl up on the bed and hold her.

Suddenly, Marvin turns the computer screen to the side, showing Sierra the little blob that's appeared. He points to the grey shape and presses the wand a bit harder to Sierra's stomach to make the image a bit easier to see.

"Is that our baby?" she asks, voice quivering. The emotion in her big grey eyes has mine glossing over.

"That's baby," Martin confirms. "You're about eight weeks along."

Pride swells inside of me. I'm immediately flushing with frustration, needing to kiss my woman and wipe away the tear cascading down her cheek.

"Eight weeks," I echo, my voice no louder than a whisper. Straightening my shoulders, I move my large, rigid body around Marvin and his fucking desk, coming to a stop directly beside Sierra.

I bend down, and she doesn't hesitate to tip her head back and capture my lips in a soft kiss, not caring that there's somebody else in the room. When she pulls away, I link our fingers and bring them to my mouth, kissing her knuckles.

Without thinking, I let my mouth linger above the skin of her ring finger for a few seconds too long.

I'm pretty sure the technician is talking again, but his voice is nothing but static flowing in one ear and out the other. Suddenly, I've found myself imagining the impossible, even just for a minuscule fragment of time.

What if instead of bare skin, my lips had met a cold silver band and a diamond? Would that really have been so bad?

An arctic breeze slams into me, and I fall back into reality.

"Remember that the date won't necessarily be when the baby arrives, but it gives you a good idea. I'll send the results to your doctor, and they'll reach out to talk about what's next." *Wait, what date?*

Marvin pulls the gloves from his fingers with a *smack* and moves his desk back before grabbing a white towel, passing it to Sierra. "For the gel," he adds when her curious gaze doesn't stray from me, and I take it from him instead. "I'm going to email you the pictures that I took today as soon as I can. You should get them this afternoon."

I nod numbly. I'm in a daze as I wipe the excess gel from Sierra's stomach and pull her shirt back down. Her eyes are narrowed and hot on my skin, watching me drop the towel in the bin full of other towels and shove my hands in the pockets of my jeans.

"Congratulations, guys. Happy New Year." Marvin leaves, and the door stays open behind him—a signal for us to leave when we're ready.

"Ready?" I ask her. She's clearly upset with how cold I've become but won't say anything here.

"Yep," she replies briskly. "Let's go."

21

Sierra

"What's wrong with you?" I snap once we get in Brooks' car and Braden turns the heat on full blast. He hasn't spoken since we left the clinic, and after a very long, awkward walk to the parking garage, I can easily say that I am *so* done with the silence.

His grip is so tight on the steering wheel his knuckles have turned a ghastly shade of white. I want to reach over and pull apart his scrunched brows before they morph into a single one.

"Nothing," he replies tersely, flicking his eyes to me quickly before looking back at the road. "Is your seat belt on?"

Feeling by my left hip, I realize that I forgot to put it on.

"Put it on."

With a huff, I'm reaching behind me and pulling it over my chest. I clip it in place and mumble, "Yes, sir."

"You can't forget to wear a seat belt, Sierra."

"I didn't do it on purpose."

"Is that supposed to change the odds of something hitting us and you being thrown through the windshield?"

I bristle at his tone. "No. I'll remember next time."

He looks at me again, and I notice that his eyes have softened a bit. "I just want you to be safe. This baby is sucking your brain through a damn bendy straw right now."

"Maybe she'll be extra smart, then."

"She?"

I shrug. "Call it a mom's instinct."

Braden turns to me when we stop at a red light, grabbing my knee. His eyes move around my face before he sighs. "I just got a bit overwhelmed back there. I'm sorry."

I feel the tension in my shoulders disappear at his apology. "It's okay to get overwhelmed. But don't take it out on me. I'm just as scared as you are."

"You don't look like it."

"Trust me, I'm freaking out enough on the inside. I don't need to look like it on the outside."

Braden keeps his hand on my knee, but his stare falls back on the road when the light turns green, and we move through traffic again.

"How *are* you feeling right now, y'know, after actually seeing . . . it."

Something about the way he stumbles over the word "it" has me chewing on my lip to hide my grin.

"Honestly, I feel terrified. I don't think that it had fully set in yet until I heard that heartbeat. Now I just . . ." I hesitate for a few seconds when a feeling of intense, brutal love crawls up my throat. "The reality of it hit me really hard. All of a sudden, I realized that I was really going to be a mom."

I can still feel the way my heart swelled and my stomach tightened up in that exam room once that strong, quick heartbeat filled the silence. There will never be a sound as beautiful as that. Not ever.

And I'm so grateful to have had Braden there with me during that experience. He gave me the reassurance and courage that I needed to keep from turning into a sobbing mess. He handled everything so well, and I don't think that I've ever been prouder of him. But maybe that's why it made me so upset once he flipped that switch and turned cold and detached.

"I thought that maybe you were upset," I confess before he has a chance to say anything. "Today was perfect—at least to me. So when you got so upset, it really, really sucked. All I could think of was, what if this was too much? What if you realized that you couldn't really do this?"

My hand flies to my mouth when the car lurches and swerves to the right. "What are you doing?" I screech, swinging my head to look at Braden.

He flies into an empty parking lot and puts the car in park. "What did you just say?"

Anger is potent in the car, becoming more and more charged until I actually start to worry that it'll shatter the windows. It fills my mouth and burns my throat.

Braden swipes quick hands through his hair, making the ends stick straight up. "It fucking guts me that I've made you think so low of me, baby."

"I'm sorry."

"Don't." The word is strong, leaving no room for argument. "I'm the one who should be apologizing. Fuck, Sierra. I've *never*, not once in my life, felt like I did when we got to see and hear our baby back there." He lays a careful hand on my stomach and watches me with glossed-over eyes. "We *created* that. We *did* that."

Covering his hand with mine, I murmur, "We did that."

"Come here," he commands, sliding our hands to rest on my hip and pulling me toward him. When I'm close enough that our faces are inches apart, he presses our foreheads together. "I'm not sure that I'll ever fully be ready for this, but who is? Being a dad terrifies me, but that doesn't mean that

I'm going anywhere. I will not abandon you. We're in this together. Okay?"

"Okay," I whisper past the lump in my throat and blink away the threat of tears. "I love you."

His eyes close softly. "I love you."

"For the record, I think that you'll be an amazing father."

"Yeah? I'll have to be to keep up with their mother. God knows that you'll put every other parent on this fucking planet to shame."

And just like that, my worries evaporate for the time being.

A FEW MINUTES LATER, Braden leads me through a small family-style restaurant with a steady hand on my lower back.

"Your stomach hasn't stopped growling for the past fifteen minutes." He chuckles under his breath and stops us beside a booth, signaling for me to slide in.

I feel a bit bad that I didn't catch the name of the restaurant on the sign outside, but there was only one thing on my mind when he pulled up: food. After sitting down, I see the menus are already resting on the table alongside a metal basket full of condiments and napkins.

"Have you ever been here? To—" My eyes find the name of the restaurant on a menu. "—Supreme Eats? What an awful name."

Braden's laugh is completely unfiltered as his head falls back. "Fuck no. It was the first place that I saw after your stomach started gurgling. Figured it was better than nothing."

"Your romantic gestures never fail to make me swoon," I tease.

He shoots me a wink as an older woman with tight silver curls and thick-framed glasses strolls up to our table, notepad and pen in hand. Her smile is warm and inviting, making me grin in return.

"Good afternoon, sweethearts," she says, the hint of an accent I don't completely recognize peeking through. "My name is Val, and I'll be taking care of you today. I hope you don't mind my candour, but I must tell you how stunning of a couple you make. You make me miss my *marito*."

My brows scrunch together at the unfamiliar term, but before I can ask what it means, Braden cuts in, leaving me a gaping mess. "*Grazie*, Val. My Sierra is gorgeous enough for the both of us. But *sei così bello*. I'm sure your husband wishes that he could be here with you."

Hold on . . . Braden speaks another language? Freaking Italian at that. The fancy words sound way too sensual on his tongue, and I know that I'm in trouble.

I'm openly staring at him with parted lips and an undeniable warmth pooling in my belly when Val says, "Oh my! You speak Italian?"

He shrugs. "A bit. My stepfather's family is from Sicily."

Val nods enthusiastically. "I have only been to Sicily a few times in my life. Have you been?"

"Unfortunately not. Maybe one day."

Val turns to me for the first time since her introduction, and I nearly wave a flag of victory. "Have you, *cara*?"

"No, but it is on my bucket list. I would love to go to Syracuse and visit the theatres. My sister went on a school trip in high school and has so many stories."

Something nudges my foot beneath the table, and I glance over at Braden to see him already watching me with a heated stare.

"You will love it," Val insists. "Anyway, I should be taking your drink orders before the boss man comes and gives us trouble."

"Water for me, please, Val," Braden says, reaching across the table and patting her wrinkled hand.

I smile. "I'll have an iced tea."

With a nod, Val slips her untouched notepad into her apron and walks back to the kitchen. As soon as I'm positive she's not within hearing distance, I'm narrowing my eyes on Braden and asking, "Why didn't I know that you spoke Italian?"

His eyes widen briefly. "I didn't think that it was important. I'm not fluent or anything. I just know the basics."

"Basics or not, I still would have liked to know that about you."

He looks a bit shocked, and I don't know if that should bother me. "Well, I don't speak any other languages besides the French we were required to learn in school, but don't test me on any of it. I can only really remember how to ask to go to the bathroom or how to say hello, my name is Braden."

I find myself laughing before I can stop myself. "That's better than me. I remember how to count to ten, but that's about it."

Braden's expression turns thoughtful. "I didn't mean to keep speaking Italian from you. It just never came up."

"I know," I say on an exhale. Maybe I was a *bit* dramatic. "It sounds kind of selfish, but I just don't like other people knowing things about you that I don't. That's crazy, right? I mean, it's not like you know every single thing about me."

He arches a brow. "And what don't I know?"

Val quietly drops off our drinks, and I take long, greedy gulps of my iced tea. "I don't know. It was just a figure of speech."

"Why don't I believe you?"

"Because you can be a stubborn ass sometimes."

Braden leans forward, his elbows on the table. "Careful, little fighter. Do you remember the last time I led you into a public washroom? I wouldn't want to ruin poor, innocent Val's ears by dragging you inside a stall and fucking the attitude right out of you."

My pulse quickens, and I squeeze my thighs together to try and dull the ache building between them. Braden's threat settles between us as I slide the hair off the back of my warm neck.

Our eyes stay locked, neither of us blinking like we're scared to lose a game we never even agreed on playing. Without realizing, I've started leaning across the table and am now just inches away from feeling Braden's lips on mine. If he just moved a bit closer . . .

A hand curves around the back of my head, holding me steady as he brushes his lips across mine, groaning into my mouth. I'm about to tell him to just kiss me already when he does, softly yet passionately. Gentle yet possessive.

It's over far too quickly, but I'm still left breathless and wanting more—needing more. The only thing on my mind as Val takes our orders and returns a few minutes later with plates of food is just *how* badly I need more. I feel like an addict, yet I can't be bothered to fight off the urge.

My legs remain squeezed shut and my cheeks hot as we eat. By the time we're finished, I'm scared to stand up, not knowing whether I have a wet spot on my leggings.

Braden must be thinking something similar because he pays the bill and says goodbye to Val eagerly, all past playfulness gone and replaced with an urgency that only intensifies the strain of my hard nipples against my bra.

When he slides out of his side of the booth and extends a hand out for me to take, I do so without hesitation and let him pull me up, wet spot be damned. His heat is a welcomed feeling despite my raging body temperature as he leads us past a row of empty booths.

We've almost hit the doors when I feel a shiver crawl up my spine, and an eerie silence envelops the few tables close by. My eyes slide shut when I hear the voice of the only person that could dry the soaked area between my legs so quickly.

"Sierra? What a coincidence. Join us, would you?"

22

Braden

Cole. Motherfucking. Travis.

My spine goes ramrod straight, a protective arm winding around Sierra's waist. She's become as still as a statue after hearing him speak and doesn't melt into me like she usually does. That alone is enough to have my fingers curling into my palms.

I didn't miss the way Cole ignored my presence beside her. But then again, why would he acknowledge me? I'm the competition. The guy he thought he got rid of after bringing her here.

Red mist teases my vision, floating in and out of my narrowed stare when I turn my body and tower over his table. The repulsive smile on his face is enough to have me aching to yank him up by the collar and drop him on the dirty floor.

Expensive black suit, shining shoes that probably cost more than my rent, another diamond-encrusted watch around his wrist. He's cut his hair since I last saw him, trying and failing to pull off a buzz cut. But that's about the only thing new about him.

Cole sits with perfect posture. His hands lie flat on his skinny thighs, head turned in our direction and dark eyes focused on Sierra in a way that makes my stomach roll.

I know that I'm glaring at him, not bothering to hide my feelings toward my girlfriend's pervy boss, but it's semantics at this point. There's no way that I'm going to pretend that I don't hate this fucker's guts.

"Sierra, it's lovely to see you out of the office. How are you doing?" the man I didn't notice sitting across from Cole asks, sounding mighty casual, like he's asked her those questions before.

Yanking my glare from Cole, I let my eyes wander to the occupied booth across from him, asking bluntly, "Who are you?"

The guy has to be about my height but maybe a few pounds lighter. A genuine smile curves his lips. "Mackenzie Thompson. And you must be Braden. I would say that it's nice to meet you, but I'm not sure that you will return the favour."

My brow twitches. "You would be right," I admit, not bothering to beat around the bush. Sierra releases some of the tension from her muscles when my thumb starts making small circles on her hip bone.

"Braden." She clears her throat. "This is Mack. Gretchen is his assistant."

"*Mean Girls* girl?" I ask, remembering the tiny woman I met outside Sierra's office building a few weeks back. I haven't seen her since, but Sierra talks about her all the time.

The Mackenzie guy makes a choking sound before covering it with a cough. "Have you called Gretchen that to her face?" he asks.

I nod, relaxing slightly. This guy could be a threat, but there's something real about him that makes me think he's the opposite.

My thoughts only solidify when he says, "You have a big set of balls, man. I like it."

"Gretchen threatened him, though. So we'll have to see if he risks it again," Sierra puts in, covering my hand with hers where it sits on her hip.

"We should take bets on whether she knees him in the dick or twists his nipples. My money is on the dick," Mack snickers.

"We were actually in the middle of a meeting regarding your job," Cole butts in. His angry words piss all over the light-hearted energy we've created and darken the mood again. "It wouldn't be wise to stay around to listen. I will talk to you Tuesday. Or will you be needing *more* vacation time?"

Sierra stiffens, sucking in a sharp breath. I bite my tongue—hard.

I'm borderline seething, teetering on the edge of letting too many harsh words slip from my lips that could get her fired right here and now. The hatred I feel sizzling in my blood must be obvious because when my eyes collide with Mackenzie's hard stare, the only thing I see is understanding.

My palms burn, and I know immediately that my nails have popped the thick skin.

"It's nothing bad, Sierra," Mackenzie clarifies, looking at Cole with evident disgust before moving his attention to her. "I'm giving him an update on the Waterton Brothers account because he's your direct supervisor. I spoke to both brothers briefly yesterday, and they told me they'll give *you* their update after New Year's."

She squeezes the hand that's still gripping her hip, and I relax it, not realizing how hard I've been holding her. Pressing a soft kiss to her temple, I watch Cole and the way his icy stare focuses on my mouth before caressing her face in a far too intimate way.

"Go to the car, baby," I whisper against the shell of her ear.

The hitch in her breath is nonexistent to anybody but me due to our closeness. "Please just trust me. I need you to go to the car."

A slight nod is all she gives me before she's walking outside without me. I shove the anxiety that erupts inside of me at the thought of her being outside alone behind a door for now. She'll be okay by herself for a few minutes. I really don't need her to see this.

I revel in the way Cole gasps when I spin on my heels and slam one hand to the table in front of him, the other to the booth behind his head, boxing him in. Anger radiates off my body, smothering the air around us.

If I didn't have Sierra outside waiting for me, I would be dragging his ass out back and kicking his teeth in.

"Talk to my girl like that again and I'll rip your vocal cords out with my bare fucking hands," I spit through clenched teeth. "Whatever you thought you were doing with her ends here. Sierra is mine. She'll never be yours. The sooner you get that through your thick fucking skull, the easier it'll be for you. This is your *last* warning."

The deep-rooted fear in his eyes barely settles the storm raging in my head, but I back away and drop my arms anyway. I put extra effort into not looking at him in case I lose whatever is left of my self-control and break his nose.

I catch Mackenzie's blank stare and hope that he can read what I'm trying to say with mine. *Don't let him ruin her career.*

Mackenzie pulls a wad of cash out of his wallet, tosses it on the table, and tips his chin at me. Standing up, he mumbles something to Cole that I don't bother listening to before walking alongside me out of that fucking restaurant.

"He won't touch her career, Braden. You have my word."

A hand hesitantly pats my shoulder before I spill our secret out to him in a wobbly plea. "She's pregnant. I need you to do everything you can to keep him away from her."

Mack doesn't hesitate. "Consider it done."

THE RIDE HOME WAS SILENT. Brutally so.

Sierra sat with her body curled toward the door and her cheek pressed to the cold window for the entire twenty-minute drive home. She didn't even ask me to change the awful music that I purposefully played in hopes of stoking the fire I knew was spreading inside of her. I wanted it to blaze, to shoot sparks in my direction. Anything to get her to cut the silence and talk to me.

The sunshine that had been beaming from her perfect smile as we ate our greasy food and talked about whatever the hell we wanted had been tucked behind thick, dark clouds, and all I wanted was to rip them apart and feel that warmth again.

At first, I thought that she was upset with me for how I asked her to back away from a fight she probably had every intention of taking part in, but Sierra isn't one to revel in her anger without speaking a word. If she were pissed at me, I would have no doubt about it.

So that left two other possibilities. One, she was embarrassed with the way Cole spoke to her in front of someone as high up on the food chain as Mackenzie, or option two, she was hurt.

Regardless of whether I was looking at option one or two, or fuck, even both, they were unacceptable. When I parked the car outside of Sierra's apartment, I actually inspected the steering wheel for my fingerprints, worried that they had become permanently indented into the leather from how tight my grip was the entire drive home.

I press those same fingertips into my thighs as I sit on the edge of her bed, listening to the shower run behind the bathroom door. My temples throb with a headache that I don't doubt has erupted because of the pile of questions running around my skull.

Sierra wanted to shower alone as soon as we got inside the apartment, and for some stupid reason, I let her go instead of prying answers out of her as to what's been eating at her.

Fuck this.

I quickly strip out of my clothes, dumping them in the hamper before walking to the bathroom and testing the door handle to see if she locked me out. When it turns easily, I blow out a breath and push my way inside.

The room is hot, steam twirling in the air like smoke and fogging up the vanity mirror, blocking my reflection. When I see Sierra's clothes forming a small pile beside the sink, the corners of my mouth tug up. *Some habits never die.*

Pulling back the shower curtain, I step in behind her. My arms form a cocoon around her wet frame before I'm pulling her back to my chest and clasping my hands at her middle. She shudders, tipping her head back and out of the water until it hits my chest.

"You don't get to hide your problems from me." My lips brush the tip of her ear. "Your problems are also mine."

Sierra doesn't say anything beneath the steady stream of water, but when I nudge her head to the side and drag my nose along the column of her neck, she falls into me, trusting my strength to keep her upright. The pulse beneath the thin skin beats fast against my lips as I kiss her throat, once, twice. My tongue begs for a taste of her, but I shake those thoughts free when my dick starts to harden against her back.

"I would do anything for you, my little fighter. Just name it."

Pushing the curve of her ass into the base of my erection,

she pulls my hands apart and urges one down between her thighs. "Touch me. *Please.*"

I don't deny her. I can't. Even knowing that this is her way of evading the conversation that we need to have.

With her hand on top of mine, I slide my fingers over her wet mound, spreading the lips and drawing circles around her swollen clit. "You're already wet," I groan, plunging two long fingers inside. "Do you want me to take you? Right here?"

Sierra bucks into my hand, nodding frantically. "Yes," she replies in a desperate gasp.

I pull my fingers from her pussy and take a step back. The hot water hits my chest before I have a chance to miss her warmth. "Hands on the wall."

She moves quickly, desperately. Her palms touch the shower tile at the same time mine settle on the smooth skin of her back. I glide them over the sharp ridges of her spine and down to the two identical dimples above her ass before kneading the thick flesh beneath them.

Her choked sound of surprise erupts around us when I spread her cheeks apart and drag my thumb between them, skimming over her puckered hole and pressing it inside her pussy. "Have you ever let anybody take your ass, baby?"

She releases a strained breath. "No."

I fuck her with my thumb. "Would you let me?"

"Let you what?"

I nearly laugh at the way she feigns ignorance. Instead of responding vocally, I ease my thumb from inside of her and slide it back up to her virgin hole, exploring and teasing. Pressing just the tip inside, I swallow a growl at the way she sucks me in.

"One day you'll let me fuck you here. But not today." Wrapping my cock in a tight fist, I line up with her dripping entrance and push inside, sheathing myself in one thrust.

"Today you'll come all over my dick," I growl into her neck, breathing in as much of her clean scent as possible. It goes straight to my head, turning my thoughts fuzzy.

"*Yes, yes*. Make me come," Sierra cries over the sound of rushing water. Her fingers are curled against the tile when she drops her head back and whimpers a contorted version of my name.

My thrusts are savage, hard, and quick. I fuck her like a man who has everything to lose and nothing to gain. Like I'm on death row and this is the last time I'll ever be inside of her.

The sounds that escape us are borderline inhuman yet mix together to form a fucking symphony that I want to hear every day for the rest of my life. My balls slap her backside with every thrust, her juices making sloppy sounds where we join.

I reach around to lightly collar her throat and pull her back flush to my chest. With her legs closed, the walls of her pussy tighten around me, strangling my cock. "You're going to come for me, fighter. You're going to own me. Fucking use me."

Sierra's nails are scratching my forearms like a wild animal when I feel her walls quiver around me. *She's going to come.*

I pinch her clit between my fingers, knowing that that's all it will take to send her over the edge.

"I'm coming, Braden. *Oh God,*" she screams so loud it echoes off the bathroom walls.

A roar gets lost in my throat as I fall with her, my face buried in her neck, our sweat mixing before getting swept down the drain. My thrusts come to a stop before I gently ease out of her, my heart throbbing when she whimpers.

I try to catch my breath as I release her throat, dropping my hand to the space between her breasts, feeling her raging heartbeat beneath my fingers.

"It's beating so fast," Sierra says softly, spinning around to face me. Warm, silver eyes shine, watching me in a way that has me fumbling for something to say.

Nothing comes, so I don't force it. Instead, I let my eyelids droop and focus on the steady thump in her chest. The feeling of every exhale drifting across my lips.

Time seems to stop as we stand together, two opposites held together by something more palpable than a magnetic force. Something threaded in her soul and mine, binding us together.

Fate seems like an unoriginal and cliché term to use to describe what I think brought Sierra and me together. But for now, it's as good of one as any. For this moment, it'll have to do.

23

Braden

The water has run cold by now, but neither of us makes an effort to leave this safe space. I hold Sierra in my arms, giving her any warmth that I have left. She presses closer in my embrace, sighing long and tired.

"I'm sorry that I tried to cut you out. That was just . . . really embarrassing for me." Her words kiss my wet throat.

"Men like Cole Travis shouldn't hold that sort of power over you. You're too strong to be brought down by that guy."

She takes a hesitant step back, just enough to catch my eyes. Her brows lower slightly, as if I've surprised her with my words.

"It's hard not to be. He's my boss, and he purposely tried to make a fool out of me in front of somebody that could fire me without a second thought. Mack is part owner of the entire company—I can't look like a fool in front of him. Especially not when he's already put his back out helping me when he didn't need to."

"Trust me, Mackenzie doesn't give a fuck about Cole. If anybody will be getting fired, it'll be him." If I have anything to do with it.

"I also hate that he embarrassed me in front of you," she says quietly, glancing away timidly. I almost don't hear her over the sound of the shower.

Cupping her jaw, I tilt her head so that she's forced to meet my gaze. There's a pink flush to her cheeks, but it's not from being warm. Her skin is ice beneath my fingers.

"Sierra, I don't care about what that stupid fuck says about you. You're my girl. Never feel embarrassed in front of me."

She nods cautiously, looking like she only half believes me.

"How about we talk about it more after we get you out of this water? You're not getting sick because of that asshole."

I grab her hair in my hands and wring the water out of it before reaching around to shut off the water. She shivers in my arms as I pull back the curtain and grab her towel from the hook. After stepping out and wrapping her up, I place a kiss on her forehead and tie my towel around my waist.

While she runs another towel through her hair, I grab her some clothes from the bedroom and place them on the toilet lid.

Not long after, she's hanging the damp towel and slipping on the clothes that I brought. My chest pulls tight at how gorgeous she is without even knowing it, all smooth skin and perfectly sculpted features. I could watch her for a lifetime and never get tired of what I would see.

"You're right," she says after a few silent moments. I lift a brow, encouraging her to continue. "About Cole. He isn't worth it. I'm sorry that I let him get to me like that. Usually it's easier to ignore his shit."

"You say that like dealing with his shit is a common thing."

She lifts a shoulder, avoiding my scrutinizing stare.

"He just likes to push his boundaries. It's an ego thing."

My shoulders pull tight, scowl deepening. "It's not a damn ego thing, Sierra. What kind of boundaries does he push? Has he touched you?"

The unmistakable flame of anger flickers across her face before she can hide it.

"Tell me what he did. Now." I seethe.

Sierra's fingers tap her hip. There's worry in her eyes. "Can you promise me that if I tell you, you won't hunt him down and stomp him into the ground?" she challenges.

"No," I say honestly.

"Then I won't tell you."

I laugh once. The sound is anything but humorous. "Simple as that, huh?"

She nods. "You're not getting involved."

"I'm already involved. You're my girlfriend. We're going to have a baby together, dammit!"

I want to pull my fucking hair out right now. Not smashing Cole's face into a brick wall at this very moment almost feels like a punishment of some sort. And the longer Sierra keeps me shut out, the more this feeling of rage heightens, and the harder it becomes to ignore.

I've always been an act first, think second kind of guy. I'm a fighter; I like to feel the surge of adrenaline in my veins before throwing a punch and the burn in my knuckles that follows.

Sitting back and letting things play out on their own is not something that I ever planned on doing. Especially not when it comes to Sierra and that butt plug of a boss of hers. He's crossed the line one too many times. I should have done more than lay a threat down at that diner, but it was too public.

No, the first time Cole is introduced to how I deal with boys who fuck with my girl, he won't have anybody to save his sorry ass. It'll be just me and him.

"Yes, we are going to have a baby together. But that doesn't mean that I need you to fight all my battles for me. I've got it handled," Sierra says, exasperated.

My stare hardens to stone. "Handled it how? By sitting back like a good little worker bee and letting him continue to make you fucking uncomfortable?"

"Don't talk down to me because I won't let you act like a caveman out to save my honor."

I run a rough hand through my wet hair, tugging on it and expelling a harsh breath. "I'm not trying to talk down to you. I just don't want you to keep quiet about this shit. If he didn't touch you, then tell me right now, and I'll drop it. But if he did, he needs to be dealt with. He can't continue to put his filthy hands on you. He won't stop unless I make him." My voice softens. "Guys like him, baby, they don't just have a change of heart and leave you alone. He won't stop until he gets what he wants, and that's *not* okay."

Something I said seems to resonate somewhere in that pretty head of hers because some of the stiffness in her shoulders melts away, and her eyes finally crash with mine.

Her inhale is shaky. "Before you got here, there were a couple of times where he touched me. Just lingering brushes on my arms and sides when we would pass each other in the halls or get pushed together in a crowded meeting."

"Fuck." Red. Deep, blood red. That's what I see when I drop my head back and stare at the ceiling, pulling in a long breath through my nose before puffing it out of my mouth. "And? There's more. I can hear it in your voice." *I don't want to hear any more.*

"There was only one time . . . that he tried for more." She has to pause to clear her throat, blinking a few times. "I was looking for extra sugar packets in the breakroom for my coffee. They're in the bottom cupboard, so I was bent over or squatting, I don't remember. But I felt hands on my ass, squeezing it roughly. I shot up instantly and just froze. My thoughts were scattered all over the place. It took me a few seconds to turn around and see that it was Cole. He had the biggest fucking grin on his face, like he had just won a gold medal for touching me like that. Some intern walked in before Cole had a chance to say anything or touch me again."

A ball gets lodged in my throat before sliding free and tumbling through my insides like I'm a living pinball machine before it lands with a splat at the bottom of my stomach.

"I'm going to break each one of his fingers," I say with a sense of calm that I don't feel. My rage is simmering beneath my skin, begging for a chance to reach a full boil.

Sierra brushes a clump of damp hair behind her ear, and I stop breathing when I see the way her hand shakes. It only takes three steps to reach her and wrap her in my arms, squeezing her tight like I'm trying to pull her body inside of mine. The need to keep her safe and protected is intense, inescapable. Nothing can touch her if she's in my arms, my frame serving as her own custom-made armour.

With her face pressed to my throat, she murmurs, "I felt dirty after. When I got home, I scrubbed my skin until it was red and sore. Gretchen is the only one I've told."

I bury my lips in her hair and breathe in her pure sunshine scent with greedy gulps in an attempt to keep my cool. Sierra needs my comfort right now more than I need to seek retribution.

"If he touches you again, I'll kill him," I whisper. The words are as soft as silk, but the promise peeking out from behind them is too sharp, too vicious to miss. "You're my everything. My one and fucking only. Nobody hurts you or makes you feel like you're less than the fierce, take-no-shit woman who I met in a line outside Sinners. Cole is done.

That's a promise, Sierra." I catch the hitch in her breathing and quirk a small smile.

She feathers a few kisses along my throat, humming against the skin. Vibrations electrify my bones. "I don't want you to get hurt or in trouble. Plus, Clark would never get rid of Cole. He carries Cole's balls in his back pocket."

"Clark isn't the only one in charge anymore. He gave up that right when he agreed to a merger with Mackenzie."

And if I learned anything today, it's that Mack isn't Cole's biggest fan. My gut tells me that there's not much going between him and Clark either beyond a simple business transaction. If I play my cards right, Cole will be on a one-way trip back to where he came from before he has a chance to snatch his balls back.

Sierra pulls back just enough to allow our eyes to collide and noses to brush. My hands travel to her hips, keeping her smashed to my chest. I welcome the constant need to touch her, soaking it up.

"You're a lot smarter than you look," she pokes fun, trapping her bottom lip between her teeth to avoid laughing.

I narrow my eyes, trailing my fingers up and down her side. "You talk a lot of shit for someone so small and . . . ticklish."

Shock invades her features before she's pushing at my chest and scrambling out of the room, a shriek echoing through the apartment. I stay where I stand instead of following her immediately, allowing myself a few seconds to grin and fully digest the swell of happiness that inflates my stomach. Belting out a laugh, I give my head an amused shake and take off after my girl.

Sierra's ability to let go and embrace that little girl inside of her just for me to see is a fucking beautiful thing. Her quick wit and humour is a hidden layer of her personality that I wasn't expecting to uncover but couldn't feel any luckier to have peeled back and bared witness to.

Soon enough, I'll have discovered every single thing that makes up the woman that I love, and she'll have done the same to me.

We have the time.

24

Sierra

WHEN BRADEN AND I FIRST MET, THERE WERE SO MANY PIECES IN my puzzle that I had forced to fit in the wrong spots just so the final picture wouldn't be incomplete.

I may have looked like a confident, know-it-all woman who had her life stitched perfectly at the seams, but that's a far-off assumption—a mask I spent too many years perfecting. In reality, there was so much going wrong in my head that those perfect seams were really bursting wide open.

Those pieces that were pushed into holes they didn't belong had begun to look out of place. I was starting to notice them, and they were ruining the image I was portraying on the outside.

My panic attacks are only one of the wrong pieces. But one that had become noticeable far earlier than the rest.

They would shake me to my core over things that had no right causing such disruptions in my head. And had been a regular part of my life since I was young. I guess I just got used to them.

I can admit now—after finally reaching out and talking to a therapist who I've grown to love—that it was shame that kept me from asking for help earlier. Dr. Tali thinks that the majority of my insecurities stem from my parents' abandonment and lack of love they gave. She believes they were one of the main reasons that I felt the need to force my life into a perfect image that in turn helped blossom my anxiety into what it had become.

I don't think she's very far off.

I met Eliza Tali in the line of a small, local coffee shop on one of the worst days that I've had since I can remember. With my stomach swelling just enough that I could no longer hide it beneath my work blouses and high-waisted skirts, a shine to my hair that I had no idea what to do with, and no more morning sickness, the beginning of my second trimester had been doing me too many favours.

My thoughts were in the clouds. I wasn't paying attention to where I was going after I grabbed my expensive lemonade from the counter and spun around so quickly my glossy hair swung over my shoulder. Right into the chest of the person behind me.

We collided so abruptly that my grip on the plastic cup tightened, and the lid popped right off. And when I tried to steady myself, the bright yellow liquid sloshed right over the rim and soaked the blouse of the woman in front of me.

An intense feeling of embarrassment flooded my cheeks and stained my entire upper body a red so bright that all I wanted to do was hide. The eyes of onlookers felt like pins in my skin. I wanted to get out. I *needed* to get out.

I knew that my hands were shaking as I fumbled through my purse looking for napkins, even though there were stacks just over on the counter. My lungs felt like they were covered in cement. I couldn't breathe, and when I did, it was more wheezing than actual breathing.

Thinking back on it now, a hot flash of shame runs through me. I know how ridiculous I must have looked getting so worked up over spilling my drink on someone, but at the time, it seemed like the worst thing that could have happened. It was such an intense feeling of misery that I yearned for an escape route. I was mortified, and my anxiety had spiked to the highest it had been since I was a teen.

But then a gentle, delicate hand covered the one sifting through my bag, stilling it. When I looked at the owner of that hand, I was met with a pair of round, emerald-green eyes that watched me with a compassion so obvious I was left reeling.

"It's okay. I was never a fan of lavender anyway," the woman had said, a genuine smile tugging at her mouth. When I blinked at her, confused, she only laughed. "My blouse. My mother-in-law bought it for me for Christmas, and I'm just getting back from our monthly lunch date. I figured that I should wear it for her today even though lavender washes me out."

I could feel the red subsiding from my cheeks and the cement cracking around my lungs. The ground stabilized beneath my feet again.

"I'm Eliza Tali." She held her hand out for me to take. I could feel her paying too much attention to how mine shook as I clasped it around hers.

"Sierra Caster," I replied, wincing at the roughness in my voice. "I'm so sorry about your shirt. I don't know what I was doing. I wasn't looking where I was goi—"

"Oh, please. You did me a favour, really. I have such an awful habit of keeping clothes that I know I'll never wear. Now I have a reason not to hold on to this," she said sweetly, as if I really had done her a favour.

I was so confused standing there with that woman, her blouse soaked with lemonade and my heartbeat still thumping in my ears. But then she had confused me even more and handed me a slim, white card with her name and number printed on it. She told me to give her a call the next time I felt like the world was shaking and falling apart at my feet.

I didn't have the words to reply, so I only nodded. And after Eliza squeezed my arm and excused herself to the bathroom, I dumped my empty cup in the garbage and got the hell out of there.

I've seen her three times and called her once over the past four weeks, and although my anxiety hasn't necessarily gone anywhere, it's become manageable and only going to get better.

It's put not only my mind but the minds of the people closest to me more at ease. Especially with my pregnancy. Sophie's weekly check-in calls have transformed from worrying interrogations about how I'm doing and handling everything to gossiping about the latest drama's in the span of those four weeks. She still worries too much, but I don't think that will ever truly stop. Not that I would ever want it to.

"You good, S?" Sophie asks, tearing me from my thoughts.

I blink away the fog in my mind and smile at the image of her on my laptop screen. It's still a shock to the system to see Sophie without her blonde hair. She's been dying her chestnut curls blonde since our first semester of college, so it threw me for a loop when she went back to her natural colour shortly after Christmas.

"I'm good. How are you and your new roommate?"

I sit up straighter against the headboard, adjust the pillow behind me to rest lower at my back, and balance my laptop on my small baby bump. The bedroom window is open again, just the slightest bit despite Braden's complaints.

I can't blame him for telling me not to keep the windows open considering it is early March and it hasn't started warming up much outside, but I'm in a constant state of sweat with this damn baby, so he can suck it up.

Sophie scowls. "I don't know why I did this to myself. I should have just built a cardboard house and slept in a damn alley."

I wince. "It can't be *that* bad."

"Oh, it's that bad. He posted a freaking bathroom schedule on the door. A schedule! Not to mention he went and reorganized all of my toiletries, so now he knows how heavy my flow is and what a menstrual cup looks like."

"Braden did mention that he's very particular."

"Particular my ass. He's compulsive."

"At least he's cleanly and not one of those guys who leaves his dishes in the sink until they mold."

"Cleanly or not, he's driving me up the wall," she sighs before looking at something behind her computer.

There's a tug in my chest at the faraway look in her eyes. "What's really going on? This can't just be about Clayton and his hearty relationship with cleanliness."

She presses the area between her brows with her thumb, and her shoulders slump. "This has just been a lot to deal with. I didn't think that I would be twenty-six with no future, a negative sum in her bank account, and a roommate who has an excessive collection of Marvel comics."

"You do have a future, Soph. It just wasn't at that school. We both know that that dad was out of line. You shouldn't have been the one punished for his blatant hatred."

My fingers curl into fists on the mattress as the reminder of that day bulldozes through my head. I'll never forget the pain in my best friend's voice when she called me after getting cornered in her classroom by one of her student's parents—a big white guy with a love for derogatory and sexist terms—after she had graded his son's test "too low."

The scene blew up, and insults that are far too disgusting

to repeat even in my head were thrown until Sophie, being the fearless bad bitch that she is, sucker punched him square in the nose. She was fired the next day for professional misconduct. The dad never pressed charges, but that was only because her student aid had recorded the entire thing, and he was terrified of his job catching wind of how big of a piece of racist shit he is.

Sophie pulls at the elastic holding her hair up in a bun, and brown curls tumble down to frame her slim face. She twists a thick strand around her finger, and her frown deepens. "He did it to provoke me. I shouldn't have punched him and played right into his hands."

I roll my eyes. "If you *hadn't* punched him, I would have been disappointed. He deserved far worse."

Sophie is a proud Latina woman who was raised by an even prouder one. She shouldn't have to back down from anything. Especially not men who think it makes them big and strong to talk down on somebody half their size just because of the colour of their skin. She's just as much of a citizen of this country as he is. As I am.

Not being there with her, especially after that, is really, really hard.

"Anyway. When are you telling your parents that you're pregnant? You're already seventeen weeks along."

She obviously wants to avoid talking any more about what happened, so I let it go. If she doesn't want to talk about it anymore, I'm not about to push her.

"How about never?" It's only partially a joke. "Just thinking about how my mother will react has me checking my skin for a stress rash."

"You just need to rip off the Band-Aid, Sierra. Your mother will have something negative to say whether you tell her tomorrow or a year from now with a baby in your arms,"

Sophie says sympathetically. "It only makes it worse that you haven't introduced them to Braden."

"That's not my fault. They haven't been in the country since I saw them before I moved," I defend myself.

"Then just FaceTime them and do it. At least then you can end the call when your mother starts to lay into the both of you."

I let out a choked laugh. "Yeah, I'm sure they would leave it at that."

"Look," Sophie says, her voice strong in a *no bullshit* way. "It's your life. It's your baby. It's your relationship. Neither your mother *or* your father has ever made an effort to be a constant in your life, so don't give them this power over you. Don't let the fear of what they'll say or do affect you so heavily. You have so many people by your side, you don't need your parents or their judgment."

I swallow the boulder in my throat and dip my chin, looking at the pillow beside me that has become Braden's. If Sophie wasn't watching me, I would have picked it up and held it close to my chest, maybe even breathed in the smell of him that always lingers on the pillowcase.

Besides our baby, Braden has been the biggest surprise of my life. He's put in so much work and become such a pillar of support for me, especially throughout my pregnancy. It doesn't matter what I ask him to do, he'll do it. Hell, most of the time, I don't even need to ask. It's like he can read my mind and body better than I can. He knows what I need before I do and does it before I even have the chance to question him.

Over the past few weeks, he's been working more than usual—coming home later and leaving earlier. But every single night, he comes home with either dinner from my favourite restaurant or plans for what to cook, curls up on the couch with me to watch *Law & Order*, and rubs my feet to the point of near orgasm.

It's become the norm, the expected. I've grown comfortable with him being with me, our lives fully intertwined. Some days—or more like every day—I think about how lonely I was before him and feel such a deep-rooted sadness. It just helps confirm what I already know.

I never want to spend another day without him or the life that we've begun to grow together.

"You're right," I admit, regardless of the burn in my chest. "There's nothing that my parents can say to me that will hurt more than anything they've already done."

"God, that's so sad. You shouldn't have to feel like that, S. I'm sorry."

I wave her off. "Don't. It's not your fault. Clare is more a mother to me than the woman who carried me for nine months. Her approval is the only one that mattered to me, and I got it."

Sophie's mouth lifts in a sad smile. "And you know that I love you and that troublemaker you're harvesting."

"Harvesting? Jesus, Soph." My eyes roll as a genuine laugh slips past my lips. It's small, but it's real.

"You've got this, Momma. And if Braden does anything to upset you, let me know."

"Oh yeah? And what are you gonna do? Jump on my back and stick your finger in my ear?" a deep, rumbling voice asks.

My head snaps up, and I find Braden leaning against the doorjamb, his arms crossed and a giant grin on his face. I fight to keep the squeal of excitement trapped in my throat as I stare at him, halfway lost in a trance.

He's all muscle and confidence right now, and I want to climb him like a fucking tree. Especially when his eyelids fall to half-mast and his stare slides down my body and bare skin, getting snagged on the edge of the sleep shorts I've worn all day.

The heat in his eyes is evident, making my legs fall open of their own accord.

"And that's my cue. I'll talk to you later, babes. Love you!"

I'm half-aware of the way I say goodbye, too busy watching Braden stalk toward me like a predator to prey, anticipation building low in my belly. A large hand presses my laptop closed before moving it to the floor.

Braden bends down, and I inhale sharply when soft lips make contact with my exposed belly and fingertips brush the skin above my shorts.

"You're so beautiful. I missed you both today," he whispers against my swollen stomach. Tears fill my eyes at the intense, unmistakable look of love on his face.

My fingers slip into his hair, playing with the softness of it. "We missed you too."

He's watching me closely when he says, "I want you to go somewhere with me tomorrow."

"Okay. Do I get to know where?"

With a final kiss to my belly, he's standing back up and running his palm over the top of my head. "It's a surprise. A good one, I promise."

"Everyone says their surprise is a good one. Nobody would agree if you said it wasn't," I tease, tilting my head back to meet his gaze. "But I'll play. It better *really* be good, though. Especially if you're making me leave the house on a Sunday."

He chuckles, shaking his head. "You have my word, baby. Now, come on. I picked up dinner."

"Have I mentioned lately that I love you?"

He shrugs. "Once or twice. Now, get your tight ass out of here while I shut this damn window."

25

Braden

Never in a million years did I think that I would be holding hands with my pregnant girlfriend in front of my own gym. But here I am. And it feels fucking out of this world.

The words *Knockout Fitness* are scrawled along the right side of the single-storey building, lit in a hard-to-miss cherry red. A giant window sits on the left side of the door, a few steps from the fob scanner we installed to ensure access to clients anytime, day or night, regardless of our official open hours.

Over the past couple of months, a few more nearby buildings have sold, and businesses have started to take up shop, making the area a lot busier than it was when the renovations began. It's only a matter of time before there's just as much traction in our area as there is a few blocks over.

"This is the gym you've been working at for the past few months?" Sierra asks from beside me after a few long minutes of silence. I nod. "It's gorgeous. Are those solar panels on the roof?" She points to the top of the building, where solar panels have been installed along both sides of the sloped roof.

When I turn to look at her, I'm surprised to see the vivid excitement in her eyes. "Yep. It was a super-last-minute idea, but I think it makes it stand out."

She hums in agreement. "I like that I get to see where you work, but working out isn't really how I expected to spend my Sunday morning. Actually, *can* I even work out? You know . . . since I'm four months pregnant?"

I bite down on my tongue to avoid laughing. I'm surprised she doesn't already know the answer to that question considering how much she loves Dr. Google these days.

"I didn't bring you here to make you work out. But if you want to, you can. I already talked to your doctor and have a list of things you can't do in case you decide that you want to."

Suddenly indignant, she grips her hips. "So you brought me to a gym thinking that I would want to stand back and what? Watch you? Please," she scoffs. "I can work out just fine, thank you very much. If you're working out, then so am I."

I'm grinning by the time she finishes her speech, not to mention incredibly turned on. Sierra has a fire inside of her that burns alongside mine. It makes me want to drag her inside my office and fuck her up against my desk.

"Don't look at me like that. I'm not sure the owner of this gym would like knowing we had sex in the changing room."

I toss her a wink. "I don't think he would care. I heard he's a pretty laid-back guy."

Her eyes flare with curiosity. "Is it someone you know?"

"You could say that." Slinging my arm around her shoulders, I pull her close and walk us to the entrance. With my free hand, I scan my key fob and open the door. The lights are off, but before Sierra can ask why, I'm flicking them on and hurrying her inside.

"We're the only ones here?" Her uncertainty is obvious,

but there's no sign of fear. She's staring at the black walls surrounding the entrance. Or, more specifically, the white-painted quotes covering them. "*We can't be brave without fear.* You have that tattooed on your bicep."

"Mhm. Muhammad Ali. It was the first tattoo I got," I confirm. "Come on, I want to show you something." I slide my hand across her back and down her arm until I can link our fingers together.

Nerves tangle in my stomach as I lead her to the back office. We walk silently down the bright hallway, the walls decorated with photos, some personal and some not so much. I'm grinning like a naughty schoolboy when I feel her pull on my hand, her heels digging into the floor.

"Why are there pictures of you on the wall?" Sierra asks cautiously. With her body barely a foot away from the first photo hung on the wall, I can't see her expression, but I would put money down on that adorable little wrinkle being between her brows. "How old are you here? You look exactly the same."

Moving behind her, I hang my arms over her shoulders and rest my chin on her head. She sighs, melting into my embrace like warm butter. Like being in my arms is the most natural thing in the world.

"Exactly the same?" I tsk. "You wound me, fighter. I'm much bigger now."

The photo in front of us was taken at my first real fight, back when I was a sixteen-year-old chump who thought his shit didn't stink.

A much scrawnier version of myself stands with a pair of gold shorts hung around his hips, ending right above the knee, and a mess of long, unruly curls on his head and curling behind the ears. My arm is lifted in the air, my hand in Dad's. I had won the fight by some miracle, but there isn't the hint of a smile nor a stitch of pride on my father's face.

Probably because I had entered the fight behind his back, but that's water under the bridge now.

I could have hung any other photo, maybe one where my dad didn't look like he wanted to leather my ass, but it was my first fight. It was memorable. It's the match that decided everything for me. Sparked the fire that hasn't burnt out yet and hopefully won't for a long time.

"Braden, why are there pictures of you here?" she repeats the question that I ignored, trailing her fingers along the top of the frame.

I'm suddenly hit with a wall of fear that causes my throat to swell and my next words to die on my tongue. I shouldn't be scared to tell her that all of this is mine, but once I do, things will become very real, very quickly. Once Sierra knows, the ball will drop. Owning my own gym will no longer be a dream but a reality. One that I have the ability to fuck up and lose.

I grapple with the handle on my emotions when she spins around in my arms and pushes up on her tiptoes, placing a kiss on my jaw. She nuzzles into the crook of my neck, palming my back with her small hands. I shudder a breath and tighten my arms around her shoulders.

"What aren't you telling me?" she murmurs. Her gentle words do me in.

"It's mine. The gym is mine."

"It's yours?" I sputter. "Yours how?"

He might as well have told me he's a born-again virgin. Surprise doesn't even cover how I'm feeling. The mix of emotions inside of me varies from curiosity, surprise, and a whole shit ton of pride.

The gym—from what I've seen so far—has a factory-like feel and is absolutely beautiful. It feels luxurious yet intimate and not at all intimidating like I was expecting when we were standing outside. With shiny wood floors and freaking chalkboard walls, it feels like a place that I would actually want to spend hours at, and I'm not a gym type of gal. I can't wait to see what the rest of the building looks like.

Braden chuckles, kissing my head. "Mine as in *mine*. I own Knockout. I've spent almost every day here for the past four months getting it ready to open."

My jaw is unhinged, but I don't bother closing it.

"I'm sorry that I kept it from you," he apologizes.

"Don't apologize. I just have so many questions."

"Like?"

"Like when did you decide to do this? What about the gym in Vancouver?"

He backs up and grabs my hand again. "It became a real idea the day after you left. Rampage is now Tyler's. He bought it, and I used the money from the sale to buy Knockout. Well, what's now Knockout. The building was empty when I bought it."

What? My brows fly to my hairline. "It was empty?"

He nods. "Four walls and a killer echo."

"Holy shit."

"Do you have any more questions you want answered right now, or do you want the grand tour?"

"They can wait. Show me. Please." I'm incredibly eager. How did I miss something this big? He was building an entire business from scratch, and I had no idea. Although, to be completely fair, I was under the impression that he was just working here.

"We'll skip the office for now. I might be too tempted to

bend you over my desk and have my way with you." With a hard smack, his palm connects with my right butt cheek. "These fucking leggings, baby. I want to rip them off of you."

Heat crawls up my neck. These pregnancy hormones have me acting like a dick-obsessed mess. All it takes is the slightest brush of Braden's skin or that gruffness in his voice to make my panties slick and an empty feeling slump between my thighs. Fuck, I don't think that I can deal with his dirty mouth right now.

"Later," I breathe.

"Later," Braden agrees, but his eyes say something else. They're dark, possessive as they sharpen on me. I can feel the tension snap and crackle in the distance between us, and I want it to suffocate me. He crowds my space, suddenly so much closer than before.

The ache between my legs is distracting. It's pulling my head in the wrong direction. I need to focus on the revelation that just took place, not the way my underwear sticks to my pussy, already so wet with my arousal.

I nearly moan when Braden pushes me against the wall, shaking the picture frames beside me. My thighs spread of their own accord, giving him room to move between them. He picks them up and wraps them around his waist instead.

"Fuck," he rasps.

I've nearly torn a hole in my lip from biting down on it by the time he tilts his hips and brushes the hardness of his cock against my centre. I throw my head back as pricks of pleasure ricochet through me. The thin material of his gym shorts do nothing to hide the ridges of his erection as he grinds against me, brushing my clit just enough to tease.

"Please," I gasp, grabbing his flexed biceps and squeezing.

Lust blazes in his half-lidded stare, warming me all over. With a tense jaw, he moves a hand between our bodies and into my leggings. Oh my God. *Yes*. Fingers slide over my wet panties, and knuckles brush my clit, making me tremble with anticipation.

"Oh *fuck*. Please." I'm shamelessly grinding into his hand, far too desperate to care about anything but getting some relief.

I cry out when he hooks two fingers under the crotch of my panties and tugs them aside before plunging two fingers inside of me. I'm so slick, so needy, that there's no resistance as he starts fucking me with his fingers.

"You have such a greedy pussy, baby. Do you feel how it sucks me in? How fucking wet and swollen you are for me?"

His dirty words do nothing to smother the flames under my skin. They're dousing them in gasoline, and the burn is pure pleasure.

The grip my thighs have around his waist starts to loosen when they begin to shake, my climax threatening to send me toppling over the edge. Braden's thigh slides beneath my ass and rests there.

"Want to watch you," he groans, looking pained. "But I need to kiss you."

Braden's mouth slants across mine, hard and needy. The kiss is far from romantic, but that's not what I need right now. His tongue presses to the seam of my lips, and I open for him desperately. He swallows my moan when his thumb applies a hard pressure to my clit before sliding around the wet, soft skin in quick circles.

My head swims, my heart rate blasting into overdrive. Black dots swarm my vision as I rip my mouth from his. "I'm coming. *I'm coming*."

"Soak my fingers, fighter," he demands, adding a third finger just before my walls start to convulse around them. A husky groan falls between us as I ride his hand, my head thrown back, sobs falling from my lips.

After the pleasure subsides, my head falls forward,

colliding with Braden's chest. I blink a few times to try and gather my bearings again and shudder when he slips his fingers out of me, wiping them on my leggings before squeezing my thigh.

The squeeze draws my attention to the quivering muscles wrapped around him, and I drop them from his waist, cursing at the soreness that pulses through them.

"Better?" The humour in his voice is thick.

Leaning back, I meet his eyes and smile sheepishly. "You're the worst."

"Your ruined panties would beg to differ."

A blush crawls up my neck as I push at his chest and slip from between him and the wall. Running a hand over my hair, I say, "Give me that tour already. I want to see the rest of this place."

I can't help but watch as he reaches into his shorts and adjusts himself. When my eyes stay locked on his crotch for way too long, he snorts. "Keep looking at my cock like that and I won't be able to give you this damn tour. We'll take care of it later. Right now, I want to show you the rest of my gym."

Nodding, I drag my eyes up to the dimple in his cheek and reach out to lace our fingers together again.

Braden leads us through the hallway, past the men's and women's locker rooms, and out toward a huge open space filled with all sorts of workout equipment. Punching bags hang from the ceiling and form a sort of divider between the normal training area full of things like treadmills and bench presses and what I assume to be the part of the room where you would focus more on boxing. A fighting ring sits at the centre of that half of the room.

Racks upon racks of weights and kettlebells are set off to the side of the workout equipment, and more quotes fill the walls where mirrors don't. There are rows of yoga mats and balls beside bottles of sanitizer and rags off by the hallway entrance. A room labelled as a Training Room sits at the far end of the gym, behind the fighting ring.

Braden's eyes beat into the side of my head as he waits for me to speak, but my tongue does nothing but flop helplessly in my mouth. I'm speechless. Completely in awe of him and this space that he's created. I don't think I could be any prouder of him.

"Sierra?"

Oh my God. He sounds nervous.

I squeeze his hand and force something, anything, out of my mouth. "I don't know what to say." His gulp is audible, and I wince, quickly explaining. "This place is phenomenal. I don't know what to say because I think I'm in shock. This is amazing, Braden. *Really* amazing."

When he tugs me toward him, his grin takes the wind out from under me. Joy bubbles in my stomach, and I giggle when he loops his arms around my waist and hugs me so tight my feet hover above the ground.

"Thank Christ," he blows into my hair.

"Did you think that I wouldn't love it?"

"I figured you would. But it feels fucking out of this world to hear you say it out loud."

Understanding floods my system. I pepper kisses all over his throat, jaw, and face before pulling back and holding his gaze hostage with mine. "You did it."

"I did it," he echoes slowly, like he's finally letting it sink in.

"When do you open?"

"Tomorrow."

Mouth gaping, I pull away. "Tomorrow? You waited until the day before your grand opening to show this place to me?"

He puts his hands—palms out—in front of him. "In my defense, the bags weren't hung until yesterday, and the weights were a day late. I wasn't about to show it to you incomplete. It had to be perfect. And now it is."

"Fine." My lips itch to pull into a smile. "Now, are you going to show me how any of this stuff works? Or do I need to find myself a different trainer?"

His eyes darken at the threat, and he takes my ass in his hands. "Not unless you want to be held responsible for the injuries I give them, you fucking won't."

I laugh loudly, blissfully. "Okay, okay. Only you."

His entire face softens. "Just me."

And it's true. It is just him. I place my hand on my stomach. It's just *us* and our future.

26

Braden

How do baby brands get away with charging five hundred dollars for a stroller? It's straight-up highway robbery at this point. I'm pretty sure a baby doesn't care that the thing pushing it around on the sidewalk has a fancy logo stitched into the handle or a special cup holder for mom and dad.

But it doesn't end there. Stroller after stroller is lined up in front of me and Sierra, and the longer it takes us to pick one, the more my skin itches like a thousand fire ants are trying to burrow themselves beneath it.

Some of them are more like luxury beds with wheels, while others are more clunky and plain. There's cream, black, pink, blue, or beige. Adjustable or nonadjustable. Meant to grow or not meant to grow. Full-sized or lightweight. And what the fuck is a jogging stroller? Oh boy, I'm pretty sure my brain is cramping.

The original plan for today had been to look around a few baby stores to get an idea of what we wanted to add to our registry. However, it's safe to say that that idea crashed and burned the moment we stepped inside the first store and Sierra burst into a fit of tears after catching a glimpse of a newborn onesie with the saying *"Strong like daddy"* written across the chest.

Not even two minutes later, we had an associate in a baby blue polo rushing toward us and whisking Sierra away. Now, a full hour later, my girlfriend is holding a scanning machine, adding items to our in-store registry and waiting on me to help decide which stroller we need to add.

"The first one is fine," I say, staring at the plain black one on the end.

I have no clue how much that one costs, but it looks like it's on the decent end of the spectrum. It's pretty plain and to the point. Nothing too extravagant.

"What about the third one?" Sierra asks, tapping her thigh with her fingers.

The third stroller is beige and lies flat like a bed. Although it doesn't have a fancy brand stitched in the squishy handle, it seems a bit impractical.

"What if the baby throws up in it? Won't it stain?"

She hums. "Good point. I didn't think of that."

I point to the last one. "What about that one?" It's still black but is a bit fancier than the first one I chose with its dual cup holders and decent storage underneath the seat. "The girl said it has a matching car seat that clips inside for when the baby is really small."

"You caught that?" Sierra slants me a surprised look.

I bump her shoulder, smiling softly. "Yeah, I caught that."

There's something about the way she's looking at me—all lovesick and content—that has a warm and fuzzy feeling setting up camp in my stomach. I want to take a mental picture of that expression and tuck it away for days when I really need it.

I try not to show my surprise when she blurts out, "Let's add the last one to the registry."

"You sure? We don't have to pick that one just because I like it."

She cuts a hand through the air. "I'm sure. It's the most practical. Plus less likely to stain."

My smile grows with the small victory when Sierra scans the stroller's barcode and heads toward the crib section of the store. I follow her behind her like a puppy scared of getting lost, my eyes not leaving her back for the rest of our trip.

We spend another hour scanning endless items to our registry before migrating to the outlet mall a few streets over. I've never had to go dress shopping with a woman before, but I'm trying not to act like the idea of it makes me want to take a nap.

A few people walk by us, but the mall is dead for a Saturday morning.

"Do you really not have anything to wear to this dinner tonight? It's not a suit-and-tie type thing, is it?" I ask casually, like I'm not crossing my fingers behind my back in hope that she'll magically remember she has the perfect dress already shoved in the back of her closet.

"It's a charity dinner, Braden." Sierra's arm brushes mine as we walk. "You have to wear a suit, and I need to find a dress that actually zips up in the back and doesn't make me look like a beached whale."

Her last comment makes me frown. Is that really how she sees herself? I can't begin to understand how it feels to watch your body change and grow in the way she is, but it pisses me off to hear her talk that way.

"You don't look like a beached whale. You're five months pregnant and still the most gorgeous woman I have ever seen."

She looks doubtful. "You're supposed to say that."

"Like hell I am," I snap. Grabbing her hand, I tug on it, forcing her to stop walking and face me. When she refuses to meet my gaze, I pinch her chin between my thumb and pointer finger and lift it, forcing her to look at me. The insecurity I find trapped in her silver eyes is enough to put my heart in a chokehold. I immediately soften my voice. "You were stunning when I met you, and you're even more stunning now. You're growing our baby, Sierra. I've never been as attracted to you as I am right now. I wish you felt the same way about yourself, but until you do, I'll be here to remind you. Okay?"

There's a slight pink tint to her cheeks, but I'm not sure if it's from embarrassment or something deeper down that she won't tell me about while we're in the middle of the mall. Either way, it doesn't matter. The only thing that matters to me right now is making sure that my girl knows how beautiful I think she is so hopefully, maybe, she'll be able to believe it too.

"This isn't the place to talk about this, I know. I'll drop it for now. But you bet your tight ass that we'll be doing a lot more than just talking about it when we get home." I press my lips to hers, feeling them quiver ever so slightly. I swallow the shuttered breaths that brush mine as she tries holding back the tears I find building in her eyes. Brushing my thumb under her lower lashes, I swipe away the rogue tear that escapes and kiss her again before whispering, "No tears."

The only sign of acknowledgment she offers me is the small choked sound that swells in her throat before her spine snaps straight and her chin lifts, this time without my help. And just like that, she's the image of confidence.

"Thank you."

I wear a proud grin when I kiss her temple and say, "Let's go get you a dress, fighter."

I THINK I swallowed my tongue. My hand drifts to my throat and massages the hot skin, like I'm actually searching for it behind my Adam's apple.

The apartment is silent, the air stiff and pulled tight, ready to snap. Lust attacks my senses, so dangerously potent in each quick inhale of air that I suck back. My cock stirs, desperate for attention from the woman walking toward me.

Sierra's hips twist as she moves. The tight black silk wrapped around her curves fits her figure too perfectly, like a damn glove. I want to tell her to go change back into her cookie monster pants and my sweater, but fuck if she doesn't look confident as all hell. It's obvious in the way her lips are quirked up in a seductive smile and her nose stays pointed to the sky even under the intensity of my stare.

I'll happily deal with a hundred sets of wandering, curious eyes following my girl all night if it means that that look stays right where it is.

You could drop a match and set the room on fire with how dense the air feels between us. And I would gladly burn if it meant that I could look at her for a few minutes longer.

Sierra stops a few feet away and spins in a circle, arms splayed out. "What do you think?"

"I think that you're far too good for me," I rasp, eating the distance between us and placing my fingers firmly on her hips. My thumbs draw circles into the silk dress. "And that it's going to hurt keeping my hands off of you all night."

Silver eyes blink innocently at me through thick, black lashes. "It's a good thing that you won't have to, then, isn't it?"

A nearly inhuman groan rattles in my chest when she

grabs my hand and slides it beneath the hem of her dress that she's already lifted to her knee. Smooth, warm skin pebbles with goosebumps beneath my fingertips as she slides them up her calf, her thigh, and to her wet, bare pussy.

"Fuck," I mutter, grazing my knuckles against the slick skin. "Where are your panties?"

She inhales sharply, and her fingernails dig into the top of my hand. "I skipped them. The lines would show in this dress. But if it's a problem, I'll just go put some on—"

I cut her off by digging my knuckles between her lips and brushing the swollen bundle of nerves hiding there, feeling her pussy weep for me. With a moan, her head falls forward, hitting my chest.

"It's cute when you try to beat me at my own game, little fighter. But we both know I'll win every single time." I pull my hand out from under her dress and slip my fingers in my mouth, sucking them clean. "Let's go, Sierra. We don't want to be late."

Her growl has me laughing like a maniac all the way to the door.

27

Sierra

Braden's hand is warm on my back as he leads us past chatting women in floor-length gowns, gawking men crowding an open bar, servers with trays of champagne, and to our designated table in the crowded ballroom. My body is already crying from the heat blasting around us, but I try not to focus too much on the sweat building beneath my arms and more so on not stepping on the hem of my dress and toppling over.

Too many tables to count fill the room, each decorated with elegant pink-and-yellow flower arrangements and a crisp white tablecloth. Number cards are hung from the back of each chair, causing my steps to falter.

"Shit," I hiss, feeling Braden's concern immediately as I dig my heels into the shiny wood floors.

"What's wrong? Did something happen?" he asks with wild desperation, reaching for my stomach.

I offer him a shy smile and urge his hands back down. "No, sorry. I forgot to look at where we're sitting."

Table and seating assignments were sent via email this

morning, but I was too busy fawning over the grey glider chair I wanted for the nursery to pay attention to much else.

I unclasp my clutch and pull out my phone, immediately starting to scroll through my emails. Mackenzie's name is pretty close to the top, so it doesn't take long to pull up the message.

"Seat fifteen and sixteen," I announce, putting my phone away.

"Over there," he whispers, nodding to the front of the ballroom.

We push our way through the sea of tables before coming to a stop at the second table, directly in front of the stage. I bristle when I see Cole already occupying one of the six chairs, his nose in the air and narrowed eyes trained on me—or rather, my swollen stomach.

My pregnancy hasn't been kept a secret by any means, but I've tried to stick with clothes that don't emphasize my bump at work for this very reason. I've already talked to Mackenzie about when I'll take maternity leave, and he volunteered to relay that message to Clark so that I didn't have to have more contact with that man than necessary.

Cole, on the other hand, received an email from me informing him of my pregnancy when he was in Vancouver last week. Chickenshit move, I know. But by the way he's glaring at my stomach right now, as if he would love nothing more than to see it explode in front of him, I can't say that I regret my decision.

Beside me, Braden is a mountain of tight, angry muscles, ready to protect me at the first sign of danger. I know that he doesn't care about where we are or the people surrounding us with pockets so heavy they would sink to the bottom of the Pacific. He's been wanting to have a go at Cole from the moment they met. And with his heightened protectiveness and the knowledge of what happened between Cole and me, it won't take much to make those dreams come true.

I reach for Braden's hand, intertwining our fingers and bringing them to my stomach. A sigh of relief escapes me the second there's something between Cole's glare and my baby.

Braden leans toward me, his nose brushing the tip of my ear. "We can go home. I can tell Mack that you aren't feeling well."

I want to take the offer. *Badly*. But I refuse to let Cole think that he's won something here.

"Mackenzie and Gretchen worked really hard organizing this event. We're not going to let that asshole take away from what tonight is about."

Over the past few months, I've gotten to know Mackenzie Thompson on a deeper, personal level that's made him more of a friend to me than just a boss. Gretchen had more to do with that than Mack or I did with all of her constant pushing, but that's beside the point. After Mack took care of the Waterton Brothers budget problem for me, I was able to help them reach their goals and secured a long-term client. It's been pretty smooth sailing since.

Braden and Mack have also been spending a lot of time together recently. I think Mack has been to Braden's gym every single day since it opened two weeks ago. They've built the foundation of a really great friendship here, and that makes me happy.

We both owe it to Mack to be here tonight. To support him and the Save A Home Foundation, an organization that he holds so close to his heart.

I was shocked when Mack told me about his history with foster care and how hard it was for him growing up in the system. His parents passed away when he was only five, and without any other immediate family, he had no choice but to fall into the hands of the Toronto foster care system.

He explained how grateful he is for his adoptive parents and the way they helped him turn his life around after spending ten years alone, without much comfort or affection. I remember tears filling my eyes and his steady voice explaining how those hard years helped him grow into who he is today.

Mackenzie isn't the type of man who looks back and hates the torments of his past. He values the lessons they taught him along the way instead. Hearing him sound so sure and positive despite everything that he's gone through was what made me realize that I wanted to get to know him. As more than just my boss, but a friend.

Knowing that tonight means so much to Mack made Braden's and my decision to come tonight a very easy one, despite our mutual dislike of this type of social event.

"You're right," Braden agrees, although he sounds pained.

He shifts his body so he stands in front of me and starts to push my unbuttoned jacket from my shoulders. I shrug it off, and he takes it eagerly, laying it over the chair farthest from Cole before pulling it out for me. He drapes his suit jacket across his chair, and we both sit. The chairs are so close together that with Braden's body being so large, we're pressed firmly against each other, thigh to thigh and bicep to bicep.

Braden places one hand on the table and the other on my thigh before giving it a comforting squeeze. He's more tense than I think I've ever seen him. The sharp lines of his jaw are more prominent as it clenches, and his thick bottom lip is thinner than usual, probably from scowling so deeply. My fingers itch to touch all of those tight muscles and relax them. Put him at ease. But it would be for nothing as long as we're here, only a few feet from the root of the problem.

"I noticed the bar when we walked in. Do you want to get

a drink before dinner?" I ask, feeling a bit helpless as to how to help him relax.

"I'm good, babe."

"Are you sure?"

He nods once, and I kiss his cheek, hoping that the subtle affection can help settle him even the slightest bit. His stubble scratches my chin. Even though I've become used to the scrape of his facial hair, it still sends a shudder down my spine that has me leaning even closer to him.

"I see you got your friend into a suit, Sierra. Is that why you were late? You missed the raffle entirely," Cole snarks, one eyebrow lifted in judgment.

A pang of guilt ricochets through me before I can ignore it. Missing the raffle was entirely my fault. After having such a busy morning and afternoon, Braden and I fell asleep as soon as we got back home before either of us could set an alarm. It's a miracle that we made it here before dinner considering we only woke up an hour and a half ago.

"I'm not her friend, bud." Braden laughs coldly. "But you're very aware of that."

Cole slants him a dirty look. "And I'm not your *bud*," he spits, putting extra emphasis on the label.

"Glad we got that cleared up, then."

Cole ignores Braden and focuses on me as he gulps back whatever brown liquid he has in his glass. "You look incredible in that dress."

Bile slithers up my throat. I would rather roll around in a dumpster than be complimented by Cole.

Braden leans back in his chair and grins smugly, like he's in on a joke that nobody else is. A nervous flutter fills my stomach as I think of what's about to come out of his mouth. Only he doesn't say what I was expecting. My jaw falls open when his brash grin morphs into something warmer, and he starts rubbing his thumb up and down my thigh. "Yes she does."

There's nothing dark or threatening in his voice, just a genuine feeling of love and appreciation that makes my heart vibrate like the ground beneath a dozen running elephants. Cole's presence fades to nothing in the background.

A buttery warmth slips over my skin and into my bones as I stare at Braden, surprised by his comment in the best way.

Braden has grown so much over the course of our relationship, and right now, it couldn't be any more obvious to see. I have no doubt that if I looked inside his head, I would find more than one crude comeback that would have pissed off Cole so much more than a simple agreement. And I think knowing that he could have but didn't makes his comment that much more satisfying.

"Thank you," I whisper so only Braden can hear.

His eyes meet mine, shining with so much affection I feel it down to my toes. "Don't thank me, sweetheart. It's the truth." He pinches the silky material of my dress between his fingers and hums low in his throat. "I can't wait to get you home and out of your dress so that I can show you just how strongly I believe it."

"Oh? Is that right?" I quirk a brow, acting tough even as my cheeks flush.

He laughs, so clear and bright, and it's the most beautiful sound in the world. It's a drug, one that I can see myself addicted to for the rest of my life.

"You already know it is. Now hush before I prove it to you right now. I think Mack's about to come on."

Releasing a tight breath, I pull away from him and blink a few times, bringing everything around us back into focus. The ballroom lights have dimmed, the stage now lit. With a megawatt smile, Mackenzie saunters across the stage toward a tall podium.

He's dressed incredibly dapper in a slim-fitting black tuxedo that I would probably puke at the cost of and shining, scuffless black shoes. His hair is buzzed neatly on the sides with longer, curly pieces pushed back on the top. Focused entirely on the crowd and rippling with confidence, he owns the stage, capturing the attention of everyone present and holding it in the palm of his hand.

All chatter ceases to exist as we watch him settle behind the podium, adjust the microphone stand higher, and pull his shoulders back. His chest puffs out as he grips what looks like a notepad and begins to speak.

"Good evening, everyone. I'm Mackenzie Thompson, one half of Brenton and Thompson Marketing here in Toronto. Firstly, I wanted to thank you all for joining me tonight. Secondly, on behalf of myself and Lilah Clevance, the founder of the Save A Home Foundation, we wanted to thank you all again for not only helping us reach our original goal of one hundred thousand dollars, but for going above and beyond. So far tonight, we've raised two hundred and fifty thousand dollars for our Toronto foster care system."

Clapping erupts around us, and Mack's smile grows brighter. I spot Gretchen standing off to the side of the stage, somewhat hidden behind a thick black curtain. Her lip is tucked between her teeth as she watches her boss, a faraway look flickering across her doll-like features.

"He's a good man," Braden whispers, kissing my bare shoulder and drowning out Mackenzie's voice. "I like him."

I laugh softly and lean my head against his. "Me too. Although I don't think we're the only ones."

Braden follows my gaze, and his shoulders shake with a silent chuckle. Gretchen thinks she hides her emotions well, but if you know what to look for, you can see right through her. There's nothing hidden in the way she watches Mackenzie—not now or *ever*—like she would lie down on a bridge of hot coals and let him walk over her just so that he didn't have to burn the soles of his feet.

"He's the same way. Stubborn fucker doesn't even see it."

Unfortunately, he's right.

With a sad shake of my head, I'm looking back at the man in question, tuning back into his speech as he finishes up.

"Dinner will be served in a few minutes, but both myself and Lilah will be around to chat and answer any questions you have. Enjoy the rest of your evening."

He exits the stage quickly before stopping short in front of Gretchen. I catch the tug of her mouth as she speaks before freezing with her lips parted. Then Mack's pulling her against his chest and lifting her feet off the ground, spinning them around.

I'm still watching them like a creep when Braden's phone starts ringing. Removing his hand from my thigh, he slips his phone from his suit jacket and answers it quickly after seeing the name on the screen.

"Hey. Is this important? I can't really talk right now."

Surprise flares in his dark brown eyes, and my spine goes ramrod straight.

"Fuck. Okay, yeah, we'll make it. Keep me updated, okay? Don't go fucking silent on me, Tyler."

I'm smacked with a thousand reasons as to why Tyler would be calling and why Braden looks like he's about to curl over and vomit. My hand finds Braden's shoulder and stays there, unmoving.

"I got it. We'll be there as soon as we can. Go back to your wife. I'll let you know when we're there . . . Okay. Bye."

"What's wrong?" I ask as soon as he pulls the phone from his ear.

Kissing the knuckles of the hand resting on his shoulder, he lets out a shaky breath. "Gracie's in labour. We need to go to Vancouver. Right now."

28

Braden

I'M GOING TO BE AN UNCLE. TYLER IS GOING TO BE A FUCKING father. We're *both* going to be fathers.

How the hell did that happen?

My head is a jumbled mess as I slip my arms through my suit jacket and help Sierra to her feet, even as she rolls her eyes and assures me she's pregnant, not broken.

I'm pretty sure that I'm grinning, feeling way too excited to get to Vancouver, but my face has been numb since I heard Tyler's voice.

Fuck, it hit me harder than I expected to hear him be anything but the arrogant little shit he usually is. His nerves were evident in the way his words shook and the loud gulps that flowed through the phone. It probably hit me harder knowing that in just a few months, that's going to be me.

"You're not seriously leaving," Cole sniffs, sounding almost offended. Of course he would be. How dare we not stay and soak in his presence all night.

Asshole.

"We have somewhere else to be," Sierra retorts while slipping her arms through her jacket.

Cole rolls his eyes so hard I wonder if they'll get stuck at the back of his head. "Convenient."

"Fuck off, Cole," I grumble.

His chair scrapes across the floor when he stands abruptly. His jaw is clenched so tight I'm surprised he hasn't broken any teeth. Who knows, maybe he's leaving that honour for me.

"Can I talk to you outside, Sierra? This can't wait for Monday morning."

My arm slips around her waist as she stiffens. "We really need to go. Maybe you can email it to me."

That's apparently the wrong thing to say because Cole's eyes flash with something violent, making me push Sierra behind me. My brows climb my forehead, this fucker's entire existence a complete thorn in my side.

"Oh, like you emailed me about being pregnant with this incompetent, wannabe fighter's baby instead of telling me face-to-face? Why would you get yourself into this mess, Sierra? He's nowhere near good enough for you."

His words settle in my stomach like shards of glass. He's so angry, so *bitter*, that I can almost smell his hatred in the air. Flat palms glide over my back, drawing my attention long enough for me to notice the several sets of eyes watching us with such curiosity it makes my skin crawl.

"You know what, big guy? I think taking this outside would be a great idea," I growl, gesturing toward the exit. When Cole doesn't move, I look over my shoulder at Sierra, softening my voice as I say, "Think you could find Mack for me? This shit has gone on too fucking long."

She looks hesitant, possibly a little scared—not like I can blame her. "I don't want to take away from his night with this drama."

I can't help but smile. "Trust me, he won't want to miss this. I'll find you after."

"Okay," she exhales. "I'll get Mackenzie. Please don't hurt yourself. Tyler and Gracie don't need to be worrying about you on top of everything else."

I grab her chin between my fingers and lift, making our gazes lock before I'm capturing her mouth in a claiming, demanding kiss. A shiver moves through her when she kisses me back just as hard. With a nip to her lips, I pull back and glide my thumb along the top of her cheekbone.

"Don't have too much fun without me," she teases lightly before slipping away in search of Mack.

With Sierra gone, I turn my attention back to Cole. Hatred swirls in my blood, making it bubble in my veins. "Either you can walk yourself out of the building, or I can drag you out in front of all of these people. Pick."

He stares back at me with a grin that has my stomach swirling.

"You're quite demanding, Braden. Sierra didn't strike me as the type to enjoy being bossed around, but maybe that's what I was missing. Perhaps I was *too* nice."

"Don't talk about her. This is the only warning you're going to get," I say slowly, with a sense of calm that I sure as shit don't feel. "Let's go."

Thankfully, he starts walking toward me before I have to toss him over my shoulder. He narrows his eyes and bumps past me, taking the lead. I squeeze my eyes shut for a few seconds and exhale slowly before following him out of the ballroom. It's easy to ignore the gawking guests now that Sierra is gone and no longer being scrutinized. She didn't need that shit.

Cole stomps his way through the sliding doors at the entrance of the hotel hosting the gala, and I pick up my pace, meeting him outside before he has a chance to shake me and take off.

The wind is strong tonight, swaying through the trees that

bend and curve awkwardly, creating loud *whooshing* noises around the parking lot that sound a lot like when you place an empty paper towel roll to your lips and shout.

I'm surprised when Cole willingly moves along to the side of the building, finding a place in the shadows that the street lamps and headlights can't reach instead of being a pussy and staying in plain view.

"If I didn't know any better, I would think that you've dragged me into the dark with plans of beating *my* ass," I shout over the wind and the few feet of distance between us.

Cole's hands find his hips, his fingers curling. He shakes his head furiously. "You're not going to touch me, Braden."

"I'm not?"

"Not unless you want me to press charges, you're not."

I can't help it. A booming laugh scrapes up my throat, and my head falls back.

"Do you know what a hypocrite is, Mr. Big Shot?" I ask with a wicked grin. Cole blinks at me, unimpressed with my question. "See, if you were to press charges against me for whatever it is I'm going to do to you, then it would be completely plausible to expect Sierra to press charges against you for sexual harassment, don't you think?"

He takes a brave step forward, fists shaking at his side. There's no hiding the outrage burning in his eyes. I've just struck a cord deep inside of him, one that he didn't want me knowing he had.

"I didn't sexually harass her!" he roars, taking another step closer.

"You touched her without permission, you fucking scumbag! She's never given you any reason to think you could lay a single finger on her. But you did it anyway. You took what you wanted because that's what you think you deserve, right?"

I don't give him time to answer.

"Well, now I'm going to break every single bone in your hand so that you won't forget what happens when you touch somebody like that without their permission. The next time you think of doing this again, you'll feel the pain of your bones snapping and hear the tremble in your cries like it's happening all over again. Because it will happen again. Mark my words, Cole Travis. Touch somebody else the way you did Sierra and I'll come back here and fucking end you."

I stalk toward him, watching with the same unwavering smile as he fumbles back a step, and another, and another until he collides with a brick wall. *Stuck*. He's stuck.

"You gave her a promotion, so she owed it to you, right?" My voice is shaking, but I'm not sure if it's from the outrage burning inside of me or the pain I feel thinking about him touching Sierra.

"She didn't tell you no. So in your fucked-up mind, that meant yes, right?"

Against my better judgment, my arm shoots out in front of me, and my knuckles collide with the bricks beside his head. He gasps, eyes bulging while I suck a pained breath through my teeth.

Fuck. I can't wiggle my fingers.

I'm towering over Cole as I tightly grip his right wrist with my non-aching hand and lift it beside his face, pinning it against the scuffed brick. The maneuver is a bit uncomfortable and leaves my entire side open and vulnerable if he decides to fight back, but I'm not about to try and test the extent of my hand injury. I definitely broke something.

"You're not really going to do this," Cole stammers, struggling a bit against the wall. I tighten my grip on his wrist until I know that he'll have bruises the shape of my fingertips in the morning.

"You're right. He's not. We both are, shit for brains," a familiar voice spits, the deep tenor swirling in the wind.

I don't turn around to face Mack—not wanting to risk Cole making a run for it—but I know he's close. Worry threatens to knock me off my feet when I think of Sierra and where she is. Is she here too?

"You can't do shit to me, Thompson. Clark won't let you touch me," Cole spits venomously.

"No? Even if a sexual harassment lawsuit with your name on it threatened to dismantle the entire Toronto branch? News flash, Cole. Clark doesn't give a shit about you. He only cares about what you can do for him," Mackenzie states, coming to stand beside me. "And your value has quickly depleted."

I can feel my friend's eyes on my busted hand but merely shrug in hopes he'll leave it alone. There's nothing we can do about it now. The sooner we get this done with, the sooner I can find my girl and get on a plane to meet my niece or nephew. I'll see a doctor then.

"You're done, Cole. After tonight, we better never see you again." Mackenzie brushes me to the side and replaces my hold on Cole's wrist with his own. When he uses his free hand to pull something clunky and shiny from his jacket pocket, my jaw nearly unhinges. He holds his hand out, palm open and face up.

"Fucking brass knuckles? You're a badass, Mack." I take the unexpected weapon from him and slip the cold brass over the knuckles on my left hand. It's not the first time that I've felt this type of heaviness on my hand, but it's never been on my nondominant hand.

I hesitate for a moment, my muscles growing tense. If Sierra is nearby, there's no way that I can do this. She doesn't need to see or hear this.

Like he's read my mind, Mack shifts his weight and leans over to me, whispering, "She's already on her way back to her place. Just take care of this quickly."

I nod, relaxing slightly. As soon as Cole realizes what's about to happen, he starts to really resist Mack's hold, struggling and clawing at him. Mackenzie has to pin him to the wall with a forearm to the throat to gain some leverage. It's about time the piece of shit realizes that he isn't getting out of this.

My fingers tingle like they know what's about to happen and can't hold back their excitement. I roll my shoulders back and close my left hand into a perfect fist.

"I warned you back at that restaurant what would happen if you so much as talked to Sierra again, but I never would have given you the chance to walk away so easily if I had known what happened while I was gone. Now you'll pay for what you did to her."

Cole's scream vibrates through the night when the brass knuckles make contact with the back of his hand, crunching the bones, leaving his hand utterly useless. Mackenzie lets go of his wrist and steps back. We watch the tears stream down Cole's face as he cradles his shattered hand and kneels over, vomiting on the pavement.

"Get the fuck out of Toronto, Cole. I never want to see you again," I spit.

My lips curl in disgust as I slip off the knuckles and hand them back to Mackenzie. He silently slips them back into his jacket as we turn around and leave Cole to figure out what to do next before somebody comes to investigate the screams.

"Did she take a cab?" I ask him, finally lifting my hand up under a stream of light flooding the parking lot and wincing at the swollen, bloody mess.

"Gretch drove her home."

I let out a breath. "Thank you. For everything."

Mack snorts. "You're welcome, man. He deserves a lot worse."

"Yeah, he does."

We come to a stop in front of a row of parked cars when he jingles a set of keys between us. "Let's get you back to your girl."

"You're okay with leaving your party so early? I can take a cab," I protest. As much as I hate cabs, I'm not about to steal him away from such an important night.

He lifts a shoulder. "They don't need me. The important stuff is over."

"Alright then. Let's go."

29

Sierra

The second I hear the front door click shut, I'm dropping the sweatshirt in my hands and rushing from the bedroom. With my heartbeat in my ears, I run through the apartment and release a tight breath when I see Braden in one piece, slipping off his dress shoes.

"You scared the hell out of me, you asshole." I'm pissed off, but that doesn't stop me from throwing myself at him or planting kisses all over his face while he binds his arms around me.

"I'm sorry for worrying you, baby," he whispers.

"What happened?" I plant my hands on his chest and push back, searching his face for any sign of an injury. When I come up empty of anything but exhaustion in his eyes, I step back, forcing his arms to drop to his sides as I search the rest of him.

"It's a long story," he replies far too calmly.

Glacier water fills my veins when my eyes fall to his hands. Or specifically, the swollen, bloody mess that's left of his right one. My breath catches.

"What the hell did you do, Braden?" I yell, gently taking

hold of his wrist. He hisses through clenched teeth when I lift it to take a closer look at his hand, but he doesn't pull it away.

His knuckles look like they've stopped bleeding, but the side of his hand is already bruised and swollen enough that his pinky doesn't even resemble a finger anymore. His left hand is a bit red and angry-looking, but nothing that has me even half as worried as his right hand does.

"Got into a fight with a wall. It'll be fine. Once we get to the hospital, I'll get it looked at. But we don't have time to worry about this right now. I'll wrap it up, but then we need to go. My dad already booked our plane tickets, but our flight leaves in two hours."

I scoff but lower his hand, releasing it. As much as I would love to fight him on this, he is right about being on a time crunch. Two hours doesn't leave us enough time to get him to a hospital.

"I'm almost done packing. Let me at least clean it up for you. You can tell me why you punched a wall and what happened with Cole while I'm doing it."

He looks like he wants to put up a fight but thinks better of it. "Yes, ma'am."

I level him with a hard stare. "Sit down. I'll get the first aid kit."

After receiving a fake salute, I go to the bathroom and collect everything I need. Braden has his eyes closed and his head resting on the back of the couch when I return.

"Start talking."

With his eyes still closed, he says, "Cole Travis is no longer someone that you need to concern yourself with."

"That's not ominous at all." I snort, dropping to my knees and digging through the first aid kit. "Care to elaborate?"

After twisting off the cap of a bottle of peroxide, I wet a face cloth and gingerly hold his wrist to keep him still while starting to dab at his blood-crusted knuckles. Braden barely flinches as I clean his hand, but his eyes are beating down on my face, watching me.

"Mackenzie fired his scummy ass, and then I broke his fingers like I told you I would."

My brows fly to my hairline. Braden did what? With my head reeling with this new information, I ask, "Mack fired him?"

He chuckles. "Yeah, sweetheart. He did."

"Did Gretchen know he was going to do that? Because she didn't say anything to me about it when she drove me home."

"Do you really think that she would have been able to keep that a secret if she knew?" I chew on the inside of my lip and shake my head once. He grins. "Exactly. Gretchen didn't know. I promise."

"Okay," I whisper. Cole being gone seems almost too unbelievable. Too far-fetched.

Braden told me that he would take care of it, but I tried not to get my hopes up about it. Cole deserved far worse than a few broken bones and the task of having to find a new job, but if that's what it took to get rid of him, then all I have to say is *good riddance.*

Blowing out a breath, I drop the cloth beside me and lean forward to make sure I haven't missed any blood. I hold back a wince when I focus on the angry bruises that decorate his skin. The swelling and crooked shape of his pinky are the most concerning parts of his injury, though.

"I'll be okay, Sierra. We have more important things to do right now than worry about a potentially broken bone," he says gently, using his left hand to palm my cheek. His thumb traces the length of my bottom lip.

I look up at him and lean into his touch. "You have to promise me that you'll see a doctor as soon as you can. You can't risk not getting it checked out. You're a boxer, Braden."

"I will get it checked out. I promise. Now please kiss me."

A laugh bubbles up my throat as I use his knees to help push myself up and lean over his lap, pressing my mouth to his. He nips my bottom lip and grabs the back of my head when I try to pull back too soon.

"Not yet, you don't," he growls before his lips are back on mine in a desperate, passionate kiss that has my toes curling in my socks. A steady arm moves behind my back and pulls me closer until our knees are knocking, and my hands slip up his thighs.

My eyes slide shut as I kiss him back, hoping to God he can feel my appreciation for him and what he did through our clash of teeth and lips.

The only person who has ever thought to do something like this for me is my sister. But Braden . . . Braden didn't hesitate to put himself in harm's way to protect me. That realization has the world tilting around me.

I lose track of how long we stay in his position, but once my lungs start to burn from lack of oxygen, I pull back again, and this time he lets me, breathing just as hard as I am.

"Thank you. For everything that you did. I still don't know what to say," I murmur, staring into his warm eyes, soaking up the love shining brightly in them. I'm not sure that I'll ever get used to being looked at like this. Like I'm *everything* to him.

He gives his head one firm shake. "Don't thank me. I would do it a million times over for you."

And without a doubt, I believe him.

GRACIE BATEMAN IS A CERTIFIED BADASS. I'm in awe of how perfect and put together she looks not even twenty-four hours after giving birth to a nine-pound baby boy. Hair held up in a bun, not a stitch of makeup on, and a grimace on her face whenever she moves around, she still looks like a runway model.

On the small hospital bed, Oliver Bateman lies curled up on his mom's chest, a head full of ink-black hair nuzzling her breast over top of her silk, baby pink pyjamas. He's fast asleep in a milk coma as his family watches him closely, several curious faces anxious to get a chance to hold him and kiss his soft, smooth cheeks.

Gracie's brother, Oakley, sits at the foot of the bed, a large inked hand wrapped around her ankle. His wife, Octavia—or Ava as she told me to call her—sits beside Braden and me on the small couch resting beneath the large window with a horrible view of the opposite side of the hospital. Tyler hasn't moved from her bedside since we arrived, and I would be lying if I said that didn't make my heart double in size.

There's such a profound love radiating off the otherwise intimidating man as he stares down at his wife and son, like he's in utter awe of them. His fingers timidly trace the edges of Oliver's face before stroking his head and the soft hair that covers his small, round head.

A quiet knock on the door startles everyone before it slowly opens, revealing another unfamiliar face.

Smiling crookedly, an incredibly wide-shouldered man walks into the overcrowded room. There's a young boy clinging to his back like a spider monkey, but he doesn't seem to mind as he tightens two large hands around the boy's knees and holds him close. With his foot, the man closes the door and joins the rest of us.

"Adam," Gracie squeaks, careful not to wake the sleeping baby. "You made it."

Humour lights up Adam's face. "You doubted me, Little H? Come on."

I must laugh a bit louder than I intended to because it

captures Adam's attention. My mouth automatically slams shut when he stares at me, seemingly bewildered at my presence.

"You're actually real," he states, eyeing me with a reserved stare, like he's trying to convince himself I'm not a damn figment of his imagination. "And really pregnant."

"Adam, dude." Oakley cracks up. "Don't be a shit."

Glancing down at my belly, I let out a very unattractive snort. "Yep. Very real and very pregnant."

Braden stifles a laugh beside me. "Did you think I was lying?"

"Can you blame me?" Adam counters. "You go from being allergic to commitment to having a baby in less than a year and expect me to believe you?"

"Everyone else believed me!"

"I did kind of doubt you until Gracie showed me some pictures after Christmas," Ava says sheepishly.

Adam feigns offence. "Why didn't I get to see these pictures, then?"

"You didn't ask."

"How was I supposed to ask when I didn't even know they existed in the first place?"

"Oh God, don't start," Braden pleads. "It doesn't matter. Just tell my girl it's nice to meet her, and go meet my nephew."

Adam's lips tug up in the type of smirk that rivals Braden's. Sly, thrilling, and dangerously attractive. His brown eyes fall on me again, more open than a few moments ago. "It's a pleasure to finally meet you, Sierra. This monkey on my back is my son, Cooper."

I smile warmly. "It's great to meet you both. I really appreciate everything that you've done for Braden and Knockout the past few months."

Adam's large hand cuts through the air. "We're family here. That's what we do for each other."

I nod, deciding not to say anything else as I lean into Braden's side, letting the familiar scent of laundry detergent and a combination of spices that I can never pinpoint make me feel that sense of home that only he can bring me.

Grasping the hand he has resting on his thigh, I squeeze it tight, like I'm scared that if I'm not holding on to him, he's going to somehow disappear. And in all honesty, that's exactly what I'm afraid of.

The feeling of Braden's eyes on me, no doubt bright with curiosity, nearly has me pulling him out of the room and into a storage closet just so that I can kiss him over and over and remind him that he's stuck with me. But I settle for the soft strokes of his thumb on my wrist, knuckles, and palm instead, finding comfort in whatever I can get.

The heaviness of these feelings doesn't subside, though. No matter how badly I wish them away. They're blasting through my head, reminding me that I've handed away a piece of my heart to someone else. Someone who could take it and run.

I've always been fine on my own. The only people that I had grown to need over the course of my life were my sister and my niece. But that's changed so drastically over the past year. Now I don't think that I could survive in a world without Braden. Without his flirty jokes and expert-level kisses. Or his burnt pancakes on Sundays and foot rubs that always lead to us spending hours in the bedroom.

The guy I met at Sinners was only a piece of the man I know now, and there's no doubt in my mind that I want to spend every day for the rest of my life falling in love with the rest of his missing pieces.

Ava uses the break in conversation to get off the couch and move toward Adam, holding her hand out for the boy that seems to have no intention of letting his feet touch the ground. "Coop, come sit with me so your dad can say hi to Gray and the new baby."

Cooper hesitantly moves his face from where it's hidden behind Adam's neck and looks at Ava with a smile so sweet I have to fight the urge to awe out loud. The young boy is a spitting image of Adam with that thick, dark brown hair that curls behind his ear and round, deep chocolate eyes that hold so much light. He's even got the same natural pout in his bottom lip and soft curve of his nose.

With a quick look of approval from his dad, Cooper loosens his hold and drops his feet to the ground.

"What have you been feeding this kid? He looks even taller than when I last saw him," she says as she walks back to the couch and flops down beside me. Cooper settles on Ava's lap and leans back against her chest.

I offer him a small smile when he turns his head and his eyes slam into mine, surprised and cautious. I'm an unfamiliar face in an even more unfamiliar place, and from what I can tell, he's a shy kid. His long eyelashes brush his skin as he blinks at me before turning away and watching his dad.

Braden's presence slams into me when he presses closer, whispering, "Coop doesn't do well with strangers, baby. Don't take it personally. His mother did a number on him."

My brows tug together. "What do you mean?"

"Later, fighter. Adam doesn't like to talk about her."

Even though my curiosity is piqued, I agree with a single nod. It's really none of my business anyway.

Adam's facing Gracie, Tyler, and Oakley now, but he answers Ava with a clear smile in his voice. "He eats me out of house and home, O. I'm sure he even eats more than your husband nowadays. Ain't that right, Mr. Vegan?" he asks Oakley while smacking his shoulder and squeezing.

"Really, Tyler?" Oakley grumbles, tilting his chin to glare at his brother-in-law. Tyler offers a shrug.

Adam moves around Oakley and kisses the top of Gracie's head. "How are you feeling, mama?"

Dropping her chin to Oliver's head, she sighs happily. "Sore. But it's nothing compared to how at peace I am. I feel complete, ya know?"

He hums in agreement. "I'm glad, Gray. Being a mom fits you."

My hand falls to my swollen stomach and moves in wide, slow circles. I might not know exactly how Gracie is feeling yet, but I have a pretty good idea.

With every day that passes, the connection I have with our baby grows, forming something unbreakable and honestly, a bit unbelievable. My excitement climbs with each kick and roll that I feel, with every baby book we buy and tiny shirt we fold.

The fear that's plagued my mind since the moment I found out that I was pregnant is fading, replaced with an overwhelming sense of longing.

Soon, I remind myself for the thousandth time.

I blink away the blur in my vision and focus on the two fists connecting in the air above Gracie. Adam and Tyler share a long look before they both break out in cheek-splitting grins.

"Who would have thought being a dad would look so damn good on you, man," Adam teases.

Tyler rolls his eyes, acting tough, but his smile betrays him. "Could say the same about all of us guys here."

"Maddox can't wait to meet Oli, by the way," Oakley says.

I shuffle through all of the information Braden shot at me about his friends and their families on the plane ride here before remembering that Maddox is Oakley and Ava's three-year-old son.

"Don't call him Oli," Tyler grunts. "It sounds like loli. Kids at school will be calling him lollipop before he even hits the first grade."

"Sorry, Ty. It's already decided. Good luck trying to convince a toddler otherwise," Oakley retorts.

"I think it's adorable," Gracie chimes in. "Plus, it's only fair. We call Maddox Doxxy, and there's no way in hell I'm going to stop once he gets older and starts to hate it. Nick-names are a family privilege."

Cooper laughs in Ava's arms.

"You think that's funny, do you, Coop?" Oakley teases him.

"I'll always call him Doxxy. Even when he strongly dislikes it," Cooper states proudly, his chest puffed out.

Everyone laughs, and Cooper's cheeks turn a deep red before he's tucking his face in Ava's shirt.

I suck in a sharp breath when the baby shifts around in my stomach and I get an intense urge to pee. After wiggling around uncomfortably for a few seconds, unable to get rid of the feeling without having to leave the room, I give up and stand.

Looking down at Braden and the alarm that flickers across his face, I say, "I'll be right back," and make sure he's relaxed again before leaving Gracie's room, the door shutting softly behind me.

The pungent hospital smell was much fainter in her room —most likely because of how many of us were in such a small space—but now attacks my nose with full force.

There's the faint sound of another baby crying somewhere on the maternity floor as I walk down the hallway, passing a few nurses in pink scrubs and a doctor with a scrub cap on that reminds me a lot of something I would find on *Grey's Anatomy* before I find the washroom.

I'm humming under my breath when I push open the

door and ram boobs-first into something—or *someone*. An apology is on the tip of my tongue before it shrivels up and dies.

The aged scowl in front of me is too familiar. I gulp. "*Mom*?"

30

Braden

My eyes wander to the clock above the door, a weird feeling slithering in my bones. It's been fifteen minutes since Sierra left to go to the bathroom, and I've been sitting here nearly the entire time squeezing my knees.

I know that there's a thin line between being protective and smothering, which is why I've waited this long before chasing her ass down. But as the time continues to tick away, the more intense this gnawing in my stomach grows. Something feels wrong.

"You look like you're the one that needs the bathroom, Braden," Adam teases. "Maybe you should have gone with your girl."

My frown deepens as I look from the clock and to the single dad. "She's been gone a long time, right?"

"She's over halfway through her pregnancy," Gracie says lightly. "It gets harder to do simple things the further you get. Give her a few more minutes."

A rumble fills my chest at the idea of waiting any longer when I have such a strong feeling that something could be wrong. I should have gone with her in the first place.

"If you're that worried, just go check on her," Tyler pipes up from the other side of the room.

He's holding Oliver now, staring down at his son with a look so warm it could melt ice. There's so much love in his eyes, so much protectiveness. My brother would burn the world to the ground for his wife and baby. Just as I would for Sierra and our baby.

I tear my eyes from them when jealousy scrapes my insides like barbed wire. It's completely irrational to be jealous over something that I will have in only a few months. But I'm getting antsy.

Antsy to hold and smell and love our baby.

Antsy to watch my beautiful woman become a mom.

"Yeah. I'm going to do that. Be right back." I'm off the couch and out the door in a matter of seconds.

My head moves in all directions as I stalk down the hallway in search of the bathrooms. Panic starts to bear its ugly head the longer it takes me to find her. Irrational or not, I can't shake this fucking feeling.

I almost shout in relief when I see the familiar stick person that marks the women's washroom. I lunge for the door, about to whip it open, when I hear a set of hushed voices from behind it.

"Don't. You don't get to say anything about this." *Sierra.* I would recognize that voice anywhere.

The other voice is high in pitch and carries the slightest bit of an accent that I doubt I can pinpoint. It almost sounds like a mix of several different ones.

"You're unmarried, you don't own a home. You've barely even started your life. How could you let something like this happen?"

The silence that follows is haunting. I want to let Sierra handle this on her own, but there's no way that I can stand here and let her be talked to like that. My muscles are taut, pulled so tight I'm afraid they might snap like an over-stretched elastic band. Pain radiates from my palms, and I release my hands from the fists they've become.

"You don't know anything about my life, Mom," Sierra exhales, sounding defeated in a way that has my feet begging to bring me to her. "You haven't known anything about me or my life since I was a little girl."

I had a feeling that the posh-speaking woman was Sierra's mother, but hearing her confirm it makes me pull open the door and join the two women in the bathroom. Shock and panic flicker across Sierra's face when she realizes what's happening, but I don't do anything more than wrap my arm around her waist and kiss her temple before facing her mother.

Anger is a dangerous emotion. It almost always has a way of bringing out someone's true intentions and feelings that they've kept hidden. For Sierra and her mother, that couldn't be a truer assumption.

Dina Caster narrows her eyes on me, on the tattoos that cover my bare arm, the scars on my face from years of fighting, and the splint on my right hand. I already knew she wouldn't like me. Wouldn't see me as a worthy match for her daughter. But seeing the disgust in her eyes still feels like a crowbar through the ribs.

"The baby daddy, I'm assuming," she sneers, venom dripping from every word.

Trying not to laugh, I realize that not only does Sierra have nothing in common personality-wise with this woman, but she doesn't look anything like her either.

Sierra's hair is a warm brown, like a cup of coffee with too much cream, while Dina's hair is so dark it's almost black. Her mother's eyes are a steely blue, not the molten silver that I see even in my sleep. Pale, porcelain skin and a bronze tan that comes from being out in the sun for hours on end. Tall and short. Curved and thin. They are complete opposites. In every way.

I don't bother holding my hand out for her mother to shake, knowing full well she would probably spit on it. There won't be any winning this woman over, but hell if I'm not going to try and help her understand the mistake she's making by continuing to mistreat her daughter. It's clear that I have nothing to lose when it comes to this woman.

"Braden, actually. But baby daddy does have a nice ring to it," I say while pulling Sierra even closer and brushing my thumb along the side of her belly. She wraps an arm around my front, keeping us close, not bothering to hide her affection from her mother. "And you're the mother."

Her glare tightens. "Dina Caster."

"Why are you even here, Mom? This is a maternity ward."

"A friend's daughter just had a baby last night. I was dropping off some flowers."

Sierra releases a sound of disbelief. "Wow. Lucky her. I wouldn't know what receiving a gift from my mother feels like."

Dina's lips pull taut. "Don't act as though you ever cared whether you received anything from me. You had Clare growing up. She's all you've needed," she snips. The frown lines in her forehead and between her thin eyebrows are deep, like they've been there for years. There's a thick sense of jealousy in her words that I know Sierra latches onto.

"No." She tips her head back and sucks in a steadying breath. "You don't get to act jealous of my sister. She was there for me when you couldn't be bothered. She was more of a mother to me than you ever were."

A mix of guilt and regret slides across Sierra's face the second those hate-filled words fall between them. Dina Caster gasps, a hand to her chest. The temperature in the bathroom drops.

"Well then." Dina straightens, suddenly wearing a mask of indifference. "If that's how you feel, then I'm glad you didn't bother telling your father and I about your pregnancy. He will be just as disappointed in you as I am when he finds out."

My teeth gnash together, and I have to press my mouth to Sierra's temple to keep from mouthing off. If this was anybody else, I would have shoved them out the fucking door by now.

"I stopped caring about your opinion a long time ago, Mom. You've never supported me a day in your life. Why start now?" My heart splits down the middle at the blinding pain in Sierra's voice. It rocks me, the ground suddenly unstable beneath my feet. "Believe it or not, I don't need a house or a wedding ring to know that I'm ready to take care of this baby. You would know that if you had bothered getting to know me over the past twenty-six years.

"You weren't ever involved in our lives. You've seen Elizabeth a handful of times. I wasn't naive to think you would take a sudden interest in my baby. And you know what? That's okay. Clare and I turned out fucking amazing on our own. And *our* baby"—she peers up at me through wet lashes—"is going to grow up surrounded by so many amazing people and so much love that they will never question how special they are, regardless of if you and Dad are involved."

Sierra finishes on a heavy breath before pressing her forehead to my bicep. A warm wetness forms on the sleeve of my shirt, and I know that means tears. Tears that her mother doesn't deserve. I move my hand from her side, dragging it up her back and cupping her neck. She shudders against me, and a broken sound slips from her mouth.

"You have no idea what you've given up," I mutter, meeting Dina's gaze head-on. "I would do anything for your daughter. It doesn't matter what or why. I would do it without a single reason and with a goddamn smile on my face because Sierra means that much to me. She's fucking *everything*."

I'm dizzy, high on adrenaline and the feel of Sierra's body molded to mine. I wait for Dina to say something, but when she just continues to stare at me, unblinking, I decide to continue, letting everything off my chest.

"I had only known Sierra for a few months before I ended up losing her. I made the biggest mistake of my life, and I paid heavily for it. We were only apart for *three weeks.* Yet in those three weeks, I was nothing more than a husk of who I was after being with her. Sierra makes me want to be a better man. A better person, friend, and now a father. So to know that you are okay with feeling even a shard of the loss I felt when I lost her and that you're *choosing* to feel that emptiness? That tells me all that I need to know about you."

The silence is deafening.

But when Sierra curls into me, her face hidden in my shirt, both hands wrapped around my body in a side hug, I know that she's not upset with me. Her swollen stomach pushes into me the closer she tries to move, making her huff. A laugh rattles my chest as I fold my arms around her as much as I can.

"Sierra," Dina scolds. "You're not going to let him talk to me like this, are you?"

My glare darkens, becoming sharp and unforgiving. I try to keep my anger locked down, but when Sierra's mother places her hands on her hips and opens her mouth again, I growl, "Leave," before I can stop myself.

Dina looks surprised, like she can't believe somebody had the nerve to order her around. "Excuse me?"

"Leave, Mother," Sierra mumbles, looking at her over her shoulder. "There's nothing else that needs to be said."

"I'm not leaving. This is ridiculous," she scoffs.

Sierra's eyes bore into mine with a silent question. I nod.

"Then we'll go."

It's almost painful to let her slip from my arms.

Dina blanches. "Sierra."

"I have all the family I need. People who actually care about me. Blood or not. Your opinion doesn't mean anything more to me now than it did ten years ago. Now, if you'll please move, we are here visiting our friends."

When her mother doesn't move, I level her with a stare that has her fumbling out of the way so we can pass.

As soon as we're out of that godforsaken bathroom, I'm pushing Sierra back against a wall and covering her lips with mine. It's a desperate kiss, a raw and vicious claim. A reminder that I'm not going anywhere. Not today, not tomorrow. Not fucking thirty years from now.

"You're mine," I rasp, nipping at her bottom lip.

Fingernails scrape at my neck, Sierra's voice just as needy and possessive as mine. "And you're mine."

31

Sierra

"SURPRISE!"

I clutch my chest as I take in my living room, now full of smiling faces, tables, and decorations. There's a large banner hung above the tables with the words *Happy Baby Shower* written in thick pastel yellow letters. The long white tables are covered with frilled tablecloths the same shade of yellow, one stacked with gifts, the other piled with assortments of snacks and desserts. My stomach goes rogue, growling loudly.

Braden's breath is warm on the back of my neck as he holds me to his chest by my shoulders. "I know surprises aren't really your thing, but I figured you might accept this one."

"It's perfect," I whisper and throw him a grin over my shoulder.

Gretchen, Sophie, Ava, and Oakley stand to the side while Gracie practically vibrates between her husband, Clayton, and my sister.

A mix of nerves and excitement taints Gracie's features before I open my arms and close the distance between us. Her embrace is warm and calming, like a sister's should be. The realization that I've begun to think of Gracie as a sister is an electric shock straight to the heart.

"I'm here too, you brat," Clare scolds teasingly.

"And me," Sophie says, beaming at me.

I'm swapping from one woman to the next as I launch myself at my big sister and wrap her up tight. My words are no louder than a soft exhale. "I've missed you so much."

Clare sniffles in my ear before pulling back and holding me in front of her. Her eyes make a long sweep over me. "I missed you more, S. Look at you. I haven't seen you since your birthday, and now you're damn near about to pop."

"It certainly feels like it. You should see my ankles after a long day," I groan as Sophie, Ava, and Gretch rush over and collect their hugs. Luckily, it's only eleven in the morning and my ankles don't resemble tree trunks yet, or I would have already flopped down on the couch with my feet up.

"Oh my God," Ava chimes in. "I was the exact same way with Maddox. I had to sleep with a stack of pillows under my feet to keep them elevated, or else I would be up all night."

Oakley visibly shudders beside her.

"When do I get to meet your little troublemaker? He's not here, is he?" I ask, looking around the apartment that feels entirely too small all of a sudden. With the body heat from so many people combined with the lack of A/C, I'm grateful for the sundress I slipped on before leaving for breakfast. It's early June, and the heat isn't taking it easy on us this year.

Ava shakes her head at me. "He's with my parents for the weekend. Planes and Dox go together as well as orange juice and toothpaste do."

"Not to brag, but Oliver slept the entire flight here," Gracie says, tipping her chin.

"That's because he's not even four months old. Wait until

he hits toddlerhood," Oakley snorts, pinching the underside of Gracie's arm. She yelps, flicking him in the arm.

Braden continues to hover behind me, kissing the top of my head. "Our baby will be the top dog in this group. So embrace it now, Gray."

Tyler laughs loudly, taking everyone but his wife by surprise. "I sure as shit hope your kid doesn't have nearly as much arrogance as his dad does." He gives me a pitiful look. "Good luck, Sierra. You're going to need it."

"She seemed to do a good enough job with Braden." Clare tosses me a wink.

Everyone hums in agreement while I lift a shoulder and grin. I'm not about to deny it. I know Braden isn't either when he cheers, "Fuck yeah she did."

"Okay, okay." Gracie claps her hands. "Enough chitchat. It's time for the guys to leave. This is a *girls-only* baby shower."

"It is?" I ask.

The five women nod.

Braden rotates my body so that we face each other. His stare is so intense it makes my breath pitch. It looks like he doesn't want to leave, but then again, I don't want him to leave either. I'm not sure if general clinginess can be blamed on an unborn child, but that's what I've been going with over the past few months.

I was expecting to find work exciting again after Cole was fired, but to my surprise, it started feeling more like a prison sentence than anything. Being cooped up in my office day after day has pressed on the wrong nerves. By five o'clock, the only things I want are a healthy dose of fresh air and to feel Braden's arms wrapped around me.

My love for my job isn't the problem, I'm positive about that. I adore my colleagues, my clients, and the work that I do. I think I just want to be at home for a while. Relaxing.

After working so hard with no breaks over the years, I think I've just become worn out and need to spend some time focusing on the people in my life.

I joke that this is all the baby's doing, but in reality, I'm beyond thankful for the sudden change in thought. The last thing that I want is to become too wrapped up in work and my career that I lose track of the other important things in my life.

Braden's words are gentle, almost raspy. "Try not to miss me too much, baby."

"Likewise."

Pushing up on my toes, I kiss him quickly, not wanting to put on a show in front of so many of our friends. But unsurprisingly, Braden seems to have other plans.

I startle when he nips at my mouth and holds me in place with a strong hand around my nape. His tongue swipes my lips, and a soft growl falls between us when I refuse him entrance.

"Open, fighter. I'm not leaving here with a cheap kiss," he whispers, sealing our lips together again, and this time, I let him in for just a few seconds before pulling back, my cheeks flushed.

Clare gags. "Yeah, I could have gone my whole life without seeing my sister get kissed like that."

Kill me now.

Ava coughs to cover her laugh before she's pushing Oakley out of the room, Gracie doing the same with Tyler. Both guys grab Braden by an arm and drag him out with them.

"Bye, ladies. Don't get into too much trouble!" Oakley shouts seconds before the door clicks shut, leaving us five women alone.

Gracie's blue eyes are pure trouble when she moves to the

front of the room. "What do you say? Is it time to get into some mama-approved mischief?"

WITH A VIRGIN MARGARITA in one hand and a mini veggie sandwich in the other, I tip my head back and laugh. My mind is clear, my heart full. Stacks of baby clothes and blankets sit at my feet, surrounded by a mountain of tissue paper that Clare is eagerly stuffing into a garbage bag.

"I didn't even know there were so many brands of bottles," I say, gawking at all of the baby supplies spread along the gift table. "Or soothers."

Ava nods and touches my arm reassuringly. "It can be a bit overwhelming. But once you know what baby likes, it'll get easier."

"I still can't believe that you don't want to know the gender yet," Clare guffaws. "Especially with how much you hate surprises."

"It's such a beautiful surprise, though," Gracie says.

I throw her a smile. "If there was ever a time to make an exception to my 'no surprise' rule, it's right now. Plus, it did make the nursery easier to decorate without having to focus on blue or pink. The yellow we chose is beautiful."

Gretchen leans forward in her folding chair, getting more engaged in the conversation. She was the one who helped pick out the colour of the nursery and started painting after I bailed on our plans and passed out on the couch. She smiles so wide her sparkling white teeth shine. "And the pastel makes it easier on the eyes."

"It's a gorgeous nursery," Ava chimes in. "And you make a good point. I know that as soon as people find out you're having a boy, they assume you want dinosaurs on everything, and if it's a girl, you must want ballerinas or hot pink sparkles. It's easier to just tell them to buy neutral."

"Personally, I think you're going to have a girl." Clare beams, finally setting the full garbage back to the side of the room and plopping down on the arm of the couch. "You might be huge, but you're carrying really high. Plus, it seems to run in the family."

"Don't start with all the hypothesizing." I wag my finger in her direction.

"I could see you having a little girl," Gracie says. The other girls hum their agreement.

"Braden is sure that it's a boy. I have a feeling it's a girl, though."

"Mother's intuition might prove itself after all. You only have a month left. Think you can make it?" Gretchen stretches her legs out in front of her and kicks my foot.

Smiling, I drop my gaze to the giant round belly stretching the material of my sunflower-decorated dress. Excitement swells and blooms in my chest.

"I can make it. We've already waited this long." I rub small circles on my stomach and laugh when something kicks against my palm. Eight sets of eyes focus on me as I continue watching my dress shift with each kick from inside my stomach.

"You said that baby was super active, but I thought you were exaggerating," Clare confesses, slightly in awe.

"I nearly peed myself when I touched her belly and felt a kick for the first time," Sophie blurts out. "I didn't think babies were that strong."

I shake my head. "She gets even crazier when Braden's close by. It seems that we're both a bit obsessed with her daddy."

Gretchen snorts. "A bit?"

I narrow my eyes on her.

"Well, if it isn't obvious enough, Sierra, Braden's utterly obsessed with you. He looks at you like you're the only woman in the world," Ava says, her eyes sparkling. "I've known him for a long time, and I honestly never thought he would ever love anyone the way he loves you."

Gracie joins in. "I second that. Not to mention the fact he's so excited to be a dad. He's surprised us all, I think."

I'm sure that I look like a schoolgirl who's just found out her crush likes her back right now, but I couldn't care less. I know how much Braden loves me and how excited he is to meet our baby, but hearing it from people who have known him for years and have watched him learn and grow and become the man he is today makes it feel that much more real.

"If I can be the big sister here for a minute, guys," Clare says cautiously, like she's scared of what she's about to say and how we'll all react. Ava, Gracie, and Gretchen look weary. Sophie just looks plain annoyed.

"Clare," Sophie warns. "Just be happy for her."

I shoot Sophie an appreciative smile but shake my head, showing her that it's okay. Clare might not have another chance to tell me whatever is brewing inside of her before she leaves again.

Nodding at Clare to continue, I try to prepare myself for whatever she's going to say.

With a weary smile, she says, "I'm always going to worry about my sister. It's my responsibility to make sure that she's happy and taken care of. And I've seen how happy you are, S, but I'm not going to pretend that I don't worry about Braden's ability to take care of you later down the road when life decides to take a shit all over you both, because it will."

The room becomes eerily silent. An ache starts to build in my gut that I immediately want to rip out and toss away. In my peripheral vision, I see the other women stiffen, their spines ramrod straight. Sliding my eyes shut, I gesture for Clare to continue before I start thinking too hard on what she's said.

"Braden still has his own apartment, right? Have you discussed him ditching it and living here with you? What about marriage? You've always wanted to get married, S. Are you really okay with never experiencing that? With giving up that piece of your future?"

It would have hurt less if she slapped me.

My face is pale, cold. A lump builds in my throat that I try to swallow down but fail. Gripping my knees in a white-knuckled grip, I keep my eyes focused on my yellow-painted toes.

I wince at the scratchiness of my voice. "Braden is here every day. Every night and every morning. For months he's been here. He hasn't given me any reason since coming here to believe he would flake on me and this baby." I fold a protective arm around my stomach. "And as far as marriage goes, I used to think that that meant forever. But I know better now than to believe a ring and piece of paper equate to a lifetime of happiness with somebody that I love."

"Are those Braden's words or yours? Because that was the excuse he told me when I asked him the same thing," Clare says tightly, a cold bite to her words.

"You asked him about marriage? When?" My questions are snipped and just as harsh as I intended.

"Christmas."

I blow out a harsh breath and finally lift my darkening eyes to my sister. Her lips are pulled tight in a scowl, her arms crossed and stiff. She doesn't look the least bit sorry or regretful, and that only fuels the anger sparking beneath my skin.

"I don't expect you to understand my choice, and I especially don't expect you to understand Braden's. But I am asking you to at least remember that I'm not someone who can't think for herself. I know that Braden loves me and this baby. I know that he wants to be with me for just as long as I want to be with him. Sure, I wouldn't complain about being married to such an amazing man, but it's also not something that I'm going to let form a wall between us. If it happens, it happens. If it doesn't, then it doesn't.

"I appreciate you caring so much, Clare. But I'm not a little girl anymore. I can make my own decisions. And being with Braden for the rest of my life is the one that I've decided to make."

My sister nods once, a look of acceptance finally slithering across her face, and I release a harsh breath, taking the small win in stride. In reality, we don't need her or anybody else's approval. But having Clare completely in my corner, especially after what happened with our mother, feels better than I thought it would.

32

Braden

THERE WILL ALWAYS BE MOMENTS IN YOUR LIFE WHERE YOU WANT to throw two middle fingers in the air and tell the universe to kiss your ass. But there are also times when you want to drop to your knees and thank whatever god you believe in for blessing you with the life you have and the people you've gotten to meet along the way.

Right now, I'm struggling not to do the latter. At least not while I have an audience.

Sierra's confession has my heart in my throat and my stomach between my legs. I'm gaping at the back of her head like a fucking idiot, but I can't get my feet to move. It's like they've been cemented to the floor in the two minutes since I walked inside the apartment.

The guys were adamant that we should stay out longer, damn near dragging me to a pub to grab a few beers for old times' sake, but all I wanted was to come home and see my girl. And now that I've heard her declare to her sister and all of my closest friends that she wants to be with me forever—everyone else be damned—the few steps between us feel like miles. Too fucking many of them.

Tyler chuckles quietly under his breath before squeezing my arm and giving me a small shove forward. That's all it takes for me to rip my feet from the floor and rush to Sierra.

I round the couch quickly, grinning at the gasp that falls from Sierra's parted lips while scooping her up in my arms and starting to carry her belly-up toward the bedroom.

Her stare is warm with affection, but her touch is blazing hot and greedy as her fingers burn through my T-shirt and brand my skin.

"Thanks for coming, everyone. I'm sure the gifts are great. You can let yourselves out!" I shout once there's some distance between us and everyone else. I turn down the hallway, my steps large and quick. As soon as we walk through the doorway, I'm kicking the door shut behind us and setting Sierra down on the bed.

She falls back, hitting the mattress. Her chest heaves, eyes droopy and clouded with a sheen of need. Pushing up on her elbows, she watches me closely while slowly parting her legs, that fucking dress the only thing keeping me from seeing between them.

I'm beyond caring if anyone's still here and within listening distance. My cock is hard and heavy between my legs—it has been since the moment I heard Sierra declare me her forever. The only thought ringing in my head is to get inside of her and show her that I return her feelings.

With a rumble in my chest, I'm pressing my knees on the bed and sliding my hands up the smooth skin of her legs, from her ankles to her knees. Then I'm pushing her legs up until her thighs brush her belly. Her dress flips up over her stomach, exposing her white cotton panties and the wet spot at the centre of them.

My scruff scrapes the inside of her thighs as I lean in and press kisses along all of that sensitive, silky skin. "Forever is a long time, fighter," I rasp, tonguing the crease of her inner thigh. "Are you sure that's what you want?"

"I'm positive," she breathes, collapsing onto her back, one hand slipping through my hair while the other grips the bedding.

I drag my nose straight up the centre of her slit, groaning when my tongue slips out and follows its path, the taste of her exploding in my mouth. "Then that's what you'll get."

She peels her eyes open, and the barely contained emotion in them has my movements faltering, my thoughts sizzling out into nothing. I stay frozen, knelt between her legs, and can't help but watch as she releases my hair and pushes herself into a sitting position. When she grabs my face in her hands and pulls me up her body, I don't fight. I roll us over instead.

She sucks in a breath that releases as a whimper when I grip her waist and settle her on my jean-clad cock. Silky brown hair falls around her face as she peers down at me and swirls her hips, lips slightly parted and brushing mine. A whisper skips across my mouth. "Are you sure you can handle me for that long?"

My hands drift to her ass and squeeze, using the soft, round flesh to slowly glide her pussy up and down the swell in my jeans. Her breaths are uneven, shuddered. With her pupils blown, she watches me with a deep, predatory hunger that has me grappling for my self-control. It's only been three days since I've been inside of her, but that's a record for us. The last thing that I want is to blow too fast, and right now, with the need I can feel pulsing beneath her skin, that's too big of a possibility.

"Do you doubt how well I can handle you, fighter? Should I remind you?" I ask tightly when quick fingers undo my jeans and gently trace the bulge begging to be released.

Watching me through a blanket of lashes, she yanks down

on my waistband, and I eagerly lift my hips, giving her the room to pull off both my jeans and boxers. I hiss when her small hand wraps around my length and gives it two gentle pumps.

"Yes. You should."

I reach toward her, but she shakes her head, tightening her grip on my cock and collecting the bead of precum that's pooled on the head with her thumb before slipping it between her lips and sucking it clean.

"Jesus fucking Christ," I grunt, barely holding on as she sucks on her thumb and moans a sweet sound of pleasure that has my balls tightening. "Fuck me, Sierra. Slip me inside before I come all over your hand."

A rebel brow lifts, and she tilts one side of her mouth. Reaching between us with her other hand, she tugs her panties to the side, exposing her pretty pink pussy. My head tips back, a raspy noise building in my throat when she slips my cock along her wetness, the tip grazing her entrance for the briefest second, just enough to make my head fucking spin and my hips lurch.

"Say please," she orders. I buck my hips again, pressing my fingers harder into her skin.

"Please," I grit out before groaning not even a second later when she sinks down my shaft, whimpering at the sudden fullness. "*Fuuuck* yes."

Sierra's head lolls to the side, her hands planted on my chest as she anchors herself before starting to move, working my cock with confidence and expertise. She moves like she knows I was made for her. Like every single inch of me is all for her and only her.

She's right in that assumption.

I am hers.

Only hers.

"Forever," I choke out, yanking her dress down to expose

the heavy tits held behind a silky beige bra. Possessiveness has me pinching at her peaked nipples through the material, craving the sounds she makes when I do. Euphoria sinks deep in my bones and ignites a fury of different emotions, all of which have me gasping for breath like I've just run a marathon.

Swiftly, I unhook her bra and toss it away. Her nipples are so hard they almost look painful, but when I roll them between my fingers, the sound she makes is anything but pained. It's pure bliss.

"Forever," Sierra echoes, tossing her head back and scratching at my pecs and thick-cut abs. I savour the burn her nails leave behind, fighting off the urge to beg her to dig deeper and leave me covered with her marks.

My thrusts pick up speed when she starts to slow, her cheeks flushed and a sheen of sweat glistening across her forehead. Brushing her hair from her face, I grasp her chin and lift, forcing her to look at me.

"Come with me," I whisper, staring fiercely into her eyes, holding them hostage.

Sierra nods frantically and makes a high-pitched noise when I slide a hand between us and apply pressure to her swollen flesh. She tightens around me, damn near strangling my cock, and I know that she's about to reach that peak.

"That's it, baby," I coo before gritting my teeth and grunting as a shock wave of pleasure bulldozes into me. Sierra releases a series of curses and bucks on my lap, her eyes damn near crossing with the strength of her climax.

"Braden. Braden, fuck." It sounds like a prayer.

"Take it, fighter. I'm coming," I rasp and thrust a final time, spilling deep inside of her. My thighs are clenched, pulsing. Sierra's uneven breaths mirror my own as her eyes fall shut, and a small smile pulls at her lips.

"I can't wait until I can just collapse on top of you again."

She laughs and pulls off me, releasing a small whimper as I slip from her warmth. Falling back on the bed, she turns her head and stares at me with wonder.

"What?" I ask, tucking myself away in my underwear and grinning wide.

"How long were you standing there listening before you came and stole me away like a caveman?"

I turn on my side and grab her hand, circling her ring finger with my thumb. "Long enough to hear you hand your sister her ass and tell her that you don't need to get married to be happy with me."

"I don't." There's nothing but honesty in her voice, and it makes my heart thump against my rib cage, trying to go to her.

Slipping a hand into the pocket of my jeans, I pull out the shiny silver band that my boys helped me pick out earlier today and swallow my fear. The smallest, almost inaudible gasp escapes Sierra when her wide-eyed stare focuses on the ring.

"Braden, wha—"

I laugh, cutting her off. "It's a promise ring. I know that it's not quite the same as a marriage proposal, but it's a step in the right direction. It means that I *will* marry you one day, my little fighter. If for nothing other than being able to call you Sierra Lowry and making sure that every other man on this earth knows that even on paper, he has no chance in hell with my woman. I swear that I will give you that dream wedding of yours. The one that you told me you dreamed of all those months ago at my father's wedding." Searching her shiny eyes for any sign that points to her not wanting this, I come up empty of anything but contentment and bliss.

A tear slips from her eyes when she nods. "Are you sure? You know that I would never force you into marrying me. I don't need that from you. I know that you love me and that you're not going anywhere," she rushes out.

Clasping her hand, I pull it to my mouth and kiss her knuckles.

"This was all me. I'm not ready yet, but when I am, you will be my wife, and I will be your husband. I was a fool to hold on so tight to the past when my future is so fucking bright. With you by my side. We're surrounded by so many happy couples, all of whom love being married. Both of my parents are happy and have moved on. It's time that I moved on too."

She blinks, and tears cascade down her cheeks. "Oh, my God. I love you."

"I love you too, beautiful." Settling her hand between us, I slip the ring onto her finger and capture her lips in a fierce kiss, one that I hope helps portray the long list of emotions that are zapping through me right now.

Love, excitement, *hope*. Our future's so bright it's blinding.

But I wouldn't dare look away. Not now. Not ever.

33

Braden

LEATHER SCREAMS AS STRAINED VOICES FILL THE GYM. THE captain of the Toronto Timberwolves is throwing perfectly timed punches at the pads covering my outstretched hands as Mackenzie does the same exercise with Laslo, one of my trainers. Sweat flows freely down our skin, soaking into our clothes and hair.

We've been here for the past two hours, training and pushing through things we would rather burn off through gallons of sweat and sore muscles than talk about.

It's been a month since I put a ring on Sierra's finger and two weeks since I dumped my apartment and officially moved into her place. There was really no point in keeping a lease on an apartment that I hadn't even been to in forever, so as soon as Sierra brought it up, I didn't hesitate to agree. We had been unofficially living together since I got to Toronto, anyway.

Sierra's due date was three days ago, and we're still waiting for something to happen. The stubborn baby refuses to come out and meet us, and that feels like a really messed-up form of torture.

Sierra's OBGYN doesn't want to induce her until the beginning of next week, which means that if our baby decides to bake for another four days, we have to just sit here and wait. I've been losing my mind, constantly doting on her, needing something to keep me busy. That's why Sierra kicked my ass out of the house this morning.

"Attention to Braden," Kyle says, smirking when I snap back to reality, barely avoiding a punch.

The confidence on the captain's face has me changing up our drills to throw him off. "Go! One-Two-One-Two-One-Two." His lip curls as his punches speed up before ending the drill with an uppercut that has me stumbling back.

"You're a cheeky fucking bastard, Lowry," he hisses, resting his gloved hands on his hips and tilting his head back, trying to catch his breath.

"Is that a compliment or an insult?"

"I'm going to shower." Tearing off his gloves, he shows me his middle finger before stalking toward his water bottle, not humouring me with an answer.

"I want to keep Lo as my trainer," Mack grunts, finishing a defense drill. "You're a fucking hard-ass, man."

I fake a gasp. "Me? Really?"

Laslo snorts loudly. For a new hire and an even newer friend, he sure doesn't hold back. It's why I like him so much. Well, that and the food his mom brings us every day.

"Stop being a pussy, Thompson. Pay attention before I knee you in the balls." Laslo lifts his gloves higher up his six-foot-three body, and Mack follows with his punches.

"Try it," Mack growls.

I shake my head at their bickering and slip the pads off my hands before stretching out my fingers. Heavy steps pound against the floor, and I spin toward the sound only to stiffen completely.

Kyle's face has gone pale—way too fucking pale—as he

stares at me, unblinking. I tear my stare from his face and drop it to the phone clutched in his hand, the screen open and glowing.

My stomach plummets, fear turning my blood ice-cold. "What's wrong?" I force the words out.

"Your phone kept ringing in your office." He's holding my phone out for me now. "Baby," he stammers.

It's Mack who speaks up, his tone showcasing how little he cares for Kyle's vagueness. "What do you mean *baby*? As in Braden's baby? As in Sierra is in labour?"

Muffled voices come from the phone's speaker. Kyle nods, his eyes clearing a bit as whatever the fuck is wrong with him slips away. "Sierra's water broke. They're on the way to the hospital."

"Give me the fucking phone," I command, rushing toward him. Once I've yanked it from Kyle's grip, I place it to my ear and exhale deeply. "Sierra?"

"Braden," she cries, the sound alone slicing me in half. "Oh my God. You need to go to the hospital. We're on our way."

"Which one, sweetheart? I'll be right there. How far apart are your contractions?"

A few car horns blare around her voice, and another voice flows through the phone. "Braden, it's Gretchen. Sierra's water broke an hour ago, but now her contractions are five minutes apart and getting stronger. I'm taking her to Toronto General. Tell Mack to drive you. I don't trust you not to get in a damn car crash."

Five minutes apart. Getting stronger. Those are the things I latch onto.

My head feels like it's underwater. I hold my mouth open, trying to get words out of it, but nothing comes. Panic is trying to drag me under and fucking drown me.

"Please get there quickly," Sierra begs, her voice sounding

wet and full of so much pain. Hearing her that way has me suddenly bursting out of the gym, not bothering to wait for Mack before heading to his car.

"I'm leaving now. I'll be there as soon as I can," I promise her before tightening my voice and addressing her friend, "Gretchen, text me all the info as soon as you get to the hospital."

"You got it," Gretchen replies as Mackenzie comes busting through the doors and rounds the hood of his car, unlocking the doors. We get in, and he starts the engine when Sierra says, "I love you. I'll see you soon."

I release a shuddered breath and whisper, "I love you, fighter," before she hangs up and Mack pulls away from the curb.

It's time to meet you, baby. About fucking time.

SIERRA'S sob rips through me, tearing my insides to ribbons. She pushes again, for what feels like the hundredth time in the past two hours, and squeezes my hand like it's the only thing feeding her strength.

She's exhausted, her eyes barely open, lips crusted and dry. I keep stroking her damp hair and kissing her clammy forehead, hoping that it's at least doing something to help with the pain she's in. By the time she got to the hospital, she was already too far along to get an epidural.

"The head is almost out, Sierra. On your next contraction, I need you to push really hard," Dr. Spetza instructs, her face firm, concentrated.

"Okay, okay," Sierra breathes, her eyelids fluttering.

"Hey," I murmur, squeezing her hand. "You're almost done, fighter. One more, yeah?"

She dips her chin, and the smallest smile pulls at her mouth before disappearing when the next contraction comes. Sierra pushes hard, a raw yell escaping her as the doctor shouts for her to keep going.

I can't look away from her, not even when the doctor tells us the head is out and the shoulders are next. My heart swells, my knees shaking at the strong tide of emotions that threaten to knock me on my ass.

This is my future wife in front of me, giving birth to *our* baby. I've managed to keep my own feelings on lock while I've been here, not wanting to take anything away from Sierra, but there's no stopping them now.

Tears stream down my face when I hear the first cry, the high-pitched wail that comes from our baby. Sierra collapses on the bed with a smile that I know I'm mirroring.

"It's a girl," the doctor says.

The second the words are said, I'm full-on crying, my shoulders shaking with each sob. My grin couldn't be any bigger as I cut the umbilical cord and return to Sierra's side, kissing her everywhere I can.

"A girl," she cries, grabbing hold of my forearms and bringing me closer until I blanket her entire side. "You were wrong."

I can only nod, not trusting my voice yet.

The baby nurse brings us our girl and lays her on Sierra's bare chest. A tiny pink hat sits on her head, covering a full head of brown hair that I can see peeking out of the sides. She's so tiny that I'm scared to touch her.

Sierra doesn't seem to have that problem as she brushes the knuckle of her finger across the smooth skin of our baby's chubby cheek and coos, "Hi, Tinsley. I'm your mommy."

Our eyes collide when she calls our daughter by her name for the first time, and I nearly choke on a sob. It's like all of the nurses have disappeared and we're the only people in the room.

"It fits her perfectly," I murmur.

I reach for Tinsley's hand and inhale in surprise when she grabs my finger in a tight fist. "I'm Daddy, baby. It's about time you made your appearance."

Sierra laughs. "It was only three days."

"Technically four now," I say, looking at the clock across the room and back at Sierra and the bundle of love cuddled to her chest.

Four a.m. on August fourteenth. That's when our baby girl entered the world and changed my life forever. In the best, most fulfilling way possible.

It's almost fitting that she would make us wait for her arrival, considering her mother had me waiting for her too. And now that I have them both, they're not going anywhere.

"Waiting those four days was more than worth it," Sierra hums, kissing Tinsley's tiny hat-covered head.

I press my lips to Sierra's forehead and whisper with absolute contentment, "Yeah, it was."

EPILOGUE

SIX MONTHS LATER

Braden

Tinsley blows bubbles with her spit as I unclip her car seat and pull her into my arms. She wiggles like a lunatic, as if being held is the last thing she wants, before I try to slip her inside the baby carrier that's hanging open on my chest. I drop her diaper bag onto the curb beside me.

"One of these times, you could at least act like you don't hate being in your carrier instead of scratching at me like a rabid animal," I mutter to the six-month-old, who's trying her damnedest to stay free of the prison strapped to my chest.

Tinsley's only response is to punch me in the chin and blow spit bubbles in my face.

"I was going to give you a few raspberries when we got inside, but after that, I think I'll give you the chicken and avocado purée your mommy sent for you. How does that sound?"

My brow is lifted questioningly as I stare down at a pair of curious blue eyes. Long lashes flutter as she blinks. "No answer to that? That's what I thought. Now, let's go inside before Daddy gets in trouble for being late to work. I'm the boss, Tiny. I have to set a good example."

I quickly flip her around so that she doesn't have to spend the day looking at me before all but shoving her in the carrier, strapping her in tight so that she doesn't end up on the floor of the gym. I throw her diaper bag over my shoulder and walk us inside Knockout.

It's just after ten in the morning, and the main gym is packed. A remix of "Toxic" by Britney Spears plays through the speakers, making me snort. It would seem that Laslo got a hold of the Bluetooth. Speaking of the asshole, he's already walking toward me, his eyes focused on the little girl on my chest.

As soon as he gets close enough, he's cooing at her. "Tinsley, baby, you are absolutely glowing today."

The little traitor has the nerve to give him a big grin, showing off her top tooth. I glare at Laslo and kiss the back of Tinsley's head.

"Take it somewhere else, Laz. This is a daddy/daughter day."

That's what I refer to them, anyway. With Sierra back to working full-time, we didn't want to have to pay for daycare when it's easy enough for me to bring Tiny to work with me most days. When I train on Mondays and Thursdays, she stays with her grandpa Brooks now that he's working from home, taking care of Knockout's books and finances, but every other day of the week, she's Knockout's little helper. And honestly, I wouldn't have it any other way. I love having her here with me.

"Yeah, okay. According to you, every day is a daddy/daughter day. You can't hog her forever," Laslo teases.

"Wanna bet?" I dare him to argue with me.

Grinning, he throws his hands up in surrender before blowing Tiny a kiss. "Your dad is a lunatic, baby girl. One of these days, I'll teach you how to kick his ass."

"If anybody is teaching her how to kick ass, it'll be me, you cocky shit. Get back to work. I don't pay you to stand around talking all day."

Laslo roars with laughter. "Got it, boss."

"I have to check a few things in my office. Let me know before you go for lunch if I don't see you before then."

With a wave, I'm heading down the hallway, a giggling baby on my chest.

Sierra

I wake in alarm, drenched in sweat. Flinging my hand out from under my pillow, I come across cold sheets.

"Braden?"

When no response comes, I shoot up in bed, blinking to try and get my eyes to adjust to the darkness blanketing the bedroom. I can barely make out the time on my alarm clock.

3:42 a.m. My lips tug up, warmth building in my chest.

Swinging my legs over the edge of the bed, I slide on my slippers and put on the Knockout T-shirt Braden left on the floor, covering my naked body. It falls to my knees and still smells like his cologne. I fight the urge to bring the material to my nose and sniff, deciding to go find the source of the smell instead.

A small plug-in light illuminates the hallway, just enough that I don't run into anything on my way to Tinsley's room. Her bedroom door is cracked open an inch, another dim light glowing behind it.

As soon as I shoulder it open enough to enter, I smile, placing a hand over the ache growing in my chest. A good ache. The best kind.

A bare-chested Braden sits in the grey glider chair that I spent far too long picking out, a sleeping Tinsley in his arms. Our six-month-old daughter is sucking away on the bottle in her mouth, all five fingers wrapped around Braden's pinky like she's holding him there, terrified he'll vanish if she lets go.

Braden's lips brush her chubby cheek when he whispers, "You eat like your mom, Tiny. Like you're scared somebody is going to take your food away if you don't eat fast enough."

A giggle escapes me, drawing his attention. Those soft brown eyes meet my tired silver ones before drifting along my body, growing more intense the further down they get. My skin heats under his gaze before I manage to reel myself back in. The last thing we need is to keep each other up the rest of the night.

This is Tinsley's only and last feeding tonight, but Braden and I will be up again in a little over two hours when our alarms blare.

I can't even begin to explain how helpful Braden has been during night wake-ups and feedings over the past six months. For some reason, I was worried that I would never get any sleep as a mother with a newborn baby, but when your baby daddy happens to be a guy who doesn't mind swapping every other wake-up with you or rocking a screaming baby back to sleep when you can't take any more, you get more than enough sleep to still be a decently functioning human being the next day.

Although, I'm sure if Braden had the deciding vote in the matter, I would never have to wake up with our girl again. He would do it all without complaint. That's the kind of father and overall *man* he is.

"She's going to hate that nickname. You know that, right?" I ask softly, walking toward him. His eyes track my movements. When I reach his side, I brush a few stray curls off his forehead.

Tilting his head so that he can still see me, he says, "That's too bad for her."

"Riiight. I'm sure you won't drop it as soon as she opens her wide eyes and flutters those long lashes at you. She already has you eating out of the palm of her hand and she can't even speak yet."

Braden shrugs, eyes sparkling with mischief. "Don't be jealous, sweetheart. You know I'll always eat from your palm. Or anywhere else you want. I'm partial to the paradise between your legs, but semantics."

I roll my eyes. "Okay, Romeo. She's done eating."

Tinsley no longer sucks on the nipple, now in a milk coma, happily curled up in her daddy's arms. Her head of thick brown curls lies messily on her head just like Braden's—another reminder that she got almost all of his genes and so far, not many of mine. We're waiting to see if her eyes lighten from blue to grey or darken to a whiskey brown like Braden's, but if I had to bet, I would say they'll be brown.

My only hope now is that she'll at least inherit my *badassery* as everyone calls it. Sophie bet Clayton fifty bucks that Tinsley will make him cry before her tenth birthday.

"Let me put her down, and we'll go back to bed."

I hum in acknowledgment and kiss his cheek before moving to the side. With heavy eyes, I watch as he slowly gets up, careful not to jostle Tinsley too much, and brings her to her crib. He sets her down like a seasoned pro. She doesn't so much as twitch, just softly coos to herself.

As soon as he turns around, he has me tucked beneath his arm, leading us out of the room and closing the door.

"Have I ever told you that you look good in my clothes?" he asks, fingers tucking under the sleeve of his shirt and rubbing my bare bicep.

"Once or twice."

"Well, you do. You look almost as good with this baggy shirt on as you do without it. I think I need to take it off to be certain."

The rasp in his voice makes my toes want to curl in my slippers.

"Once tonight wasn't good enough for you?" I nearly purr as we walk into our bedroom, the sheets messy, the blanket lying half on the floor. *4:05*, the clock reads. "We have work tomorrow."

I gasp when he pulls me in front of him and walks us toward the bed. The backs of my thighs hit the mattress before I fall backward. Grinning, I push myself up the bed, yanking the blanket over me and tucking it beneath my chin before he has a chance to make good on his threat.

"You're a little shit." He chuckles and crawls in beside me.

I sigh contently when he pulls me to his chest, my head beneath his chin and arm over the ripped muscles of his abdomen. His heat wraps around me, and my eyes fall to half-mast.

"We won't end up going back to bed at all if you get my shirt off, and you know it."

His hum buzzes in my ear, and his hand slides beneath the hem of the shirt, pushing it up so that he can draw circles on my side. "You make it sound like a bad thing."

"It is when it means I'll be showing up to a day full of meetings looking like a freshly fucked zombie."

"That's my favourite type of zombie." I pinch his side, and he flinches, laughing. "Okay, okay. Just sleep."

I kiss his left pec, the skin above his newest tattoo—Tinsley's name, birth date, and handprint from when she was only a few days old. The cursive writing is the perfect mix of both elegant and simple. I'm still not over it, and it's been months. More often than not, I find myself staring at it, all dreamy like, imagining something similar on my skin.

"I think I want to get a tattoo," I blurt out. "Something for Tinsley. Like yours."

The fingers drawing circles on my side freeze for a brief second before moving again. They start drifting to the area right below my right breast.

"Yeah?"

I nod.

"Okay, fighter. I can call my guy tomorrow."

"Thank you," I whisper.

His calloused fingers continue to stroke the skin over the paw-print tattoo I have beneath my boob.

"You know, I've never asked what your tattoo means. It's your only one."

A small smile tugs at my mouth. "It's honestly pretty stupid. I got it on a drunken night that I don't really remember."

"Tell me anyway."

"A group of football players dared Sophie and I to get matching tattoos at a party our freshman year of college. I remember convincing Sophie that we don't need our names tattooed on each other and that matching pair of paw prints will have the same meaning. Don't ask why I chose paw prints—I'm still not sure why I did. Anyway, she got hers on her left ass cheek, and I got mine under my boob."

Fingers brush the underside of said boob. His laugh is raspy, giving away just how tired he is.

"I really fucking wish I knew you back then. Maybe if I did, I wouldn't have dropped out. Seeing you on campus every day would have been more than enough motivation to keep suffering through class."

My grip on him tightens, and I breathe him in, unashamed with how addicted I've become to how good he always smells. "I still can't believe that we went to the same school. Even if it was only for a few months. Something tells me that you were even more arrogant back then than you were when we met, though. I would have hated how attracted to you I was knowing that you were an arrogant asshole."

"You're right about that. I was awful back then. But that wouldn't have stopped me from pursuing you. Once I saw you, you would have been as good as mine. And once I had you—shit, baby. One night wouldn't have been enough. It never was. I knew as soon as I got you in that cab that I would be back for more."

An overwhelming sense of nostalgia floods through me. That first night in Sinners flashes through my head like a picture reel, bringing back memories that I know will never fade.

"I think I knew it too. That's why I took off before you woke up. You reeked of heartbreak, and I had no clue if I was up for the task of taming a player."

His chest rumbles. "Well? What do I smell like now? From how often you smell me, I think it's safe to say I no longer reek."

I move to pinch him again, but his hand captures mine, holding it tight. A thunderstorm of emotions swells in my chest as I link our fingers and finally let my eyes fall shut.

"You smell like mine."

A shuddered breath slips through my hair like a warm breeze. "Good, sweetheart. I am yours."

Forever.

EXTENDED EPILOGUE

FOUR YEARS LATER

Sierra

I GASP WHEN BRADEN'S GLOVE MAKES CONTACT WITH THE underside of his opponent's chin, flinging the bulky man's head back as a collection of blood and spit flies from his mouth and hits Braden's face.

My boyfriend's grin is wicked, making him look more like a naughty schoolboy than the thirty-one-year-old father I've watched grow over the past few years.

Overhead lights flood the room, illuminating Braden's body and the elegance and expertise with which he maneuvers it around the ring. Toes tapping silently, arms fixed in their perfect position. He's as skilled as he is cocky—without limits.

I didn't think that it was possible for him to get any bigger than he already was when we first met, but I should have known better. He's a brick wall of powerful, lean muscles that I won't ever get enough of.

Braden never stops working, never stops trying to get bigger and better than he was the minute before. And he has done exactly that. In every aspect of his life.

I've never been prouder of him.

"Finish it!" Tyler shouts from beside me.

Brooks grunts his agreement before adding, "Stop playing with your food, boy!"

I risk a glance at Braden's father and fight back a smile when he grabs the long, grey hairs on his chin and pulls hard enough to wince. My shoulders shake with a silent laugh.

It was a year after Tiny was born that Grandpa Brooks went full silver fox, and he still hasn't recovered it. Our family sure hasn't made it easier for him either. Not with our constant teasing and poking at him for being so old that he can no longer hide his age behind his youthful complexion. But that's just what we do. We tease and poke and laugh, because we're family.

If there's anything that I've learned over the years, it's that blood doesn't equate to family. And the family that I have now . . . it's everything I've ever wanted. Everything I've dreamed of.

With a scowl, Brooks bumps his shoulder roughly with mine and slants me a look. "Stop laughing at my grey hairs."

"Come now, Brooks, I would never," I reply, looking back at the ring with a grin just in time to see Braden's nose spurt blood before he delivers a punishing blow to the other boxer's lower stomach. Subconsciously, I grip the chain—his lucky chain—hanging from my neck in a tight fist. Braden's opponent curls into himself, stumbling back until he hits the red ropes.

An easy win for Braden.

I've watched enough fights now not to be surprised by the bloodshed or moments of brutality, but watching Braden in pain never gets easier. He lets the referee lift one arm in victory before wiping away the blood staining his lips with the other and grimacing. His eyes catch on me, and I wave wildly, relishing in the barely noticeable softening of his expression as we hold each other's stare.

Even with a gruesome-looking nose and splattered with another man's blood, he's the most beautiful person I've ever seen.

"Ready to go?" Tyler asks, turning to face his father and me. I nod, sending Braden a wink that he swiftly returns with the addition of a blown kiss before focusing on his brother.

"What's the time? We should be getting home to Gracie and the kids soon," I say as we start moving through the crowd and toward the locker room, where Braden will meet us.

Tyler and Gracie have been in town for the past two days while the Vancouver Warriors play the Toronto Timberwolves. And with Braden's match landing during their stay, Gray offered to babysit Tiny so I could come watch.

Tyler and Gracie's newest addition to the family is now a year old, and compared to their eldest son, Oliver, Jamieson is on a whole other level of crazy. He's a spitting image of Gracie, inside and out. And with even more attitude.

Add Tiny into the mix, and I don't even want to begin to imagine what mischief they've caused while we've been gone.

"It's not that late," Tyler replies casually, lifting a shoulder.

"She's got Lana with her too. I'm sure those two can handle a few kids," Brooks says.

"You sure about that?" I ask, laughing.

Brooks is silent for a second before he nods, suddenly a lot tenser than he was a few seconds ago. "You're right. We won't be here much longer."

Tyler taps his fingers against his thigh but doesn't say anything else the rest of the way to the locker room. Neither of them does.

A cold wave of nervousness crashes inside of me when we reach our destination and they still haven't spoken. The men in Braden's family aren't always the most outspoken, but they're never this quiet. Especially after a winning fight.

With my brows two hard slashes on my face, I pull open the locker room door and storm inside. The scene in front of me has my knees quaking beneath me.

All of our family and friends are packed into the room, their faces beaming with a sense of unfiltered happiness that I feel like a sucker punch to my chest. A high-pitched giggle that I would recognize anywhere has me searching for my daughter in the mass of bodies.

"Momma," she giggles, bouncing in place.

Tinsley grins up at me from her place between Oakley and Ava's sons, Maddox and Noah, a mess of dark brown curls and red-sucker-stained lips. Her silver-coloured eyes are wild as she watches me expectantly, like she does when she knows something that I don't.

My curiosity swells, reaching a peak when I don't see Braden in the sea of loved ones.

Someone places a large hand on my back, and I look over my shoulder to see Brooks tip his chin, smiling softly. I tilt my head, preparing to ask him what the hell is going on, when the fighter-only entrance door opens and my bloody man saunters into the room.

"What's going on?" I ask him when he walks my way, swallowing the space between us with confident, determined steps. My breath hitches as he comes to a stop a few feet in front of me.

"Daddy!" Tiny shrieks, clapping her hands furiously. Braden blows her a kiss, and she catches it with a giddy smile.

I take a second to inspect him for injuries and release a breath of relief when I don't find anything that I wasn't already expecting. His nose is swollen but doesn't look broken, and all the blood has been wiped away besides a few dried flecks left on the hard curves of his cheekbones. He's grinning at me by the time I finish looking him over, two rows of perfectly white teeth winking at me.

"You seem nervous, fighter," he teases. His grin grows incredulously bigger, and a set of matching dimples pop in his pink cheeks. "I just won. We should be celebrating."

A compelling force has me moving closer to him. "We should. But can you blame me? Why is everybody here? Have they been here the entire time? And why haven't they spoken a word? It's like being in a room full of wax figures."

A snort resonates from somewhere in the room.

Braden gives his head a quick shake, chuckling low and free. Our eyes meet, and the intensity in his has the air solidifying in my lungs.

"They only got here ten minutes ago. And I made them promise me not to speak before I got here. I knew that if they did, one of them would crack and spill my plans."

"What plans? You're not making any sense."

"Well, if you would just give me a second to explain," he chastises me. I throw my hands up in surrender, and he smirks. "I've been planning on doing this for months now, debating how and when. But with Tiny and our busy schedules, I realized that there would never be a time that I thought was perfect enough for this moment. So I decided that this would be as good a time as any. Now I can finally do this."

Shirtless besides his usual pair of gold shorts, he takes a single step forward before dropping to one knee.

My hands are shaking and ice-cold when I bring them to my mouth in absolute awe. The image of Braden knelt down before me becomes blurred when tears fill my eyes.

"What are you doing?" I inhale sharply, shaking my head in disbelief.

We've talked about marriage over the past four years. It's been an impossible topic to avoid. But I was—*am*—still content with the ring already on my finger. There's been no rush. No pressure laid down at his feet. He knew that if we got married, it would be because he *was* ready for it. I have been ready since the moment I fell in love with him.

Even without a marriage certificate and a wedding ring, there has not been a day in the past five years where I didn't know how much he loves me or doubted his intentions for the future.

We've bought our first house—a small three-bedroom bungalow in Scarborough, only a half hour from both our jobs. Tinsley will be starting kindergarten soon, and we've been discussing trying for a second baby.

Braden's sat beside me, holding my hand as my career blossomed into what I always hoped it would, and when I was promoted into the position left empty by Cole Travis' departure, Braden was the one beaming, telling me, "I told you so."

I've gotten to watch Knockout swell in popularity all throughout Ontario while cheering from my place beside him as Braden finally started to understand just how much potential he's always had hiding beneath that thick layer of self-doubt.

My life is perfect. I'm content. The only thing we could have possibly been missing is this. This moment right here and the prospect of what that could bring us.

Braden's hair flops across his forehead, teasing his brows before he blows it away with a harsh breath that I'm sure was full of nerves. I've forgotten Brooks was behind me until he reaches around me and hands his son a dainty, square velvet box.

I'm standing just close enough to the two of them to vaguely make out the warm, hushed words spoken between the two men.

"I'm proud of you, son," Brooks says.

Braden's eyes shine for the slightest second. He centres himself quickly, blinking furiously. "Thanks, Dad."

All too quickly, his eyes are on me again, making me the centre of his attention. Of his world. My once broken playboy, now an amazing father and partner, looks at me with a stare as soft as cotton. A stare that portrays everything he's feeling but hasn't yet said.

He opens the delicate box with long, calloused fingers, revealing a gold-banded ring with a handful of small diamonds nestled around a large oval-shaped one. My chest feels too small to contain my expanding heart when the first tear splashes my cheek.

"Fuck, baby. Don't start crying on me yet," he laughs breathily. His eyes sparkle and shine when I give him a watery smile. "Never in my life did I plan on feeling love like this. The kind of love that both consumes a person and stabilizes them. But you brought me exactly that. You're my strength when I'm weak and my calm when I'm scared. You are every good, honest part of me. And I want you to be my wife. I know that now more than ever."

"Braden," I whisper incredulously.

He shakes his head once. "You changed my life, little fighter. You've been so patient—even though this has taken me far too long. I was serious when I told you that I would marry you one day. And now, I'm more than ready to be your husband. So, Sierra Genevieve Caster, what do you say? Do you still wanna marry me?"

"Yes, of course I do," I breathe. With two steps forward, we're only a finger's length apart, but it's still too far. In this moment, we can't be close enough.

I grab his forearms, pulling him up before throwing myself at him without a second thought. He catches me with ease, as if he was expecting me to wind up in his embrace.

With strong arms, he pulls me in close to his body, holding

me tight. Pressing his face into my hair, he exhales slowly before saying, "I fucking love you."

"I love you, Braden." I can't hold back my laughter as it slips free.

After holding me for a few seconds longer, Braden pulls himself free, taking the slightest step back before moving the ring box between us, the lid still open. It's nearly impossible to hold back my tears now as I stare down at the beautiful piece of jewelry that I'm going to wear every day for the rest of my life.

He carefully plucks the ring from its holder before handing the empty box back to his dad. I hold my left hand out for him, and he holds it more delicately than he ever has. The gold-banded engagement ring glides up its designated finger, fitting perfectly. The diamond catches the light, and my heart skips a few beats.

"It's gorgeous," I say, finally looking away from the ring and toward my fiancé. A shiver travels up my spine at the new label. It's going to take some time to get used to that one.

I'm not surprised when I find Braden already watching me. His eyes blaze as he says, "It has to be. Look at you."

I tip my head forward, connecting my forehead to his chest and laughing. His arms bind around me again, trapping me in his hold.

"What would you have done if you lost tonight?" I ask.

His scowl is instant. "Not like that would have been even a possibility, but I still would have asked you to marry me, baby. I just would have been a lot uglier when I did."

I laugh. "You and ugly don't even exist in the same universe."

"You don't have to flatter me, Sierra. I'm already yours." He tosses me a wink.

"Can we speak now, Braden? Because I would really like

to congratulate my sister," Clare says from wherever she's wound up in the crowd.

"Yeah, Mommy. When do we get hugs?" Tinsley asks.

Braden's arms loosen just enough for me to be able to spin around in them. As soon as I do, our little girl is sprinting toward us. She hits my legs and releases a small *oomf* from the impact before wrapping her arms around my knees.

"Hey, baby girl," I murmur and smooth a hand over her unruly curls.

She tilts her chin to look up at me at the same time Braden nuzzles his head into my neck, kissing the warm skin there. Our family starts closing in on us, a symphony of congratulations adding to my bliss.

"Do you get to wear a pretty princess dress now?" Tiny asks.

"I sure do. And so do you," I reply.

She gasps. "I do?"

Braden's laugh kisses my jaw. "Of course, Tiny. Both of my beautiful princesses have to wear their best dresses."

"I will, Daddy. I promise." Our daughter tips her chin to the sky. *Gah*. She's adorable.

My sister is the first of the group of people to reach us. Tiny lets go of my legs when Clare steps in front of me. She doesn't hesitate to bring Braden and me into a tight hug. Tears prickle my eyes again.

"It's about damn time," she mumbles. I can hear the wobble in her voice.

Clare has come around more to Braden over the years, but there was still a lot of distrust on Clare's end. I was beginning to worry it would never go away, but maybe now it will. She should have no doubt now that he doesn't plan on going anywhere.

I wouldn't let him even if he tried.

Braden's body jolts when he's slapped on the back before

he's wrenched away from me. Clare drops her arms, and I twirl around to see Tyler, Clayton, Oakley, and Brooks squeezing the life out of my man in celebration.

"How does it feel to know you're about to join the marriage club?" Tyler asks.

Braden's eyes catch mine over the crowd that's formed between us, and his grin is everything. "I've never been more ready for anything."

I soak up this moment with a smile stretched across my face.

If this is how the rest of our lives are going to go, I can't wait.

THE END

Playlist

Come Back To Bed — Sean Stemaly	3:15
Heartless — Diplo, Morgan Wallen, Julia Michaels	3:08
Just Friends — Virginia To Vegas	4:14
Think Of Me — Olivia Lunny	3:39
Sex — Eden	2:30
Side Effects — Carlic Hanson	2:54
Whoever Broke Your Heart — Murphy Elmore	3:04
Shh...Don't Say It — Fletcher	2:40
Like No One Does — Jake Scott	2:42
Beautiful Mistakes — Maroon 5, Megan Thee Stallion	3:16
Hard Boy — Frawley	3:39
Like This — Jake Scott	3:37
Maybe — Jake Scott	4:07
Shivers — Ed Sheeran	3:36
Hate u cuz I don't — Bea Miller	3:09
The Only Exception — Paramore	4:28

Playlist

Exchange — Bryson Tiller 3:15

Single Saturday Night — Cole Swindell 3:08

LOVE IN THE DARK — Jesse Reyez 4:14

Hold You Tonight — Gryffin, Chris Lane 3:39

Love You Still — Tyler Shaw 2:30

As I Am — Justin Bieber, Khalid 2:54

MIDDLE OF THE NIGHT — Elley Duhe 3:04

Every Kind Of Way — H.E.R 2:40

Know No Better — Justin Bieber, DaBaby 2:42

If It Weren't For you – FINMAR 3:16

One More Night – Maroon 5 3:39

Kiss You Inside Out – Hedley 3:37

High For This – The Weeknd 4:07

Still Into You – Paramore 3:36

I Don't Do Drugs – Doja Cat, Ariana Grande 3:09

Thank you so much for reading Player Of Mine! This is the end for Braden and Sierra, but not the Amateurs in Love series.

If you enjoyed Braden and Sierra's story, please consider leaving a review on Amazon or Goodreads. Reviews help authors more than you know!

Clare and Max's second chance romance is coming 2024, and Tinsley's story is coming in 2023 in my new second-generation series!

Join my Facebook group, Hannah's Hottie's, and chat with other readers like yourselves over all things books!

Interested to learn how Gracie and Tyler met and fell in love? Or want to get a glimpse at Braden back in his college days, playing hockey alongside the famous Oakley Hutton? Check out my new adult, hockey romance series!

The Swift Hat-Trick Trilogy

Lucky Hit — Oakley and Ava
Between Periods
Blissful Hook — Tyler and Gracie
Vital Blindside — Adam and Scarlett

BLISSFUL HOOK

Swift Hat-Trick trilogy book #2

Everyone knew the rules.
Gracie Hutton was off-limits.
But Tyler's never been one to follow rules.
And now she's about to become his ultimate sin.

Tyler Bateman doesn't know what easy means. He's never had an easy day in his damn life. Everything he has he's worked for. Blood, sweat, and tears.

Hockey is his escape, a passion he never knew he could possess. He wants to succeed. He wants to prove that he's worth something.

He wasn't expecting her to matter. He didn't want her to. But she had other plans, and now his best friend's sister is about to ruin his life.

And he might just let her.

VITAL BLINDSIDE

Swift Hat-Trick trilogy #3

Adam White is many things, but a single dad was one that he never planned on becoming. He was twenty-three when the plan he had for his life crumbled at his feet. In the blink of an eye, he went from a flirtatious playboy just getting his new business up and off the ground to a struggling father of a two-year-old boy that he never knew existed.

Still, he did it. Adam accomplished what he thought was impossible. And now, at the prime age of thirty-three, he doesn't think that his life can get any better. His twelve-year-old son, Cooper, is his world, and his business, White Ice Training, is one of the most known hockey training facilities in Vancouver. But when he posts a job listing for a new hockey trainer, he gets a response that lights a flame inside of him that he never realized was burnt out. One that he refuses to go without again.

One terrible game was all it took for Scarlett Carter to lose everything. After a career-ending injury destroys her chances of ever playing professional hockey again, she finds herself lost in a mess of guilt-stricken "what-ifs" and broken dreams. Moving back home to Vancouver was never in the playbook, but neither was letting herself get tricked into taking a job working for a man who seems to want to stop at nothing to see her play the sport she loves again.

Scarlett wants to forget about the world that broke her, but the single dad refuses to let her move on. The more time she spends with Adam, the harder she's finding it to resist him and the sly grins he seems to only give her. She can't help but wonder why he cares so much about her. And more importantly, why can't she bring herself to make him leave her alone.

Acknowledgements

Writing a book is never easy, and this one was no exception. Without the team of people that I have around me, surrounding me with so much positivity and encouragement, I wouldn't have been able to show Sierra and Braden the ending they deserved.

My plan for Braden and Sierra was always to have two books. At the end of Craving the Player, they both had so much growing to do. In my mind, they needed more than I could give in a single book. And 180 thousand words later, I can finally say that I am so incredibly proud of how far they've come and what they've both accomplished. I hope you all feel that way too.

The risk that comes with writing a duet is scary, and I'm so grateful for the love that I have received. To every single person that read Craving the Player and fell in love with Braden and Sierra, this one's for you. You gave me the push I needed to finish this story the way I wanted to from the beginning.

I want to say a huge thank you to my beta team for being so excited to help me with this book, and for loving Braden and Sierra so much. Your help meant everything.

I am so happy to have found my editor, Sandra (@oneloveediting). You are such a lifesaver. Thank you for doing such a great job with this book.

To my ARC readers, you rock. You help so much more than you know. Thank you for everything.

About The Author

Hannah is a twenty-something-year-old indie author, mom, and wife from Canada. Obsessed with swoon-worthy romance, she decided to take a leap and try her hand at creating stories that will have you fanning your face and giggling in the most embarrassing way possible. Hopefully, that's exactly what her stories have done!

Hannah loves to hear from her readers, and can be reached on any of her social media accounts.

Facebook reader Group : Hannah's Hotties
Instagram : Hannahcowanauthor
Facebook / Twitter : Hannahdcowan
Website: hannahcowanauthor.com